THE ENIGMA WRAITH

BREAKFIELD AND BURKEY

The Enigma Wraith
by Charles V Breakfield and Roxanne E Burkey

© Copyright 2017 ICABOD Press

ALL RIGHTS RESERVED

With certain exceptions, no part of this book may be reproduced in any written, electronic, recording, or photocopying form without written permission of the publisher or author. The exceptions would be in the case of brief quotations embodied in critical articles or reviews and pages where permission is specifically granted in writing by the author or publisher and where authorship/source is acknowledged in the quoted materials.

This book is a work of fiction. All names, characters, places, and incidents are the product of the authors' imaginations or are used fictitiously. Any resemblance to actual events, locales, or people, living or dead, is coincidental.

Published by

ICABOD Press
972-283-2383

ISBN: 978-1-946858-09-2 (Paperback)
ISBN: 978-1-946858-30-6 (Hardback)
ISBN: 978-1-946858-10-8 (eBook)
ISBN: 978-1-946858-11-5 (Audible)

Library of Congress Control Number: 2014917746

The Enigma Wraith was previously published under a different ISBN

Printed in the USA

ACKNOWLEDGMENTS

We are grateful for the support of friends and family during the efforts to create this story. We will endeavor to bring you more stories that incorporate technology and, of course, personal opinions. We want to make you enjoy, think, laugh and perhaps tear up just a little. If an individual gets three out of four of these, then we consider that success! Four out of four and we do somersaults.

Thank you, Sandra Breakfield, for your tireless editing efforts. Your observations and recommendations have helped us build better stories and products to be proud of. We would be remiss if we did not recognize your support.

With this the fourth volume in The Enigma Series, the comments and contributions made by our pre-readers were, as always, appreciated. Our primary pre-readers, Kaye Behrens and Tyler Burkey, provided that extra set of eyes that kept us focused on the story. The honesty they offer is always refreshing and hopefully will continue with the next story. A long time mentor, John Costello, provided some Irish view that we hope we captured correctly. Thank you, John. We did take some liberties with your namesake.

A few of our readers offered focused comments and we wanted to thank Jon Shaw, Jim Hughes, Tara McCain and Lee Smith for your astute comments. Budding author, Jim Hughes, in particular offered great support and constructive feedback to us.

We offer a special thanks to our friends, Evan and Gary, along with others at the Red Caboose Winery, for sharing information about the process of wine making in Texas where their success has grown over recent year due to their efforts and really outstanding wines. The extra time spent helping to pick the grapes and share stories with others that enjoy the beauty and continued growth at Red Caboose Winery reminds us of how excellent Texas wines can be. We also appreciate their letting us take a bit of creative liberty with the property which we needed to round out the story.

Specialized Terms are available beginning on page 330 if needed for readers' reference.

Other stories in The Enigma Series by Breakfield and Burkey:

> The Enigma Factor
> The Enigma Rising
> The Enigma Ignite
> The Enigma Wraith
> The Enigma Stolen
> The Enigma Always
> The Enigma Gamers – A CATS Tale
> The Enigma Broker

Full copies of the reviews for the following excerpts were selected from and are available on their associated websites, major book-selling outlets, and at *www.enigmabookseries.com*

Awarded Best Techno Thriller Series for 2017 by TxAuthors – Enigma Book Series

KIRKUS REVIEW – *The Enigma Factor*
… Breakfield and Burkey's novel is a thriller for the 21st century. A complex thriller with a hacker-centric plot and polished technological descriptions that may attract new fans.

READERS' FAVORITE – *The Enigma Factor* **- 5 Star**
… is a very well written story about technology professionals and the financial organizations they are empowered to protect and serve with the utmost integrity…

READERS' FAVORITE – *The Enigma Rising* **- 5 Star**
…I enjoyed the way technology is presented in this work, but it's the investigation that will leave most readers breathless….

KIRKUS REVIEW – *The Enigma Ignite*
… This time around, however, they've amped up the suspense, as R-Group has very little time to find Keith and EZ. There's also considerably more humor in this third outing, including a number of tongue-in-cheek acronyms (such as Su Lin's "Polymorphic Operational Programing of Technology to Aggregate Recurring Temporal Synergies," or "POPTARTs")

READERS' FAVORITE – *The Enigma Ignite* **- 5 Star**
… They also are adept in writing about the human element—for example, the interaction between Su Lin and her students.

KIRKUS REVIEW – *The Enigma Wraith*
…The authors' latest novel—their fastest-paced yet—dives headfirst into the plot and maintains an engaging mystery based on the R-Group's investigation. The person responsible for the Ghost Code, they discover, is Mephisto, corresponding with hacker Callisto, though the true identities behind the handles aren't initially clear.

KIRKUS REVIEW – *The Enigma Stolen*
… The authors focus on characters in preceding books, but this time, they've breathed new life into the series with Julie's CATS. Her subset, of sorts, allows for the introduction of unfamiliar faces, like employee Brayson, and fresh storylines. Breakfield and Burkey once again deliver the goods, as returning readers will expect—intelligent technology-laden dialogue; a kidnapping or two; and a bit of action…the romance between Julie and husband Juan is unparalleled.

READERS' FAVORITE – *The Enigma Always* **- 5 Star**
Fast-paced and gripping, there is no waste, not of words, not of a single plot element…The characters are well-developed, the complicity between some of them lived through very threatening and dangerous moments… Breakfield & Burkey are expert storytellers, entertainers who create a story that will have readers oblivious to their immediate reality…I enjoyed the excellent writing, the complex plot, and the monumental conflict.

KIRKUS REVIEW – *The Enigma Gamers – A CATS Tale*
In this spinoff of Breakfield and Burkey's (*The Enigma Always*, 2015, etc.) techno-thriller series, someone's hacking companies and places with automated services and demanding ransoms.

READERS' FAVORITE – *The Enigma Gamers* **- 5 Star**
…Breakfield and Burkey have written a thriller that should catch the attention of cyber-lovers and online gamers, but it is a story that will be of great interest to everyone with a computer, an internet, and access to anything online. The topic is crucial and very relevant.

KIRKUS REVIEW – *The Enigma Broker*
The main storyline is energized by its formidable villains: …. The authors also sprinkle welcome touches of romance throughout, involving quite a few couples—one of whom plans to get married. The humor is more subtle but equally satisfactory, such as Mike's private insults regarding his boss, the ePETRO chairman. Another exciting thriller entry in a series that shows no signs of slowing down.

As civilization leaves the Industrial Revolution behind, humans are diving into the Internet of Things. As machines talk to increasingly more machines, a new digital predator appears on the landscape, much like the early carnivores did on the African Savannah. This world of technological interoperability we are immersing ourselves in allows for the launch of a new class of vulnerabilities. We are primed for the digital to strike out at the physical instrumentality in our lives. Now comes the helpless feeling in our physical world of phantoms attacking from within the digital realm.

...The Enigma Chronicles

PROLOGUE

THE END ARRANGEMENT ALWAYS COMES FIRST

This outrageous opportunity that had unceremoniously arrived swirled in her mind as she waited for the call. For the last three days she'd reviewed all the information sent to her from one known only as Mephisto. It was both intriguing and intimidating, plus she'd lost more than a few hours of sleep as she had picked the information apart. When the encrypted file had appeared at the designated location, with no way to trace it back to the sender, she knew she had met a technical better. The combination of the contact, method of file delivery, and the actual file contents were fascinating and more than she had ever imagined as close to feasible. This could change the balance of power in the cyber warfare game.

After she launched the embedded program file on a clean laptop, it had taken less than a day for the code to morph and to complete the stated routine before it simply disappeared. Even her elaborate trace files that she had established to capture the activities of the program were wiped clean. She'd filmed the screen with an external camera, as well as watched the screen as the event occurred. Had that not been the case, she would have reviewed the laptop and sworn that nothing had occurred. Simply stated, she would have categorically argued that the program had failed. Yet it hadn't. The goal had been accomplished with no trace left behind.

As she'd mentally explored the potential uses of such a program method, she'd found that the targets outlined were only the tip of the iceberg. It seemed clear she was at the ground floor of a disruptive technology that could change the world. The feeling of such power surged through her veins and created a natural buzz. To keep her end of the bargain in this arrangement, she had to accept the high risk potential of imprisonment.

She'd unsuccessfully tried to penetrate to the code level and determined it simply wasn't possible. That left her frustrated at being unable to steal or copy the information to use on her own. Her frustration reminded her that their group was only a rag-tag band of hackers dropping ransom-ware code onto unsuspecting Internet surfers, encrypting all their hard drive files, and blackmailing them for only digital currency to unlock their machines. This new offer, however, was intoxicating and dwarfed her group's technical efforts. Her role in this arrangement would be high risk and hypothetically could result in high monetary gains. Her decision point was whether the remuneration exceeded the risk factors. This was a very tough decision. If she agreed to the arrangement, it would give her more time to study and capture this unique code.

Questions still raced through her mind. Why had she been contacted? Was she really prepared for the first set of insertions requested? And who was this group that created this type of code and what were their long term goals? For her, this was a blatant seduction that she'd likely accept for far less money than suggested. The code names being suggested were from Mephisto, and she suspected they held some meaning to him, meanings that he would likely never share. Honestly, she didn't care about a name. She had been forced to play many roles in her life.

Today would be the third and final call in their planned discussions before the contract would be finalized, or they parted on friendly terms. If she accepted the contract, then she had to fulfill a commitment cancelled only by her death. She was reasonably sure that Mephisto would insist on helping her keep that end of the bargain, if she screwed up. She wasn't permitted to tell anyone of the details, the targets or the timings. She only needed to provide the access points, introductions, and then simply walk away. Success or failure was to be monitored and then conveyed to her by

Mephisto. As the phone rang, she answered in mid ring, then chided herself for being too eager.

The man on the phone softly chuckled as his rich baritone voice suggested, "Ah, I see that you were ready for the call. That is good. For our arrangement to work we need communications between us to be prompt and succinct. All too often people in this business forget their customer service manners, which only sours a relationship.

"I saw that you retrieved the package. May I presume you completed the actions as requested?"

"Yes sir, I did. It performed as advertised. I don't quite understand how, but it did."

"Let me be perfectly clear," he unwaveringly warned, "you do not need to understand the how in any of this. Your role is to deliver what I provide to you, where I say, and convey the information requested within the timeframe for each test. Any attempts to copy, decode, or penetrate the program will be tracked and result in immediate forfeiture of the contract with the ultimate penalty. Just as I know you tried with this code as it was being monitored. That, my dear, is not negotiable. Is that understood?

"I have a great deal of patience for my work but almost none for people who don't follow instructions. This will be the only time we have to go over this particular rule."

His deep voice had a malevolent edge to it that made her feel like she was about to be punished. It took all of her mental and emotion strength to resist the physical chill she was experiencing that threatened to make her teeth chatter.

With a few deep breaths to bolster her mental acuity, she responded, "I understand." Along with everything else, she now had to check her anger at being caught. She shifted the discussion. "I believe that I have outlined the way to effectively enter the first group of scenarios. Do you need that detail?" she asked.

"No. My dear, if you agree to be my Callisto, you will have the freedom to choose how to inject each of the programs into the targets." His voice tempered as he encouraged, "Be creative. This is a task I want you to have fun with, as long as you provide the entry information and adhere to the timeframe prescribed."

She nervously laughed and then asked, "I gather there is no traditional user acceptance testing needed? User testing based on your scenarios would be hard to track."

He chortled as he replied, "That is not a critical factor from your contract perspective. Meeting the performance criteria is the responsibility of others and not your concern. I did like your joke though."

"So, do we have a deal then?"

She paused to form her question carefully, then she inquired, "I would like to know, how you knew to contact me? I have worked to maintain a low profile. Protecting myself is as important to me as protecting yourself is to you."

"Callisto, if I may be permitted to test how it sounds in our discussion, you were recommended a long time ago for detailed and discreet work by someone who is no longer of this world. I kept this information to myself until the right opportunity for your talents was presented. I did not wish to squander someone such as yourself for mundane and routine assignments. In addition, I was assured that you never broke your word once given. I recognize you learned that lesson the hard way. Furthermore, I know you are and have been relentlessly ruthless in pursuit of your stated objective, and that I have need in my line of work.

"I believe you are the one true Callisto for me. Shall we complete our arrangement? Ten thousand Euros for each of the first group of tasks, payable upon successful time and placement as outlined. Fifty thousand Euros to be paid to your bank account electronically for our finalized agreement. The next series of payments will be determined when those scenarios are identified."

The answer wasn't the one she had wished for, but his vague reference to her past hit home. She had no desire to dig up her history, and this arrangement was one she felt able to control. Funding her other projects required this type of money. Her confidence rose as she reflected upon her goals and desires. Her fears subsided as this venture's possibilities flamed her imagination.

Callisto then suggested, "The cash payments you are offering are attractive, but it occurs to me that they might be dwarfed by what you intend to do with the code after your trial period is over. I would suggest you consider that I be brought in as a junior partner for a percentage of what you think you are going to get, in exchange for just covering my expenses? You said yourself that I have value beyond a simple series of transactions. My female intuition tells me there is much more value to both of us if I receive a percentage, Mephisto."

Mephisto paused slightly and with a chuckle replied, "I prefer to rent rather than buy my resources. It is why I am still a single male. I can pay more for the pleasure of temporary companionship with none of the long term burdens of ownership. I will consider your offer only after your performance on my designated tasks. Prove your value and worth during the upcoming exercises and perhaps a partnership of sorts will be considered for more than a few gratifying transactions."

"Mephisto, I am not looking for a full time relationship, but I am interested in a percentage of a larger piece of any future action, and you have agreed to consider my offer. So yes, we have an agreement. Each subsequent group of scenarios will be negotiated for a fee after I review the targets, correct?"

"Excellent, Callisto, we are agreed. This first group will be completed over the next four weeks at the targets indicated. I will provide you a minimum of three days advance notice as to the due date for each of these. The first is due in four days from today and the code for that target will be in the prescribed location with a link to the location for the next source code for target two. The locations will not be repeated. You may work on your plans of how to deliver my information to each source to help prepare you for the targets on the list. No event should occur except on the prescribed due date."

She assertively replied, "As you wish, Mephisto. I will not fail."

"We will not fail, my dear."

As he disconnected the call, an uncomfortable tingle rose up her spine. In that moment, she knew her acceptance was a one way trip to an uncertain end that she had to control.

CHAPTER 1

WHICH YIELDS BETTER RESULTS: BRUTE FORCE OR BRUTE THINKING?

Jacob's palms slapped the desktop at the sides of the keyboard as he watched the screen in frustration and then shouted, "Damn it!"

Abruptly standing, sending the wheeled chair back five meters at a high velocity, he started pacing as he watched the idiotic character as it hopped around the screen. The character he'd nicknamed She Devil probably had laughter as well, but the laptop was set to mute for his concentration. This personal animated coach, delivered based on his logon credential, was annoying enough, but the real insult came from the box in the lower right hand corner.

> *Ha, Ha, Ha!*
> *You missed, JACOB. Do you want to try again or is it time for milk and cookies?!*

He reached over and pressed a key combination that removed the annoying creature his coworker and alleged friend, Quip, had inserted for entertainment. His pacing continued as he mentally replayed the steps of his program for this stage to see what he might have missed. The whole purpose of his efforts was to create a deflect program that morphed faster than the base code that a random hacker had created. As he shortened his pacing track in front of the monitor, he randomly ran his fingers through his thick, wavy hair before he stopped, retrieved the chair, and retook his seat. His blue eyes would have pierced the screen, if that were possible, to get past this step in this program. The latest program being dissected was open, and he reviewed it until he reached the point where he'd inserted his changes.

This program and the associated logs were part of the information detective hunt that Quip and Jacob had continued gathering from multiple sources across the Internet. The programs, logs, and information they'd gathered seemed to have the running theme of changing code that resided at the root of the system. It was like an extremely vicious virus with a mind of its own. How it was activated, deactivated, and sometimes vanished was his focus. The maddening part of the exercise was that he had no clean example to work from but only small residue pieces of code and a few overlooked log files, along with his imagination and experience. By all reports, this program was one that was lifted from the onboard computer of a very high-end smart car.

According to the information in the blog posting of the driver, this was from someone who had recently purchased a luxury vehicle. The driver and his female passenger were taking the new vehicle for a leisurely weekend drive. Jon and Carol Shaw, named as the owners of the car, hadn't expected the random smart car behavior they had experienced with less than five hundred miles on the odometer. Driving along a scenic road near Tuscany, the driver had modestly set the cruise control at the posted speed limit rather than risk receiving a ticket from the automated Italian speed traps. For half an hour or so they chatted and took in the countryside, which was awash with summer color and dotted with various animals on the hillsides.

It was quite a pleasant road trip until the accelerator started to increase and then abruptly decreased before the driver could respond. In fact, controlling the steering wheel seemed to be the driver's focus as the brakes completely disappeared. Then the wheels seemed to lock-up before the vehicle came to a stop. According to the post that had accompanied the smart car downloads, the driver had barely missed a head on crash with a Braunvieh, who had been calmly chewing her cud as she'd swatted flies with her tail, just before the vehicle crashed through a fence.

The Internet posting became a bit more interesting when the Shaw couple was issued a reckless driving citation by the police. The police maintained the driver had foolishly set the cruise control, expecting the car to drive itself, while they had a *grope and feel* in the back seat of the driverless vehicle. The Shaw couple vehemently denied the allegation that they were too stupid to ride in a smart car believing that it would drive itself while on cruise control. The police maintained they found no faulty on-board computer code and no mechanical anomalies to explain the accident. The Shaw couple had taken their complaint to the social media ranks to see if anyone else was experiencing the same kind of issue.

Jacob had recovered a portion of the program from the hidden registry files, recreated the scenario, and had found another thread in the puzzle he'd been assembling. There was no real *code residue* and no log activity to check against as the program file was gone. However, on his closer inspection, the log time date stamps looked odd so Jacob had opened them up to compare them to each other during the questionable time frame. He noticed they were all identical. Something had indeed run on the smart car on-board systems, replaced actual logging files with manufactured ones, and then deleted itself, thus giving the impression that nothing had been done in the on-board computer. However phony the logs were, there was no real proof that rogue code had been executed on the smart car.

He had a partial tendril print from the programmer. It contained the same characteristics he'd isolated from the other incidents and pointed back to portions of the *grasshopper-loop* he had unraveled, be it nearly too late, from the former Professor Su Lin. He had his suspicions, which was why he continued to poke at the problem from each of the odd incidents randomly revealed as he and Quip trolled for data. This was what he measured himself against in this sixteenth scenario. He was on the verge of completing and confirming at least a similar tag in the strings he was trying to connect.

He was further annoyed as he and Petra had both looked at this type of vehicle to purchase for their travel while in Europe. However, after studying this series of events he was beginning to lean more towards more traditional rather than this new trend toward smart cars which could be readily hacked. He sent off a quick email to the poster of the incident to verify if the on board systems had received any automatic downloads, and if so when, in relationship to the events.

The door to the machine room tweeted as someone entered. Jacob looked up to the monitor that showed the live feed to the operations center entrance and smiled as he saw Petra enter. She was not only his coworker but the love of his life. She was short and petite with her long blonde hair tied up in her work bun, as he liked to think of it. She was beautiful.

In her lyrical voice, Petra gently asked with the amusement reaching her dark brown eyes, "Honey, should I ask what the score is or presume the crazy new hairdo is due to your doing calisthenics while waiting for the program to compile? Judging from the amount of scalp tissue under your fingernails, I'm guessing your scalp is kind of tender," she added with a grin. "I'd hate to think I couldn't run my fingers through your hair later if the urge struck."

"Sweetheart, you can, but all that will do is remind me to be pissed off again.

"Actually, I sure am glad we broke these program forms into steps. I can see they are related based on the similar tags from the programmer. The style is similar although it shows as less complete with each event. I believe it is the same programmer growing their skills over time. It is much easier to feel a small taste of success with each of the scenarios isolated. Out of the fifteen or so steps for this phase, I have twelve completed. They do seem to build upon the maturity of those programs we broke apart before, just as we suspected. I just cannot find a definitive link, though I am tracking some inconsistencies. It is a time thing. I have confirmed the replacements of the registry files and creation of hidden ones and some rootkit like behavior.

"How are you doing with the enhanced encryption for hiding these beasts? We need to understand how these beasts are introduced, as well as to understand how we introduce the cure."

Not only were they friends and lovers, but they were a powerful programming and encryption team. Petra was foremost in the encryption field and constantly pushing the limits even further, as with this effort. Jacob was the lead programmer and system tester. They were talented enough to switch tasks when needed but very adept at their specialties.

"I have a new modification that takes my high end standard into the 256 encryption method and then leverages in a multi-form factor authentication. It looks promising, and heck, my She Devil beast scored a ninety out of one hundred. So not perfect, but at least in the very good range."

Jacob frowned and then asked, "I don't get it. Why does my She-Devil-Layla count points, which, by the way, are Jacob zero and Layla twelve, instead of giving me points for effort? Quip, with his toys and warped sense of humor, is really getting annoying. Argh!"

Petra laughed. "Well, I guess Dad just likes me better than you. But I didn't come in here to gloat or trade point, my darling," she emphasized as she rubbed his shoulders briefly then continued, "Dinner is in a scant hour, and you asked me to remind you. We leave in five minutes, please, so get it compiled and let's head out.

"Quip had sent me a text that he had uploaded the latest *net* noise he captured from the Asia Pacific region, and ICABOD is analyzing the consolidated data."

Jacob briefly reflected on the changes that had occurred since he had found Petra and was invited into the family business. Petra was the daughter of Otto, one of the former key people of a group created during World War Two with a charter to preserve individuals' wealth and protect them from governmental tyrants. Jacob's grandfather, Wolfgang, was a second key person in the group who focused on the financial aspects of this family organization fondly referred to as the R-Group. The third leader of the R-Group was Quip, who had taken the reins less than a year ago from his grandfather. Quip specialized in leading edge technology and maintained the Immersive Collaborative Associative Binary Override Deterministic system, or ICABOD, as it was fondly called. Quip was also considered the project manager for problem projects like this one.

"Sounds good, sweetheart. I've about had it for today. Yep, some progress, but simply not there yet."

They closed down the unnecessary lights, locked up and headed to Petra's car. Jacob figured they'd have time for a quick shower, together of course, before drinks in the library.

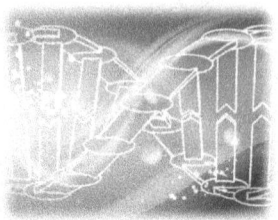

CHAPTER 2

IT'S JUST ONE DAM PROJECT AFTER ANOTHER

Pavan, the hydro operator, was completely absorbed in his book and failed to notice his supervisor headed straight for him. Pavan almost looked his twenty-something with his scruffy hair and loose fitted clothes. As Pavan read, he absent-mindedly pulled pieces of his sandwich off and munched on them, oblivious to his rapidly approaching, red-faced plant supervisor.

The slightly winded, overweight supervisor startled Pavan into focus when he demanded, "What did you do? Why do you have the gate locks wide open and the turbines on max while you are at lunch?

"No one has requested that we boost the hydroelectric output. Plus, with the drought situation, we need to conserve all the water we can. Again, what the hell are you doing?"

Jolted back to reality, Pavan stared blankly and blinked several times, then responded, "Here in Brazil, union rules clearly state that I get my full hour for lunch without a supervisor hunting me down or swearing at me. Now unless you want yet another union grievance to address, I suggest you calm down and try to make some sense. What are you talking about?"

The supervisor was now seething and angrily replied, "Don't you feel the turbine vibrations or hear them whining at their high revolutions per minute? What did you do? Did you decide to launch everything on a mass destruction setting so you could come back and save the day after finishing your comic book?"

Pavan was now incensed as he insisted, "It is NOT a comic book! It's a graphic novel, expertly written and flawlessly drawn to achieve...

"Hey, wait a minute! What's wrong with the turbines? Why do they sound like they are ready to take off and leave the solar system?"

"That's what I have been trying to tell you, Pavan! Come on. Let's get back to the SCADA controls and try to reign in this looming disaster!"

They double timed back to the master control area that housed the supervisory control and data acquisition (SCADA). Pavan stared in disbelief at the settings and then the output gauges. He'd worked at the hydroelectric plant for over three years and really knew the equipment despite his cavalier attitude of a few minutes ago. He'd worked hard to earn the trust and respect he had at this critical operations area. Pavan was extremely proud of how he contributed to the businesses and people of this region of Brazil.

Pavan clarified, "I personally set all of those turbines on low RPM levels based on the minimal water flow we agreed to this morning.

"These settings are... Boss, I can't even get the settings this high through the SCADA terminal! How in the hell did the settings get amped up to one hundred and twenty percent? Basically every gate is wide open and the turbines are set to maximum output which will destroy their bearings if we don't immediately bring everything back under control!"

Pavan frantically logged into the SCADA master control terminal, only to discover that the terminal wouldn't accept any commands. Finally some words painted across the screen, *Ghost Code-patent pending*. The words sent an icy chill down both their spines.

The supervisor grabbed up a desk phone to make an emergency alert call only to find that the phone system failed to connect to dial tone. He reached for his cell phone. The hardened bunker holding the turbines made it nearly impossible to get any bars indicating cell service.

He looked at Pavan imploringly as he suggested, "I'm going up top to try and get reception to call in an emergency alert. You stay here and keep trying to login to the SCADA terminal to see if you can get the gates closed."

Then the circuit breakers started tripping. Pavan looked slightly relieved as he mumbled, "At least the downstream power stations won't start melting from all the extra power being pushed onto the grid."

The phones were obviously back on, as one rang. The supervisor picked up the inbound call which, as it turned out, was from the home office.

An angry voice on the other end shouted, "What in the hell is going on up there? We got people downstream screaming that water levels are rising way too fast. The people upstream want to know if the drought is over based on all the water we are cutting free. The power division wants to bill us for all the sponges they have to buy and use to sponge up their melted power and switching stations!

"If it's not too much trouble, can you stop screwing around up there and bring this mess under control now?"

Just as the frantic supervisor was about to scream help, Pavan looked down at the SCADA terminal with its familiar login prompt. He accessed the system and began corrective actions. The supervisor watched the activity and saw marked improvement as it occurred with each command Pavan entered. He witnessed the catastrophic pitch of the hydroelectric dam as it started to respond to the entered terminal commands. Slowly each of the systems was brought back under control. Their pulse rates in turn slowed as well. The supervisor almost calmly recounted the situation to the headquarters' caller. It would take a few hours to restore everything to the pre-event operational levels, but they were past the danger point.

Then as system diagnostics were begun, Pavan's SCADA screen cleared again and another message was displayed that read:

> *The Ghost Code exercise has completed.*
> *Please gather up all your possessions and leave by the nearest exit. The theater management hopes you enjoyed the show.*

The screen cleared and displayed a shadowy smiley face that dissolved after a few seconds back to the regular command terminal screen. Astonished, Pavan turned around to see that the supervisor had also witnessed the event.

CHAPTER 3

IT'S LIKE PLAYING WITH HALF A DECK OF CARDS

Quip contemplated several different things over his drink as he watched the others slowly gather and make their drink selections. He could sense that both Petra and Jacob were tired. After weeks of trying to determine the full solution to the code issue and gather all the available information, the team was no closer to a solution to any of the code issues. Even though the R-Group was highly effective at information gathering and analysis, this problem seemed to have many isolated yet related tendrils. There was no home source that they'd been able to identify. Things were randomly occurring. The only thing they could honestly say was that the events seemed to be increasing in scale and yet the locations were random as were the affected industries.

Quip was a unique male, to say the least, with his untamed hair and elegant demeanor when he stood to his nearly two meter height. Tonight he was well dressed in that casual finished manner that only a born and bred European seems to readily pull off. Most times he was dressed in jeans and casual shirts. If it weren't for his advanced degrees in applied mathematics and physics, combined with the ability to speak six languages, he could easily be mistaken for a typical computer geek. As the project manager and keeper of the R-Group infrastructure, he was responsible for providing direction to the group.

Admittedly, he'd found himself somewhat distracted as his current love, Eilla-Zan, or EZ as she was more fondly referred, had arrived in Zurich as the team had begun this project. He was getting that brief respite he knew the others needed as well. This was simply not a short term activity or contract. This was for much longer term and far higher stakes. He knew this, without a doubt, to his very soul.

Quip had been delighted when EZ had arrived in Zurich, groomed and perfumed with a touch of sass, to find out where their fledgling relationship might go. It was his first real adult relationship. Until she had entered his life, he had spent his time on his education, learning the family business, and adding huge layers of technology for the organization's use. Currently, Quip's distraction with his long, wavy red haired goddess, EZ, was such that he'd limited his work time. The recent uploads were necessary to keep abreast of the traction this rogue code seemed to be getting.

EZ was a pretty, tall, intelligent Georgia Southern Belle and was actually related to one of the R-Group's communications subcontractors. Quip was making daily trips back and forth to her Zurich hotel or simply spending the night and calling in or working remotely when EZ was sightseeing. Bowen, Wolfgang's long time butler, had agreed to help show her the sights as well as act as her personal driver. Since EZ was really not part of the current family business, Quip wisely restricted some of her exposure to the operations and locations. Tonight, Bowen had been dispatched to pick up EZ and return her to Wolfgang's chateau for dinner.

Quip, Wolfgang, Petra, Jacob, and Julie discussed some of the issues they had faced during the week, hoping to spark ideas on the avenues that needed to be pursued. They'd had some positive discussions in the chateau's study.

The chateau was quietly elegant with furnishings that were rich and tasteful in that older European styling. It was immense and included several bedrooms allowing most of the family to reside there when in town. Most of the larger rooms, including this study, had fireplaces that burned warm and inviting in the colder months, which was the majority of the year. The gardens of the property were heavily laden with roses in summer and had beautiful walking paths with minimal nighttime lighting. The property was inviting at any time of the year.

Wolfgang was the current patriarch of the R-Group and held one of the voting rights for overall direction and projects worked by the R-Group. His specialty was financial matters, and he had an instinctual ability to correctly follow the money to the sources. He was a tall elegant male, a little under two meters, with salt and pepper hair and blue eyes that could flip between interrogations focused, or twinkling with merriment to match the situation. He was a patient man who had lost his daughter but gained a relationship with his grandson, Jacob.

The chateau had been the family home since it was acquired during World War II as his family escaped Poland. He was always delighted to share his insight of the war, honor, and the family business beginnings. He was thrilled to have family close after so many years of no family.

Quip had the second vote, having succeeded to his position when his grandfather had passed away. He'd been immature when he received this elevation, but Quip was filling the shoes with guidance from Wolfgang.

Petra and Jacob currently shared the third voting right, because Otto, the former third and final voter, had recently stepped aside for health reasons. Otto was father to both Petra and his adopted daughter, Julie.

Everyone's thoughts were interrupted when Julie looked at the screen on her cell phone. Julie, the sister of Petra, was most renowned for her megawatt smile. She was a master at cyber identity remodeling for the team and targeted people they protected. Julie helped with specific clients and was quick witted, yet professional head to toe.

After catching the number from the screen, she looked up, flashed her smile and explained, "Please excuse me. Continue your discussions, but I think I need to take this call. I'll be back shortly."

They nodded at her as she turned and went out of the study, shutting the door as she left. Each of them refreshed their drinks and sat down again to collect their thoughts.

Wolfgang suggested, "Do we need to look a little closer at the new advanced computer arms race that China just took the lead in? We know that they have been pouring money into a program to build the fastest supercomputer in the world and they have made their goal. Their Nuclear Asymmetric Binary Operational Ballistics system, or NABOB, is now the fastest supercomputer among the sovereigns. However internally the Chinese refer to it as the IQ 5678 supercomputer. The United States, by all appearances, is taking a really critical look at their technological capabilities.

"However, unlike the other developed nations that are using these massive processing monoliths to predict climate change, or map the human genome, or correctly identify the sub-atomic components such as the *God-Particle*, the Chinese have kept their agenda a secret. We believe that their secret project has to do with what Jacob received from Su Lin via an email account used by Daisy."

Quip stepped into the discussion as he added, "After we found Su Lin's unauthorized hack into ICABOD, we also discovered she used it to then penetrate the cyber-wall around the Chinese's NABOB. Jacob and I both suspect she went nosing around as we found some log files that were missed when she was cleaning that link into NABOB. She must have found some fairly interesting routines because of what she had built.

"We also believe Su Lin, or Master Po as she was known then, headed up the framework for NABOB with her former colleague Professor Lin at her Cyber-Warfare College in China. We presume that he took over much of that college and associated projects when Master Po was removed from the scene."

Jacob nodded, then suggested, "The foundation of the π-R-Squared DP logic was apparently one of the more interesting things Su Lin created when she ran the Cyber–Warfare College. The logic is currently in use by NABOB. We had never seen anything like it before. I have also confirmed that it is what Su Lin used to build the kill-switch inside the *grasshopper-loop* code which we still have not been able to completely disable or repurpose. Annoying, but there it is."

Petra then added, "All good points and some of the blanks are filling up though far slower than we'd like. We received that email from Daisy, which she was instructed by her professor to send to us after she returned to finish her studies at Texas A&M. We presume it is the last email from Su Lin on the subject we are investigating and the erratic behaviors we are finding."

Looking at her tablet, Petra read the email contents.

"Dear all,

Thank you so much. I am sorry I am not with you, but I'm fairly sure I don't want to face what you will have to resolve. I gave you all the tools you will need. Jacob, you are probably the best warrior at winning the contest. You will need what you have learned from our training sessions and the grasshopper-loop to combat the people who are pushing the NABOB system to build and launch genetically engineered vanishing code.

The premise is that if you had taken the amino acids found in the Earth's earliest primordial soup of an ocean and mapped them to present day life, one could build their own synthetic type of life in a digital construct. In theory, with enough processing power one could build their own self-aware digital army to attack their enemies' informational driven society. It should begin showing up soon, but I am not certain of the format.

Focus on the possibilities totally outside your normal frame of reference. There is little time to dwell on what could have been. I am dismayed at what I have seen my old students creating that will wreak havoc on whole societies. Please believe, as quickly as I could, I delivered all the raw tools you should need to win in the coming conflict. Take care, my young ones, as you have much to offer each other and the rest of humanity. I know you can correct this problem that I fear I started, my friends.

With true affection, Su Lin"

Quip stated, "I agree that these are the pieces we need to use as our starting points. What is our best guess as to who we are up against in this race against the NABOB?"

Petra offered, "I can't tell you exactly why, but some of this has a lot of Chairman Chang's fingerprints on it. But his mode of operation has been mostly money laundering schemes. It could however be other sources from the Iranians or Russians which could have begun with cyber thievery. I want to see if I can get Julie back in here as she may have some insight as well."

"Of course," said Quip, as he grinned, "go ahead. We'll just keep working and take notes for you girls."

Petra and Julie returned a short time later, deep in conversation as they approached the gentlemen. Julie finished her thoughts to Petra quietly, and they both looked up as they joined the circle.

Flashing her megawatt smile, Julie apologized, "Sorry for my delay. I needed to finish a conversation with Juan before he went into a meeting. Petra brought me up to speed with the findings today from both her efforts and Jacob's.

"I'd have to agree, it sounds a bit like Chang, but his teams have been doing identity and money laundering. This would be a new avenue if his team was involved with advanced programming, especially with Master Po out of the mix. How much background do we have on her second in charge, Professor Lin?"

Quip answered, "That is a very good question, Julie. I know that he was good and studied diligently under Master Po. How much progress he could have made with what Master Po left behind would be a guess. We know in doing her training of our team as Su Lin she did access some of their systems. Jacob believes that was why the email warning was important to her."

Everyone nodded. Then, they launched into discussions about the pros and cons of the different groups currently doing advanced hacking, such as the Middle Eastern groups and others out of Korea and Japan. The rumors of the Chinese supercomputer and the team's deep knowledge of the former cyber warfare college in China seemed to give credence to some of the suppositions.

Jacob then quickly summarized his current verifications of different elements from each of the code elements he had pieced together and the possible signature characteristics he'd assembled. Bottom line was they needed some additional first-hand information to supplement the information gathering from the posts and blogs. It seemed like some information really needed to be gathered first-hand from the sources, perhaps with some extensive interviews. They agreed to continue the discussion after working through the other promising examples that had been located.

The door to the study opened as Bowen announced the arrival of EZ. She entered and greeted everyone with hugs and handshakes. Bowen announced dinner would be in half an hour as he closed the door behind him.

EZ asked, "Do I have time for a drink before dinner?"

Quip responded, "Of course, honey. What can I get you?"

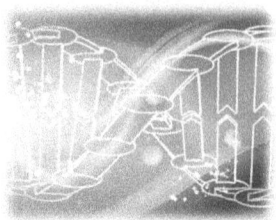

CHAPTER 4

FIRST THERE WERE ASSETS AND THEN THERE WERE NONE

John C was thoroughly annoyed at yet another call and a second text message. Didn't they realize this was his pub time with the lads? It was Thursday. Why couldn't this annoying issue wait until tomorrow morning's technical briefing? John C seriously considered dropping the cell phone into his creamy pint of Guinness, which was being infused with the shot glass full of fine Irish whiskey in the bottom, and simply report tomorrow that he needed a new phone. John C smiled as he recalled how his old Texas friend had introduced him to drinking whiskey with his brew and being told these were called *depth charges* because when consuming your Guinness you never knew when you would be torpedoed by the whiskey in the base. It occurred to him that just maybe the Texas boys might be on par with his Irish mates but quickly dismissed the idea as too forward thinking and probably an erroneous alcohol induced notion. He also dismissed the idea of ruining a perfectly fine pint, and thus the phone survived.

Finally, upon receipt of the fourth direct call, John answered, "John Champion here! What's holding up my take out order? All I wanted was two Guinnesses, three vodka martinis thoroughly shaken, two rum and cokes, and four peppermint schnapps all loaded into one bucket for this party I'm invited to, because I am bringing everyone their drink order! And don't forget the straws since you won't let me take the individual glasses they were mixed in!"

The bank vice president, Wallace O'Sullivan, responded, "Ah, John C, you do know how to answer your phone! So if it's not too much trouble, my lad, can

I drag you away from your customary brain cell elimination efforts at the pub to come back on-site now?"

John C mentally scrolled through his litany of sarcastic and vulgar responses, but finding nothing appropriate for his boss's boss, almost contritely replied, "Sir, you wound me with your allegations! I was in consultation with my favorite tattoo artist trying to decide which lewd image I should add to my body art collection. The crowd on the street side of the glass display window seemed to favor my left buttock over the right, and I'm trying to get a show of hands for the voting. Can't this wait until tomorrow or at least until the ink has been applied?"

O'Sullivan was always annoyed when he had to deal with John C. If John C wasn't one of the most sought after bank security experts in all of Ireland, he would have dismissed him a long time ago.

"When you wouldn't answer your phone, John C, I called one of your running lads who told me you were with him at the pub knocking back marginal beer with disappointing whiskey because you were probably too far gone to drink them separately. Or worse, perhaps you think you're a Texan. If you're not completely arseholed can you get down here, now!?"

John C grinned as he said, "Yes, sir, I can do that. I should be there in twelve minutes, if I stop to pay before leaving. But since you are most anxious to have me there, I will have the weasel you called pick up the tab and be there in eight minutes.

"Ordinarily, I could make it in six minutes, but I would like to empty my bladder before our meeting. I trust you will permit this small luxury. If not, I shall feel obliged to use the elevator on the way up again. Do you know if they have installed toilet paper in the elevator, per my previous request?"

"Fine! We'll wait while you go potty, John C! We'll be waiting in the main meeting room when you are finished."

John C was a little puzzled by the request as it sounded like this was more than a forgotten password or a computer log file that hadn't been archived properly. After sticking Ciaran with the bill for telling O'Sullivan his location, John C left the pub. En route, the thought occurred to him that maybe something really was wrong since O'Sullivan hated to call. He usually just had someone else summon him to a meeting. It also validated that the old bloke knew how to use a phone.

When John C arrived, it was obvious that indeed something really was wrong. All the vice presidents, board members, the chief information officer, the data center manager, and the operational technology leads were crowded into the main meeting room. The mood was very tense and everyone seemed on edge. John C saw that none of his standard humor would be welcomed at the table, so he quickly took a chair, determined to figure out what was going on.

O'Sullivan, who had called John C, took a mental inventory of the attendees and then stated, "Okay, put the overhead projector on and bring up our current status. Let me review where I think we are, which is, I believe, totally screwed.

"A bank works on debits and credits with customers and other banking affiliates, and everything, and I mean EVERYTHING, is currently at zero! As of three hours ago, we don't owe anything. Nobody owes anything. We have no assets! We are a business that is now *persona non grata* as if we never existed and are welcomed nowhere! Does anyone care to explain how it might have happened that this bank was electronically robbed?"

The Chief Information Officer and the Data Center Manager stood up, while the former clarified, "We were simply cleaned out. As far as we can tell, nothing came through the edge and all the systems' logs show that they are electronically clean. There are no anomalies on the servers, and the edge logs, as well as the firewalls logs, show no penetration. So I will tell you, if something got in, it left no fingerprints and no trail."

O'Sullivan then asked, "Okay. What about our backups? How about restoring everything from yesterday or last week? We have to have something to at least restore our records to a last known positive configuration."

The panicked looks exchanged between those present, both standing and sitting, clearly told the depth of the catastrophe.

With a resigned fatalistic posture, the Data Center Manager stood rigidly at attention and admitted, "Ladies and gentlemen, without going into all the gory details, we have no backups to restore that will give us our institution back. Everything is zero. There is nothing going forward and nothing to go back to. The electronic assassination of this bank is total."

The statement echoed through everyone's mind as it produced the same sick feeling in all of them.

O'Sullivan tersely asked, "Are you telling me that we have no system backups, no history, no off-site storage of tapes, and absolutely no telemetry in any other location or media type to restore from?"

The Data Center Manager took a few seconds to bring his anger under control before he replied, "That is correct. The off-site storage of our data backups was terminated due to budget constraints late last year, and we were instructed to simply use secure on-site storage. I remember the instruction quite vividly since it was not long after that the Vice President or VP bonuses were announced. The banks' cost reduction schemes had generated unexpected profits.

"Oh, yes, and that's when it was decided to terminate the backup administrator since we didn't need that position based on everything being kept on premise and on-line for a quick restore. As it turns out the easy restore access also meant easy destruction of this bank's backups."

The irony of the bonus payout after eliminating the backup/restore personnel and eliminating the off-site storage of the backups was not lost on the VPs in the room who shifted very uncomfortably in their chairs.

John C let all the information sink in and then went to the computer that was projecting the banks' account status and began to login with his credentials only to have his login sequence interrupted with the screen image;

> *Ghost Code*
> *Patent Pending…*

John C bristled with some indignity and hit the enter key that promptly displayed the banks' restored inventory of debits and credits, with a smiley face after the screen display. With everyone's attention now focused on the projected screen image, John C hit the enter key again and revealed the following screen image;

> *Thank you for doing business with our banking corporation. Would you like to take a satisfaction survey for a chance to win a €10 gift card?*

Then the words dissolved into an ironic smiley face that also vanished. The room was completely still. No chatter. John C had no glib remark for the attendees - he too was uncharacteristically speechless. He performed a quick inventory of the systems and the bank accounts, and everything appeared as if nothing had happened. John C rocked back into his chair and wondered, what would my ex-wife have said if they got into my knickers without me knowing? Then it occurred to John C that she probably couldn't care less since she and the solicitor made off with his Porsche at the divorce proceedings. The bitch.

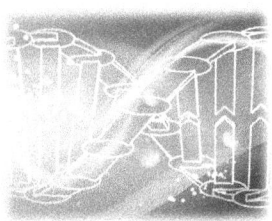

CHAPTER 5

FOCUSED OR DISTRACTED. WHAT WAS THE QUESTION AGAIN?

The light dusting of snow outside the Zurich Operations Center from the night before had been a late spring surprise but provided some interesting visuals for everyone. The clouds had moved out, and the crisp morning air was even more vibrant with the sunlight glistening off the snow and ice crystals. The mixture of radiant heat from the sun and the cold air gave everything a moist yet crisp look and feel. It made it hard to concentrate on anything outside of the sheer beauty of nature.

The team seemed infected with some unexplained reluctance to head into the operations area and get into character. Quip was texting with EZ like a pre-teen on a school bus ride. Petra was holding Jacob's hand and talking about their next getaway vacation. Julie was staring out of the window completely lost in thought. Even Wolfgang seemed absorbed in his pink copy of the Financial Times of London to the exclusion of solving the computer problems that seemed to be mounting daily from what they were now calling the Ghost Code.

Quip prodded the team into the meeting room and asked, "So what do we know so far? It appears like we have some identifiable fragments that give us a general direction to look forward toward solving; we have the unsolved riddle of the *grasshopper-loop* that is a work in progress; and we have what appears to be a collection of seemingly random events categorized by appearing out of nowhere, flaring up like a supernova, and then imploding into nothing but not before offering one last taunt on the computer screen. Is that about it?"

Jacob added, a little annoyed, "Quip, you make it sound like we haven't done last night's homework assignment. We are not getting engaged early enough to capture the code breeding sequence or to get a full picture of its demise because it is cleaning up after itself. I can tell you what we do have is someone painting annoying messages on the computer screen when a coding routine that I wrote fails here in our center."

Petra noted the strained comment and interjected, "Quip, we need more Ghost Code examples, not just snippets of fragments, if we are going to work this backwards to the source. The banking example in Ireland is the most recent one, but we are facing the same problem: it came, it delivered chaos, and it left with no evidence that it was even there. While this looks like a teenage hacker prank, it is a Proof of Concept exercise. If the code was fully baked then I can imagine our Ghost Code not restoring everything but instead painting ransom demands on the screen of every bank terminal until paid. I mean, why restore what had been taken, if the source code was fully evolved?"

Wolfgang and Quip both nodded in agreement.

Quip then questioned, "Are you suggesting these events are training exercises prior to a full scale onslaught?"

Discarding his earlier irritation, Jacob now observed, "That is an interesting observation, Petra. That might more easily explain why everything gets restored and the program cleans up after itself. That suggests that the program creator has further ambition for the code but is not willing to tip their hand."

Quip considered the statement from Jacob and then asked, "Julie, do you have some observations on this topic?"

Without moving her gaze from staring out the window, she said, "Quip, I'm an operations and delivery technician. While I find all this discussion interesting, I'm not going to be able to help write encryption code or debug the *grasshopper-loop*. I can comment on the delivery issues I see. From what I've heard on the hydroelectric plant, the bank, and even the smart car, they all have the same thing in common from a delivery perspective: rogue code is delivered into a system that does not usually lend itself to being penetrated. As a cyber-assassin, I am always looking for ways to get in, deposit the payload, and leave with no one the wiser.

"This is precisely what these episodes have demonstrated and to points you are all raising. We are up against some very well trained cyber assassins."

Wolfgang suggested, "We also need to start making inroads on following the money. There is always money in this sort of multi-layered activity."

"May I also make a recommendation here? Since we are not getting enough information remotely, perhaps we would be more successful if we had resources go to site? In that way we can do some forensics activity first-hand."

Quip nodded in agreement then proposed, "I would like to see Petra and Jacob take separate road trips this time so we can get the most value from you individually in the shortest amount of time. Jacob, I need you to go to New York and retrieve some equipment at our Ronnie, Ltd. offices and have it shipped here. You might want to also check-in with your former employer at PT, Inc. Petra, I'd like you on the hydroelectric gig in Brazil. I know you prefer to work together, but I really believe we need to split up to shorten our time horizon. Are you two alright with that approach?"

They both nodded agreement with his plan.

Wolfgang interjected, "Petra, I have some contacts that we can leverage in Brazil to make your entry go smoother, and I'll reach out to them after this meeting."

As they were about to wind up the meeting, a text came through to Quip's secure phone.

After reading it, Quip smiled and stated, "Well, that was good timing! Apologies, but I have an impromptu lunch engagement so I must dash. I'll be back early afternoon all."

With that, Quip hastily headed for a common-use auto that was kept handy for just such an occasion but not before he called out to everyone, "Ladies and gentlemen, the Quipster has left the building, woo-hoo!"

The team members all lowered their heads but peered at each other, with knowing looks and raised eyebrows, which left nothing unsaid.

When Quip returned that afternoon he seemed completely distracted and unfocused. Petra was the first to notice and pulled him aside to ask what was wrong.

Quip sadly responded, "Petra, EZ needs to return to Atlanta to help Andy. I asked her not to go but stay a while longer to see if we could make us work. She said that was one of the things on her mind now and that was why she wanted to leave. She felt she needed time to think things through, and I asked if she wanted more space. She indicated she did need more space, and then I asked if more permanence would be possible.

"Well, that got her a little teary and of course that made me feel even worse. You know it would be better for couples early in their relationships to have flash or cue cards that females could use to indicate what they are thinking and how the conversation should go next. They would need at least two hundred cards to cover their range of emotions."

Petra, somewhat indignant, chided, "Oh, so males don't need flash or cue cards to convey their pent up emotions?"

Quip was astonished at her lack of understanding. "What? What? We males only carry one card that has writing on both sides. The front side says, Sex then Beer, and on the reverse side it says, Beer then Sex! Oh, do come along, Petra!"

Petra simply rolled her eyes as she reminded, "Well, she couldn't have wounded you too badly, since it seems your sense of humor is still intact."

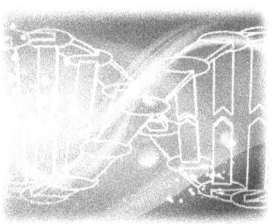

CHAPTER 6

THE SUBTLETY AND OWNERSHIP OF BEING DELIVERED

She answered the cell phone with some hesitancy, "Mephisto, I was not expecting your call. I understood I had more proof points to complete before our next discussion. How may I help my benefactor?"

Mephisto placated, "Ah, my Callisto. You should understand that when I call I want more, if not better. This call is about needing better from someone of your skill level."

Callisto swallowed hard, then allowed, "Mephisto, I have delivered everything you tasked me to do and on time. Where is the problem?"

Mephisto smiled as he explained, "I gave you latitude to enjoy the assignment, but I see far too little imagination in your efforts. More importantly, I see a lacking in your approaches to our attack vectors. Can you tell me when you plan to do something inspired?

"I was led to believe you had imagination. All I see is someone focused on the payment. We had talked about you becoming something of a junior partner for a percentage, but I'm not seeing any compelling arguments toward that end with your actions. How immensely disappointing!"

Callisto bristled while she calmly justified, "I seduced. I danced. And I vanished.

"I persuaded the target vectors per our agreement and introduced your payload as instructed. May I know specifically why you are dissatisfied?"

Mephisto confidently stated, "Because you were caught on film and by someone who knows what an assassin now looks like. You are now no longer an asset but drifting towards being a liability. I was led to believe you were more competent than this. Can you defend your actions? I really need better than what you are delivering if you are going to persuade me to buy rather than rent your considerable properties. I expected to see something far more inventive that this marginal work! I am not a benefactor that needs below average students."

Callisto sensed her trial spiraling out of control, with the judge and jury as one in the same. She explained, "Perhaps your attack on my efforts is about getting full valued information for no cost.

"I can appreciate that, my Mephisto. I am, however, not willing to bend over and take what is delivered simply because I have receptacles for the length that you want to offer. I would suggest that you have made an error because I can take on more than one male at a time and in more than one place at a time. So stop with the gamesmanship stance and simply state what is on your mind.

"I am used to satisfying men at a very basic level. When I am working with more advanced males, such as how I view you, I sometimes need more contextual clues for what inspires you. I am willing to go the distance, as they say, but your vagueness is not helping me reach that potential."

Mephisto grinned as he agreed, "Sometimes it is important to know if I am dealing with a weasel or a lion, my Callisto. We have not dealt together very long. I need to know how you think. You have performed adequately so far, and for rented assets you are meeting my expectations so far. However, my challenge to you, if you want an equity position, is that a bit more imagination needs to be demonstrated. You should understand that I am not interested in being delivered on, but seeing the objectives of your trials exceeded.

"I do want you to continue your efforts on my behalf. Your next group of events need your creative side. I will let you know when I am truly dissatisfied. In that case, you won't ever stop looking over your shoulder. Good night, madam."

And he was gone.

Callisto lowered the phone and cursed, "Oh great, another demanding male! Just what every female dreams of! Crap! This reminds me of where I came from. Too bad he is essential to my future!"

CHAPTER 7

SOMETIMES SEEKING LIES IS AS VALUABLE AS SEEKING THE TRUTH...
THE ENIGMA CHRONICLES

Chairman Chang said over the phone, "Professor Lin, sir, I appreciate your concern, but let me point out that I am responsible for the necessary funding that allowed you to build the IQ supercomputer. My computer resource requests come first, so other departments will have to wait.

"I understand, Professor, that our efforts are pushing the limits of the IQ 5678 system...

"No, you may not know the nature of our program. It is on a need to know basis.

"When I send in my director and her deputy, I expect more cooperation and less hostility to my program...

"You, above all, should understand that programs are not simply finished. There is always additional ongoing refinement for every project. However, I will say that our early proof of concept applications have proven quite satisfactory. I wouldn't expect our program to be quite the same level of burden on your supercomputer...

"No, I didn't say you could put off my application development in favor of improved food production based on changing weather patterns or taming our air pollution that has grown out of control...

"I don't care how belligerent he got with you. Unless you would prefer to have your family, parents, yourself, and your pets retrained in a quaint little village near Mongolia that gets its water delivered once a month whether it is needed or not, as I did with your Master Po. I suggest that you exercise the authority I have invested in you and tell him to have patience."

"Ah, now we are communicating! I'm glad we had this discussion and could arrive at an amicable arrangement based on what I told you to do. Oh, and this is the only pep-talk I will provide on this topic. Good day, Professor Lin." He finished in a satisfied almost cheery voice.

Looking up from his desk phone, Chairman related, "I am fairly confident that Professor Lin will now extend every courtesy to you both for our computing needs. Again, work on this program is classified, and anyone expressing too much interest is to be directed back to their own affairs."

Arletta Krumhunter, also known as Prudence in some circles like this one, had supported some clandestine operations for a United States agency before being demoted. She gave a mischievous grin as she asked, "Or they will be subjected to retraining instructions in a quaint little village near Mongolia? Your motivational lectures are an inspiration to us all. Right, Major Guano?"

The now deputy director, Major Guano, was too distracted to respond as he tried to watch for Chairman's white tiger, Nikkei. Nikkei was Chang's pride and joy acquisition from a former employee who wanted out of Chairman Chang's sphere of influence. Chairman Chang always enjoyed the effect the magnificent animal had on most people. Watching Major Guano squirm, like now, was always enjoyable. However, Prudence seemed to delight in caressing and scratching the 160 kilo animal until she purred.

Prudence got along so well with the animal that Chairman was a little bit jealous. He consoled himself with the fact that no one got to wrestle with Nikkei like he got to, and he had the scars with some fresh wounds to prove it. However, Chairman felt that Nikkei could remain penned up today while they finished their business.

Comforted that Nikkei was not out prowling, Major Guano finally volunteered, "Chairman Chang, sir, let me brief you on where we are at with the Binary Adaptive Interjected Holistically Unconquerable, or BAI HU project."

Prudence raised her hand as she interrupted, "Major, let us recall our positions, shall we? I'm the Director. Therefore, I will brief Chairman Chang while you just nod your head."

The two exchanged very intense looks, as she openly dared him to contest the statement. Without saying a word, he quite obviously wanted to choke the life from her.

After a few tense seconds, the Major stoically replied, "My apologies, Director! Please would you be so kind as to deliver your briefing orally to Chairman? Your oral talents have lead you to the top of your profession. As we all know your oral delivery is much preferred by Chairman to all other reporting."

The innuendo that Prudence always delivered orally to Chairman wiped the smirk off her face.

Prudence turned to face the now grinning Chairman as she explained, ""Chairman, we have so named this in honor of the Chinese Bai Hu or White Tiger. I would be most pleased if this was for your white tiger, Nikkei.

"Our work on the BAI HU project has yielded some very positive results, Chairman. The first proof of concepts showed that our mutating code, genetically engineered for infiltrating host systems, can then assemble itself and grow dynamically to complete the embedded tasks.

"Our original prototype code is now greatly enhanced to penetrate every defense system we have introduced it into. The BAI HU project has been greatly accelerated with the access to the supercomputer that you arranged. The first generation of our code, as you will remember, was simply encrypted with self-destructing algorithms to be launched if it was detected.

"This new generation of code is self-generating, opportunistically adaptive, and self-propagating, which is very much more to our purposes. We can program in the ultimate assignment, the time parameters, mile-stones, and exit protocol and simply launch it. It builds with internally generated material and grows at a rate suitable to meet the time deadlines."

Chairman enthusiastically asked, "And what of the forensics team efforts after the fact? Can the digital fingerprints be re-assembled to understand how it is put together or where it came from? Most importantly, can it be traced back to us?"

Prudence smiled a Cheshire cat smile as she responded, "We have seen to it that the dispatched code suffers from *digital decomposition* the same as its biological counterparts. Basically, nothing is left to analyze since part of its genetic makeup is to remove all traces of itself from the point of its inception to the last digital breath that it takes. It comes from nowhere and leaves without a trace. Genetically engineered code designed to vanish when complete."

Chairman was thoughtful for a few minutes, then asked, "And what of the BAI HU project while it is operating on its mission? How does it defend itself while it is operating on assignment and thus essentially vulnerable?"

Prudence confidently replied, "We have given it a couple of defense mechanisms which includes functioning at the operating system level, much like a standard rootkit in encrypted mode. It is, though, greatly enhanced by the IQ 5678 supercomputer. You would have to know when and where the vanishing code had been introduced and have an equally powerful Chinese supercomputer to be able to try and break the encryption algorithm.

"To vet our encryption algorithm, after we built it, we fed it into the IQ 5678 supercomputer to see how long it would take. Because of its genetic design and adaptability, the Chinese supercomputer had no small amount of difficulty in breaking it. Basically, the IQ 5678 consumed all its processor resources, which was undoubtedly what Professor Lin was referring to with regards to consuming all his resources.

"We had to terminate the program request to break the encryption algorithm and requested an estimated projection of processing time to do the job. The IQ system indicated that it would take two to the twenty fourth power in centuries to break the code. I am quite confident that we should be done with our program objective by then."

Chairman agreed, "Madam Director, I am glad your ability to deliver results was not an idle boast. I am pleased with the progress. Let's speak again at the end of the week. I am anxious to hear the details of the next proof of concept test you have planned. We will talk again then."

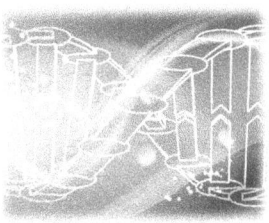

CHAPTER 8

GOOD OLD DAYS ARE NEVER LIKE PEOPLE RECALL

Zara clarified, "Our customers are paying a lot for these services, so we must make sure they get their money's worth."

Dante asked, "What more do they want? The proof of concepts entry strategies you ordered went as promised. I do not give away more free samples. Your unidentified customers must deliver on their promises in advance, not after the fact. I am a professional and proud of the work I do. I will be known someday as the most incredible hacker."

Zara placated, "We have talked about this, Dante. We can't be our new customers' prime store front for this line of work without some collateral show of good faith. Besides, as I market this technology expansion, we will more than make up for the loss of revenue from the retail buyers who need someone or something crushed electronically. I am positioning us to take over preeminence as the top line information gathering organization, not just give you a showcase for your ego.

"We are getting new customers looking for discounts over their previous providers. Perhaps working with these unknown investors has muddled your survival skills. Your skills are now being better appreciated than ever before by me, but only when you do as I request."

Dante grinned as he agreed, "You're right, Moya Dushechka. We are better than any other group, and our code access abilities are proof. We are every bit as good, definitely even better than, we were under Grigory. So what do you next want to do?"

Zara smiled then replied, "Why, we recruit the best talent and steal the best resources, of course! There is talk of an amazing computer with leading edge artificial intelligence technology. If we can locate it and steal the talent that has used or supported it, there won't be anything we can't do or anything we can't achieve.

"Grigory provided me with the number to reach the information broker named Otto, along with the process used when working a project with him. I think I want to contact this Otto to open a request for identification of this computer and the list of talent used to support it. Trying to locate specific people without inroads is not efficient. I am all about being efficient, ever since my surgery. Now that we have regained our direction, I want to make certain we continue to gain ground and lose none. No other group can match our management abilities."

Dante looked incredulously at her as he questioned, "We can take on anyone. I would like to acquire the man that I almost had in Las Vegas and again in Zurich. He keeps falling out of sight, almost like he reinvented himself. It would be good to locate him. I believe he has talent in complex programming.

"It is also said that the group that holds the computer you speak of is headed up by a genius geek that has squandered his power like a drunken Cossack, except he didn't rape anybody! He may have adequate programmers in his group, but are they vicious enough to do combat with us? No, I say. We select the star that is rising but unknown and wouldn't offer much more than a bone to escape their fate. This is the way we succeed."

Zara smiled affectionately at Dante while she stroked his jawline like the family dog. He was a powerful enforcer who had cultivated a few programming skills that made him useful in his role at the Dteam. However, Dante was never the kind of person who was capable of a brainstorm. He was more likely to experience a light drizzle. He lacked many things, but she protected him even when he angered her.

She looked into his eyes then warmly stated, "Yes, of course, Dante. These other groups are merely adequate, you profess. That is why these merely adequate programmers dismembered your code and posted the corrections and very poor evaluation to our internal website, which no one should be able to get to, much less edit!"

"I was phishing and was almost able to track back to their location when you spoiled it."

"You fool!" admonished Zara. "Don't you understand un-harvested talent when you see it? Besides, every time we deliver new solutions to our growing base of customers, they always say the same things: 'Oh, that many lines of code? My previous support provider always delivered solutions in fewer lines.' What that tells me is we could be better and be doing better with that talent working for us. Perhaps if we think in terms of mergers and acquisitions with new processes you would see what I am saying. I want to locate them and force them to our will. We would be unbeatable!"

Dante appeared disheartened, but clapped his hand to his chest as he argued, "I am senior programming architect. I do not need their processes. If you bring them in, they must report to me and follow my instructions, or no one will be happy. This is not as good as the old times. Your ways are difficult. You are very young."

Zara smiled sweetly as she replayed the past. "Oh, you mean like when Grigory was running the Dteam? The rogue group engineered his demise and sent our Dteam into a tailspin. You were working a spamming network of a whopping ten personal computers, when I rescued this place after that crazy Chairman Chang's disruptions. So don't tell me about the good old days!

"There was nothing good about the old days. I will tell you what needs to be done. Your only question back to me is, how soon? Got it?"

Dante's temper flared. At more than forty-five kilos and almost a half a meter taller than she was, she should have been afraid of this powerful enforcer and his capabilities. Dante reached to grab her arm to put her in her place, but she moved and his big hand ended up on her breast. Her move was deliberate, and the action launched her into her favorite game of cruelty.

Zara smiled a terrifying smile as she asked, "Did you need more instruction? Was the last lesson inadequate in knowledge for you?"

Dante pulled back his hand, but the icy chill she emitted had already traveled down his spine as he was reminded of the last exercise he had received.

Zara closed her eyes and recalled her beginnings.

> She had come from a large but poor family. She was told that she would be moving to another home that had more room for a growing young girl who needed some privacy from her brothers. The new family was very nice, and the room was so wonderful she could hardly believe that it was all for her. The reality started to set in when she asked one of the other girls there what they did there.
>
> The girl had given Zara a fatalistic smile as she clarified, "We do whatever they tell us, to whoever they tell us. Just remember, never cry and always pretend you enjoy it."
>
> Zara learned quickly to satisfy the male patrons and even made them believe she enjoyed it. Then one day a patron asked for specifically rough treatment and even brought his own whips and chains. The learning experience was quite fascinating for her. She soon realized that this she, in fact, did enjoy.
>
> She excelled at delivering bondage and discipline but moved quickly into sadomasochism treatments which brought more customers with more abusive demands. By the time she was seventeen, she had a stable of customers that only wanted sexual abuse and she no longer had to submit. She was now an expert on dishing out humiliation and pain as a dominatrix to regular customers that paid handsomely for it.
>
> Zara had built quite a clientele in those years, and she learned early on to have friends in important places, particularly in her line of work. She might have eventually run the place if it hadn't been for the little accident that occurred. The coroner protested that the patron's face could only have been frozen with that distorted look of consummate pain from the heavy use of her tools of the trade. The coroner insisted that, based on the heavy bruising, open lacerations, and scarring, there must have been foul play. But the investigating detectives and even the judge were sympathetic to her plight based on the favors she had bestowed on them. Since she was still under eighteen years, Zara was remanded to a childless couple that the courts felt would give her a normal life

again. Too bad the husband was her regular Thursday afternoon attorney customer.

The couple tried to create a normal home life for her, even with the husband's side benefits. The computer training that she received at this stage offered her a glimpse into the high tech world which she embraced more than her previous trade. Something about going from being a blue collar day laborer to a high tech white collar worker seemed very compelling to her.

She might have made this life work a bit longer, but the husband couldn't let their past go. She made certain that the wife caught them and made it look like it was all his idea. Ruining the attorney gave her great satisfaction, but the real treat was thoroughly seducing the wife before taking the new laptop they had just bought her as she walked out the door. She had another job offer based on her new found computer skills, and she loved her new Internet name that the Dteam had given her, Moya Dushechka.

Dante pouted as he reluctantly agreed, "I do not like bringing in these unknowns. But yes, you are boss, Zara. How soon, boss?"

Zara smiled then patted him on the head as she responded, "You see how much better things are when you do like you're told?"

Dante frowned then said under his breath, "I liked it better when she was pulling triggers rather than pulling strings!"

Thinking to himself, he reflected that he might have more to fear if she was pulling triggers again.

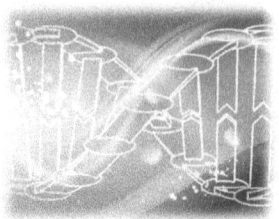

CHAPTER 9

FOLLOWING ORDERS DOES NOT MEAN YOU UNDERSTAND THE BIG PICTURE ...
THE ENIGMA CHRONICLES

Petra was about to book a return flight due to customs refusing her entry into Brazil. The customs people were annoyed that Petra didn't have any of the usual paperwork or even a work visa required to enter the country. While they argued, she dashed off a quick email about her being detained at Brazilian customs at Sao Paulo International Airport. Within a few minutes the Brazilian customs supervisor was called over to take an important phone call.

After the supervisor picked up the telephone handset, his anger quickly changed to fear and groveling while standing at attention. All the people who worked for the supervisor and all the people trying to get into Brazil saw the supervisor's demeanor change to an apologetic posture of a person being thoroughly dressed down. While no one could hear the exchange behind the wall of glass, the constant mopping of his brow and the continuous head nods as he listened had everyone smiling and some even snickered.

Petra tried to remain undistracted by the event and waited patiently for the supervisor to return to the customs station where the agent and she had remained in silence. Finally the supervisor replaced the telephone handset, mopped his brow one more time, and then tried to collect himself before returning to the customs agent where Petra was.

The supervisor curtly stated, "Madam, we had a good conversation with your sponsor, and your missing paperwork is being processed as we speak. I hope you understand our need to strictly follow orders on work visas in Brazil. I have all assurances that the proper paperwork is in transit. You will of course be allowed to proceed based on my recent phone conversation. I hope your being detained here at customs will not incline you to grade us poorly in this matter when you speak with your sponsor."

Petra smiled slightly as she reassured, "I don't think the issue will come up, but if it does I don't believe it will warrant additional details."

The supervisor, now somewhat relieved, added, "I understand that a car and driver are waiting for you outside. I have been asked to help get your bags and act as your escort."

He extended his hand to indicate the way, then gathered up the luggage and led the way.

Once they were out of earshot of the regular customs agents, the supervisor said in a low terse voice to Petra, "Why didn't you tell me you were here at the request of the Minister of Energy and Thiago Bernardes? You will explain, please. I was not hostile to you, only the circumstances under which you came to this country. All of this could have been avoided if only I had been notified, but I understand the need to maintain state secrets. Again, please forgive me."

Petra added a warm smile of understanding as she promised, "When I am engaged by a client, I am to maintain client confidentiality. This meant I could not tell all the reasons that I was here. We were both at a disadvantage in our first meeting. Our next meeting will of course not have this issue."

As they reached the car, they were greeted by the driver who accepted the luggage from the supervisor.

Petra then asked, "Since you have been so very kind, sir, please allow me to return the favor. I might recommend that you change your shirt? The one you are currently wearing seems quite wet from perspiration."

And with that she got into the car which then left the area.

brightened at the thought of being in a one on one conversation with Petra and promptly left, with his male imagination working overtime.

Pavan strained to reel in his disgust of the plant manager and tried to focus on the discussion with Petra. He could tell Petra was there for nothing else but the assignment. He couldn't understand why Javier was trying to hit on her.

Petra asked, "Pavan, can you tell me, in your own words, exactly what happened that day the hydro-system went into over-drive? Please do not leave anything out no matter how mundane or trivial it may seem. I want to go step by step over the event, then I would like to see and access the SCADA terminal under your direction."

Pavan provided a thorough description of all the events. He found Petra easy to talk to, and to his delight she even spoke a little Portuguese.

As he concluded, she queried, "Did you by chance get a picture with your cell phone camera of the taunting message from the computer screen?"

Pavan dropped his head a little and remorsefully replied, "No, I did not. With everything going on and all the turmoil, I confess that I did not have the presence of mind to take photos. I was only focused on trying to get back into the SCADA terminal and bring the system under control. I am sorry."

Petra smiled as she reassured him, "No worries. I was just hoping for some visuals for my report.

"Can we go see and review the SCADA terminal now? I'd like to see if there are any residue files on it that we might be able to retrieve for further analysis."

Pavan agreed and of course acted as her escort.

As they were heading to the SCADA terminal, Javier quickly caught up with them and stated, "Madam, I thought I made myself clear that you were to be escorted when out of the meeting room!"

Petra canted her head a little and calmly responded, "Pavan is my escort. I am complying with the rules. I wanted to review the SCADA terminal."

Javier was a little impatient but reiterated, "What I meant was, I am to be your escort when you are out of the meeting room. Since I may not have been clear in my instructions, I will let this indiscretion pass and will accompany you both."

Pavan, now more embarrassed by the circumstances, looked away from the supervisor.

Petra smiled a disarming smile as she almost apologetically added, "Of course, please forgive my indiscretion, and we will follow your lead."

At the terminal Petra requested, "Can you log into the terminal and run the full diagnostics on this ……

"How old is this terminal? And, just for the record, when was it patched for security vulnerabilities? Does it have Internet access to the software manufacturer for software updates that are available the first Tuesday of the month?"

Javier grinned and clarified with some arrogance, "The SCADA terminals are *air-gapped* and therefore have no accessibility to the Internet. In this manner we keep viruses and other malware off the system. We even removed the network interface card so it can't even be inadvertently attached to the network and be infected. With no access by other computers and no access to the Internet, we don't even need anti-virus software so we save money as well."

Petra nodded, then thoughtfully asked, "So how do you get device drivers and key software updates for this operating system, that is no longer supported in this decade?"

Pavan answered, "We are forced to use the USB analog transport system also known as 'sneaker-net' in North America. An analog operator takes the USB drive to a machine that does have Internet access, downloads the files, takes it to Javier, he scans it using our virus scanning software program also from the last decade, and once it is passed the files are uploaded to the SCADA machine."

Javier quickly interjected, "That is no longer the proper sequence since I am the one who downloads the software updates to the USB drive. Once that is done, I insure the drive is given to the operators to apply. See, it is this USB drive labeled TONS for tons of important stuff."

Petra then questioned, "How often do you schedule system reboots of the SCADA systems? Do you reboot them after uploading the patches?"

Javier smiled proudly and stated, "These systems have not been rebooted since 2006! They are very robust machines as is evidenced by how long they have been up!"

With a quizzical look Petra asked, "How does this program know to re-read the updated files and the edited registry without a reboot?"

Javier, again pleased with his unique approach, said, "We stop and restart services rather than try a reboot! Our up-time availability of the SCADA systems are the envy of all South America! Our bonus system is predicated on system uptime, and since 2006, we have not failed to receive a bonus!"

Pavan didn't say a thing about the flawed process nor about the bonuses only being paid to the supervisor and manager types. The look of frustration and dismay were unmistakably displayed on his face at something he had argued about many times before but had always lost the argument.

Petra didn't miss Pavan's unspoken sentiment and then inquired, "So any and all computer poisoning comes from the USB analog transport system managed by the plant supervisor? Is that what I'm hearing?"

Pavan struggled to suppress his smirk as the supervisor darkened with rage from the accusation. The conversation was no longer agreeable from Javier's perspective.

He argued, "Everything that goes into those systems is scanned thoroughly by the book! If any virus code is getting onto those systems, it is the operators using the SCADA systems for games they put on the machines which they should not do!"

Pavan now bristled and explained, "You think we are bringing high end, graphic intensive, sixty-four-bit processor video games to try and run on a sixteen-bit, brain-dead chip set, with 640 kilobytes of RAM? Is that your accusation?

"The damn things don't even have DVD drives so the only way to get the game code on them is to copy onto antique 3.5 inch floppy disks to feed the routines in! Don't you think someone would notice and report us trying to carry in 520-floppy disks to try and upload 750 megabytes of games? The disk drives aren't even that big! And not only that….."

Petra calmly raised her hand and agreed, "Pavan, I think you have provided enough information in your defense.

"Now I'd like to speak with Javier in the meeting room so I can be in front of my PC. Would you excuse us, sir?"

Petra's warm smile helped settle Pavan down, as he also took the non-verbal cues to take a deep breath as he nodded in ascension. Javier smiled at what he interpreted as a feminine invite into a private room. Javier escorted Petra back to the meeting room as quickly as he could without running and promptly closed the door behind them once in the room.

Javier took a seat close to Petra who was entering something on her PC when he put his hand on her leg.

Petra, without flinching or showing any alarm in her voice, questioned, "Do you always grab at women who are trained in defensive combat, Javier?"

She then threw a fast moving strike with a closed fist but extended knuckles right into his windpipe, causing him to gasp and grasp his throat. Then she smiled a sympathetic smile and continued, "Javier, I don't think you are to blame for the computer virus you gave to Pavan that was put onto the system.

"It will be a few minutes before you can talk so I will simply do a monologue for the time being. Agreed? Oh, that's right, just nod your head."

Javier struggled for air but nodded at Petra.

"You see, you told me how the virus got onto the SCADA systems, but I was puzzled as to how the virus got onto the USB analog train system. So I accessed the video files that are captured on this place, and I think I figured out how you got tricked into delivering the virus by using a USB drive labeled TONS. I did a reverse analytical lookup on TONS, which actually reads Systems Now Operating Transparently or SNOT as the program is called. So armed with that piece of info, I searched your on-premise video surveillance footage, and I found something very interesting."

She turned her PC around and ran some footage of two people sitting in the same room she was currently in, with one of the people being Javier.

Petra then explained, "Now I can see your face in the camera. However, all I can see of the other individual is the back of what I assume is a dark haired female. She seems to be loosening your trousers, pulling them to the floor, moving in close between your legs, and performing what appears to be average oral enjoyment. I say average because she is exchanging a USB drive for one in your trouser pocket, which begs the question how good was it? Oh, that's right, silly me. You're still trying to breathe. Sorry.

"Anyway, it doesn't appear that your theory of the lead operator installing games on the SCADA terminal will be taken seriously after seeing your seduction and the introduction of a group of infected files into a manual process with no checks or balances. So I would like to scan that USB drive to see if there is anything left on it, and I need you to tell me who the delivery service was, so we can start to look for her.

"Additionally, the video storage that has this particular video probably ought to go into restricted storage so it can't be accessed by the operators. It needs to be preserved as important evidence. Don't try to erase it since I have a copy already for my report. I am confident that it will need to be reviewed by the authorities, and if you erase the images you will be guilty of tampering with evidence.

"Oh, and one last thing: never touch me again."

Javier shuddered at the cold smile she gave him. As she walked out the door, she signaled to Pavan to escort her out.

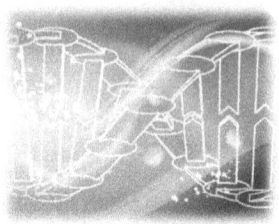

CHAPTER 10

FORTUNE ALWAYS SEEMS DAUNTING WHEN YOU ARE AT THE END OF THE LINE ...
THE ENIGMA CHRONICLES

Jacob had arrived in New York the night before and had spent a couple of hours with his former boss in the morning. He had two reasons for the trip. The first was to touch base with his former company and see if their financial customers had been experiencing any similar events as related to this Ghost Code. The second was to visit the Ronnie, Ltd. offices and retrieve some gear for shipment back to Zurich, which he planned for later in the afternoon. Julie had also texted him that while he was in New York, he needed to go to the tax office and make certain that his property name transfers were correct in the records.

The discussion with his former boss, Brian Smythe, of PT, Inc., had gone well. There had not been any incidents in New York like the one that had happened just recently at an Irish bank that had prompted John Champion to call Brian for assistance the week before. Brian indicated that John C then admitted that he really was looking for Jacob, based on their past associations, and wanted to know how to get in touch with him. Based on the high regard for John Champion, Brian had forwarded the request to Jacob as a professional courtesy.

Jacob was pleased that Brian had thought enough of him to forward such a difficult assignment for a respected colleague to him. Brian agreed that Jacob should interact with John and simply keep Brian and his team in the loop. Brian didn't know the organization that Jacob worked for in detail, but recognized his commitment to good treatment of customers. Jacob planned a preliminary call with John C to set up times for Jacob to go to Ireland as soon as he completed his New York trip. What Brian was able to relate on the event seemed very interesting.

As Jacob entered the tax office, the conversation with Brian was replayed in his mind, with nothing making sense. Then he looked up. What was Petra doing here and looking like that? Her hair was cut, now dark brunette, and she was almost vulgarly dressed. But her movements and facial features were intact. There was no mistaking her, she was his Petra! She was supposed to be in Brazil. It was a total surprise seeing her here in New York sporting a full makeover. Her clothes were so tight fitting, low slung everywhere, and no underwear he was certain. If they weren't in the tax records area for the city, he would have sworn she was trying her hand as a lady escort. His overt staring, albeit in disbelief, finally got her attention.

The dark haired beauty smiled at him and closed the distance between them, then said in a sultry Russian accent, "So perhaps you can tell me why you are doing the hard inventory of my person, with your mouth open? I must assume you American males don't mind being scoped as thoroughly as you just scoped me. At this range, I can see that you too have a hard inventory firmly packed into those jeans. Do you mind if I ask you to let me see your going away view?"

Jacob tried, yet failed, to match this sultry Ukrainian Russian accent with his Petra. Up close, she didn't exactly match with his love. He must miss her more than he was willing to admit. He also wasn't willing to comply with this beauty's request to turn round to show off his definitely male physique.

After a brief pause, Jacob licked his dry lips and refocused his blank stare as he offered, "Madam, a thousand apologies. I thought you were someone else. You see I, er, um, you, we, oh. That is to say ..."

The dark beauty smiled mischievously, moved closer, and lowered her sultry voice as she seductively stated, "Ah, good. You have mastered your vowels, and I'm sure the consonants will be forthcoming, and dare we hope perhaps full sentences after that?

"Tell me, is this what you Americans call, hitting on a lady? If it is, then I suggest you should try more practice. But, I must admit, it was flattering being given a visual physical by what we Ukrainian girls would call a male who is easy on the eyes. Now if you will excuse me, I have urgent business elsewhere."

As she turned to leave, Jacob blurted out, "No wait! I meant no offense! You looked so much like my lady that I forgot my manners. Please at least tell me your name so I can apologize properly, madam!"

The dark beauty turned back, smiled and moved closer to his ear and in the most seductive tones intimated, "Ah, so you do have oral capability, you gorgeous male! In my country we like to reward quick learners with small treats. My name is Zara."

Jacob, nearly undone, responded, "Zara, my apologies for staring and mistaking you for my lady. I meant no offense, nor was my intent to hit on you, as you suggested."

Zara smiled as if musing to a different conclusion. Then she replied, "Oh, what a shame! Does that mean my responding staring leer was no good and not compelling? Perhaps I should be more agreeable to American males staring at me. Another time, you gorgeous male, when your mind is not otherwise consumed with my presumed rival."

As she turned to leave, he blurted out, "Jacob! My name is Jacob Michaels, Zara!"

Without looking back, she smiled as she left the property and estate records area.

Just as he was giving himself a good mental dressing down for ogling another woman, who made him feel like the first time his mom caught him looking at a men's magazine, the records area exploded in anxiety and concern. A quick glance allowed him a view of what was being displayed on the computer screens.

One clerk behind the counter loudly asked to no one in particular, "What's happening to the electronic records? Why is there no downtown block of tax records? What the hell is going on?"

The commotion in the records area was soon matched with other records workers who seemed to report similar types of issues. As the level of concern and anxiety continued to escalate, Jacob moved his head to stare out the door that Zara had left through. He thought briefly about how odd that this started just after she'd left.

Just about that time, someone hollered, "Hey, where did this USB thumb drive come from? It isn't mine. Where'd this come from? And what the hell does this mean? Why is the screen flashing this crazy message?"

Ghost Code
Patent Pending...

Jacob reacted quickly and jumped over the counter while he urgently pleaded, "Please don't touch the keyboard! Let me take a picture of the computer screen!"

Before he could capture the image with his fruit phone the image dissolved, leaving only the mental imprint he had captured with his own eyes.

Over the phone Jacob asked, "Quip, do you still have that facial recognition/identification program on ICABOD, though I cannot think of any reason you'd remove it?"

Quip responded, "Of course. You have something you need me to run? Just send me a digital photo and I'll run it. Is something going on? You sound off, my friend."

Jacob answered, "I don't have a picture of her, but she looks like Petra's evil twin. I mean almost exactly like her except with dark hair cropped short to her shoulders, and a sensual voice complete with a Russian accent that I rightly placed from Ukraine, maybe around Kharkov or Kiev."

Quip asked, in his usual deadpan voice, "So you want me to hunt down some babe you met at a gentleman's club? Let me guess, she was in the ultimate vacuum packed pants with no VPL, a spray-on top with no bra and her head lights on? Does that about cover it?"

Jacob was distracted replaying Zara's image in his mind but managed to ask, "Uh, no VPL?"

Quip, pleased to have derailed the conversation, stated, "Yes, no visible panty lines. Anything else you can tell me about your exotic dancer? Did you happen to see what color her eyes were or were you completely distracted by the fact her head lights were on?"

Jacob, in a thoroughly annoyed voice, replied, "I wouldn't be in that type of club without you, so back off.

"She said her name was Zara, just before all the computers in the city tax office got infected with a computer virus. She was also clothed, be it ever so trashy. Not at all like my elegant Petra. Up close there were lines around her eyes and very faint, almost scarring near her ears close to her jawline.

"Also she didn't have a blouse on, per say. What she had was painted on to distract all the males and outrage any females," Jacob admitted upon reflection.

Quip thought for a moment and then asked, "So you know the old joke about the attractive female who goes into the gambling casino and asks to place $5,000 on a single spin of the roulette wheel? She convinces the pit boss to accept her bet, but she insists on being naked because it is very lucky for her. The croupier looks at the pit boss, and they both agree to one spin of the roulette wheel while she is buck naked. When the marble stops, she is jumping up and down, hugging everyone, and shrieking, 'I won, I won'. She gathers up her winnings, then her clothes and goes to cash out. The pit boss turns to the croupier and asks what the marble landed on. The croupier responded with 'I thought you were watching the table.'

"So she went topless but painted and nobody noticed the deception. Am I right?"

Jacob said, "I did see her eyes. They were dark brown."

Quip grinned and then asked, "What kind of earrings did she have?"

Jacob said, "They were a pretty pink stone, I think."

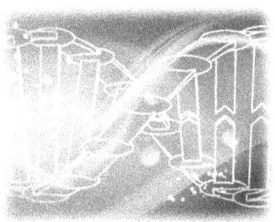

CHAPTER 11

GAMESMANSHIP, COMPARISONS, AND PERSPECTIVE

Quip acknowledged into his cell phone, "I got the video from the hydroelectric plant you sent. What did you want me to have ICABOD try to match this against?

"Oh, okay, so I should run it, and… Geez, Petra, you sent me something from your porno collection! This is some guy with his britches down around his ankles getting his gander gobbled by some babe! You must really miss Jacob. What am I supposed to do with this?

"What do you mean, ME being vulgar! This is from your porn collection, not mine! Talk about your poor timing! With EZ headed home and me on my lonesome, you have to send me poor quality porn of some fat guy getting his pecker puckered! Now I'm really lonesome!

"Okay, okay, okay, I'll stop it, but can we at least fast forward this part so all I have to look at is the few frames in question? Well, thank God for that!

"Yes, EZ left this morning.

"No, we didn't talk about that. She wanted to think things through and not with me in close proximity. She wanted some space and a little time, so I suggested she head home to be with family and consider things.

"Hmmm, I see where you are talking about in the video. She is not just giving…, uh as you say oral enjoyment, but she is stealing something from his pocket.

"Okay, yes, she could be swapping something out of and into his trousers pocket while he is otherwise distracted."

"Oh, yes, that's a male distracted, alright. So you want me to see if we can get any facial recon on Veronica Vacuum here?"

"Alright, I will stop with the crude comparisons. But I have to make one other observation here. She is clearly in no danger of volume choking or gasping for air from mister under-endowed. I mean it's pretty obvious that there is no candy left on that lollipop stick."

"Petra? Petra? Hmmm, you must be going through a bad cell zone. I think the call is dropping."

CHAPTER 12

NEVER BE SO PROUD THAT YOU CAN'T ASK FOR HELP

John C checked his email again and found the response he was looking for. He and Jacob had met at DEFCON and other security shows a couple of times, and they had always seemed to hit it off, particularly after a few customary pints of the black stuff. The difference was that after four or five of said pints, John C was always ready to chase the ladies who were hoping to find a new beau whom he would ultimately be divorced from in the not too distant future.

John and Jacob both worked in digital security for banking systems in different countries, but their security problems were the same. Cyber crooks attacked the banks because that was where the money was. In all honesty, it was also the reason John C was in banking security. It was no secret that whenever he sent an email to close associates, John C always signed his email digitally with 'because that's where the money is'. Obviously, bank management wouldn't let him use it on his official email correspondence because of the unprofessional message it conveyed.

The email exchange had bounced back and forth several times but finally John C had won out. Jacob was on a retainer to work with John C and his institution on their near digital death. John C had taken all of his usual expertise and all the suggestions from Jacob to try to find how the cyber assassins had gotten in, wiped everything clean, and then put it all back with no trace of how it had been accomplished. It was a humbling experience for him and even more so when he had asked for additional expertise to be subcontracted to assist.

It irritated John C to have to hand-carry the purchase order for Jacob's services to O'Sullivan for his signature. It couldn't be routed through the normal process because O'Sullivan didn't want anyone outside of the people who had witnessed the event to see that another security guru was being parachuted in to sort out the bank's mess. In addition, O'Sullivan wanted a dig at John C for having to beg for funds to assist where he had failed to find anything.

O'Sullivan suppressed his gratified smirk as he lorded, "Well, Johnny, do we need some money to bring in a digital security expert well versed in forensics for the banking environment? I trust you will be able to take care of his access to the facility and work on-premises rather than from the local pub?"

John C was not about to let the comment go, so he challenged, "That's right, sir! These are exciting times! I bet once this mystery breach is thoroughly researched, we will expose these cyber assassins for the economic and social criminals they are and hand them over to the appropriate authorities who can pack them off to jail until well into the next century!

"Surely after that the VP's can get their bonuses just ahead of the next wave of layoffs. Efficiencies breed VP bonuses, which underscores the need for fewer employees and less security around here. I for one cannot wait to see who will be executed next, then compare later to who we should have kept!"

O'Sullivan barely restrained his annoyance as he looked over the top of his glasses at John C, who always seemed too delighted at speaking his mind to him. O'Sullivan had already grown tired of the game of needling and quickly signed the purchase order to get John C out of his sight.

John C grinned from his successful verbal combat, took the signed purchase order, and, with a light-footed step that ended in a pirouette at the door, turned to bow in each direction before leaving the office. It was noted that he spent much more time bent over with his posterior pointed at O'Sullivan than he had in the other directions which could easily be interpreted as a *faux-mooning*.

O'Sullivan's secretary was always amused by John C's antics, and her laughter at the display had the desired effect of infuriating the VP beyond measure. John C had always been a good dancer which had previously earned him a nice scholarship for his advanced degree studies. He claimed that dancing was a sure footed way to get close to a lady. Dancing well on the floor usually led to a subsequent merry dance between the sheets. He had successfully used that technique with each of his first three wives.

John C caught up a little with O'Sullivan's secretary before heading back to call Jacob about the signed purchase order. Once the purchase order was in the system, Jacob could start charging against it. John C felt a little nostalgic at the prospect of working with Jacob again and was actually in a hurry to get ready for his work with him.

John C asked on the call, "Okay, now that we have sorted all of the logistics, when and where do you want to start?"

"John C, I've added my associate Quip into this conversation. We have been seeing this type of phantom attack in diverse locations, and he has been feeding the forensic evidence into our main computer to help build a more complete picture. I have to be honest here, we have not trapped this beastie yet as all we really have to go on are fragments so small as to be almost useless. All we have is anecdotal evidence that people claimed to have seen. We don't even have any useful screen shots to prove that they actually saw '*Ghost Code-Patent Pending*' on the computer."

Jacob continued, "Now, John C, you're pretty good at forensics, as I recall. If you haven't found anything significant and we have several examples of the same kind of attacks with nothing to show for it, I am reluctant to fly to Ireland, rack up a bunch of expenses, and have no real Root Cause Analysis to make everyone happy."

John C nodded and replied, "I appreciate your candor and honesty in this matter. You know that sometimes a fresh set of eyes can trigger new thinking that leads us to prowl in unexplored areas. I need that fresh pair of eyes to help me trawl through this institution's data to hunt for what you already know to look for. Besides, if you are here working on a purchase order that covers your expenses, I can have you pay for the consumption of my favorite beverage. There is something gratifying about having the bank pay for my drinking problem."

Jacob puzzled and asked, "…Uh, you have a drinking problem?"

John C responded with a chuckle in his voice, "Well, not really a drinking problem, but I do need constant re-hydration of fluids derived from fermented hops. At least that's what my ex-wives claimed when they filed divorce papers.

They maintained that Guinness ruined our marriage, but I do have a slightly different view on that issue. Either the right lady helps you forget about drinking, or the Guinness helps you deal with the lady. So far Guinness is winning with a score of three to zero."

Jacob then questioned, "So, were they right?"

John C, now tiring of the line of conversation, said flatly, "No, they were just poor choices on my part, and I dealt with them by not dealing directly with them. Hey, enough forensics on my personal background! Are you going to work on this or not? I came to you for help, so are you going to help?"

Jacob, taken aback at the abrupt shift, said, "Hey, lighten up, man! I'm just trying to figure out the business environment and how to best help you out here. I withdraw the question about needing constant re-hydration."

John C was chastened. "Jacob, I'm sorry but they are all over me to find the root cause of our near digital death, and this has me at a severe disadvantage at the bank. I'm used to running the show my way, and now they are taking me to task for not solving this extremely disconcerting problem. Jacob, I need your help. Will you do it?"

"I'll schedule my travel as soon as I disconnect from this call. Does it sound like I'm here to help you now?" replied Jacob.

John C breathed deeply then said, "Yes, Jacob, it does. Thank you. Talk soon, my friend."

After disconnecting the call, Jacob phoned Quip back. "Well, I've never heard him this stressed before. Usually, he is fairly confident and is almost never intimidated by anything or anybody."

Quip's eyebrows were very arched as he said, "Yes, he did sound like he was wrapped around the axle on this issue. I do like the way you tried to set expectations on this because we simply don't have much to go on. However, I think it would still be of value for you to go on site as requested. We are finding a few fragments here and there so maybe you will find something else. Finish up the tax thing and go to Ireland. We might get lucky."

"Yeah, I need to get that issue resolved, thanks for reminding me. With Petra on travel to Brazil, I can work John C's issues and then return to Zurich from there."

"Jacob, before the tax office, can you go by the Ronnie, Ltd. offices? I need the gear left there shipped here. I am glad you touched base with your old employer, PT Inc. More pieces to the puzzle. Keep me updated."

"Sure."

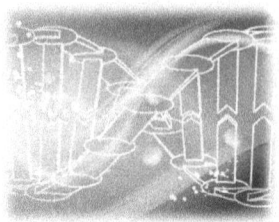

CHAPTER 13

HAVE I GOT A CRUSH ON YOU

Petra took the call after seeing the caller information on her fruit phone and stated, "Quip, I am kind of busy here in Brazil. I am trying to meet up with Lara before I head back home. What's up?"

"Petra, I am sorry to interrupt you, but this is what looks like another of our strange code exercises. This guy contacted us on Otto's number. He wanted to speak to Otto, but I said you were helping out while Otto was on an extended vacation. Do you recall a Gary Kibben from a trip to Texas with Otto? He claims he met you when Otto took you on a motorcycle trip around Texas.

"He and his son Evan apparently own a winery. He said he had contacted Otto some time ago for a recommendation on some technology additions to monitor soil moisture for his grapevines. Otto had recommended some programs and connections that were a bit over Gary's price tag, so he ordered something on-line he thought was similar. However, now they have a weird issue, as he put it."

Petra paused for a few moments then replied, "I do recall meeting with a gentleman in Texas in a barbeque restaurant after he had assisted us. Like always, the conversation began and continued, including an invitation to Gary's property where we pitched our tents for a couple of nights. The property was pretty, and Gary spoke about his sons. I can't recall his sons' major in college, but Gary, I think, was an architect. Nice man. It doesn't surprise me that he and Otto kept in contact. Otto has never met a stranger and always takes care of his friends."

Petra remembered that wonderful summer trip she and her Dad had taken through Texas. They had rented Harleys in Dallas and simply gone riding for two weeks, camping out and meeting some very memorable people. Petra's Harley had gotten a flat tire just outside of a small town in Texas, and that had grounded them to a halt. They decided to call for a tow and perhaps enjoy some local food while the tire was repaired. Cell phone coverage was a little spotty, and she had trouble calling the emergency towing service when a man stopped his pickup truck just behind them, then kicked on his emergency lights to alert other drivers of a problem.

Gary introduced himself and offered to take them to the garage in town. Otto was apprehensive about leaving the gear on her Harley unattended, so they put all of her stuff in the back of the pickup. Otto followed Gary into town to the promised garage on his Harley. They'd made arrangements for the tow of Petra's Harley. The owner of the garage thought he would be able to get it fixed the next day or the day after that at the latest. The local restaurant was the next stop as Gary and Otto quickly became friends. During dinner Gary had mentioned his son and the property he had purchased with some wild idea to maybe grow some grapes and perhaps make it into more. His son Evan had fallen in love with the property and been out every chance clearing the land and learning all he could about grapes.

Gary had led them to his property after supper, suggesting they were more than welcome to camp there. The gravel road was something of a challenge for Otto on the motorcycle, but he took it slowly and after a mile into the property they came to a stop. The view was wonderful, and the ideas that Gary shared sounded like a wonderful dream. He'd even shared the idea for the name being discussed, the Red Caboose Winery. Petra had not kept up with Gary or whether his winery ever took off. Obviously, it had passed the dream state and become a productive business.

As she returned from her tour down memory lane, she asked, "So what is the weird issue he is having?"

"Well, he pointed me to the posting his son had made on-line, regarding the recent random behavior of the application and associated equipment they'd purchased. The company could not be reached as the number was out of service.

Evan apparently had Googled and not found anyone yet that had purchased the product and had any issues.

"A few days ago, the computer the application was working then started doing some strange messaging, which he failed to capture or even read clearly as he was watching his grapevines as the water turned on in the heat of the day. He unplugged the computer and powered it off, then he'd run out to shut off the water valves, taking control away from the computerized application."

"Okay, well that does sound suspiciously like other random events we have been reviewing. What did you tell him?"

"Petra, I promised him you would call, rather than Otto. I hope you don't mind."

"There was also the fact that the name of the application is Ghost Water, which is way too close to Ghost Code for me to ignore."

"Wow! Agreed. I am happy to call him. Sounds like I need to go see this, but it will need to wait until I am finished here."

Petra waited while the number connected and then introduced herself, "Gary, this is Petra, Otto's daughter. I believe we met when Dad and I toured Texas. How are you, sir?"

"Petra, how nice to hear from you. How is Otto?"

"He's doing quite well but on a well-deserved vacation with my Mom. I understand that you have really continued down your path of creating a Texas winery. By the looks of your website, you are doing quite well."

Gary laughed as he said, "The winery is doing well, thanks to Evan and his vision of combining the majority of the year as a farmer of the finest grapes in the area, and the rest of the year refining his wines, now as a renowned vintner, winning several awards. It is simply a dream come true."

"I am so glad to hear about your success. And your son helping you. That must really make you proud."

"It does. And not just one son, but both. My other son is a chef and his culinary creations are matched perfectly with the fine red wines Evan creates."

"Gary, I am at a customer site but wanted to call as I heard you were having some strange issues. As it turns out, strange issues are my specialty this month. My background is in computers with a focus on security types of problems, which is what sounds like you're having."

Gary responded almost relieved, "Oh, thank goodness. I had hoped that you continued down the path Otto spoke of. I would really appreciate your coming here, and we will afford you every courtesy. Honestly, Evan can give you more details on the events that have occurred than I can."

"Let me work on my schedule and let you and Evan know when I can be there. Ask him to not even turn the machine back on at this point. I will do that while I am there. Would that be alright, Gary?"

"It is perfect. Thanks very much for calling me back."

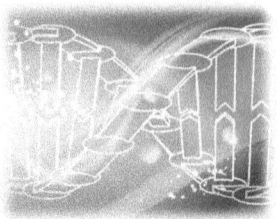

CHAPTER 14

PRECIOUS MOMENTS CAN QUICKLY VANISH WHEN YOU AREN'T WATCHING

Juan grumbled, "Where is that stupid co-pilot? Badger me to get on as a co-pilot, and now he seems to have vanished. I need to learn to be less helpful to whiney people with funny foreign accents. Ah well, I can get my pre-check done a lot quicker and leave on my schedule without having to wait for someone to go potty. I had better get started if I am going to pick up Lara on time."

Juan ran his hand under the aircraft as he walked and smiled affectionately at the Gulfstream jet that he flew for Destiny Fashions of Brazil. He thought about all the beautiful models he had flown to so many exotic locations for extended photo shoots. Talk about your dream job! Running babe-e-luscious models to magazine shoots where they need to change constantly and almost wear clothes to show off not to cover up! On top of that Lara paid him too!

He chuckled to himself when he thought about how many males would pay to have his job. Of course, the irony of it all was that while the models were for the most part very pretty and usually nice, when not parading in front of a camera, it was just a job for both of them. Anyway, he already had a special, steady lady that kept him focused on her inventory. He thought it odd that she never warned him about having Roman fingers or Russian hands. Frankly, it never entered his mind to try out the goods, as it were. She was who he really wanted, and his philandering days seemed a thing of the past. Anyway it wouldn't do to be sampling the wares since the owner of the company, Lara Bernardes, had given him this job at the request of his brother, Carlos.

Carlos was a communications specialist with a focus on using satellites. He worked all over the world as a contractor. Carlos was Lara's full time night male, so any stupidity on Juan's part would cost him his flying job and possibly his beloved Julie. Not to mention the whipping he'd receive from Carlos. While all were powerful motivators, he frankly liked his life the way it was currently arranged. Nothing else seemed interesting.

With the aircraft checklist completed, and after he topped off the tanks, Juan made one last area review looking for the missing co-pilot, with no success. He decided he'd likely never see the guy again. Odd though, the guy was so insistent to learn the trade, asked so many questions, seemed so eager, then had simply vanished. Juan climbed in the cockpit and started the engines after closing the door. The ground crew pulled the chocks away, and he moved the aircraft into takeoff position.

He followed his filed flight plan out of Acapulco and headed out over the Yucatan to see the ocean. Everything looked so good at 28,000 feet. He saw the waves as they broke over the barrier reef off the Yucatan Peninsula. The waves were catching the sun's rays and sending reflected light bursts like a myriad of tiny stars flickering, floating on the ocean. Gratified by the spectacle, it reminded him that this was why he had always wanted to fly. Also it felt good to be working a legitimate job and not having to worry about being chased by the *federales*. Things had worked themselves out, and finally everything was going his way. Juan chuckled and then thought to himself, when everything is coming your way it's a good indication that you are in the wrong lane of traffic. And then it started.

The on-board computers flickered, then blanked, then returned momentarily only to go dark except for a red line centered on the screen that said;

Ghost Code
Patent Pending...

The radio chatter stopped, and all electronics that were computer dependent simply spun. Only the analog driven old school instruments, running on vacuum pressure and one analog compass, gave any useful information. Juan was alarmed but didn't panic. He went through the emergency checklist trying to bring the computers, which drove practically everything on the aircraft, back on-line. Precious minutes passed, but nothing seemed to help.

Then he noticed that the analog speed indicator showed that he seemed to be dropping and accelerating at the same time. He hadn't noticed it was approaching the danger zone for the aircraft. By the time he started to struggle with the stick controls, nothing made any difference. Even though the hydraulics almost worked, he had enough upper body strength to move the rudders and ailerons. He realized the air was now being pushed out around the aircraft such that the rudder and ailerons no longer had any airflow over them to correct his direction. The Gulfstream moved so fast that the air simply could not be affected with aileron activity.

After a few more frantic minutes trying everything from the radios to reviving the computers, he settled on one revelation; he was doomed to ride this out. After he had gained enough control to maintain attitude, he resigned himself to this fate as he retrieved his cell phone. He was able to use it the way Carlos had instructed him, with a satellite, to make a call to Lara.

Lara promptly answered, "Hello, Juan. Please don't tell me you are going to be late for this photo shoot? You promised me no more missed deadlines."

Juan swallowed hard and then with tenseness evident in his voice he replied, "Actually, Lara, that is exactly what is going to happen. Can you conference in Carlos, so I can hear him dress me down too, please?"

Lara wasn't quite sure what was wrong but quickly called Carlos.

"Carlos, my darling, I need to bridge you onto a conference call, right now," Lara insisted without any preamble.

Carlos, somewhat bewildered at her demanding request to join a conference call, responded, "Sure, Lara, but can you tell me what's going on?"

Lara said nothing until she joined the three of them and indicated, "Juan, Carlos is now on. You want to tell us what is going on now?"

With a resigned smile, Juan fatalistically responded, "Yes, Lara, thanks. Hi, bro. I'm glad you had time to talk. Well, let me be brief, since I don't know how much more time I have left. I just wanted to tell you both I'm sorry, but this time it really isn't my fault. I also apologize for your aircraft, Lara."

Carlos knew that tone and asked, "Juan, what's wrong? Where are you calling from?"

Juan drew a deep breath and succinctly replied, "I am at about 27,000 feet, the on-board computer systems are gone, and there is a strange message on the screen that I took a picture of then texted to your special fruit phone number before I called Lara. I have no on-board air controls that work, except manually with great effort. I don't know if the screen shot was received, but it had this cryptic message, *Ghost Code - patent pending*. I have no idea what that means. Carlos, I am in *Mach tuck*."

Carlos closed his eyes and grimaced at the cruel information.

Lara shook her head, very puzzled, and asked, "What is Mach tuck?"

Carlos's stomach knotted and his mind raced as he responded, "Mach tuck is where the aircraft has accelerated to the point that the plane is pushing air out so far around the plane that air necessary to stay close to the wings, tail, and ailerons to control the craft cannot be used to steer.

"Juan, we've talked about this before. Can you cut the fuel or drop the gear to slow the aircraft down so that the air control will respond again?"

Juan replied, "The computer controlled fuel efficiency system went with the twin computer systems. While I was fighting to get them back on-line, I noticed the aircraft was gathering speed and dropping altitude.

"I won't say I panicked, but I tried to manually lower the gear and sheared off the crank handle, which gave me a sick feeling. If I had the computers and electronics back, I could conceivably lower the gear. However, nothing is responding. It occurs to me that I am about to reenact the deep space meteor impact that caused the extinction of the dinosaurs 65 million years ago. Of course I am not the size of the meteor, which I expect was the size of Bolivia, so we shouldn't worry about a nuclear winter ensuing from my impact."

Carlos said nothing but dropped his cell phone down to conference in someone else to the call. While the call was connecting, he continued to try to locate the Gulfstream with his systems and based on the cell signal Juan's phone was emitting. He was grateful that Lara caught him in his work environment surrounded by vast computer resources. He'd known the scheduled flight yesterday, as Juan had copied him on the flight plan as always. As the call was answered, he located the aircraft signature and began tracking its course.

When she answered, Carlos said, "Julie, I need you to join a conference call right now, please."

Carlos completed the bridging action and asked, "Julie, are you there?"

Julie was confused as she answered, "Carlos, hi. What's up and who else is on the call with us?"

Juan smiled broadly at her voice and said, "Hi, babe. It's me, sweetheart. It is so good to hear your voice right now. Carlos and Lara are both on with us, so we'll need to keep the conversation clean, okay?

"Listen, honey, I am having some aircraft trouble, and I may not make our special date that we planned for after this trip. I know you wanted to keep it a surprise, but can you tell me what the doctor said this morning? I think we all would like to hear the results."

Julie was confused and started to panic as she tried to speak, "What, umm, huh, no…"

Carlos intervened, "Julie, Juan is caught in *Mach tuck* with all the computer systems gone. He cannot slow the plane down to control it. …em …There may not be much time to talk to Juan, Julie. Please tell him everything that you want him to hear about you and the doctor, whatever it is."

Julie was desperately frightened and felt helpless as she asked, "What about kicking the door open to see if that will help slow down the aircraft so you can regain control?"

Juan responded, "Good idea, honey. I thought of that but as long as the engines are running the gangway is locked in place.

"Even if I could get the gangway down, I would have to leave my seat and buckle to open it. Once opened, the aircraft would decompress sucking me out the door, which isn't a whole lot better than what I'm facing now. Lowering the landing gear was also a non-starter solution.

"So honey, will you tell me what the doctor said? I really want to hear what was said."

Julie, as tears streamed down her face, managed enough courage as she replied, "She said, we two are going to be three, just as we suspected, my love. Please tell me you are coming back. Please tell me there's a way out of this?"

Juan struggled with tears but fought as he levelly responded, "Oh, honey, such good news! I am so pleased and proud! Very few males get as good a female as you, babe. But you must promise me that when he or she arrives that you will say that I would love him or her as much as I love you. Will you do that for me, honey?

"Carlos, I have a request of you, my brother. Will you find these people that are breaking Julie's heart and destroy them?"

Julie screamed, "Juan, don't you leave me! I need you. Our baby needs you."

Though Carlos's eyes were overflowing with tears, he resolutely pledged, "Yes, little bro."

Juan then said, "Julie, I don't know …"

It took everyone a few seconds to realize and accept that there was only three of them on the call now. Juan had just vanished.

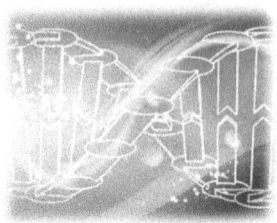

CHAPTER 15

REACTIVE MEASURES PRECLUDE YOU FROM DECISIVE ACTIONS ...
THE ENIGMA CHRONICLES

Carlos sat for moments, which seemed like eternity, in shock over the events that had just unfolded. His blind rage was only slowed by his now desperate need to find his brother. He pushed his feelings of acute loss into the background in favor of taking action. Juan deserved better than his falling apart. Whoever had messed with his brother had earned an attack vector that Carlos would relentlessly deliver with a cold, calculated smile. Action was required, and it would take more than just Carlos to locate and destroy these perpetrators. Regardless of how long it took, Juan would be avenged.

With at least a starting point for a plan forming, Carlos systematically captured the flight path data and zipped it into a file. He then gathered the recording of the conversation from the point Lara had bridged him into the discussion. As he glanced at the photo of the cockpit screen Juan had sent, tears threatened his vision, so he breathed deeply and regained his control. Right now he needed to keep his head, no tears, no remorse, he internally berated himself. In the back of his mind memories played while he worked to put together the information at hand.

They had been born into a family that seemed to have bad fortune stalking them. His grandfather had been one of Trotsky's followers. He was killed when all were assassinated along with Leon Trotsky in 1940. Carlos and Juan's father had been killed by stray police bullets in the Mexico City University protests in

1968. They both had near incarceration experiences with the U.S. authorities and had been trying to move to legitimate lines of work.

His younger brother, Juan, was a strong, powerful man and looked the part of his Mexican heritage with his black hair and swarthy complexion. Quick to tell a funny, yet often times a male focused story, Juan was adept at flying, karate, enjoying females, and getting into trouble. From the time Juan had come into the world, Carlos had looked after him and trusted him like no one else. Even Lara, the love of his life and soul mate, maintained a different place in his heart. He brushed the thoughts away as he focused on the task at hand, where perhaps he could make a difference.

As he reviewed each of the elements he had gathered so far, nothing made sense. The plane was on the filed flight plan, although he could tell from the mapped data that the speed was way above normal, though the altitude was good, relatively speaking. During the tracking it was far higher than the 28,000 feet Juan had suggested. The signature of the plane disappeared at the same time as the voice communication. He could not see anything regarding a crash, though that was what he suspected. He gathered the data files together and emailed them at the same time as he dialed the phone. The call quickly connected.

"Hi, Carlos," responded Jacob, slightly distracted by his ongoing efforts with the *grasshopper-loop* code and all the incidents he'd been reviewing. "What's up, man?"

"Jacob, I just sent you some files, and I need you to open them now so we can discuss them. Is Quip around close to you, and maybe Petra?"

Jacob sensed the demanding tone and knew that Carlos had a problem. "Yes, Carlos, your files are downloading. Quip and Petra are both around though working in other areas right now. I will alert them. What's wrong? Are you okay? I've never known you to call and launch into an accelerated discussion with only you doing the talking."

"You're right. I would tell you I'm… I'm fine," Carlos responded as he raked his hand through his long black hair. Then he insisted, "The problem is with Juan. His plane just vanished. I need you to help me, right now, to locate him."

Jacob started to record their conversation as he rapidly sent messages to Petra and Quip to join him. They were in the Zurich operations center with all the resources at hand. Carlos and Jacob had a history of respect for each other as professionals and friends. Carlos would not call for help without good reason. Jacob completed the file download and opened them.

"Alright, Carlos, my friend, I have the files up. Let's start with the details. Where do I need to look first?"

About that time, Quip and Petra joined Jacob on the call, and Jacob switched to speaker phone to be hands free. Jacob alerted Carlos that they were all present and he was on speaker phone.

Quip and Petra greeted Carlos, and then Quip said, "ICABOD ran a cross media trace of all known instances of *Ghost Code – Patent Pending* to see if there are any references in this quadrant of the galaxy and cross referenced with other known sabotage efforts. I seem to recall some other events that sound vaguely familiar in the Net-Chats."

Quip had programmed the ICABOD computer to respond to either keyboard input or to verbal commands, and it was capable of translating very complex dialog. However, even though ICABOD was capable of using recordings to respond, Quip was always changing the voice recordings to imitate famous movie stars or talking computers from landmark movies. Quip insisted that this was to exercise the minimal Artificial intelligence (AI) attributes of ICABOD which helped promote learning in his circuitry.

However, wide spread use of the American 1950's radio detective investigator voices had Jacob and Petra pleading with Quip to change it. Quip had relented, but the new female voice with her sweet southern drawl sounded suspiciously like Quip's EZ. The consensus was to let it go for now and let Quip stay with the voice of EZ.

"Carlos, this may take a little time to locate meaningful cross-references for Ghost Code," suggested Quip. "But we will let you know as soon as we find something with our big data search engine that ICABOD has access to. Is there anything else we can whack on while that is working?"

Staring intently out the window of his high tech computer area, Carlos responded, "Yes, there is, Quip. I need a bogus *breadcrumb trail* built for a computer hacker that is on the lamb from the authorities. I will need an identity to match the running thief's persona. Can you make it look like he stole enough to have the U.S. cyber heavies after him and that he can't go back home? He can't be too bright, since they know who he is, but he has to be good enough to elude his pursuers. Oh, and this time can you give me an interesting Internet identity that I can use that will not track back to anything we are currently involved with, yet unique enough that when it pops up on the grid you can geo-locate it and monitor?

"Whoever did this is smart, vicious, and likely a small group, I think. Between your tools and my former contacts, someone will know something useful. They hit Juan in Mexico and that is a place I know quite well."

Quip and Jacob looked quizzically at each other, but Petra stepped in and stated, "Carlos, I will have Julie work it up as soon as possible. I know you are in a hurry for this. However we need to make certain it is the correct background."

Carlos's resolve was hardening by the moment as he replied with conviction, "Madam, you have no idea!"

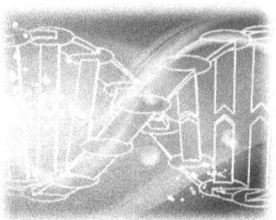

CHAPTER 16

THE BEST WAY TO COMFORT OTHERS IS TO GATHER YOUR OWN STRENGTH

Lara set down the phone and let the tears fall. She was angry, sad, and ached for Carlos, Julie, and herself. How had this happened? How could Juan just be gone? Over the months that Juan had worked for Destiny Fashions, she had grown to love his sense of humor, his respectful way with the models, and his dedication. She stood and started pacing in a random, unfocused manner. Carlos, the strong anchor of her life, would be inconsolable. She knew her prince well enough to understand he needed time to gather his strength before she encroached or offered any help. She stopped pacing and sent a quick text to him.

> *Carlos, my love, I am here when you need me. Anytime!*

Whether she received a response now or later, he would know. That was the most she could do for him until he reached out. She recognized, without a doubt, that Carlos would somehow find these people and extract his revenge. It would not be pretty when the culprits were located. Carlos was a powerful male who refused to have his family, however extended, hurt by others. He would take his time deciding what steps to take, and she respected that.

After reviewing her options on where her actions could make a difference, she decided support for Julie should be first and foremost. Julie had been so

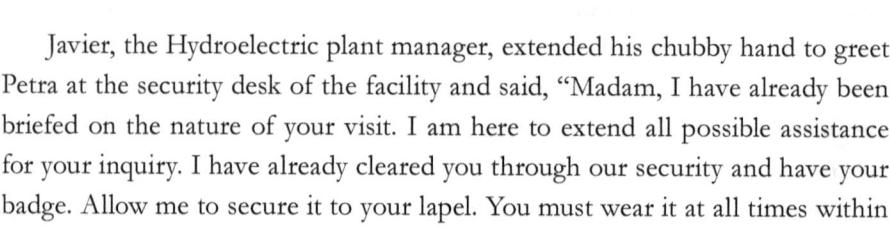

Javier, the Hydroelectric plant manager, extended his chubby hand to greet Petra at the security desk of the facility and said, "Madam, I have already been briefed on the nature of your visit. I am here to extend all possible assistance for your inquiry. I have already cleared you through our security and have your badge. Allow me to secure it to your lapel. You must wear it at all times within our facility."

Pavan, also in attendance, rolled his eyes and wondered if she would ever get out the grease stains on her blouse left by Javier's hands. He muttered under his breath, "Yes, thank you, your grubbiness."

Petra intercepted his hands before Javier had a chance to fumble with the security badge and with her professional smile in place clarified, "You would understand that I am familiar with the complexities of a security badge clip as engineered to attach to clothing."

Pavan grinned at the sarcastic remark but let the smirk vanish as soon as the supervisor turned to him.

Javier was slightly flustered but managed to ask, "Well, where would you like to start, madam? I have our lead operator Pavan here to help answer any operations questions you may have. I also have a meeting room reserved for quiet discussions as a work area for your activities. However I must request that you be escorted in any activity that requires that you leave the meeting room including the restroom or break room for security reasons. We had something of an incident here of late, and we now require all visitors be escorted once past the main security desk."

Once Petra was set up in her operational meeting room, she asked to speak with Pavan. Javier plopped himself in a chair at the meeting table so he could listen. Petra politely asked him to leave, giving the reason that each interrogation should be done one on one and that he would have a turn as well. Javier instrumental in helping Lara to start Destiny Fashions. She had become such an important contributor as the business thrived with her unique fashion designs for casual and loungewear for women. She'd recently started socializing some ideas to add in a line for men. This innovative Brazilian company was quickly winning attention and more customers all over the world. Julie needed support quickly, and Lara wondered if she should simply go to Julie.

After she'd wiped her tears, she reset her resolve, and she scrolled through the contacts on her phone and pressed to dial. It took several rings before the call connected.

"Hello, Petra. It's Lara. Do you have a few minutes to speak with me? Are you free?"

"Hi, Lara. Jacob, Quip, and I just ended a conversation with Carlos. I am so sorry about Juan, Lara. We are going to try to review the information that Carlos sent to Jacob and work on a plan to find Juan."

"At least you know that part, so I do not have to explain. This is about another aspect of this horrible thing that I would guess my prince left out. His focus is correct on Juan at this point. Others, however, are also impacted and well, frankly, you may not know. Please, call me back when you have some time alone. Okay?"

"No, Lara. Wait. I will make now good. Give me a second to step into another room."

Then speaking away from the phone, Lara overheard Petra as she said, "I need to take this call now. I'll catch up with you later," followed by steps and a door opening and shutting.

"Lara, you still there? I moved and the door is closed. I should have stayed in Brazil it seems. How are you doing? I am sure this is hard on you. Carlos sounded, I don't know, resolved I think. I heard the revenge in his voice."

"Oh, Petra. The conversation with Juan before we lost him was so desperately sad. I know that Carlos is furious at an enemy he can't identify yet. He probably feels he let his brother down, which he did not.

"What you may not know, though, is that three of us were on the phone with Juan. Carlos added Julie into the call when Juan explained how dire his situation was.

"Petra, I was so focused on trying to grasp what Juan was saying and not saying, that I almost fainted when Julie told Juan her news. I felt so empty. I know how awful I would feel if I were in her position. She offered up suggestions for Juan to try and was being supportive. But when she said he couldn't leave her, well, I just broke down for the pain she must be feeling. I am not certain where she is, but I know she had planned to join us at the shoot site, so she and Juan could take a few days together. Sort of a celebration that now won't happen." Lara inhaled and tried to stem the tears that began rolling down her cheeks. This was harder than she thought. "Poor Julie. She is all alone, Petra."

"Lara, I think I am missing something."

"I didn't realize Julie was on the phone. I know how much she loves Juan so I know she is likely in shock and grief stricken at his loss. She isn't one to give up hope though. Certainly not without some evidence which means finding him or portions of the aircraft. We aren't at that point yet.

"She should be at our family house. She isn't here in Zurich. I will call her after we finish. I had planned on it when Carlos explained what happened to Juan."

"Petra, it is much more than just Juan missing, though that is terrible. Julie announced, at Juan's insistence during the call, that she's pregnant. I don't think she's told anyone else. She had just been to the doctor to confirm. He insisted she tell him, well us, on the phone. Oh, Petra, she was so trying to hold herself together as she begged him not to leave her. I am so worried about her."

Stunned, Petra sat down and stared into space. She couldn't even respond to Lara. Julie, her little sister, pregnant and alone. The tears welled up in her eyes and overran her cheeks. How unfair for anyone, especially Julie.

Taking a breath, she asked, "Lara, are you sure you didn't mishear her? She made no mention when she said she was going home about any doctor's appointment or even seeing Juan soon. The only thing she asked was if our parents had already taken off on a trip, which they have."

"I'm sure. Juan had to beg her to tell him. He sounded like he knew he couldn't fix the issue with the plane. He wanted to know she would be protected. He wanted someone to look out for her, like Carlos and me," sobbed Lara.

"Okay, stop now. You and I know very well that tears do not fix anything. We know that we need to make a plan and then execute it."

Lara took a deep breath and replied with some confidence, "You're right. Let's look at our options."

"Do you think that you need to go to Carlos, Lara, or can you maybe come to Europe? I could speak to Julie, and she could be with you while the team works on finding Juan. I'd know then she is with someone that cares. Our parents are on a much needed holiday, and I'd hate to pull them back if there are alternatives. Plus, I'm not certain Julie is ready for that. What do you think of those options?"

"Carlos is going to be focused on his brother. He won't even speak to me until he's got some plans in place. It is just how he's put together. I did text him, but I don't expect a response. He trusts me to take care of me, so the less distraction and whining I do at him the better.

"The shoot is scheduled to start in two days, so I need to get the models on location. I could really use some help. What about Julie helping me? As I recall, she does hold her pilot's license, because Juan joked about letting her fly while he slept."

"Yes. She has always kept current on her licensing and physicals. I don't recall the aircraft that she feels comfortable in, but she and Juan did co-fly a flight not too long ago. Now whether, with all this, if she will even fly or not, I have no idea. She's tough though."

"Alright. My Papá has three company planes here in Sao Paulo. I would need to get his permission, which I believe I can do, and then if Julie is willing, I will get her to Sao Paulo on the next commercial flight. Just tell me which airport to have the ticket waiting at."

"Lara, that sounds good. I will call Julie next. No promises, but I'll get back to you."

"I am off to call my Papá and update him on the events as well. Thank you, Petra, for putting it into some perspective. I am glad we're friends. We just don't spend enough time visiting. We'll make up for that after this."

"Yes, we will, my friend. You take care, and thank you for letting me know. I'll call you back."

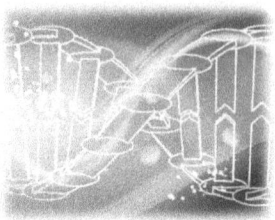

CHAPTER 17

IT IS SO HARD TO PUSH AHEAD OF THE GRIEF

Julie was totally shell-shocked. Her entire life had stopped as she'd gone from an incredible high to desperation. She stared at the phone for what seemed like hours yet could have been only minutes, waiting for the screen to light back up, and Juan to laugh and add some flip comment about yanking her chain. But nothing happened. Tears she had when she'd pleaded with him had vanished. She had no capacity to cry. No capacity to feel anything but numb. She protectively placed her hand over her stomach and closed her eyes, waiting for something she couldn't classify.

Here she was alone in Luxembourg, while Otto and Haddy were traveling to Rome and Paris on a well-deserved sabbatical. She loved her parents and her sister. She enjoyed working in the family business as a cyber-assassin nicknamed JAC. She wondered, as she had earlier in the day before the nightmare, what her family would think. Quip would have some comment, that's for sure. Her heart ached but still no tears.

She had planned to meet up with Lara and Juan at their next shoot and show off some new designs. She had come up with a new idea for men's wear she'd hoped Lara might add into the Destiny Fashions line. She had connected with Lara on an assignment for the family business. Ever since then, she had been close with Lara as well as found an alternative outlet for her creativity. It matched so well to her sunny disposition and trademark mega-watt smile. Now this. Julie felt she'd never truly smile again until she located Juan.

Suddenly the screen on her cell lit up just before the caller name and customer ring tone kicked in, letting her know it was her sister. Julie thought to ignore it, but suddenly she wanted to hear her sister's voice.

She pressed accept on the call and, mustering as much nonchalance as possible, answered, "Hi, Petra. How are you?"

Not one to pull a punch, Petra responded, "Hey, Julie, I am sort of worried about you. We just ended an unexpected call from Carlos a little bit ago. How are you doing? I understand you were on the call when communications with Juan ended."

"I am sure he just entered a bad cell zone. Actually, I thought perhaps it was him calling back when I answered you."

"Okay, we'll go with that, my sister, for the time being. We have started to review the information that Carlos sent as well as what we began retrieving. Any thoughts or ideas that we should keep in mind?"

"I don't know. It was so weird. We talked about the various steps to take, which of course he'd already done.

"There was no explosion or crashing sounds, just silence. Like he'd hit a bad cell zone. No static though. It was almost eerie, that pointed silence."

"Well, that aligns with what Carlos suggested as well. He was tracking the aircraft until it vanished, almost like Carlos had done before to mess up tracking aircraft signatures. But Carlos said that made no sense based on the systems that were and were not operational. So far we have no debris field, but we are reaching out to other sources for data."

"Petra, he did not crash. There is no way that happened. Do you hear me?" she admonished, then the tears filled her voice. She sobbed, "He wouldn't leave me or our baby. He simply wouldn't do that to me."

"Oh, sweet Julie, he would not leave you, if he had a choice. I agree. I knew you guys were very close. I had no idea about a baby though," Petra paused.

"I just found out this morning. I wasn't even going to tell him until we met up at the shoot day after tomorrow or so. I was so ecstatic when the doctor told me this morning, I danced around. I wanted to call you and Mom and Dad, but I had to wait and tell him first. You understand, right?"

"Of course, I understand. I don't think I could keep that kind of secret for days like you were planning. This is wonderful. I'm going to be an aunt. Wow! How are you feeling? Any morning sickness?"

"None. At least not yet. I feel great. Doctor Ingles did some blood work and gave me some horse pill vitamins. He also insisted that I maintain a very healthy diet, which I plan to. I am only five weeks along, so very early. I set up some future appointments and filled the prescription right away."

"I just want him to hold me," Julie added with a whisper.

"That all sounds very good for my niece or nephew. Any idea which one?"

Julie laughed a bit. "No silly. It is too soon for that."

"Okay, well you are going to have to give me all the details, because I have no clue on this. This is all new ground for me."

"Me too! So I think I will fly back to Zurich and help out in the operations center on piecing the information together to locate him. I am sure it is something really easy."

"Julie, I don't think this is simple or easy. It seems to tie into all the incidents that Jacob and I have been working on. I think it ties back to Master Po and maybe even the school she ran. I also think that you are too close to help here, right now."

"Petra, I have to do something. I won't sit around just waiting and wondering. That is so not my style."

"I agree. Do you want me to come home, or call the folks?"

"No, I want to be involved and contributing. I will come to Zurich. I can leave in the morning."

Petra waited, then decided to be honest, as was her nature. "To be honest, Julie, I also spoke to Lara. She is devastated and worried about Carlos. Carlos is going to focus on Juan to the exclusion of all else. He wants to find him at least as much as you do. Lara has lost her friend, her pilot, and the love of her life is not going to turn to her until he finds his brother.

"Lara is worried about the shoot and getting the models on site. You know how easily that girl internalizes situations and blames herself. I am concerned she will ignore her responsibilities to Destiny Fashions. It is having great success, but is not to a point where Lara can ignore it.

"Could you perhaps help her? You know the business, she mentioned you planned to join the shoot, so I suspect you have some new designs to show off. She is also going to be in a bind transporting the models on commercial flights, unless maybe you could help with that. You are still current, right?"

"Hmm," sighed Julie. Then warming a bit to the idea, she replied, "Of course I am current. I never know where or when our business will take me. That would be very irresponsible of me.

"I could go help her. Juan was going to share the flying with me anyway. So I can help. He would appreciate my holding onto his position rather than Lara hiring someone else."

"As if Lara would do that without more evidence. What am I going to do with you, Julie?"

She flashed a bit of her renowned smile, as she replied, "Help me get a plane, of course!"

Petra laughed, as she said, "Okay. Let me call Lara and let her know you can help. I will have her call you directly.

"You give my niece or nephew a pat and say how much I love them. Almost as much as I love you, Julie. You are the best sister in the world."

"I will. You have to call me though and update me every day. Good or bad news. Do you promise?"

"I promise daily updates, probably in the evening.

"By the way, may I tell the family about the new addition, or would you rather?"

"Go ahead and tell them. Saves me for the funny looks later with the cart before the horse comments."

"There won't be any comments, just lots of love and support. You know this family. I will let you tell our folks though. See you later."

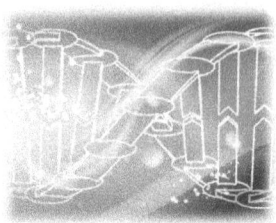

CHAPTER 18

BEING THE GATEKEEPER, YOU GET THE RESPONSIBILITY AND THE BLAME ...
THE ENIGMA CHRONICLES

Jacob held out his hand to greet John C as he said, "John C, it's been ages! How the heck are you, sir?"

John C smiled politely and replied, "It has been a while, hasn't it? It is good to see you again. I just wish it wasn't under such dire circumstances."

Jacob studied John C a bit then admitted, "You do look a little ragged, my friend. I don't think I've seen you look this way since that time you took that product marketing job to get out of the security business. I read your social media page and the pictures that you had uploaded, but I never quite understood why you left that gig. The comment in your posting about 'fundamental marketing direction differences that rely on short term tactical actions to affect long term strategic goals' necessitated your ethical action that led you to submit your resignation, didn't quite sound right. I somehow sense there was more to that story than your posting offered the readers. And just for the record, what was this product you were managing that you had this ethical issue with?"

John shifted his gaze downward and, as his eyes cut around so as not to focus on any one thing, somewhat defensively replied, "Yeah well, it sure looked like a way out of what I was doing in the security field. I juiced the resume a little and knew someone there to put in a good word for me to make the jump to a big pharmaceuticals company. I had a good final interview, and they said, 'Blimey, man, where have you been? We want you to manage products for us, but we want you to start with suppositories and work your way up, so to speak. They complained their sales in suppository product lines had stagnated, and they were looking for someone to drive sales growth.

"I admit that suppositories are an unglamorous product. However, I thought with some out of the box thinking I could increase sales and move to something more high profile, you know. Well, everything I wanted to do got rejected or distorted, so nothing helped.

"Finally, I had just launched a product makeover with an entirely different approach. When they found out that we were changing suppositories to look like shamrock mints, with just enough spearmint flavor in them to also be tasty, they simply wigged out. I even had the instructions printed in Swahili so no one could tell which delivery mechanism of the medication should be used. What I was offering was an expedient marketing solution to their sales problem. They called it a mega lawsuit in a childproof box. We exchanged a few un-pleasantries, but in the end I was released from my contract."

Jacob stared blankly at John C for several moments before he offered condolences. "I am now really sorry I asked about that period in your life. I doubt seriously we would have had a chance to work together if you had been able to make a go of marketing suppositories that looked like lucky mints. In fact, now that I think about it, I wish I could unhear that story because I will never look at candy mints again without serious suspicion. What say we delve into the world of bank security?"

John C nodded and agreed, "Yes, of course. I think the first order of business would be to introduce you to the Vice President of this portion of the operations. You are welcome to refer to him as Mr. Candy Mint, based on the story I just told you from my previous job. He is a sweet enough fellow, but after a few minutes of talking with him you will agree that all of his thinking is of the suppository kind. Shall we?"

Jacob now recalled why he hadn't kept up with John C as he clarified, "John C, I have never known you to lie to me. At the same time though, I have a difficult time believing what you offer up as the truth. I know that I can trust the purchase order you sent me so let's take a look at the problem."

John C and Jacob took seats in front of the Vice President's enormous, yet immaculately clean desk. Obviously it was to impress visitors, but even visitors could see that no work was done on this desk.

Jacob studied the desk after their introduction and stated, "This is quite a desk. I don't believe I've ever seen a business desk quite so large, sir! Was it custom made? It is very nice."

O'Sullivan beamed as he agreed, "It is nice, isn't it? It is the largest desk here at this institution based on length and width measurements."

John C, not about to let a good line go to waste, added under his breath but loud enough for all to hear, "Large desk sizes tend to compensate for being under-endowed in other areas, or so I am told."

Jacob could feel the animosity in the air but tried to keep the conversation from being derailed from the bank's security breach. "Sir, perhaps you can give me your overall view of security processes here at the bank, and let me make a few notes? I of course have been briefed by John C already, but sometimes a different perspective can help flush out new details.

"For instance, how are administrative rights granted? What are the safeguards for these all powerful ID's?"

O'Sullivan warmed to the subject and said with a sense of pride, "We changed our administrative policy a while back and removed administrative access from all accounts and replaced it with one administrative ID. That way we only have one super-user ID to deal with, and the password is automatically changed every four hours. It is like a library book that people have to come to me for the password, so I know who is doing what on the system."

Jacob puzzled for a moment then inquired, "How is the password delivered to you? Like a hardcopy or word of mouth? If it is being changed every four hours, then reliable delivery mechanisms must be in place, correct?"

O'Sullivan grinned again as he replied, "We have a program that changes the administrative password and then sends an SMS text to my smartphone. Thus we never operate with the same password for more than four hours. We have tight control of the password and thus tight control over our administrative user ID with its omnipotent power. I am the gatekeeper."

Jacob nodded thoughtfully and wondered, "Is it a single purpose phone for only this activity, or your personal phone, sir?"

"Why, it's my personal phone. It is always with me and if someone needs the password during off hours I can be called to give it to them over the phone. There has not been a time when the password was needed that I couldn't be reached to provide it. I didn't want to have all important passwords going to a second phone that might not be where it could be immediately accessed. Besides, I don't want to carry two phones."

Jacob then asked, "Would you mind if I could take a look at your phone? I would like to do a little experiment with it, but nothing harmful, I assure you."

O'Sullivan unlocked the phone and handed it over to Jacob for his closer inspection.

Jacob then requested, "John C, will you send a SMS text message to this phone but make up a bogus security message using the word 'kumquat' somewhere in the message. I want to attach a USB device to the phone so I can watch the behavior of the unit when the message arrives."

John C nodded and did some activity on his phone. "Okay, it's on its way to the phone."

Jacob watched the phone and the program running on his laptop, with the phone connected via USB. Almost as quickly as the SMS text message arrived, another SMS message was sent from O'Sullivan's phone. The outbound message was erased from the phone after transmitting. Jacob grinned as his program captured the outbound information for playback and review. Jacob turned the PC around to show both John C and O'Sullivan that the phone had been compromised.

Now stunned, O'Sullivan was momentarily speechless but finally managed some words filled with bluster and justification. "That is not possible! My phone received a SMS text message, sent it to another destination, and then deleted that transaction without my noticing! That means the administrative bank passwords that we change every four hours is known to these bastards as soon as we know them! How could this have occurred?"

Jacob nodded in agreement as he added, "Looks like the hacker handy work of a Russian consortium we've bumped into now and again. Basically, they did a drive-by Trojan download to your smart phone that intercepts SMS text messages and sends them back out to the mother ship. If the information is important to them, it is mined and exploited by that team or sold to the highest bidder on the open market."

O'Sullivan sputtered and explained, "That is not possible! I am very careful with this phone and never let it out of my sight."

John C then sarcastically piped in, "It doesn't have to be out of your sight but only has to accept a drive- by download to be compromised. You said you use it for everything. The device was exposed to all your smart phone applications and their updates. The net of this is someone downloaded a Trojan to your phone that captured and used the administrative password to get into the bank systems. A very complex leave-behind virus code is deposited and is now hiding on our systems. The log files are useless since there is only one administrative user ID that we all have to use, but we should look at them anyway to see if anything pops to light. I don't suppose you remember any peculiar phone activity that might give us a probable infection date to work backwards from?"

The now chastened O'Sullivan hung his head and said, "Well, I did notice some unusual activity on it a few weeks back when I stopped for an evening drink. This cheeky tart asked me to buy her a drink and kept standing too close to me while playing with my phone. My phone was on the table in front of me. It never left my sight."

John C rolled his eyes, then dared, "Which phone was she playing with? The electronic one or your undersized one that is augmented with a desk enhancement?"

O'Sullivan's eyes flashed angrily as he responded, "The electronic one. Before I could retrieve it, she picked it up and it slipped down her top between her um…her uh…."

John C helped fill in the lost words, "Her antennas? You of course offered to retrieve it, I presume?" John then thoughtfully added, "So thinking about it, did you go after it the way it went down or anticipate that it might fall further than the antennas were capable of stopping its descent? In which case, a prudent male would start from the bottom and work his way up to retrieve said instrument? I can see more research being required on this topic in the very near future."

O'Sullivan, again more irritated, explained, "I didn't have to retrieve it! She did it for me and gave me an apology. Then she bought me a drink for my trouble. That was the curious part. At first I couldn't get rid of her, then I couldn't get her to stay."

John C looked toward Jacob and questioned, "So it doesn't sound like she actually installed a payload then, does it?"

Jacob again handled the phone. "This fruit phone appears to have the Near Field Communications or NFC enabled. She most likely used the NFC capability of the phone to do the drive-by download. She just dropped the phone down her top long enough to execute the installation without you seeing the activity."

The three were quiet for a few moments, and then Jacob said, "Well, this session has been very enlightening. John C, how about you and I go over the logs and do a little forensics on the systems to see if we can find some residue?"

John C nodded and took Jacob out of the Vice President's office but stopped short of the entrance and asked, "Jacob, would you mind if I had a private word with the man? I'll be right back. Please wait right here?"

"Of course, John C. Whenever you are ready, I'll be right here."

John C walked toward O'Sullivan after he closed the door and asked, "What are we going to tell the board of governors about this?"

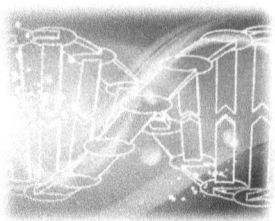

CHAPTER 19

HUMANS MAY NOT BE PERFECT, SO THEY MUST EMBRACE BEING FLAWED ...
THE ENIGMA CHRONICLES

Jacob groused, "Man, this program is just kicking my ass! I used to be able to code, breakdown instructions, analyze intrusions, and, on occasion, even order pizza. This code mocks me and my ability to decrypt and leverage the known universe. I wish Petra was here to give me her counsel, because I feel somewhat lost without her."

Jacob had called Quip to see if he'd had any luck with the file fragments uploaded to ICABOD from John C's machines. He was going to head back over to John C's bank to see if there was any other information available from the suspected drive-by infection. He wanted to get some thoughts from Quip and vent before meeting up with John C.

"I have analyzed this code with every forensic tool I know, and it still seems like Cro-Magnon man trying to do advanced calculus to plot celestial star movements. I suppose I'm simply outclassed by what I am looking at. Frankly, I don't know what I'm looking at. Feeding these code streams into ICABOD isn't even registering anything I can use. This is light years ahead of what we can do, and yet here it is, staring me in the face."

Quip didn't say anything but was quietly thinking. Jacob sensed something was on Quip's mind, but it wasn't the code being worked.

"So, Quip, how are you and your lady, the pretty EZ, getting on? I know she left to get things together, but I haven't heard any next steps. Ever since she headed home to think, you seem, shall we say, distracted? I got the impression that you would have liked to house her and change her last name. To that end, we all think she's an excellent professional and would make a great addition to the family. Petra even asked me if I would stand up at a ceremony if need be. I said yes of course, but reminded her that your brother might be offered that honor first."

Quip deftly evaded, "So, speaking of Petra, have you heard from her? I always figured you two to be the perfect couple and always together, but there you are, on your lonesome. Is she having too much fun at the winery with her tire-changing friends? Or did she take issue with the babe-a-luscious exotic dancer you were seen with in New York?

"Which reminds me, I still haven't found anything on a Zara related to Ukraine yet. Oh, that's good! You didn't find anything on her either! Har! Har! I crack myself up! Don't you just love listening to me?

"Anyway, are you going to patch things up between you two? I mean, I can do without you, but I can't do without her. She seems conspicuously absent and not anxious to return here. Let me just put the moose on the table. What precisely did you do to piss her off? Or is she simply running away from you, which would beg the why?"

Jacob was thoroughly annoyed at the question and defaulted to obscure banter. "Well, I asked her if we could do the rent-a-female thing for a threesome sex experience. You know, with lots of erotic and kinky stuff. I read somewhere that erotic is where you do it with a feather, but kinky is when you use the whole chicken. I enquired of Petra if we could do some empirical research on this theorem."

Quip stared blankly at nothing in particular, simply unable to conjure up a response. He searched for an appropriate comeback to the 'so *not Jacob*' statement. He shook his head in acknowledgement that Jacob was often a mystery.

Then with Quip's continued silence on the phone, Jacob solemnly admitted, "Actually, I asked her to marry me. I said we'd raise as many children as she wanted to breast feed until the male drawbridge would no longer raise to let the ships pass."

Quip waited a second then replied, "I liked the first story better, Jacob. So allow me to translate. You miss her and not just in the pejorative sense?"

Jacob, rather deadpan, responded, "Yes, Captain Obvious. I miss my lady, and I don't know what is delaying her return. She's keeping me in our work loop via email, but I can't reach her on the phone to just talk. I realize being in different spots on the planet right now doesn't help, especially with the major time zone differential.

"Honestly, things seemed to go sideways when Juan vanished and Julie announced her pregnancy. I want to give Petra the space she seems to need now and not pester her with questions of how she is dealing with everything. I've left a couple of voice mails and sent a few text messages so that she knows that I'm here for her when she needs me."

He lowered his gaze as he added, "I don't want to be a parasite like some males can be."

Quip smiled as he replied, "You know, one day a few years from now I might even end up liking you, Jacob.

"Julie seems to be taking this pending motherhood in her stride, albeit she's not cutting any slack on locating a defining answer on Juan. Otto and Haddy are simply beside themselves spoiling the girl. She has several months before this miracle baby appears. That child's feet will never touch the ground.

"If everything was perfect, who would need organizations or people like us? So what is the old phrase? We may not be perfect, but we are uniquely flawed."

Jacob winced then asked, "Again with the pithy sayings? Are you writing for a greeting card company in your spare time? I am having trouble dealing with a powerful female, and you are quoting an ancient TV show with refurbished Lao-Tzu teachings. Remind me to feed that sentiment back to you when you complain about EZ leaving the building! Yes, Julie has some time, but her focus is equal on the baby and Juan fronts."

Quip was a little ashamed as he admitted, "I'm sorry, Jacob. I actually admire you both. I love Petra like a sister. But each of you is asking about the other. I'm tired of the nonsense that your relationship seems to be generating, so my advice is to go to your woman and love her ... after you solve this code issue. Now, how difficult is that?"

Jacob sat thoughtfully for a few seconds, then responded, "So easily said but so difficult to accomplish. But, thanks all the same."

Quip smiled and asked, "Remember how passionate and easy it was at first with Petra? Try doing that again. I'm pretty sure she wouldn't refuse your advances."

Jacob smiled and agreed, "Sound advice, sir. Thank you."

"Now, something you said earlier about you being a parasite has made me think about a different approach to this Ghost Code program. What if we were to look at this program from a different point of view? What if we approach it as if it was organic in composition, and we were looking to develop an antidote, much like they are doing in the immune-oncology category of drugs?"

Jacob puzzled over the idea and then said, "You mean build our own virus to attack the virus? By the way, I meant you were the parasite, not me."

Quip disregarded the latter statement and spoke as if in a trance. "No, not really a virus. More of a product that can attach itself to the rogue code and interrupt the cancerous growth of the beastie. Would it be possible to provide some tasty, binary tidbits to the Ghost Code for its consumption that would interrupt its programming and render it benign to the host computer?"

Jacob, now on the same thought trail, agreed. "What we have seen so far leads me to suspect that the Ghost Code has its own binary DNA instructions of replicating and using materials from its surroundings to accomplish its growth objective and final program orders. So, if it is growing from copying or absorbing neighbor code, then why wouldn't it be willing to consume something that we manufactured?

"Following that line of reasoning, all we should have to do is build an attractive piece of code full of our own disruptive code and induce the Ghost Code to consume it. Once consumed, it would be rendered ineffective or disrupted by our Ghost Code killer. I've never written a virus before with a parasite. That is a fascinating approach to the issue. It has merit, Quip."

Quip came out of the trance-like state and illuminated, "So the π-R-Squared code that Su Lin gave us is the product to build the Ghost Code antidote with, just as she postulated in her email. We can leverage the artificial intelligence of our own ICABOD computer to help engineer this antidote. Everything we have learned about it means we need a competing product that will do only two things. First, interrupt the Ghost Code as it is building itself. Second, leave both inoperable so we can collect the specimens for further forensics. Ultimately we want our Ghost Code killer to vanish without a trace, but not disappear like a rootkit."

Jacob's eyebrows went up as he asked, "You think the Ghost Code may be incubating on the host machine like a rootkit? I had been working on that as a theory but can't prove it on these machines here in Ireland yet. It occurs to me if that is true, then just maybe we might find some code residue on these victim machines. I've only casually scanned one victim's machine for something very insidious, so perhaps I need to dig a little further on John C's bank computers. Petra's copy of the winery computer should arrive tomorrow. Let's set up remote access for me to that machine, otherwise I will be back in three days."

Quip nodded in agreement. He then questioned with a furrowed brow, "Did you call me a parasite?"

Jacob arrived at the bank, and John C provided him with the badge that allowed him to enter their secured server rooms. However, when they reached the bio-metric station, the reader failed to recognize Jacob's thumb print. Then it barked at them when John C held open the door to let them both in at once. That action summoned lots of security personnel who asked a lot of questions. The head of security insisted that Jacob be re-scanned so the bio-metric reader would record him correctly before they proceeded.

John C was annoyed and a little embarrassed by the incident, but Jacob said, "There is no need to apologize for the security procedures. That tells me that the cyber assassin didn't just walk in to do a drive-by download to your servers. So physical security appears to be fairly robust here, buddy."

John C had a sour face when he replied, "Well, who needs to come here when they can use legitimate credentials to simply remote in with the keys to the kingdom knowing that using the one admin ID we all use would render it untraceable? I can't wait to hear the 'spin' O'Sullivan puts on his excuse when we go before the board of governors. I hope they do more than the standard Sister Teresa punishment I got in Catholic School."

Jacob was a little apprehensive but figured he might as well go ahead, and he asked, "Okay, what is the Sister Teresa punishment, or am I going to regret this line of questioning?"

John C looked almost wistful as he related, "Sister Teresa was so pretty, and all the lads were in love with her or at least forever having lustful thoughts about her. But boy, oh boy, if you screwed up, she took this wooden ruler out and whacked you with it. If you answered incorrectly, you got whacked across the head. If you hid or stole something, she whacked your hand. If you wanted to be a silly ass, you got whacked on your own ass! The lads got together one day and drew straws to see if we could change that in her. I got the short straw so I was elected to be caught playing with myself to see what would happen. The result was that she demanded that I hold out my maleness and she proceeded to, as she said, 'whack my pee-pee' to remind me that masturbation was no longer an acceptable practice.

"As young as I was, I imagined all sorts of suggestive visions, clearly invisible through a nun's habit, while she was administering the punishment. It quickly became a recurring erotic dream for weeks afterwards. Whoa! Of course, I led everyone to believe that it was an enjoyable experience. As I recall, every one of the lads took a turn at getting caught so they could have the same treatment. Odd, no one admitted to the stinging pain so as to entice the next victim.

"To this day whenever I do the rent-a-female thing, I still request they start off wearing the Nun's….."

Jacob blinked repeatedly and held up his hand as he said, "Alright, I get the picture! You want justice done and something more than junior high discipline with a ruler! How about we focus on the possibilities of rootkits being deposited on your servers, shall we? We can always stroll down memory lane at the pub later."

John C shrugged then agreed, "Okay. Where do we start? As memory serves, rootkits install themselves at a very low level so that they can lie to you when you ask if they are there. They intercept requests from programs and offer up answers to make you think everything is running correctly. I like the way some of them simply tell you that there are no files in a directory and that the directory isn't there either.

"These things are nasty, but if they are using rootkit cloaking techniques to hide executable code that then acts like a thinking cyber ninja being with financial accounting skills, how are we supposed to detect it?"

Jacob held up a bootable USB drive and clarified, "I want to do a random sampling of the servers, bring them down, and reboot them with this as the bootable partition. After that, I want to run an inventory of the files with the known good file sizes and hunt for any new directories that aren't part of your institution's standard install.

"I then have another program on here that will read down to the byte and sector level of the disk drives, from start to finish, the open, deleted, and written-to sectors so we can have a complete picture of what was on these server drives. I'll take all of those results and run an analysis on them."

John C flatly stated, "You're daft, lad. You don't have that much processing power with you to do that in our lifetimes."

Jacob smiled and agreed, "Correct, I don't have that much processing power with me. But I do in my home offices. The reason is that with ten server's worth of information we should statistically be able to capture enough of the program to do some useful forensics and maybe even recreate this beastie. May I begin?"

"Jacob, let me alert operations that we will be re-booting servers and to hold the alarms on the ones we are working with. If you think our security people were anal about their jobs, you won't want to cross with the after-hour's operations team.

"It was worse before the halon fire suppressors were removed. Those madmen would hit the halon discharge button and THEN go see if it was a fire they were dealing with. I once staggered out of here unable to breathe from the gas. Thank the maker that the halon has been removed! Now it's just the fire sprinkler systems to deal with, but frankly I am not in the mood to be soaked again, so let me call them."

Jacob stared in astonishment at John C then added, "I can hardly wait for the pub stories after these other events in your life that you have recounted to me, my friend. When the hostess asks if we are a party of two, I will be inclined to say that we are more of a riot than a party."

John C just smiled, winked knowingly, and stated, "Let me make that call."

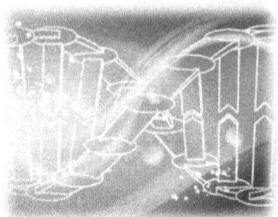

CHAPTER 20

WHO'S DRIVING THIS TRAIN?

Petra phoned Gary when she was about thirty minutes from the winery. As she entered Bosque County she saw cattle dotting the rolling hillsides. Wildflowers of purple, yellow, and white were sprinkled along the roadside on the farm-to-market highway. The beautiful countryside was interrupted with lavish homes with customized fenced driveways that displayed what she suspected were ranch or farm names. The Rockin' J made her chuckle and think of Jacob. She missed him but needed to quickly evaluate this newest potentially related event so she could return home.

Finally, reaching the metal gate embellished with the Red Caboose, she turned onto the gravel road. As she remembered the fun trip with her Dad, she recalled how tricky gravel driving was with a motorcycle. The road was now wide enough for two cars with rows of grapevines on either side that emphasized how much Gary and his son had done with the property since she'd been there. Acres of grapevines were laden with fruit that, to her untrained eye, looked almost ready to pick. Texas growing season, she suspected, was longer than near her family home. As she rounded the last bend, she came upon a huge structure and an area that seemed natural to park in, yet without lines or curbing.

Chairs, tables, and pots of flowers were artfully placed on the huge patio area. This must be where visitors lounged during tastings or the annual grape stomp she'd seen during her research of the winery on-line. It was beautiful and complete with the friendly dog that bounded toward her. As she stepped out of the car, a youngish man approached, who sported a beard and ready smile with a medium frame, around one point seven meters and maybe 60 kilograms. He had a pleasant but determined set to his jaw. She bent down to pet the friendly dog and was rewarded with finger licks.

"Careful, she'll make you continue that for hours," he chuckled, then extended his hand. "I hope you're Petra. My name is Evan. Dad suggested I meet you and show you around, as well as tell you what I can about the water program problem."

Petra offered an easy smile to Evan as she confirmed, "I am Petra. Thank you for taking time out of what I am certain is a busy day, Evan."

"Glad to meet you. I understand that you are something of a technology wizard and can help me figure out this watering program. I honestly thought it would be helpful until it went crazy. Let me show you around first, and then take you to the offices."

"I would enjoy that, thank you." Petra smiled and then pictured her and Jacob here in this beautifully alive place.

From the vantage point of the parking area, there were more rows of grapevines in every direction, save where the enormous building sat. Everything looked so inviting. Evan described the acres planted and plans to expand further with additional grapes. They purchased some of their grapes but were pleased with the increased crop yields year after year that reduced those purchased grapes. Their soil was conducive to tempranillo, port style, and viognier wines, for which they were gaining notice and winning competitions.

As they talked, Evan had led them to the back of the building, which included a huge covered patio complete with more chairs, tables, and an outdoor barbeque area. The view from the patio showed more rows of thriving grapevines. With Gary's background in commercial architecture, it was no surprise to Petra that the winery itself was totally energy efficient with advanced geothermal cooling and photo-voltaic cells.

"Your property looks amazing. My Dad and I visited here several years ago, well before your hard work. Dad and Gary talked about dreams and plans for the future of this place. I remember your Dad's passion for this land. It definitely shows. I gather that passion is infectious. He failed to mention his son would be the vintner. You seem so very young."

Evan chuckled, then explained, "I am actually a farmer for most months of the year and a vintner for only a couple. I'm certainly not from the traditional mold, and I didn't train for years as an apprentice with a seasoned winemaker. I studied chemistry and have read a great deal. At the ripe old-age of twenty-one, I began making wine. It seems to have worked, based on the continuing notoriety we receive. My wife and children love the country and the slower life.

"Would you care to sample a couple of wines now or later?"

"Yes, I would. But we better make it later, if you don't mind. I want to get into your computer and see if I can find anything in your application to explain your problem."

"No worries. You fix this program, and I'll provide the wines." Evan continued and explained, "The application seemed fine when I completed all the Wi-Fi connections for the program to control the water valves. I successfully performed all the tests that the instructions indicated. I set up the timing schedule I needed for the water valves to turn on based on the moisture levels in the soil.

"As we plant more and more grapevines, I wanted to potentially keep the costs down by automating the watering process. Most watering is conducted at night or pre-dawn to get the roots to absorb as much as possible. I had planned to still walk the rows and check my vines, but I estimated it could save a few workers with this program. When Dad spoke to Otto, he agreed that such programs were used in drought areas, like Spain, to optimize the moisture. In Spain, they happen to also use different types of plants that remain closer to the ground. Otto had recommended a vendor product that was widely used in Spain, France, Italy, and even California. The costs were higher than the application I purchased, but with hindsight that might have been smarter.

"I found the water system application when I searched the Internet. The price was almost half, and so I bought it. It arrived in a week from New York. I thought I had found a bargain as well as an American made system. Once I completed all the connections and testing, the application ran perfectly for about thirty days. Then, during the hottest part of the day, the valves in two areas started watering. I was ten feet from the first area so I ran to the valve to shut it down, but by the time I reached it, the water had stopped. I noticed a bit of water on the adjacent area, but that valve was off.

"I went to my office and opened the application on the computer and found an error message that said, **_mis-calibration occurrence – auto adjusted_**. I checked and the two valves were the only two that opened and each for seven seconds. I figured the application had an issue, but it looked okay. I rechecked all the times for possible watering and verified the moisture content allowance. All was good. Or, so I thought."

"Great detail, Evan, and good job writing down the messaging. Would you mind if I looked at the computer?"

Evan showed her the laptop and logged in, then provided Petra with the password. Petra began pouring over all aspects of the application. She was surprised when she found that the program executable elements were non-existent. The application was not in a mode to run at all. It was an incomplete program. She searched all the directories, verified with Evan how he had initially loaded the program. She copied some items from the various directories the program had created onto a thumb drive.

Evan watched, but outside of responding to questions, he remained silent. Admittedly he was not a technologist, but he paid attention and took everything in. Petra asked for the DVD that Evan had received with his easy to install instruction booklet. Using one of the two laptops she carried in her bag, she tried to view the contents of the DVD. Her intention was to load it onto her machine.

Evan handed her the booklet, DVD, and a fresh bottle of water which she immediately opened. The bottle was sweaty with cold water drops and looked delicious. As she smiled and acknowledged his thoughtfulness, she picked up the booklet with her other hand. She opened to page one and started to read when several drops of water from the bottle dripped onto the pages. To her amazement, the pages simply started to melt. She quickly tried to blot the water off the pages but failed as all but the front cover were gone in a matter of seconds.

"Please tell me you saw that, Evan," Petra calmly stated, totally amazed.

"Petra, I have never seen anything like that for any instructional document. I am so sorry about the water. Why such poor quality of paper? I might expect it out of a third world country, but not domestically."

"Yep, we are in agreement. I was thirsty, and the water wasn't the problem. The only time I have seen this sort of paper is for secret messaging, usually depicted in the movies."

"Okay, I'm going to take a look at this DVD. Let's move the water far away."

"No problem. I am going to go check on some things, Petra, while you're working on that. I'm sure watching you would be about as much fun as watching paint dry."

Petra laughed and replied, "That's funny. You go right ahead and take care of what you need to, I'll be fine. I am glad you called us. We will talk later, I promise. Plus, I want to sample your wine."

After Evan left, Petra concentrated as she loaded the DVD and tried to find any real files. What she found was roughly a hundred folders all of which were empty. No files, no executables, no nothing. One folder caught her attention. It was labeled Ghost_Code but was also empty. The only thing she now knew for certain was that the creator of this program at the winery was somehow tied to the other events.

Petra logged in her other computer and started a secure instant messaging session with Jacob. She quickly outlined what she had found and asked for his advice. Short of taking Evan's entire laptop, Jacob suggested she do a complete copy of the machine's content onto her spare machine.

She finished her discussion and then phoned Evan. When he answered, she asked, "Evan, may I make a copy of your laptop contents, please? I want to make certain we have the information to complete an entire forensic diagnostic. I didn't think you wanted to part with your machine."

"Yes, I understand and appreciate your thoroughness." He then carefully caveated, "I will expect you to keep my winery information confidential."

"Of course, Evan. Only my team will look at the data. I just hesitate to delete anything that might help me locate the source.

"I plan to be finished here in half an hour. Then I would like to sample and hear about your wines. I also need to find a motel for the night, as I try to avoid drinking and driving."

"It would be my pleasure to discuss the wines, Petra. I'll meet you on the patio. I might even offer a suggestion for your overnight accommodations."

Petra finished copying the information onto her laptop, then sanitized all of the application residue from Evan's machine. After she'd exchanged messages with Jacob and they'd agreed this was yet another key event, she sent an email to Wolfgang and asked permission to authorize the expenditure for the programs that Otto had originally suggested to Gary. She wanted to make certain that the graciousness of her host would be rewarded. With all her activities completed for the day, she easily found the patio.

Evan brought out samples of wine to a table that had a great view of the property. The sun had started its slow drift to the horizon which changed the entire view. Evan was very animated as he treated her to a litany of stories about the wines, the labels with local artist's artwork, and some of the awards they'd received. The reds were particularly smooth and full-flavored, and impressive at the very least. Several of these were earmarked to be shipped home to Wolfgang for his cellars. They discussed some of the events the winery held and the contributions made by his brother who was a chef.

After several pleasant samples, she settled on a very nice glass of Merlot and then asked, "I need to see if I can get a room close by for the night. With this wonderful wine, I hardly want to move from this patio and certainly not back to the airport for my flight tomorrow afternoon. Any suggestions, Evan?"

"Actually, Petra, I was hoping you'd consider simply staying here. We moved a coach car onto the property and refurbished it for essentially a suite. Currently, we have several within walking distance down the lighted path to the right. I took my wife there for our anniversary a month ago, and she declared it very romantic."

"No kidding. Wow, I would love to stay here. What a wonderful way to extend the nice glow from your Merlot. Thank you, Evan."

Petra immediately outlined all the reasons to bring Jacob to Texas. It reminded her of the wonderful conversations they had when they'd first met. The seal on that deal was the list of Texas wineries along with their supported wines. She'd no idea of the vast amount of wineries scattered throughout the state. It was a delightful late afternoon and evening visit with Gary, Evan, and Evan's wife and children.

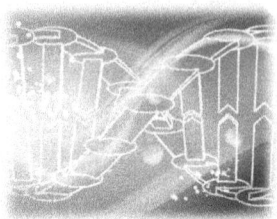

CHAPTER 21

TELL ME WHAT YOU SEE IN THE INK BLOTS ON THE CANVAS

Jacob had secured a semi-quiet booth, while John C excused himself to go to the, as he called it, *Wee Leprechaun* place. The dimly lit, smoky little pub was rich with friendly conversation and laughter. It was totally relaxed, and suddenly he understood the draw of the pub. After a tough day at work, the pretty barmaids, lively banter, and the glow of a soft fire towards the back were impossible to resist. New patrons arrived and the noise grew, though a steady din continued. Must be a special group he thought. He suspected that the size of the place was deceiving, given the way the walls were constructed. John C had earlier said that the pub's original floor plan had expanded significantly since it was a travelers' stopover during the 1600's.

When John C returned, Jacob said, "The waitress came by, and I gave her our drink orders."

"Great! What did you order?"

"I ordered two pints of the black stuff of course. What else did you expect me to order? I haven't forgotten you telling me that Guinness is good for you!"

John C expressed his annoyance as he accused, "Oh swell, you ordered two Guinnesses, but you didn't get anything for me!"

Then in a voice loud enough for the waitress to hear over the din in the pub, John C said, "Miss? I'll have two Guinnesses over here as well!" Some heads turned to look at them, and John C clarified, by way of apology, "Well, me mate here is from across the pond. As we all know, they don't show a talent for ordering to support two-fisted Irish drinking!"

The locals knowingly nodded in agreement. A couple raised their mugs and offered cheers to Jacob in an effort to try and reconcile him with his drink ordering deficiency.

Jacob gave John C a sullen look then tried to change the subject. "I'm glad that we have the data capture routines working on the servers. They should run all night, and we can collect the information tomorrow. So there is nothing to be done but go to a quiet Irish pub and sip a little brew.

"There seems to be an increase in activity, even since we arrived. Is it always this noisy in Irish pubs, or is this just guys arriving after work? I was expecting a little more peace and quiet than this."

John C agreed, "It is noisy in here. Let me see what's going on and get a few shillings owed me from that lad that just passed by.

"Oh, after I ordered that way, you seemed a little undone. In the future, do you want me to be more discreet and less vocal in the discovery process?"

Jacob grinned and replied, "I'd like a little less attention for our pub time, John C. But I certainly can be taught."

John C nodded and said in an almost whispered tone, "Very well, I understand." Then with all the gusto of a hound dog, he hollered out, "What the hell are you lot making so much noise about? If you're all having an orgy over there, at least have the decency to invite us in!"

About that time, the waitress showed up with the drinks John C had ordered and admonished, "John, me lad, we've talked about this before, and it always ends up the same! You get thrown out, and I lose out on me tips. So tip me now, before I lose my chance of making a few bob!"

John C was in an argumentative mood as he responded, "Listen, love, I'm happy to give you the tip you want, so long as it is attached to the rest of me shaft. In fact if you're not doing anything later we can….."

Jacob interceded and tactfully asked, "Miss, we were only wondering why it was so loud here. Is there some special activity going on that would account for the extra background noise?"

The waitress was a little disarmed at Jacob's polite manners, but smiled sweetly and replied, "We do have a guest tattoo artist visiting and taking orders. His portfolio is quite impressive, and the audience that is engaged with him are somewhat vocal. He boasts fast tattooing and his portfolio indicates quality work. I myself have asked for a nice Claddagh ring to be located in a very discreet spot for my man to enjoy."

"And what is that, madam?" inquired Jacob.

She giggled and yet looked a little dreamy as she explained, "It has a heart in the center to represent love with Mick's initials, a crown on top to represent loyalty, and two hands on either side holding the heart showing friendship or, as like to fancy, Mick taking care of me heart."

She sighed and continued, "The artist is from America and only here tonight. He did a quick sketch and promised to reserve it for only me, if I get it tonight. But he is expensive. Therefore, all I'm asking for is generous tipping this evening, gents."

Jacob's curiosity was piqued, so he asked, "Who is so famous that he takes his tattooing skills on tour?"

The waitress smirked and stated, "Ye mean, ye don't know of Gentleman Josh, the tattooist? He's one of your own. My, but you do lead a sheltered life, kind sir!"

Jacob looked thoughtful as he accessed something he couldn't quite grab from his memory banks. He added a generous tip for the waitress and then absently said to John C, "I seem to recall just such a tattoo artist when I was in New York. If it's who I think it is, let's go over and introduce ourselves to Gentleman Josh."

John C smiled and wholeheartedly agreed, "I've been longing for an interesting one-of-a-kind tattoo that I could use for conversation purposes. Perhaps this Gentleman Josh is the proper destination. Besides that, I can ask where he will put the tattoo on our lovely waitress."

Jacob gave John C a moderately incredulous look then asserted, "Ummm, a professional would not discuss what he put on another person or where, if he ever hoped to be called a gentleman tattoo artist."

John C studied for a minute and then asked, "Why does this sound like another one of your lectures, Mr. Jacob? All I want to know is what the graphic looks like and a close proximity of where, so I can ask to explore! That's all! I'm not looking to bear her children! I'm not looking for Miss Right. I'm simply looking for Miss Right Now! Geez, if the morality police need a new grand potentate, I'm nominating you, budrow! And besides, she'll need another male opinion with Mick at University for six more months."

Jacob, tiring of the verbal sparring, suggested with a grin, "How about we go look at his portfolio and see if there is something for you? Maybe we can get a nice tramp stamp for you that someone will enjoy when you're on all fours, shall we?"

"Is that how you see me, lad?" John C grinned. "I didn't know that about you, Jacob! It doesn't work for me, but I honestly didn't realize that you were of such a persuasion."

Over at the portfolio table, way at the back of the pub, Jacob and John C looked at the drawings and listened to the patrons' conversations with the well-tailored tattoo artist Josh. The drawings seemed detailed and well done. Jacob was surprised at the sheer size of some of the artwork and bold colors.

Josh smiled at their approach and asked, "Gentlemen, do you see a motif or graphic that inspires you? My dance card is filling up rather quickly, so if you are inspired by something or want to explore alternative sketches, then we should talk. How about you, Jacob? You still seem to be gravitating around that dragon graphic again, so how about it this time?"

John C looked puzzled, and Jacob was taken aback by being called by his name by the tattooist.

After recovering from being startled and finally recalling why Josh seemed so familiar, he said, "Of course! Now I remember you, Josh. You did a lot of work on a friend of mine. He was always trying to get me in to see you to fix this old tattoo I had done as a lark, one weekend when my mom was traveling."

Josh grinned and agreed, "That's right! We were going to do a cover-up on that blob you were stuck with on your shoulder. I suggested then and still advocate it now that a good tattoo should be an image easily discernable from across the street.

"As it is said by both genders, size does matter! Are you ready for that beautiful graphic to spill across your back? I promise when I'm done with that dragon it will have that real and malevolent look that will say to everyone viewing it, 'mess with my consort and I'll come off of here and jack you up, buddy'! You know I am only in town for a few days, but I can stay over to work the dragon for you if your answer is yes."

John C was aghast in wonderment at the topic of conversation and retracted, "Jacob, I take it all back about you being the grand potentate for the morality mob after hearing about this! I was beginning to feel self-conscious about having a small discreet Christian graphic in Irish motif on my arm while here you are planning a giant dragon across your whole back with the tail probably wrapping around, then going down your right leg! Whoa, color me impressed, laddie-buck!

"Josh, how much time do you expect to take for something that size? You claim to be fast, but I can see that as several sessions, each at several hours a piece."

Josh explained, "I know the look that he is expecting from the graphic, probably better than he does. The first session will take four to five hours, depending on his fortitude. I would let it heal at least two weeks before putting the fiery colors into it. I am fast, but I want quality work for my customers. No one is likely to go the distance for all of it at one sitting. It's just too hard on the body. Besides, there is no hurry if you are looking for quality work.

"I'm not going to push too much ink onto you like I did a couple of weeks back with this crazy demanding female. Brother, talk about insistent and driven! She had to have this tramp stamp done, colored, and wouldn't listen to reason. I don't know how I let her talk me into pounding that much ink into her, but I guess those sultry European accents are hard to resist."

Jacob looked skeptically at Josh, then quickly roughed out a sketch on a piece of paper and handed it over as he asked, "Did the tat look like this?"

Josh then went through the graphics on his phone until he found the picture he wanted by date and compared it to Jacob's drawing. He studied the sketch quickly and looked up over the top of his glasses and nodded.

"That is my work." he explained, as he handed the device to Jacob, "Yep! That is what I put on her about two weeks ago. But for you to be able to see it, she had to be….."

Jacob filled in the blank easily, "Topless."

"Yes, that is correct," laughed Josh.

John C was now speechless, his mouth wide open with slight movement as he attempted to learn to talk again.

Jacob turned to John C and quietly said, "It's not what you think. But it is related to your issues at the bank, John. This is the tat I saw but did not remember until just now. She was present at the New York tax offices just before all of their records were wiped, just like what was done to your institution."

Josh remarked, "You know it's funny. She was the one who gave me the idea to come to Ireland and do some guest tattooing. She complained that she couldn't get the kind of work she wanted while she was in Ireland which is why I guess she was so impatient to have it done all in one setting. Odd set of circumstances. Tough broad,"

John C and Jacob looked at each other in that 'ah-ha' moment.

Jacob said quietly into John's ear, "She came through here and went on to New York to wreak havoc there after whacking your bank! It's funny what you can find in a quiet Irish pub."

Trying to get their attention again, Josh asked, "Gentlemen, can we discuss some ink for the here and now, or are you only interested in what someone else owns?"

"Let's get John C here some ink so he can show it off to the babes. I, on the other hand, need to talk to my babe to see about me getting a tattoo. Besides, you will need more time for me than I can spare on this trip. But no worries, I know where to find you in New York, and I'll be back soon enough. This served as a great reminder, sir."

John C was a little apprehensive at discussing his tattoo requirements with Josh, but said, "I think I would like some work from you, but I lied when I said it was for my arm. How much discomfort would it be if the target destination is my left cheek?"

Josh grinned, then said with all sincerity, "That depends if you want it to reach the right cheek as well?"

Jacob laughed a bit and added, "I'll leave you to it, John C, since I don't want to see the ink going on that part of your geography. I've got some email and conference calls to attend to. I'll see you in the morning. Josh, make sure my friend here gets all the quality you can deliver."

As he left, Jacob could hear John C ask Josh in all earnestness, "And you're sure this graphic will help me get more babes?"

To which Josh grinned and replied, "Ah, my man, you have no idea how much your male endurance will be tasked by the ladies once you have one of my tattoos! Trust me on this, sir!"

Jacob wondered what Petra would say to his idea of a full dragon across his back. He rightly considered that he needed to discuss it with her before laying down any ink.

Then he was startled by the thought. *What if she wanted some body art as well? How would he deal with that discussion?* His mind wandered all over the mental image of her, trying to imagine what kind of graphic and exactly where it should go if she in fact liked the idea. Jacob wistfully thought about his Petra and couldn't wait to speak with her, hoping that she would take his call from the hotel room. He promptly left to return to the hotel.

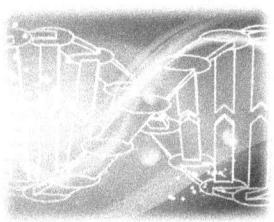

CHAPTER 22

STARE AND COMPARE......JUST DON'T GET CAUGHT STARING AND NEVER ADMIT TO COMPARING

Jacob began, "Thanks for joining the conference call, Carlos. I've got Petra, Quip, and Wolfgang on the call as well. We are all in different locations, but we wanted to exchange information on our findings at this point.

"Obviously, the big thing is that Juan and his aircraft are missing. From there, we have only small pieces and parts of clues that have a similar look, and we feel these might be related. The one common thread here is the term *Ghost Code-Patent Pending* that loosely ties these events together. What we have confirmed so far is only anecdotal information, with only one fruit phone camera shot of the Ghost Code message on a screen to do forensics on."

Quip interrupted, "Until today. I've had ICABOD running data gathering routines twenty-four, seven. I added the high profile facial recognition algorithm against a massively large Big Data warehouse across the Internet looking for someone who matches the physical description that Jacob gave me, along with a grainy video of someone shamelessly exploiting another human being and giving all of us managers a bad name."

Petra innocently asked, "Jacob gave a physical description of this person that we only have a partial facial recognition on that ties them together? What other detailed description was captured that leads to this alleged cross reference?"

Jacob now sensed a cross examination he would just as soon side step and clarified, "We actually now have three possible corroborating visuals. The first is your indiscreet videotaping of the hydroelectric manager being seduced into delivering a computer virus into an air gapped system. The second is me spotting your evil twin making a hasty exit from the New York City tax records department, just before all hell broke loose. The third is providing a carefully doctored photo of you, my dear, which resembled the cyber assassin according to the VP in Ireland at John C's bank. He confirmed the female in the picture was the one who dropped his cell phone down the front of her blouse, which provided the necessary time to install a drive- by virus via near field communications. The VP also indicated she had an eastern European accent and wasn't a Yank."

Quip said, "Right! Actually, we've come a long way since then. At first we couldn't find anything on her, right, Jacob? Anyway, the main difference between the VP episode and yours, Jacob, was that she was wearing a blouse in the VP episode."

Again Petra innocently interjected, "Oh, Jacob, I don't remember hearing that particular detail when you recounted the New York incident with my evil twin."

Jacob closed his eyes and with great restraint said through gritted teeth, "You could have talked all day and not said that, Quip! Just for the record, others in the tax records office also noticed she was only wearing a painted blouse, not cloth material, as Quip indicated! Anyway, the point is….the point is…..well, I don't remember what the point is anymore!"

Quip, now satisfied that he had flustered his colleague enough to make him lose his train of thought, intervened, "The point is we have a facial that was good enough to hunt against. Based on Jacob's auditory evaluation of her Russian accent, her admission of being Ukrainian, as well as his physical assessment of our suspect, on a lark I ran a passport photo search of international travelers going into the U.S. for the last ten days, and curiously enough I got a hit. Not only did we get a photo back of a Petra look-a-like, but she is also Ukrainian entering the United States recently from the United Kingdom. Now you know what I say about coincidences always being highly engineered. Well, this looks highly coincidental. Put together the fact that we have what appears to be the same individual in two target vectors of our interest and passport photos to begin shopping with."

Carlos, somewhat distracted by the awkwardness that Jacob was having under cross examination, reiterated, "Am I hearing something of a lead on a person that might be able to point us in the right direction of the Ghost Code, and the last known position is somewhere in the United States? That does brighten our hunting picture, but the United States is a big place."

Quip grinned as he admitted, "I thought you might say that. The entry point into the United States was LaGuardia Airport in New York. As I dug a little deeper on the evil twin of Petra, it turns out she left a residence address in New York as part of her visa contact information. Turns out it is an address ICABOD had stored as a known address for the previous leader of the Dteam. The now deceased Grigory used this address for his residence when he was in New York conducting business. ICABOD also came up with the corollary address of the Dteam operations center."

Jacob then asked, "Can we use her passport name of Zara instead of calling her the Petra evil twin with brown eyes?"

Petra innocently asked, "Oh, she had brown eyes?"

After a brief period of uncomfortable silence, Petra asked with some incredulousness, "And you know her name too?"

Jacob again closed his eyes and gave a grimaced sigh that echoed across the conference call. Before he could respond, Quip said, "I showed the passport photo to Jacob so he could confirm she was the right lady. We both hit on the idea of socializing it with the bank VP for his confirmation. It was an additional cross reference to make sure we had the right gal.

"Petra, passport information only includes information on what can be seen wearing regular clothes like eye and hair color with height and weight. They do not recount a lady's cup size or the fact that she had on a set of hot pink earrings."

Jacob's mouth went completely dry while he tried to extricate himself from this soon to be death spiral explanation.

Carlos unmuted his phone, laughed briefly at the episode and offered, "My friends, these sound like good working clues. Petra, were you and Jacob able to build a new bogus identity that I can use, or should I ask Julie? Julie assembled the last one for me. Even though I resented it at the time, I would very much like her expertise in manufacturing another ID that I can use for my hunting expedition. Only this time, can I have a more engaging name than Bobby Joe? I really want a cool sounding name that will stick out when you hunt for me, or when I am signaling something while I am undercover."

Petra smiled and replied, "As I recall, you wanted this ID to have certain attributes to give it the illusion of someone running from the authorities and that it needed some breadcrumbs that would be discovered on further research. I hadn't forgotten. Yes, we have most of it worked up but were waiting for the last few details to finalize it. I think we can come up with a suitable name for you, Carlos. When I finish my review of a Texas incident, I will be seeing Julie. Please give it a couple of days, and let us do a bit more verification on what we have so far."

Quip, unable to resist one last dig, said, "We had discussed the name Twin Aerial Hunter. But that name is going to be Jacob's new cover ID since he has become a top line-of-sight communications expert. That is, of course, provided he survives the interrogation that will likely be occurring in the near future."

Petra grinned, giggled, and then responded, "Okay, Quip. You can stop teasing Jacob now. I think my man has had enough for a while. Carlos, do we need to help arrange transportation and funding for this expedition of yours? The clues we are seeing strongly suggest the Dteam operators are involved, and if they are, you should understand they have no sense of humor nor honor in how they deal with people who cross them."

Carlos smiled confidently and intimated, "Petra, that is what makes it fun!"

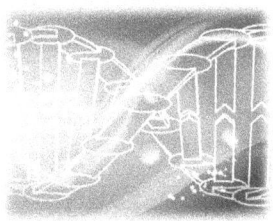

CHAPTER 23

TREASURE HUNTING CAN TAKE YOU TO SO MANY PLACES

When Petra arrived at the shoot location at the Treasure Reef entrance to Dolphin Cove, she immediately started to relax. The day was absolutely perfect with the blue of the sky complementing the greenish-blue hue of the ocean that sparkled as if emeralds were on top of the water waiting to be plucked up by a passing mermaid. The squeals and laughter from the beach caught her attention in time to see a beautiful girl with wavy brown hair trying to make her escape from a pirate. She shook her head slightly at the traditionally dressed swashbuckling pirate and the modern female in a flimsy lounging cover-up in vibrant orange and purple. The color offsets were actually marvelous.

As she got a little closer, she spotted more models, makeup artists working on a couple of girls, photographers capturing what appeared to be different perspectives, Lara and her assistant with a clipboard obviously comparing notes or checking them off, and Julie off to the side sitting in the sand. Petra showed her identification to the security staff member and gained entrance. She started to walk toward Julie, yet waved to Lara on the way. She noted that at least Julie was smiling and taking in the scene, rather than crying her eyes out, which was what she'd feared.

Suddenly a pirate was beside her, matched in step. She looked over and grinned.

"Pretty lady, can I take you to my ship and show you my chest of gold? We could sail away across the seven seas."

"Ah, Captain. As tempting as your offer is, I am not one of the models. I'm afraid that I must decline with some regret."

The faux pirate laughed and said, "That, my dear, was the nicest brush off I've ever received." With that he kissed her hand, bowed, and headed back toward the rest of the action.

She watched him saunter over to the rest of the pirates and wanted to ask Lara what she was thinking of with this motif.

Petra smiled and chuckled as she arrived beside Julie and joined her in the sand. She reached over and hugged Julie as she asked, "How are you feeling, Julie? I must say you look wonderfully relaxed."

"I'm okay. Not a twinge of morning sickness, and my energy is great during the day, though I do find I sleep just a bit longer. Eating right, taking my vitamins, lots of walking, and no more serious, twisty workouts. And you, Petra, how are you feeling?"

Petra snorted as she explained, "I'm a little travel weary to be honest. I have been from Sao Paulo to Dallas to here in a short period of time, chasing a wraith. This code is just crazy. It appears out of almost nowhere, wreaks havoc, and then vanishes for the most part. It is just taking so long to locate the root cause. It is very frustrating."

"Well, I can relate to the frustrating part. So cut to the chase, Pet, how much progress in locating Juan and the plane?"

Hugging Julie a little tighter around the shoulders, she quietly said, "Not much. We are working each piece as fast as possible."

"He's not dead, Pet. He's just not. I would know if he were, and my heart says he's not, so promise me that we keep at it."

"We all promise. If you believe it, then I believe it too. I just want you to be realistic.

"The other reason for my coming here, other than I wanted to see you and see if you even had a bump yet, which you don't, is to discuss a new identity for Carlos. If determination counts for anything to locate Juan or his assailant, you and Carlos lead the charge. We found some evidence that links some of what we see with this ghost code mess back to the Russian hackers, the Dteam. We linked back to a female out of Ukraine. We suspect she has a significant role, though

Jacob doubts she is the base code programmer, but more of a manipulator and identity hacker, which has been that group's focus over the last couple of years."

"Petra, I thought with that nasty Grigory gone, that group had died out."

"Evil doesn't die. You know that. It just adds in more people and perpetuates. We believe that they did split off part of the operations with Chairman, but still worked in their field of expertise with credit card fraud and email scamming. They have been operating in security reviews for some unknown organizations without a great deal of success."

"Okay, so what does this mean exactly, and how can I help? Pet, I will not be kept in a box, so don't try that protecting stuff."

"I wouldn't dream of keeping you out of the loop unless it would risk my niece or nephew. I need you to do the identity change for Carlos and help him get into character. We also need you to help maintain some level of contact with him and update us. One touchy issue, however, is that Carlos really doesn't want Lara to know where he is located or what he might be facing. Since we are also friends with Lara, this becomes a fine line for us. I think you get my meaning. Those outside of the family are on a need to know, just like always."

Julie nodded as Petra continued, "Jacob and I have been going to each of the incident sites that we can to gather more information. Quip is doing the endless data mining and analysis through ICABOD, and Wolfgang is prowling suspicious financial transactions. In short, everyone is hunting and no one is keeping you out. So get that clearly in your mind."

"Okay. I'm sorry. I know you wanted me to help Lara with transporting the models, and we have two more days until we are finished. I can get Carlos's ID framework tomorrow afternoon. I just need the details of what we want when someone checks. The building of the data and the verification steps will take a few days. I will call him and let him know it will be about a week. I can meet up with him and review all the details. The timing should work well with the ending of this project.

"I know what we can and cannot share with our friends about business, so I will honor his request. I sure won't tell Lara I will be seeing Carlos, as that would really bother her. I think she misses him but has stayed too busy to worry about it."

They were both comfortably silent for a while.

"Pet, look over at that girl with the rainbow flowing skirt and top," she said as she pointed to a pretty blonde walking with a pirate. "Do you like it?"

"I do. It flows well, and I like all the colors. Why?"

"It's one of mine, and I thought of you when I designed it. All that elegance and the molded top that works when a female is as pretty as you."

They both laughed as they watched the work with the models continue. The pirates looked to be more props than anything else, like the ocean, sand, and blue cloud-dotted sky with the occasional seagull. As the sun dipped closer to the horizon, the pirates and models were released, and the equipment was rapidly packed up. Lara came over and sat down, looking happy but tired.

"Welcome to paradise, Petra. I am so glad you could join us. Can you stay for a couple of days so we can all catch up?"

"I can. I don't plan to leave until day after tomorrow. What's up with pirates? It looks really interesting and very different."

Lara laughed a bit, then revealed, "This idea actually came from a trip Carlos and I made here. This area was once a big stopover for pirates, and they say there is still gold buried in some places along the Jamaica shoreline. The pirates attract the tourists and give them some sense of times past. Certainly not like the horrible pirate incidents that we have heard about for cruise ships in the media, but the romantic side, I guess.

"I thought it would be fun to have the entire fall release be about treasure hunting for the perfect outfit for all the various activities. Capture your man instead of being captured. The woman in demand and so forth. I thought it would be fun to put together an advertising campaign that would allow women to capture hints toward finding the treasure from various outfits and spreads in three of the magazines that rave about Destiny Fashions of Brazil. If they assemble all the puzzle pieces to the treasure hunt, then they can enter to win a trip to Jamaica for a week for two and see their own pirates. Julie's designs are the most prominent in this spread, and the colors she chose are bold."

Julie chimed in, "The flowing lines are perfect to go from sun and sand, to the yacht or country club, to dinner with a group or alone. All the outfits have two or three components that can easily dress it up or dress it down. Very easy, wearable, and wrinkle-free fabrics so great for travel or capture." She laughed and the other two joined in.

"What a fun idea. Challenging fun for the woman that likes treasure hunts. Now I can't wait."

"Yeah," voiced Lara. "If you like it, then other ladies will too. Come on. Let's go back and get changed and enjoy dinner. I want to hear everything that Carlos is doing since he won't tell me, but I bet you've heard. Julie is still staying through the end of the shoot, right?"

"No worries, Lara. Julie will stay and help get the models and your team back to where they need to be. I am glad you two are together and a bit jealous that you are in near paradise. I'm definitely ready to eat and laugh. It will be great to catch up in person."

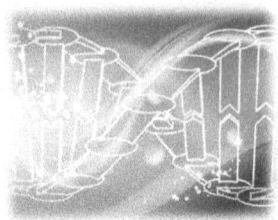

CHAPTER 24

CAN I GET THAT ORDER TO GO, PLEASE?

Major Chu Guano was startled at the sudden appearance of Chairman Chang at the cyber warfare facilities where he worked on Chairman's pet project. He snapped to attention and said, "Chairman, this is an unexpected honor, sir! If we had known you wanted to see us, we could have easily made the trip to your offices. How may I be of service, sir?"

Chairman didn't respond at first but studied the situation area and finally asked, "Where is Miss Krumhunter? I thought I might receive a briefing update on the projects' status."

Major Guano was not anxious to give details on Miss Krumhunter's work ethic, but any fact that could be mentioned in casual conversation to discredit her with Chairman was always a welcomed opportunity.

Guano offered, "Sir, I am sure she is close at hand, just taking a short break after her long hours last night."

Chairman brightened as he stated, "Oh, you two worked all night here last night on the project. I see. Excellent! I am looking forward to a briefing update on your progress."

Major Guano's eyes cut back and forth as he lowered his voice and admitted, "Well, not exactly, Chairman. Miss Krumhunter complained of a sick headache early yesterday afternoon and left the facilities for some well-deserved rest. I offered to cover off on our next generation testing and to document the results for her review early this morning. Our schedule is rather tight since Professor

Lin is constantly trying to squeeze us out of his computer facilities in favor of other programs."

Chairman was a bit disappointed but asked, "So has she been in to read your report and provide the briefing I am expecting?"

The Major shifted uneasily in his stance and explained, "Well, no, sir, not yet. I thought perhaps she may have come in and was working on our overall documentation, but the security checkpoint only shows where she left yesterday at two pm with no new check-in time for today."

Chairman now showed some concern, then asked, "So you two must really be hitting hard to keep this project on its timeline. I am sorry that Miss Krumhunter has not been able to keep up with your pace and seems to be fading here when we are so close to being finished."

Again Major Guano shuffled uncomfortably and, not meeting Chairman's gaze, offered, "I'm sure the work demands have been more than what she has been used to since this seems to be overwhelming her. Not to worry, sir. She dutifully copies all our day's work to a USB thumb drive that she takes home to work on every day. I am confident that any missed work time here is more than made up for at her studio flat."

Chairman was agitated and demanded, "Let me get this straight! She leaves at two in the afternoon, and she makes it in most days by eleven? For the love of my ancestors, I hope she takes enough time to have a little something for lunch to keep her strength up!"

Guano hesitated to volunteer any more information but then added, "Actually, she confesses to allergic reactions to Chinese food, so rather than get something from the cafeteria she dashes out for an order of preformed extruded chicken components with sugar and caffeine enriched dipping sauce. I usually give her money to bring some back for me as well, but she doesn't always remember."

Chairman ignored the glib comment as he roared, "And what do you mean, she copies everything onto a USB thumb drive to work from at home? No one takes work home from this facility! That is a breach of security! How is she getting it past the security people since no one is supposed to bring USB drives in or out of here?"

Major Guano, starting to wilt under the cross examination, suggested, "Sir, as the director she claimed the right to not have her things rifled through coming in or going out after a couple of weeks, and the security people acquiesced. It is a charming device actually as it also doubles as a nice writing pen in addition to being a high capacity USB storage device."

Chairman was now breathing a little heavier and had trouble keeping his temper in check as he questioned, "Have you reviewed some of her contributions to the project notes? And more specifically, did she say what she was doing with all that information?"

Guano looked surprised and stammered, "Chairman, I presumed she was emailing you updates on a daily basis, as you had requested. We are coming up on the second phase of our program after all the successful prototypes we have used in the various proofs of concept, so I am focused on the mass delivery mechanism. Have you not been getting our reports from Miss Krumhunter?"

Chairman was now thoroughly vexed and shouted, "Why do you think I came down here? I have not gotten anything from either of you, so I am here for a briefing on our project and you have given me more than I dreamed of!"

Major Guano was terrified that he would be turned over to Nikkei as a new play toy after this briefing. He quietly waited, afraid to speak.

Chairman, now calm again, stared into the Major's eyes and stated, "My dear Major. Is it possible that I have underestimated your value in this role and not fully expressed my satisfaction in your dedicated work ethic? I feel that perhaps there could be rebalancing of responsibilities on this project that I believe you will find more agreeable than your current role. However, I would like to discuss this matter with the current director just so there is no misunderstanding between all parties, particularly me."

Major Guano struggled to contain his exuberance and consented, "Chairman, I would welcome the opportunity to serve in any capacity that you deem fit."

Chairman nodded his head and smiled in a paternal way as he then added, "Yes, I can see that. We'll talk later."

Major Guano then said, "Oh, I almost forgot. As a precaution, a little insurance policy was embedded in the programs that were being copied onto the USB drive, just in case they fall into the wrong hands. Those programs that went onto the thumb drive are separate code stream than our production programs. If they are moved to another media or emailed we will know where they went and who received them."

Chairman was immediately pleased and smiled as he said, "You know I would really like to know more about this *phone home feature* added to our project. I see a very positive future for you, Major. Thank you for your advanced thinking in this matter. Now, if you will excuse me, I have some arrangements to make."

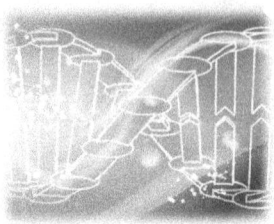

CHAPTER 25

TO FIND THE EVIL ROOT, FOLLOW THE MONEY

Wolfgang seemed satisfied as he checked over the accounts and numbers again. There was definitely recent activity in the account that had been used to fund the airplane in the incident where EZ and the government contractor were taken hostage. As he recalled, this account had been tracked back to their old customer and adversary Chairman Chang and the Arab terrorist with the pilfered *Freedom Fighter Funds*. It was the first pattern he'd found in the nine hundred plus accounts he routinely watched. He had segregated twenty accounts out and plotted the activity during the most recent four month period. There were a few that had some questionable activity and might prove starting points for finding the source programmer.

Financial accounts and money movement were areas in which the R-Group had historically specialized. Several of the financial institutes they owned, including the one here in Zurich, were tracked in several ways to minimize infiltration by unwanted people. Historically, this infiltration had been from a few hackers, but with the growing experience of the hacker communities from Russia, China, and increasingly the Arab states like Iran, the technical process to avoid the infiltration required continued sophistication. Many of the services that R-Group provided helped increase the security of their client institutions as well as to alert appropriate governments in special cases of known criminal activities.

The account in question, which Wolfgang returned to multiple times, had funds which had remained static until recently. Then, steady withdrawals had

THE ENIGMA WRAITH

occurred over recent months. The amounts weren't large, but they were all lump sums which rarely occurred. Curiously, the sums were then electronically transferred to an account in the United States to an institution that was not an R-Group customer. Additional access to this trail would take some special efforts which Wolfgang felt the team needed to agree to in advance of the doing. Patterns were Wolfgang's specialty, and this one hit a nerve. Chairman Chang had taken over a portion of the Russian Dteam's operations including their identity theft and cleansing operations. Chang had also been responsible for the removal of Master Po during her safe sanctuary rescue by Otto. Otto had always said to keep this enemy closer than most.

Wolfgang put together the logical flow of his current findings which he would present to Jacob and Quip later that morning. Tracking funding trails was always a key element to large operations. This was a large operation that touched several points and seemed to interconnect with some previously encountered disreputable characters.

Wolfgang leaned back in his chair and thought about the rest of his energetic young team. Jacob had finally returned from Ireland last night which meant they could continue their chess matches. Petra was meeting up with Lara and Julie at the fashion shoot on some island, specifically to see how Julie was doing. Quip would already be working at sifting through the information gathered by ICABOD overnight, looking for any other reported incidents that might be attributed to their challenge of the Ghost Code. From his experience, the overlap would present itself over time.

Jacob arrived in the operations center and immediately began the review of the data he'd captured from the root directory of John C's machines. It wasn't much, but more than before. He noticed the package from Texas addressed with Petra's handwriting, which he suspected was the copy of the winery machine. Hopefully, she'd return to Zurich soon. He simply wanted to see and hold her close. As he focused on the fragmented data from John C's machine, he saw elements of a wrapper. The wrapper could have been used to deliver the code rather than be the code itself. If he located at least the signature of the wrapper creator, they'd have a real starting point.

It was certainly possible that Dteam was involved. Carlos would become the eyes and ears within that organization if the plan worked as designed. But the transformation and adaptability of these programs required rarified skills as well as an approach more along the lines of the *grasshopper-loop*. He had learned and used the software coding methods that Su Lin had developed when she was Master Po, head of the Chinese Cyber-Warfare University, and that she had refined after relocating to Texas A&M. He knew that the programs he'd used to halt the *grasshopper-loop* were key to this adaptable program code originally called Polymorphic Operational Programing of Technology to Aggregate Recurring Temporal Synergies or POPTARTs. Su Lin had provided some intense training on the new programming approach. He'd learned his lessons well and understood how one could take the base process and readily modify it to become environmentally adaptable. He used that knowledge as he worked on the forensic review of the data.

He shook his head sadly as he replayed in his mind Su Lin's dangerous and foolish choice to prove her programming superiority. Su Lin had initiated a human kill-switch program that had resulted in her almost dying. She was alive and residing on the family farm in Georgia with EZ's dad Andrew, but she was very far removed from her previously brilliant self. His mind then replayed the letter from Su Lin sent to his team after her incident. Su Lin had prowled around the systems in her cyber warfare college. The wrapper was one aspect, but the code was the true prize. The more fragments he was able to extract and examine, the more he felt that the author of the code was someone who had also learned from Master Po.

Based on the incidents to date, Jacob felt the computer power required to test this code would be substantial. It would not necessarily be to the ICABOD level, but it could be close. He'd try to verify that with Quip later. He carefully segregated the wrapper pieces from the code fragments he located in the root files. As expected, the target was within the hidden root files, as was done with rootkits. They'd been right to look here on the systems. He started on the machine from the winery to further prove his suspicions and worked diligently until Quip called to meet in the conference room with Wolfgang for updates. At least he had a contribution, though not as much as he wanted. It was progress.

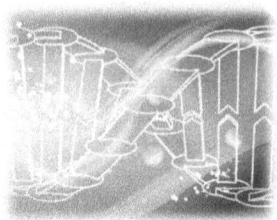

CHAPTER 26

REGARDLESS OF WHICH ROLE TAKEN, EQUITY PARTNER OR SALARIED EMPLOYEE, YOU NEVER GET THE VALUE EXPECTED...
THE ENIGMA CHRONICLES

She was startled as she heard, "Good morning, Mistress. We are pleased that you found the location promptly and at our appointed time. Our employer sends his regards and is appreciative of your adaptability to impromptu meeting requests."

Callisto regained her composure and replied, "It is a little off the beaten path, but your directions were quite good. I had my GPS device enabled just in case but didn't need it."

The men both bowed slightly and looked knowingly at each other as if to maintain insider knowledge. The one in the grey shirt explained, "We are to be your escorts during the next phase per our employer's instructions."

At that point she noticed that her male escorts were identical twins except that one of them was scarred down the left side of his face. One also wore a grey shirt, and the other wore a black shirt.

Callisto exchanged light banter with the one that had initiated the conversation. After a few minutes, she asked, "Do you always do all the talking? Does your quiet brother get a chance to add to the conversation?"

The man in grey explained, "Mistress Callisto, my brother has little to say, and his injury can get irritated with extended speaking."

Callisto was enchanted by the quiet male and moved closer to him as she confirmed, "Indeed!" She slowly reached for the gentleman's damaged face to touch the rake marks. The man reluctantly held still while she gently touched the large deep wounds that had left him noticeably scarred. Callisto then teased in a sultry voice, "I can tell that the scars don't stop at your collar –line so perhaps there is more to the story and to you as well, sir? These wounds don't seem to be from a common injury. The wounds look to be about twelve centimeters across. So will I get at least one word of encouragement from such a powerful male with a very noble scar wound?"

The man in the gray shirt, now a little unsettled, interceded, "Mistress Callisto, my brother had the serious misfortune of provoking our employer's pet. The animal responded, as you can see from the scar tissue. Yes, the rake marks that you see also damaged his tongue, travel a ways down his torso, and, no, he would prefer not to give you one word."

Callisto was now alarmed but continued to show no fear as she said, "Oh my! That's too bad, my dear. I was so looking forward to getting to know you better, but without a tongue how can you possibly deliver any oral satisfaction to a lady? And I will admit that oral satisfaction is a prerequisite for you to get to know me better. That is a shame!"

The man in grey was now vexed at the taunting by Callisto and was about to do his own verbal assault when the man in black reached into his coat pocket and retrieved his cell phone to take a call. He answered, said nothing, but instead after a few seconds handed the cell phone to Callisto who was confused but accepted it.

Callisto said apprehensively, "Hello?"

The deep baritone voice chided her, "Enough. You can stop the torment of my agents, Callisto. Is this how you get my attention when you haven't gotten enough attention or payment? If you are going to slip back into your old ways as a *strip farmer*, perhaps we are not ready to move on to an equity stake in our ongoing project."

Callisto was nearly frozen with fear, hearing the voice, but managed to respond, "Mephisto! I am so pleased to hear your voice again! About your agents here, I'm sorry to tease them a little since I anticipated that you were watching and, as it turns out, listening as well. But what a curious phrase you used just now. May I ask what a *strip farmer* is?" she tried nonchalantly to ask.

Mephisto chuckled lightly and replied, "Callisto, surely you must understand that I know of your past lives, and how you built your trade after being sold to the large house at thirteen years of age. And actually, I believe the phrase *strip farmer* was actually coined by you. I believe you described it as when the male patrons paid money to plow a feminine field, and the chosen female had to strip for them. You see, you may have outrun that past, but you have not outrun me. I did tell you I had my eye on you for some time, and this is that project that I want you for. Do not torment my associates with something you wanted to distance yourself from. Are we clear?"

Callisto swallowed hard and acquiesced, "Perfectly, Mephisto. However, since you bring it up I believe there is the small matter of my last few payment**s**. I assume you have not made up your mind on having an equity partner yet, so my fee for services rendered still stands. I have expenses that need to be covered after my last delivery."

Mephisto collected his thoughts for a moment and countered, "I need some additional work completed before I can answer the equity question for you. I have an errand that needs attending to, and I want you to accompany my associates on this adventure. You may call them Mr. Grey and Mr. Black as well as treat them with the utmost respect.

"My new jet should be rolling in soon, and I have an exercise that will require all of you. You will need to remove the code residue from it and make it fully serviceable as soon as possible. This is a replacement aircraft for one that I didn't get to take delivery on, so I am very anxious that it be 100% serviceable before I ride in it. I was able to get it for a very good price and settle an old score at the same time.

"Callisto, make certain you extend every courtesy to my associates to help them get me my aircraft. Anything less would be extremely unfortunate for you."

Callisto, somewhat relieved that she would not be taken to task, agreed, "Of course, Mephisto. I will provide all assistance required."

Mephisto smiled and said, "Oh, and my associates have your last payments with them, so they now are your bankers standing in front of you. Good day, madam."

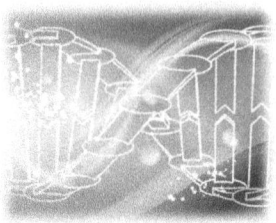

CHAPTER 27

NEBELWERFER (ROCKET LAUNCHER)

After Jacob, with comments from Quip and Petra, explained what they knew about the code to Wolfgang, they became quiet to let the information sink in.

After a few moments, Wolfgang commented, "Odd, isn't it, that as sophisticated as this program is, we have only seen evidence of a single operative delivering or introducing the code in one-off scenarios. The way you have described the code as polymorphic--*enabled for adapting to the target environment and progressing to execute a predefined agenda, then expiring*--seems lacking and unfinished.

"Most of the viral code we have seen works in one of two scenarios; either you load the code up on multiple machines to blast away a target website or firewall, or you try to install it on as many machines as possible to gather login and/or password information to get into as many target bank accounts as possible. What if there is a third target approach? What if you wanted to introduce specialized code to a particular control group concurrently for a collaborative and synergistic onslaught against affiliated targets?"

Jacob turned his head while considering the question and then reasoned out loud, "We have no evidence to suggest this is industry specific virus attacks. But to your point, we have not seen anything indicating an advanced delivery attack system either. We have only seen what I would call one-off attacks delivered only by a single person or method."

Petra then asked, "So, Wolfgang, you are suggesting that, based on the sophistication of the program, there is probably another as yet undetected component for sophistication delivery?"

Wolfgang nodded his head and explained, "Yes, I'm thinking what is missing is the *Nebelwerfer Mechanism*."

Quip questioned, "Uh, Wolfgang, can you explain your NM technical reference? I don't believe I'm familiar with how a rocket launcher would be the missing link."

"When Nazi Germany invaded Poland in September 1939, there existed the first, second, and fifth *Nebelwerfer Battalions*. Each were equipped with twenty-four, ten centimeter *Nebelwerfer* mortars in three batteries. The 1st and 2nd Battalions participated in that campaign, while the 5th remained in Western Germany. By May of 1940, five more battalions had been formed to participate in the Battle of France. The Nebelwerfers started out in the 1920s as smoke or gas launchers but were soon adapted to fire rockets into a targeted area and then quickly move so as not to be targeted by return fire. These Nebelwerfers were not designed to be far ranging or highly accurate like standard artillery but were designed instead to deliver a tremendous amount of explosive ordinance very fast to a localized area in support of fast moving ground troops.

"The first fifteen centimeter rocket launchers were delivered in July 1940 and were used in the Nazi Germany invasion of Soviet Russia in Operation Barbarossa when it began on June 22nd, 1941. Even the Soviets had their own version of the Nebelwerfer that they used against the Germans called the Katyusha Rocket Launchers, which followed the same principle.

"So is the history of a Nebelwerfer. The next question is how and/ or why am I comparing World War II rocket launchers to software delivery of poisonous code?"

Quip jumped in and exclaimed, "I get it! You load up a bunch of virus code into your software distribution machine, aim it at a group of highly affiliated organizations, and cripple them all at once. Just like the Nebelwerfer rocket launcher. After the payloads have been delivered, you make your ransom demands or announce some bullshit political statement. While you wait for your blackmail ransom to be delivered, you drive off with your Nebelwerfer rocket launcher to re-arm them for your next target, making it difficult or impossible to return fire."

Wolfgang smiled at the team and suggested, "My observation is that the matching Nebelwerfer delivery mechanism is being withheld or still being created, which is why we only see single operatives working to deliver these payloads. It may be that the responsible person or group has yet to determine the optimum delivery method."

Jacob nodded and reasoned, "That means we should expect, not single attacks, but attack groupings that would leverage the Nebelwerfer delivery of poisonous code. It follows that we need a comparable system of delivering our antidote just as fast to the same targeted group."

Wolfgang was now quite pleased as he commended, "Well done, Jacob! It appears that our chess sessions have stimulated new attack strategies in the constant war against the cyber criminals. However, I am sorry that I have just pointed out that the team has significantly more work to do. Before that work begins, how about some supper and a little wine?"

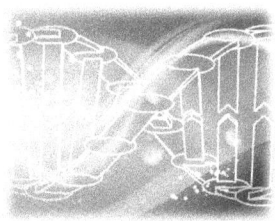

CHAPTER 28

THE DILEMMA OF HUNTING - TO DISAPPEAR YOU MUST FREEZE BUT TO BLEND IN YOU MUST KEEP MOVING...
THE ENIGMA CHRONICLES

Julie had worked with Lara to complete the shoot activities. Even though Jamaica had been a delightful venue, she was far more anxious to meet with Carlos and review his new identity. When she'd spoken to him, he'd voiced annoyance at the delay in their meeting as he waited for his new identity. She could totally relate that he was tired of not making something happen toward finding Juan or at least finding the responsible culprits.

Miguel 'Dakota' Vasquez's identity elements had fit together well which really pleased her in her role as Cyber assassin Julie, aka JAC. While JAC worked on these history changes, she'd laughed because not that long ago JAC had created very good boy identities for both Carlos and Juan. Though Juan's was still intact, Carlos' was parked and replaced with this very bad boy identity. Any direction that anyone could check or poke at this identity would show the same results.

This man, JAC had created, was capable of capturing, redirecting, and disrupting communications transactions. He had done prison time in more than one country because his abilities resulted in facilitating robberies from military bases, national museums, and private organizations. The history portrayed that he'd worked alone as well as a part of teams all over the world. As a loner, with no family and no long term friends nor a permanent residence, he could easily blend into any surroundings.

Once the history was established for Senor Vasquez, she created the identity documents, credit cards and various financial trails. His personal traits were aligned with his known behavior, but he'd need to learn his history cold.

She thought the greeting would be the toughest part as they'd had no contact since Juan had vanished. The last thing she wanted to do was to breakdown in front of him. This was neither the time nor the place for her to behave like a girl.

JAC had arrived in New York City the night before. They planned to actually meet at the Ronnie, Ltd building for their briefing. It was considered safe as well as out of the normal area of Dteam operations. They had planned to meet both this afternoon and then tomorrow to make certain the history was a part of his very being. She had constructed a full regimen of testing and questions that would help him get up to speed quickly on the new him. She had arrived in the offices that morning and was using the conference room as their staging area. Coffee was brewed, and lunch was planned to arrive shortly from a local deli. She didn't want them out together in public, just in case someone was watching.

The deli had promptly delivered at 11:30, and she finished putting it out in the conference room for easy access. Her cell phone buzzed which alerted her to a visitor in the reception area. No one worked in these offices on a regular basis though the R-group owned and maintained the building. As she entered the lobby, her breath caught when she saw Carlos. Juan and Carlos shared some family characteristics, which momentarily added misting to her eyes. Carlos was slightly taller and leaner than his younger brother. He also looked like he'd spent way too many days without a shave or even bothered with his slightly longer, unruly black hair.

He easily looked the bad boy part in a scruffy, yet mildly appealing way. It was a nice touch with the black leather fitted pants and jacket that showed just enough wear to not appear new. The white gold watch and chain were visible but not too much. Carlos sauntered like a powerful man that feared no one. His eyes were dark and missed nothing. It was totally understandable that Lara was enthralled with the man. Though his heart belonged to Lara, she also knew he could potentially gain some ground with this Dteam female. He saw Julie and formed a lazy smile as he opened his arms. Julie walked into the arms of her lover's brother. Her eyes threatened to tear up, but she stayed strong as she stepped back and displayed a rather weak impression of her classic megawatt smile.

Carlos began, "Hello, little sister. How are you? How are you taking care of my brother's offspring?"

Julie laughed and said, "Very carefully, of course. It is precious cargo."

"Do you know if it is a boy or a girl?"

"Not yet, Carlos. You will be an uncle regardless." She kissed him on the cheek, locked her arm through his and walked with him to the conference room. "I know that you are impatient to get going on this, but we need to review and drill on your identity. It is critical, I believe, that you are believable with no missed statements. You will, I suspect, be watched like a hawk until some level of trust is earned, but you should assume they will continue to study you even after it appears they have let their guard down."

"I agree with you, JAC. Reminds me of when we first met, you know. Juan was very apprehensive about changing his identity until he met his cyber assassin."

"I remember. You two put up such a fuss with how wonderfully normal you became in your new identities. Well, that's definitely changed. Your wardrobe fits this new role perfectly. I am glad you took my messaging seriously."

"All of this is very serious to me. You will find no fault with my not following directions to get to those that hurt my brother. I will find them and him, I promise you."

"Good, let's get busy. No one will bother us."

They spent the rest of the afternoon and into the early evening reviewing history, going through questions, resolved planted spots in his background and the whys. They repeated it over and over with no complaints made by either of them until it finally sounded like he had lived this identity, not just memorized it. The credit cards, pin numbers, email activity, passport, and receipts from recent activity were reviewed and safely tucked away in his wallet and black leather satchel.

They planned his random meeting with the Dteam member known as Zara. For days, they had planted Carlos in chat rooms on-line and monitored different transactions and chatter, searching for the teams. They'd had five offers to meet and potentially leverage his services, but there was only one in New York. This was the one they pursued the hardest while keeping the others on a chain just in case.

Using first Zara's background and entry to the United States, Quip had monitored the video cams located around the area, extracted the data, and built a group of places she frequented. The meeting place in the request he'd received aligned with one of those spots. Also, some of her history was being filled in with the help of Quip and ICABOD. She was a pretty enough female from what they had captured where she'd been spotted so far. Julie related to Carlos some of the places she'd been seen and only as much detail about the other incidents that he needed to create a viable reason for the Dteam to want him added to their staff.

JAC's methods for contacting and updating each other were established. Easy and simple worked best for these two. Julie planned to stay in New York for at least the first month or two, depending upon his progress. She planned to be handy if something was needed. Carlos had two goals with this infiltration activity. One was to gain access to the Dteam systems, and two was find any other information with regards to the ghost code and Juan's incident. This was serious business to them both.

"Alright, Dakota, you've done a great job today. I really think you have it all down, but I want a review in the morning just to make certain that nothing is lost overnight."

"Agreed, JAC. I am glad you are planning to stick around locally. That way I can see how you and the baby are doing. No risks, little sister."

"No risks. Which reminds me. Petra indicated that you didn't want Lara informed of what you were doing. I am okay with that as long as you promise not to put yourself at risk either. These people have no scruples and don't fool around if they think you are taking something that belongs to them. If you put yourself at risk, I promise I will find you and kick your ass. Got it?"

Carlos laughed and then added with a straight face, "You know, JAC, that threat might actually have some teeth in it. Juan told me you had worked together a lot on your martial arts techniques and were a force to be reckoned with. So I got it. Plus, I don't want to upset the little mother."

They both laughed and wrapped up for the night. Carlos wanted to escort her back to her hotel, but she insisted they separate. He would go out the side entrance of the building, and she would get her car from the basement garage and drive to her hotel.

They parted at the elevator adjacent to the stairwell and agreed to meet in the morning. Julie giggled as he hugged her then patted her tummy, which was barely a bump, before he left.

"Good night, little baby. Rest well."

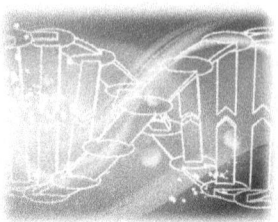

CHAPTER 29

SOMETIMES DISTANCE ISN'T A PROBLEM. IT'S JUST DISTANCE.

Jacob had awakened early and silently watched Petra while she slept. She had arrived in so late last night that other than a brief hug in greeting, she'd taken a quick shower and was asleep before her head hit the pillow. The sunrise was starting the inevitable shift from dark to gray, and he watched her silhouette become more defined. Her hair, spilling over the pillow, changed to blonde as the light increased, to the point he had to reach out and feel the silkiness between his fingers. She was a quiet and typically calm sleeper with no tossing or kicking, just rest. He loved to watch her, especially while she slept.

Petra sensed being watched as she returned from a pleasant dream to reality. Sleeping here was so much more restful than the myriad of beds she'd had while traveling. Being deliciously close to Jacob always made her rest better. She did find that she dreamed about him always while he wasn't in her bed. She opened her eye and locked onto his as she smiled.

"Good morning, Jacob."

"Good morning, sweetheart. You looked so pretty sleeping. Are you rested and ready to get up?"

She smiled mischievously and whispered, "I am awake and rested, but I don't really want to get up yet. I was hoping I might persuade you to hold me, and let me feel you."

"I can do that." Jacob pulled her close into his arms and kissed her with all the passion of a male who had missed her with all his heart. He murmured, "I missed you so much."

"Hmmm. I missed you too. Now kiss me, honey."

Later, wrapped around each other, sated, breathing returning to normal, and obviously comfortable, neither of them moved.

"Jacob, you do know we are good, right? I get the sense that you are worried about us, and I want you to know that is needless from my perspective. In fact, I had a wonderful idea when I visited the winery. We need to take our next vacation there. It was serene and beautiful with acres of grapes and a view of rolling hills. The wine was really good. They let me stay in this totally luxurious repurposed train car. It was old time elegance with all the modern conveniences. I pictured us there. It also would make a wonderful venue for a family party. It also reminded me of that wonderful day of wines we shared in Long Island, when we first met. Would you go with me?"

He pulled her just a bit closer. "I am very glad you know me so well, honey. I have been a bit worried, but I think it was more because we were far away from each other. I would be happy to see this fun place as long as I am with you. I frankly like you close by, especially in bed." He nuzzled her neck and inhaled the scent from her hair and skin while gently running his hands down her length. "Also, I would like to stay here all day and make love to you over and over again. That won't resolve any of the looming issues we are all working on though, so help me be strong and let you get up. I will, of course, follow you to the shower."

Petra giggled and shimmied out of bed, making a rapid retreat to the bathroom. "Come on, big boy, let's take a shower. We have a lot of work to do, so we need to play fast."

After breakfast they went to the operations center. Jacob was anxious to update Petra on the additional findings, especially those from her copied winery machine. He had assembled each of the fragments into an order that made some logical progression. Petra applied some of the encryption algorithms, and some portions were further revealed. They were able to confirm that the breakdown of the code and removal was almost perfect. However, the residue that remained in the registry files was not cleared, and therefore with some very tedious separation and rebuilding, they could determine that it was a programmed array that was applied. The failing was that, by the time the execution of the final registry files was in process, the rest of the code was gone. Thus it couldn't quite erase itself. Looking for code elements buried within the registry files, however, was not a common search point for most trouble shooting teams, so these would be easily missed.

From the winery machine, they were able to assemble enough to then compare it to the data Jacob had extracted from the Ireland systems. The similarities were there. They were dealing with a common programming method at least, and it had what appeared to be elements of what Su Lin had shared with them. They were both totally absorbed in assembling more fragments that seemed like putting together sand particles to make a picture, when Quip interrupted them.

"Ah, there you two are. How nice to see you back, Petra. I hope your travel was not too awful."

"It was tiring, and I'm glad to be back. Feels a bit like home, especially when you make me jump out of my skin sneaking up on us."

Jacob, with a private smile for Petra, added, "Yep, it is very good to have her home. We were actually discussing that thing earlier this morning." He then looked up in time to catch a flicker of sadness cross Quip's eyes.

"Well good. I am glad things are happy between two of my favorite people. Where are we at on this vanishing code, and have we made any progress toward understanding who is involved?"

Jacob rapidly moved his fingers across the keyboard as if playing a jazz tune on a piano. Both screens on the wall displayed two different viewpoints. The one on the left was the winery data, grouped together as logical segments. The one on the right contained the elements from the Ireland financial institution. As he explained the correlations, he interconnected the two events.

He explained, "You'll recall when we approached the *grasshopper-loop* problem, we had the relational segments of a program that were logically rather than physically connected. The same seems to hold true with this code or, as we postulated earlier, a virus.

"Further, the π-R-Squared DP logic, which I applied to interrupt the *grasshopper-loop*, I used against two of the more complete fragments found in the winery computer. Watch what happens when the small routine I created interacts with the fragment. I also created a watcher routine that illustrates each step taken for a better visual view. This is the third time, however, so I believe it works."

As they watched the small routine run its execution, it essentially opened the file where the fragment resided, and the fragment took on an entirely new digital appearance. In a sense, it grew into something whole and not recognizable back to the fragment where it began. Then it relocated itself into a different directory, which it also created.

Quip looked stunned and asked, "You've really done this twice before? Were the results the same?"

Jacob responded, "Interesting you should ask that particular question. The answer is no, but I'm not sure why. It seems to have a relationship to something else, but I can't see what that is. It is like it is part of the fragment's DNA.

"The first time I did it, the directory it created was different. When I did the second one, the directory was the same, but the size of the whole data record was different. In this one, both are different than either of the other two."

Petra described, "When you came in, we were discussing how similar this is to a genetic evolution process in that two things can evolve from the same parents, and the end results are not equal. Children are a great visible result of that.

"The common factors that would cause the differences in a digital evolution are perhaps size availability, processor speed, or other environmental conditions. Time, other than for human relationship to a given task, has no inherent relationship in a pure digital sense. Other things might be security elements, utility class routines on a computer such as anti-virus or back up programs. It is fascinating and elusive, as it seems adaptable to where and when it is.

"We think from what we have traced from these two events that two separate activities are involved. One is the program routine itself and what its instructions say it should do, how it should do it, and the exit strategy. That program seems to be workable only on a single machine based on what we uncovered from the multiple systems in the Ireland financial institution. The program seems to be flawed in not being able to totally erase its presence, as Jacob has extracted some element in each case he has worked on.

"The other activity is the method to install or deliver it to a device. I think it could be delivered through a mass distribution as Wolfgang explained with Nebelwerfer, but for now it is one-off distribution. There has to be a target list and various methods to access the targets as a conceptual proof point. If we go with that theory, then multiple groups could be involved. At a minimum, there is one to create the problem, another to deliver the payload, and the mastermind to identify the best value targets."

Wolfgang, who had entered during the discourse, interjected, "Which brings us back to the why. I am still working on the money trails. The activity is up, to a degree, for the funds I mentioned before. I think we need to get some tracking on some specific voice communications if possible. I am not certain of the end points, but certain our friend Chang would get my vote.

"Quip, do you still monitor his computers as well as those in the Cyber-Warfare College?"

"Yes, sir, but only for those I know about. We have not done a serious review of the systems that might be up and running for a while. Since beginning this project, I have not updated those at all. I have an update review for all of these scheduled for this weekend which includes the College, Chang's and several of the other public and private touch points we monitor. I believe this project is number one, and the gathering of the various data sources and analytical review of them has had my full time attention."

"Quip, I agree with you. No criticism intended."

Quip chuckled, "None taken, Wolfgang. Just wanted you to get the answer before you asked."

Wolfgang said, "Petra, by the way, welcome home. You were missed. Jacob, with what you have uncovered, what is our next step?"

"I think we need to run a couple more tests to fully understand the behavior we can expect, and then I will begin work on how to counteract it while it is in process. Petra will need to work with me for a fully encrypted delivery package that we can deploy en masse without detection. I think the mastermind has very evil intentions. We will find out who it is, but first I want to find out how to stop it."

"Agreed!" Wolfgang continued, "I think you've made some positive progress, but you have all been at it for a very long day. That is why I came here to let you know that we need to go home, relax, and start again tomorrow.

"Is Carlos planted yet, Petra?"

"No, not yet. Julie is heading up that effort and updating me daily. You will all be happy to know she looks happy and healthy, especially since she is back in the thick of things. She refuses to consider that Juan may be dead, so we need to continue to help locate him or the wreckage of the plane."

They all nodded and began the shutdown routines. Wolfgang was right. They needed some rest and a fresh outlook for tomorrow.

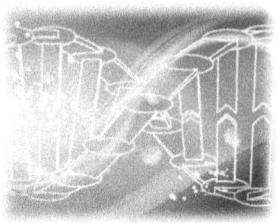

CHAPTER 30

PUSHING THE ENVELOPE IS GOOD, BUT ALWAYS EXPECT IT TO PUSH BACK...
THE ENIGMA CHRONICLES

Zara had watched the stranger enter the lounge and how quickly he sized up the people and the room. This was a man that was very cautious. Since they had exchanged only a small amount of information over their on-line chat, she'd done as much background checking as she could. She sat in the corner in the shadows while he stepped to the bar, presumably placed his order and then turned slightly to survey the room. He wouldn't spot her unless she moved. The only reason she'd agreed to this discussion was because of the Internet chat room he'd gained access into and the background he'd provided.

His beer arrived. He paid the bartender and turned around again to look at the people. His advantage was he also knew who he was looking for, but she didn't know that. When he'd stepped in, the woman in the corner was his target. Her pale skin framed beautifully with her ebony hair. The unmistakable feeling of her eyes that followed his every move verified his conviction that this was the woman. The man with her was hardly as observant, but a new character to be identified. After he retrieved his phone, he turned as if trying to hear better, then pressed the button as if accepting a call but was actually capturing what he hoped was adequate shots of both of them. He sipped his drink and nonchalantly waited. A few minutes passed, and she stood and strolled the short distance to the bar.

After she positioned herself next to him with hardly any space between them, she smiled and purred, "Okay, you said you didn't want to do this over the Net in a chat room, so here we are. Come over to the table where we can speak more freely." She turned and strolled back with an exaggerated swing to her hips.

She sat in the chair with her back to the wall which forced him to take one that exposed his back more than he liked. The man with her remained silent with no emotion on his face.

Zara stated, "You said you had skills in Unified Communications. So tell me, you bronze beauty, what should I know about you?"

He openly gazed at her and continued the appraisal of her face and countered, "So are you the one called Moya Dushechka, the inspired driver of the renowned Dteam? If you are, then I am honored to meet you and your bodyguard. "

Zara smiled at the powerfully built male.

Dante was annoyed as he responded, "I am not just her bodyguard! I am the technical lead for a powerful computer consulting group, and we are only here because you said you had something of value. If you have something of value, show some evidence or stop wasting our time. Russians have no time or need of idle braggarts."

Without turning his head to look at or acknowledge the man, he said to Zara, "You know, I typically only find such impatience when dealing with Americans. They are always in such a rush to *do the deal*, they never seem to spend the time to get to know their counterparts. Are you Russians now living in America or second generation?"

The man struggled to maintain his silence.

Zara smiled, amused at the impudence of this man, as she soothed, "You must forgive Dante's manners. He didn't think this meeting was of value. But Dante does have a point in that while I was curious to meet you, I have much on my plate to deal with, so we do need more to go on before our relationship can move forward.

"To your point, my Internet name is Moya Dushechka, and this is my associate and technical lead Dante. We are currently working in America but don't refer to it as home. Perhaps after we have had fruitful business dealings together, I might tell you more.

"So tell me, my bronze beauty, who are you, why did you seek us out, and most specifically what are you selling? However, you must understand I am not buying anything today."

The stranger's mustache curled slightly at the edges as he tried to suppress a smile and ignore Dante, as he replied, "Moya Dushechka, I am pleased to meet you, madam! I was told you had spirit and wit, but I was not given any hint that you were also a well sculpted lady with graceful moves. Permit me to say the honor is most definitely mine in our meeting.

"As to why I am here, I should tell you that my former employer grew tired of my borrowing his computing resources and satellite communications time for personal gain, and so my tenure there was abruptly and unfairly terminated. I was barely given the time to clean out my things before the government secret service agents showed up to arrest me and take back my winnings that I had worked so hard for. Alas, my 401-K savings were confiscated as well, modest as they were.

"I would likely describe myself as under-employed at this stage of my career and looking for new employment opportunities where my talents will not be under-utilized and under-appreciated. Tell me, is any of this story finding favor with you?"

Dante interrupted, "You got caught milking the corporate cow and are now on the lamb. Is that what you are telling us? You have soiled your nest, and are now looking for a new home? We don't need clumsy computer hackers with the secret service after them!"

Carlos maintained his gaze on Zara as he asked, "So, how does one get to be the head mistress of the Dteam? I am understandably interested in hearing how people rise to powerful positions in this part of the world."

Zara provided a disarming smile and asked, "So, bronze one, you suspect that to be the head mistress I must be giving head?"

He was taken aback with the forward question and said, "Madam, if I gave you cause to be offended, accept my apologies! No disrespect was intended for a lady such as yourself. I avoid any disrespect of people I am only meeting for the first time."

Dante was now even more agitated and interrupted, "How dare you infer she has climbed to a preeminent position with the Dteam merely by deep throating those who would promote her! Moya Dushechka does not need to buy her way up because she has earned that status!"

Again, without moving his gaze from her eyes, the man said, "But for your bodyguard I could easily make an exception at disliking someone on first meeting. That is, of course, unless you are with him, madam."

Zara quickly dismissed the statement. "Oh, no, of course not. I am not with him!"

This only served to infuriate Dante even more. "You've become rather tiresome, Westerner, and when people in our world wear out their welcome, we....."

As Dante was about to completely lose all restraint, the man suggested, "Tell me, Moya Dushechka, is Adagio, I mean Allegro non Troppo. Sorry, I meant the Andante person. Is he better at music, as his music tempo handle might suggest, or is he just disagreeable all the time?"

As Zara tried to suppress a smirk, Dante was already reaching for the bronze stranger to prove a point between two powerful males as they decided the pecking order of dominance. However, Dante didn't count on the stranger being so quick as to securely grasp Dante's hand, wrench it over and then bring it up behind Dante's back, forcing Dante to stand and face the wall with his nose firmly pressed against it.

Turning his gaze back to Zara, while still holding Dante pinned against the wall, he said, "As for my name, Moya Dushechka, it would please me if you would use my handle, Dakota."

Zara smiled sweetly and responded, "You're an interesting man. I'm sure we will meet again. Unless of course your former employer or the secret service finds you first.

"Just so you know, I don't do business on the spur of the moment. So you will forgive me if I take my now chastened associate and depart at this point. I will send word when we have more to discuss, Mr. Dakota.

"Dante, are you alright, Hon? Did the big bad bronze mongoose-fast unified communications specialist hurt my AnDante?"

Dante felt the grip on his arm loosen and stepped away so that Dakota was out of reach. Dante slowly turned around and, rubbing his arm, he snarled, "Be careful you do not think that you will get to do that again. You should count yourself lucky that Moya Dushechka has let you leave unharmed this time, Dakota!"

Carlos smiled at being called by his new name, Dakota, as he informed Dante, "My friends get to call me Dakota, but you can call me Mr. Dakota."

Once outside, out of listening range, Zara said, "Dante, I want to know everything there is about this Dakota. Don't stop digging after the first lie because clever people usually have more than one lie, and he is obviously a very clever person."

Dante vehemently protested, "Moya Dushechka, you cannot be serious about this charlatan! It is obvious he has an agenda that we do not yet know. I was going to research him anyway even if you hadn't asked because my nose tells me something is wrong."

Zara struggled to suppress her giggle then instructed, "Yes, I am sure your nose told you something was wrong as it was pressed up against the wall. I agree with your instincts on this one. For some reason, the school girl in me hopes he is only what he says he is. Let me know what you find out, please. And yes, start planning his exit strategy in case I am disappointed. Do you understand?"

Dante beamed, grinned and said, "With much joy, and goodly gree, Scheherazade! We will add another story to the nights! Leave it to me!"

Zara suppressed a smile at Dante's enthusiasm. "For the time being, don't get within reach of him." She turned and walked away, leaving Dante with his mouth twisted in anger.

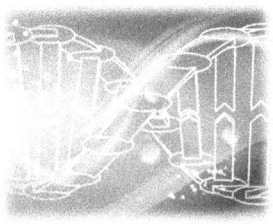

CHAPTER 31

AT SOME POINT IN YOUR LIFE, TAKING RESPONSIBILITY BECOMES DUTY AND HONOR ...
THE ENIGMA CHRONICLES

Prudence countered, "Chairman, I don't understand this line of questioning. I've been sick the last couple of weeks, and, well, I have struggled to maintain my original pace. I mean, I am sick every morning, with intestinal cramps resembling dysentery in the afternoon. It has just been debilitating. And, no, it is not morning sickness due to not loving safely, so put that out of your mind! I try to watch what I eat here in your country, but as it stands with these types of digestive disorders, I'm wasting away, Chairman!"

Major Guano rolled his eyes and loudly remarked, "Yes, we can all see that your weight has plummeted to seventy-five kilos, barely enough to sustain your one and a half meter height."

Chairman raised his hand to intercept any more distracting banter between the two and said, "Based on the research conducted by my associates, Miss Krumhunter, it looks as though you have been delinquent in your duties on my project. Conversely, Major Guano, it looks as though you were sabotaging poor Prudence's diet, then using her email logon and password to confiscate her work and resubmit as yours. That is why you were able to promptly catch me up to date with all the missing correspondence so quickly."

Major Guano's mouth hung open in disbelief as Prudence slowly turned her head to confront the Major's treachery.

Chairman smiled a knowing smile as he explained, "Yes, I had the situation looked into. It was found that you had purchased some $\text{\$¢}\square\tilde{\omega}\tilde{\Omega}$ from the local Wapothecary that specializes in rare herbs to add to Miss Krumhunter's morning breakfast and lunch. The $\text{\$¢}\square\tilde{\omega}\tilde{\Omega}$ herb is used for bodily cleansing prior to fasting but has the useful attribute of being odorless and tasteless which is useful for digestive sabotage."

Prudence was livid and exclaimed, "You bastard! Thanks to your prank, I'm either throwing up my toenails or camped on the porcelain convenience, wondering if I will be able to make it to the next toilet on my way home! May I know why?"

The Major was still unable to articulate any words, so Chairman interjected, "I think I can say without fear of contradiction that the good Major here had some professional jealousy creep into his relationship with you, my dear Prudence, which led to his clandestine attack against you.

"Major, do you want to tell us if you had another motive for your actions that turned Miss Krumhunter into a galactic event known as a pulsar? The result of which is sending all internal matter out at a high rate of velocity, in two opposite directions, nearly simultaneously?"

With supreme effort, Major Guano finally articulated, "How did you discover all this about her condition, and why do you think it was me? I have always pledged my loyalty to you and always tried to rise above the assignment you have given me to deliver the best possible results in the shortest amount of time."

Chairman said, "The receipts for your purchases of $\text{\$¢}\square\tilde{\omega}\tilde{\Omega}$ were easily traced. As far as the work you intercepted from Miss Krumhunter, you had the bad manners to simply preserve all her poor grammar, run-on sentences, commas where they shouldn't be, and spelling errors by just copying and pasting them into your documents. Not very creative and easily tracked between her email reports and your efforts. Anyway, that is the closure to a disappointing chapter in your career, Major Guano."

Prudence sneered and said, "It would seem, Major, you and your pets are about to be retrained in a quaint little village near Mongolia that gets its water delivered once a month whether it is needed or not. However, let me give you a little something to remember me by while you are retrained."

Prudence went to slap the Major, but he easily intercepted her clumsy movement which then threatened to devolve into a knock-down-drag-out fight.

In watching the spectacle, Chairman simply shook his head and said, "Now you've gone and done it. Your scuffle has alarmed Nikkei.

"Oh honey, I am sorry that they upset you! Now you two kiss and makeup so Nikkei doesn't fret over you."

Nikkei now moved out from behind Chairman's desk and seemed to be in a highly agitated state, complete with small snarls and a few growls. The Major was immediately frozen with fear, but Prudence smiled at the sight of the beautiful white tiger until she realized that Nikkei was not in the mood to be petted. Prudence backed away from the now hostile gestures Nikkei was offering up and clung to the Major out of fear.

Chairman gave a paternal smile to Nikkei then said, "These are the indiscretions of the Major, for which he needs some remediation and atonement.

"Now we come to you, my dear Prudence. We found your unsanctioned USB thumb drive that was cleverly cloaked inside a pen. I will remind you that using it to copy key files on premises to be reviewed outside the facility is very, very naughty.

"My problem is that if I continue to push Nikkei to play with you two to death, using her agitating collar, then I'll have no one to do the work I need to complete for the second phase of my pet project. I put it to you both, do either of you have any valid suggestion to help me reach my goal of a successful project? And your goals, I should think, would be something other than being retrained in Mongolia."

The Major was unable to focus on anything other than the snarling, agitated Nikkei and could not even acknowledge the Chairman.

Prudence had the presence of mind to deal directly with Chairman as she explained, "Chairman, if you have the means to access my personal computer, then it is logical to assume that you also broke into my email account, in which you will not find any electronic evidence of me sending off copies of anything from this facility. Yes, I always make copies of my work but only for backup purposes, not as a mole in your organization exporting key information.

"May I offer an example of my intentions by providing some new testing grounds for the Bai Hu project? My agency user ID and password are still valid and will allow you to test the program's capability on the U.S. military. They pride themselves in running a second but cloaked information network that is extremely hard to get to, much less gain access to. As a show of good faith to you, I will offer up the user ID, password, and random token generator that generates the third piece of information you need to enter the secret U.S. network in exchange for maintaining my current position as director. I wish to continue to serve you, but I want it on my terms."

Slightly smiling, the Chairman disabled the agitating collar which then allowed Nikkei to come down off high alert. Her mood improved immediately. Prudence bent over to pet the white tiger and offered some words of comfort to her. The Major resumed normal breathing again but remained cautious.

Finally Chairman asked, "Well, that seems like an acceptable trade, but what about the good Major here? What should we do about his indiscretions?"

Prudence, still caressing the white tiger, and without looking up said, "Oh, you mean my new food taster? I think we can continue to have him support my activities. I mean, after all I am your director, and I still need someone to type our reports so I can send them to you. However, I believe it would be appropriate to have security personnel assigned to us just so we play fair with each other. How about one of those cute security guards you have stationed outside?"

The Major smirked, and the Chairman struggled to keep from rolling his eyes as he asked sarcastically, "Which one of the female guards did you favor, madam?"

Prudence, now thoroughly embarrassed that she had unwittingly asked for a female bodyguard when she clearly thought they were male, remarked, "Oh, well, I did think that they were remarkably clean shaven. I only meant that as an example, but I would be expecting a male as our bodyguard, Chairman."

Chairman retorted, "Miss Krumhunter, I will put both of you under surveillance by a pair of my trusted associates, and they will also function as protection for both of you. I want to launch another attack vector using the three factor authentication you have in your possession. Major, you will assist with readying the package. I want this to be launch-ready within twenty-four hours so I can leverage our delivery personnel.

"Oh, and one last thing, if either of you makes a mistake or fails in the delivery process, both of you will be reclassified as organic fertilizer. If either of you tries to sabotage the other, you will both suffer, so your collective survivability absolutely depends on the other, because it now does. My advice is to function as a team whose lives depend upon helping the other. Any questions, or is anything I've said too vague to understand?"

Prudence slyly remarked to Chairman, "So this is much like sleeping with the enemy?"

The Major blanched as Chairman replied, "Prudence, I don't think you need to threaten the Major anymore today. He's been through quite enough."

Chairman sent the file over the secured exchange. The timing was better than he'd hoped for. He then dialed the familiar number. When it answered, he said, "Good day, Professor Jinny Lin. Professor, I have decided the next target for your program and sent it to you via our secure exchange. Open it now, I'll wait...

"No, there is no mistake..."

He cocked his head as he listened. "Of course, you can complete the focused revisions today...

"Professor Lin, either this is completed today as I have requested, or we will discuss your new job vocation...

"No, I am not threatening you, I am promising you...

"Yes, you have done well thus far...

"That is correct. The past is no guarantee of our future success....

"I know that there are a few issues with residue code which you have been focused on. This however takes priority...

"Yes, you have design and execution authority…

"Yes, you have the high powered resources…

"Yes, you have the technical ability…

"And yes, I have the final say…"

Chairman, now tired of the conversation, finally shook his head and ordered, "Enough! I provide the funds for your technical toy land. I make certain you have the equipment and the surrounding resources to design to your heart's content as long as my requests take priority. That was and is our deal. If the terms are no longer to your liking, then we should arrange for you to meet and greet your predecessor. I will not alter my target, nor my time line. Is that perfectly clear?…

"That is a vulgar statement used by early hominids to refer to a primitive concept they barely understood. I would rather describe one's personal ending as wielding a beautiful Katana samurai sword while riding a huge white tiger into battle in another dimension…

"Agreed, the imagery is so much more inspiring…

"Good, I will tell our madam director to expect to receive the package by end of day…

"Yes, then you can resume your focus on the clean-up…

"No, I am not angry, providing you meet the time line…

"Yes, you are privileged to bask in my shadow of great benevolence…"

CHAPTER 32

PRACTICE MAKES PERFECT SENSE, IN ALL THINGS

As the plane landed in Frankfurt, Zara almost chuckled as she considered this new assignment. It was a special target that she had expected, but not as quickly as it had arrived. In less than a day, she'd outlined the steps that needed to be taken once they reached the location. She was uncomfortable with the extra help of Mr. Grey and Mr. Black, but as they had outlined the steps they would take to accomplish the goal, their extra talent was welcomed.

In retrospect, she needed a better understanding of her benefactor. Trusting Mephisto was harder each time he called or sent her assignments. It seemed unbalanced for him to know so much and her to know so little. To date, she had kept Dante at arms' length with regards to her Callisto activities. As she worked on the various targeted assignments, she had merely informed Dante she was meeting with a customer and offered minimal details. As long as the coffers increased following her activities, further explanations were unnecessary.

Besides, Dante's real role was to keep the rest of the Dteam business of extracting funds through credit card tampering, interception of banking information, and some identity thefts running without issues. He was sufficient for running the modest team in the New York office and the four people that were positioned around the globe. Extending the business into other areas and generating new customers had been her focus.

The one hole in talent that they faced was, in fact, tapping into communications. If the communications were over just the Internet, then Dante and team could and did intercept on a routine basis. Other more traditional communications were not viewed or used. She really needed some talent to fill that void and then start to identify her benefactor. Zara had been warned not to mess with the programs and not to try traces. However, since the two gentlemen obviously knew more than she did, it had renewed her curiosity as to the true identity of Mephisto and whether she would ever hope to gain partnership.

The driver arrived at the designated hotel near one of the military bases. Taking her overnight satchel, she paid the driver and retrieved her key after she signed in at the desk. The place was far better than she had imagined when Mr. Grey had provided the instructions. In two separate conversations they had outlined the plan for the operation, but they planned to rehearse at least twice before tomorrow morning. Thankfully she had slept on the flight.

No sooner had she entered the room and set down her satchel, there was a knock at the door. She opened the door to find both men as she expected.

"Well, Mr. Black, Mr. Grey, what a delightful surprise. You set up a nice room and arrive, hopefully, ready to play. Do come in, gentlemen." Zara seductively smiled at them both as she eyed them top to bottom.

Without showing any emotion at her comment, Mr. Grey said, "Mistress Callisto, I hope your travel was not too inconvenient. Your arrival here was quite timely. Are you ready to begin our run-through exercises?"

"Mr. Grey, though I have a particular fondness for Mr. Black here, you can do run-through exercises with me anytime. Just let me get out of my travel clothes." She then grinned as she slowly removed every stitch of clothing, and then crossed over to retrieve her satchel. She displayed a lovely view of her backside, but neither of the men moved or made a sound.

"Mistress Callisto, did you bring the outfit you described as guaranteed to stop a whole battalion of soldiers?"

"I did, sirs. I was going to model it for you, unless you would prefer some different exercises first."

Now clearly disappointed, Mr. Grey explained, "We only have a short period of time left tonight to practice this, Mistress Callisto. We are, after all, business associates, right?"

Zara laughed and said with a tone of resignation, "We are." She slowly dressed and transformed into a beautiful lady in a low cut top with a flowing sheer skirt, along with five inch heels. The look was unmistakably 'come hither' to any male with a pulse. Even Mr. Black and Mr. Grey appreciated her sculpted form and smiled warmly.

Zara resigned herself to the fact that she couldn't tempt them as she once again came the total professional. "Okay. Let me recap. We are headed to the main road that leads outside of the base. You two will be positioned very near to the operations center building, which you have confirmed. Ordinarily we would be able to drive on base to deal with the Captain in charge of supply, but since this is a NATO base, security will be tighter. Understand being too close to the fence will allow you to be spotted.

"They will insist that the vehicle be parked in visitors parking, and the Captain will be forced to come to the gate entrance to sign me in. I will flirt with any and all those coming and going to make a nuisance of myself. The dress material is light enough and designed to flow which makes it easy to have a breeze catch it to send it up around my neck. Distractions will be numerous and are designed to have eyes focus on the wrong thing.

"Once inside, I will retrieve the hot-spot-Wi-Fi-enabled cell phone that doesn't get confiscated at the gate based on my antics while waiting for the Captain. Since this is the only visitor friendly building in the compound, it has been relegated to the edge of the base so no one can take a photo inventory of the armaments. I will place the hot-spot-Wi-Fi-enabled cell phone in a discreet area but in close proximity to the computer on the Captain's desk. The hard copy file I am required to bring, since I am not allowed a computer on base, will be deliberately flawed so it will need to be edited. The USB thumb drive I conveniently bring with me, which has the contract on it for reprinting, is the key to getting onto his computer via the Wi-Fi hot spot with your computer. Of course, my job will be to recommend we make the changes in an expedient manner so the contract can be reprinted there on their systems and thus giving you the bridge you need to introduce our package. My efforts, of course, will include some accidental touching, bumping, and of course re-adjusting my garment so as not to be so immodest but distracting none the less.

"If the primary distraction does not go as planned and I can't get the USB into his machine, then our plan B is to deliver the package to the network printer and let it navigate to the target area. Once we have our signed contract, we are done. If you require more time, I will need to flirt a little longer to delay long enough for you to complete your frequency hopping payload delivery. The one-time phone needs to go into the trash after I get the SIM out. Then even if it is discovered, there is no cell activity or residue to do forensics with. At the very least, I am to launch the *'Wipe'* program before disposing of it. I am to make my way out the way I came in, making sure I leave a visible female trail behind me that will help discredit the Captain once the payload has run its course. Have I missed anything? Does that cover it?"

"It does, madam. Thank you for your thoroughness and support on this effort. Mephisto indicated you would be ready and on time to perform your role. We will, of course, pass along your cooperation. I suggest we go to our planned location and see if there is anything we missed in our planning."

"Thank you both. We will complete this task, and I will be on the afternoon flight home tomorrow. We are still agreed my funds will be transferred before flight time, correct?"

"Yes, Mistress Callisto. If we are successful, the transfer will be completed before your departure."

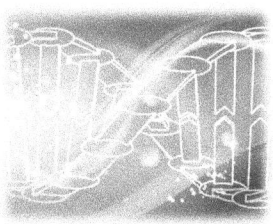

CHAPTER 33

TRY TO SEE IT FROM MY POINT OF VIEW, ONLY MY POINT OF VIEW

Dante remarked, "Moya Dushechka, you seem out of sorts. All you have done since your return is pace. What is it that has you distressed? What can I do to remove the distraction that has afflicted you?"

Zara, annoyed that Dante had picked up on her mood, snapped, "Where are you with the background check on Dakota? What have you learned of him, and is he the communications specialist he claims to be?"

Dante realized that he had intruded on one of Zara's dark and hostile moods, so he tried to respond as pleasantly as possible. "Moya Dushechka, you were not here to discuss my findings on Dakota, but I have done my first run at him. He is as he appears to be. He is running from past problems of his own doing but does have a varied history of telecommunications expertise with multiple organizations. I am surprised that some of his employers allowed him to leave. I was about to dig further into his background, as you had asked, to see if there are any new surprises."

Zara, now in better control of her annoyance, said, "Dante, with what we now know about him, let's meet with him again and see for ourselves if he is as his background claims. Between the two of us, we should be able to discern any false behavior while he talks about his past. Reach out to him for a meeting tomorrow. If everything rings true, then I want to bring him in for some hunting I want done with a telecommunications signal."

Dante was now uncomfortable again but asked in a gentle manner, "Moya Dushechka, your timeframe seems somewhat compressed from what we originally discussed. May I know what has changed? Why the hurry to bring into our organization someone we are not one hundred percent sure of?"

Zara reeled in her anger and replaced it with her trademark iciness that Dante had learned to fear and said, "Dante, I'm tired of being an errand girl with no informational knowledge of our clients. We have no leverage over one in particular, and it does not suit me to be so vulnerable.

"A communications specialist will help us gain access to background knowledge on those who think they only need summon me for a job, with no insightful explanation. I want knowledge of those smug bastards. This knowledge will give me the leverage to push their buttons. Are you finished grilling me on what I need done, or is a more persuasive debate required?"

Dante, concerned that Zara didn't see the error in her thinking, tried again to have her reconsider and soothed, "But, Moya Dushechka, this is not a wise course of action bringing this character in after only a light background scanning! It is almost as if you want, not just his skills as a communications consultant, but as a male who....."

Zara smiled with the confidence of a predator, as one after the other her hands shot out and drove deep into his throat, dimpling his windpipe. She almost cut off his air intake which silenced his protest.

While Dante struggled to breathe, she calmly unfastened his belt, loosened his trousers, and placed her hands inside his trousers and underwear to slowly pull them down. She was very careful to rake his loins with her now ragged nails which resulted from the punches delivered to his throat. This left a trail of blood oozing down his legs. After getting his trousers down, she deliberately reached down to collect his male pair in one hand and his manhood in the other.

Dante now winced from the rake marks down his thighs, but finally able to almost breathe again, was most agreeable to her coaxing him to sit closer to the edge of the chair so his male pair could be held with a little more pressure. Once Dante was properly on display, Zara continued to roll, squeeze, and firmly handle his male pair while prepared to take his manhood into her mouth after gently nipping him up and down his shaft. Without releasing her firm grasp and tugging effort on his male pair, she drove his manhood as far into her mouth and down her throat as possible until she was gasping and choking for air herself. The choking sensation brought back old memories of when she had first relocated to the big house and been given her first tutorial on male gratification.

Zara slowly withdrew Dante's manhood from her throat, making sure that she lightly drug her sharp teeth over his skin again making him wince and slightly flinch. She clamped down on his male pair, always applying more pressure, and began reaching for her favorite accoutrement, a leather flail she liked to use for swatting. Then she reached for his big hand and began licking his palm and fingers getting them very wet. Zara stared mischievously into his eyes, guided his hand to his manhood, smiled and said, "Bubi, I want to watch you stroke yourself, but you know the rules, you cannot climax until I tell you to."

Then she took his male pair in her hand so that she could swat them while he was stroking his manhood. The pain of the pressure she exerted on him along with the increasing number of stinging swats was as exhilarating for her, as it was painful for him. As an additional enticement for him, she took her free hand and pulled open her top so that he could see her breasts and how hard her nipples had become.

There was no mistaking her enjoyment of his punishment, and she continued swatting his genital area with more stinging hits and reminded, "Don't climax yet, I want to see how you handle yourself more!"

Dante was now over the top with excitement and pain, as he breathlessly said, "Oh, Moya Dushechka, it hurts so good! I can't stop!"

Zara moved out from between his legs but, still pulling and squeezing his male pair, swatted him faster until he erupted into a final climax. "There, you see, Bubi. You don't need a female, just your imagination and hand to do the necessaries. But now that you are spent, perhaps we can go back to work, yes? And arrange the Dakota meeting, yes?"

Dante nodded in resigned agreement, still gasping from the near torture and ecstasy, and finally said, "But I wanted you!"

Zara, in an almost contemptible tone, replied, "I will let you know when we can go to bed, and no sleeping, Bubi. Right now I want our communications specialist to help me turn the tables so I can dictate terms that are agreeable to me."

She bent down to get a quick taste of him and then added, "Go get cleaned up, and I will meet you back here in ninety minutes. Make sure that we have a meeting scheduled by that time, Dante."

As Dante shuffled off, he pulled up his trousers.

Zara looked down at her damaged nails and decided, "I think I can get my nails repaired in that amount of time." She smiled a chilling smile and gathered her purse and put herself back together. Then she reflectively mumbled, "They are right about sex being just like reading a murder mystery. It is always best just before it ends."

CHAPTER 34

PROBLEMS ARE PAST TENSE, SOLUTIONS ARE FUTURE TENSE ...
THE ENIGMA CHRONICLES

The Colonel screamed into the phone, "What do you mean, the support columns aren't coming here? We are on war game maneuvers here in the middle of nowhere. I need diesel fuel for the generators, ground communications repair equipment since nothing is operational, and provisions for thirteen hundred soldiers. You aren't really telling me that my support column was sent somewhere else! I don't even have enough fuel to bring everyone back to base, and all you can say is sorry! We are supposed to be doing field exercises to simulate a full scale alert, which means we scramble everyone, supplies and all. We are not on this exercise to practice stupidity! I can get that by just staying at the base and dealing with a dangerously incompetent quartermaster!"

The Quartermaster bristled at the accusation but evenly replied, "Colonel, we are trying to find out why all your support gear was sent to the wrong location. More importantly, we are trying to discover why the exercise was even called. At first it looked like the support gear was sent to the right location, but you were dispatched incorrectly. Then it looked the other way around. Now we are unsure of who or what actually called the alert in the first place."

The Colonel was taken aback by the statement and, with his temper now in check, asked, "You don't know who or what called this alert? You mean this is a false alarm or worse? Someone got into our security deployment systems and launched us all out to a one way destination with no operational support?"

"As I said, we don't know yet what we don't know. I suggest you sit tight until the situation gets unwound at this end."

The Colonel, now angered again, roared back, "Well, just call the operational support group like I'm doing right now and have them move everything here, goddammit! How hard is that?"

The Quartermaster, now dreading his own response, clarified, "Well, I can't. Protocol is to debug the SNAFU and follow proper procedure. I can't circumvent the troubleshooting procedure because this could be a fake call in which case that would only make things worse. We could be sending operations support into an ambush if the problem cannot be properly identified before moving the supplies."

The Colonel was now livid. "So here I am calling you, telling you where I am, my operations support group was sent to the wrong location, and my military deployment for a high alert simulation is basically crippled. Now you won't redirect my combat supplies needed by thirteen hundred soldiers until some computer glitch can be diagnosed?

"What I am supposed to do in the meantime? Order take-out to be delivered since we don't have enough fuel to do the drive through?"

The Quartermaster pondered the question for a few seconds and then queried, "Uh... Colonel, do you have a charge card you can use? You might want to tip the driver a little extra based on your location."

The phone call came in just as he was heading out to a meeting. "Dr. Eric PettinGrÜbber, here."

Eric listened for a few minutes and then said, "Yes, Colonel, I'm the one who ordered the alert investigated...

"I can appreciate your annoyance at being dispatched on high alert, having your supply column misdirected, and then told to sit tight while we figure this out...

"I'm not sure what you mean by your recreating the role of the Don Quixote travels with a donkey....

"Oh, now I see the parallel with your circumstances. The part where the radio narrator says, well, *we are out of time this week so until next time we will leave Don Quixote sitting on his ass*. Really, Colonel, I don't think this level of sarcasm is called for...

"With all due respect, Colonel, this is a major issue of concern, and it has our utmost attention. We cannot allow our alert systems to be tampered with and have these kinds of results, if national security is to have any meaning...

"If you must know, I was about to step into a meeting when I took this call, knowing the seriousness of this situation...

"We're having a luncheon meeting with the director for his secretary who is retiring after...

"Colonel, that type of vulgarity is totally unnecessary and frankly repulsive! After I get back from the luncheon, I will launch into high gear all the assets I have in my command to get to the bottom of the events that led up to...

"Colonel, I can assure you that we will not be gathered at this meeting--to paraphrase your coarse statement--*to engage in sexual self-abuse*! The secretary has put in her years and is leaving the agency. She is due this respect, and I need to get there before her afternoon nap. So if you don't mind, I think we are done here!"

After he hung up the receiver, Eric drummed his fingers on his desk, considering the tirade of accusations the Colonel had leveled at him. He then picked up the phone to make an outbound call to one of his favorite resources.

The voice on the other end of the call answered, "Ah, Dr. PettinGrÜbber, I presume! I see you didn't want to go to the luncheon for sleeping beauty either, so let's get down to the assignment, shall we? Which one of the mental dwarfs are we to be supporting now?"

Eric took a moment to collect his thoughts and then replied, "Stalker, we have a situation that really needs a fast but in-depth look into why a high alert scramble was launched only to be derailed as it unfolded. And I mean now. You have done a lot for this agency, and you are frankly the best at digging into the scattered details to piece together an accurate picture."

Stalker thought for a second and countered, "But you just gave me something else to work on. Which one has priority?"

Eric quickly decided. "This one has the highest priority since it has the most far-reaching consequences. We have to know how it is possible to infiltrate our systems, launch a high alert scramble, but then send support column resources to the wrong location. Ground troops and, for that matter, any military personnel are only as good as the material support we surround them with. Without ammunition, food, water, fuel, and medical supplies, our troops are nothing more than unprepared weekend campers. Stalker, I need answers and I need them yesterday. Investigating the disappearance of Arletta Krumhunter can wait for the time being."

"I understand, Eric. However, the longer that trail goes unexplored the easier it is to lose track of her altogether."

"Agreed, but it can't be helped. I need you to focus on this one first since it is in the interest of national security."

Stalker nodded his head and offered, "I understand the position of home soil over foreign soil, but may I make a suggestion? What if you ask your foreign contractor friends to initiate their hunt for Ms. Krumhunter? You know the ones who helped me a while back? That way, if they get any information on her disappearance, I can jump into the fray that much farther along than if I started from scratch."

Eric bobbed his head up and down and then agreed, "Point taken. After we finish this conversation, I'll make that call."

Stalker briefly chuckled. "I thought you might be persuaded to accelerate the hunt for your protégé. I always suspected that you had a soft spot in your heart for the lady even after that office episode with the copy machine. She must have really been smitten with you to try and seduce you with photocopies of her...."

Eric immediately paled to a soft shade of green at the thought that someone else knew of the photocopy incident, and cut Stalker off as he insisted, "Alright, that's enough of that!"

Stalker snickered and continued, "You know, I can't get that image out of my mind of her setting her plump bottom on the copier and riding it back and forth to get just the right exposure....Oh hey, that's good!"

Eric suffered the flashback and knew he was still unable to approach any copy machine without gloves. He practically shouted, "Enough! Stop it! Or I won't be able to suppress the gagging reflex for an hour! Just take the assignments in the order I told you! And keep me updated every four hours on the military deployment problem. Got it?"

"Got it, boss."

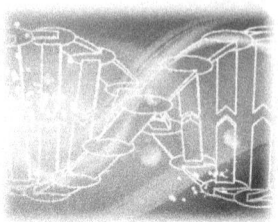

CHAPTER 35

IT IS MORE FUN TO WORK SMART THAN TO WORK HARD

When he returned from the retirement celebration, Eric was still annoyed at the potshots Stalker had taken with regards to Arletta. She was a piece of work. Most people, after working around her for a month or two, were perfectly happy to ignore or forget her. Part of him hoped she was gone for good, and then his human side kicked in so that he hoped she was someplace with amnesia. He mused that perhaps she had found someone and had simply quit to be at home as a wife and mother, too arrogant to resign. That would be an extremely unlikely end to their business relationship. The downside was she also knew how slow some things were in government agencies, and her clearance levels were fairly high. She didn't need to fall into the wrong hands.

As he refined the statement of work modification to use in his discussion with Otto, he pondered the military issue. The Colonel deserved a situation update call. He trusted Stalker to get to the cause and seek resolution. The man had been in the field and appreciated all the trials and tribulations. This was peace time, wasn't it?

He read over the services request one more time and the defined timeframe allocated to the effort. The timing seemed ample. He authorized the purchase order for up to the amount based on the last rates used by the R-Group and then dialed his special number.

"Hello, Monty, I mean, Eric. It is nice to hear from you. How can I help you?"

Eric was totally surprised at the voice. It was clearly not Otto. He regained his composure and replied, "Quip, I am surprised. Did I somehow misdial the number? I was expecting Otto."

"Eric, Otto is on leave. To make things simple, I am handling his calls. And just so you know, I am not going to be nearly as cheeseball with you anymore. Were you calling to socialize with Otto, or did you need some help?"

"Ah, about time the old man took a break. I hope he enjoys himself. I didn't think he ever stopped working.

"Actually, Quip, you were going to likely supply most of the support for this request anyway. I have a bit of a delicate problem that I could use your team's support, as well as ample discretion, to resolve."

"Okay, so who do I need to find for you, Eric?"

"Funny you should ask that specifically, Quip. How did you know it was a person and not a thing? We do both types of services with your teams. Never mind answering as, like Otto, I suspect you won't, or you'll be forced into your typical smartass role that I know so well, and I don't want to blow your transformation. I need you to find Arletta Krumhunter."

Quip extended the silence as a myriad of nasty comments came to mind. He took a breath and evenly asked, "Eric, are you certain you want her found? I thought she was some major pain in your ah…emm… side. I would think you'd be doing the happy dance to have her missing. Heck, I wouldn't mind taking credit for her missing, umm… ah, sorry. Out of scope."

Eric laughed until tears threatened. Those really had been his first thoughts when she was thought to be missing. He cleared his throat and stated, "Yep. Just between us, those were my initial thoughts. However, she is a high ranking person in the organization and cannot turn up missing without some explanation. If nothing else, the bureaucratic paperwork needs to be completed."

"I feel your pain, Eric. So let's get specific. What details do you know for the starting point? How long has she been gone? And what do you want to happen when she is located."

"Nice ending on that, Quip. Your confidence in locating her is remarkable. I hope you're sitting down. This could take a few minutes."

"Eric, I have time for you, no worries. Let's hear it!"

"Otto and you are aware that Arletta was reassigned to the operations team on the Aleutian Islands. You know, close to Alaska to cool her jets down," he laughed at his joke, and Quip did chuckle some.

"Internally something changed, and they quietly closed the facility down. It was a very slow close, and the actual day for the personnel leaving is plus or minus thirty days. Everyone left sort of in waves. I hate to say it, but the rules were lax and the follow up non-existent until some wife started trying to locate her husband.

"Apparently, this guy took the lack of public notification of the closing as a chance to take a holiday of his own. His wife was use to him being out of pocket for up to a month at a time. But as the month turned into two, with the phone disconnect then in place on the office number she'd been provided, she started up the command structure. There is nothing like a spoiled congressman's daughter to raise a ruckus.

"After she pushed all the right, or as some would suggest wrong, buttons everyone started to account for every person assigned to that site. Six people had not received a forwarding assignment with the closing of the operations center. Arletta was one of the people that hadn't been reassigned. So rather than call me or her boss to ask, it seems she simply vanished. It would be just like her to show up at some plum operations site and insist that she was assigned to some role. So that is where we have been checking. So far we have zero results. She is a salaried person, and her pay is being automatically deposited into her account. In checking those accounts, no withdrawals have been made except those set up for auto pay.

"She had some crazed shopping spree, it seems, around five years ago that maxed all her credit cards so she set up auto pay to help insure they paid first. The apartment she had used for her time in Virginia was a one room furnished. The keys were returned to the landlord when she left with two suitcases, according to an interview with the man. She had taken up residence at a by-the-week hotel on the islands. When it was checked, one suitcase was there. Those owners hadn't even cleaned her room as they were scrambling to fill vacancies when the operations center closed. Apparently, it was a major economy booster for the region, hence the quiet shut down.

"From there, Arletta was tracked, using her passport, to board a flight to Paris. Interpol confirmed entry into France with subsequent entries in and out of countries over a week, as she made her way by car into Russia. That is where we are stalled."

"Eric, it seems that your Arletta is quite resourceful. Perhaps she is just on an extended vacation across Europe to see the sights? Or maybe just driving to work the long way around to be through being mad? Any idea?"

Eric tilted his head to think about the possibilities. He and Stalker had done the same thing but from a different perspective. After a bit he continued, "I think your idea of driving through your mad is more Arletta than touring. She toured all those places as a spoiled child. Travel to her was mundane. Part of her rise through the agency, was due to her multi-lingual capabilities, as well as her Father's military career influences. You knew she was, to a degree, an untouchable."

"Oh, yeah. We all knew that. She is definitely a different type of female. But you say you still want to find her, right?"

"We need to locate her and find a way to fire her or tell her parents we have no clue and they make her some kind of martyr. She would be totally useless if that happened, and I'd be forced to work with her again. That is part of my reason for modification to your contract which is, I believe, still in place, to locate her. I sent both the modification and the purchase order authorization to the usual secured email."

Quip interrupted, "Eric, how long has she been missing?"

"Almost six months, Quip. No one gave a damn, for almost six months, where she was or what she was doing. I had my best working it, but another event that needed investigation took him away from looking for Arletta. You have the resources, I believe, to make inroads on locating her. Heck, she could be dead, but she needs to be definitively found. Sooner or later her parents will ask about her, and I would like an answer available."

"Six months is a very long time with a very cold trail. Can you send over the information that was collected by your lead guy? That helps avoid rework though we will look under every rock, Eric. Er ...Umm." Quip cleared his throat and quietly asked, "When we find her, Eric, what do you want us to do with her, assuming she is found alive?"

Eric chuckled as he replied, "Okay, Quip. The image of your team dragging her back kicking and screaming just popped into my head. That would be awkward. Once located, call and we can decide on the removal and return. Thanks, Quip, I appreciate your taking this on."

"You are welcome, Eric." Quip hesitated then asked, "Er...Eric, I do have one other question."

"Sure, what's that?"

"What happened to the husband that took off? Where was he located?"

Eric laughed, "I forgot, Quip. You like the details and closure items. The guy was found with one of the secretaries on a beach on Oahu drinking margaritas. A gorgeous blond with a great body and white bikini is hard to resist, right?

"The files are on their way to the secure email. Keep in touch, Quip. Good job too. Otto would be pleased."

Quip had received all the information and reviewed it. He set up a special routine in ICABOD for the Prudence Pursuit. If nothing else, he would have some fun with this as a slight distraction to the bigger problem. Sometimes stepping away from one problem and then returning provided improved perspective. He called a meeting with Jacob and Petra to review this new assignment. He reflected for a moment that Eric's last comment about Otto being proud of his behavior felt great.

Jacob and Petra entered a few minutes after the scheduled time, looking tired but clearly together. Previous concerns about the state of their relationship seemed gone. Too much stress with all the events and separate travel. He tucked that away for future reference. He was also reminded for a second that it had been a week since he'd spoken to EZ, and he made a mental note to call her later. He missed her but tried to let work take priority until she decided their fate. He hated that females always chose.

"What's up, Quip?" Jacob asked. "Something about a new assignment?"

Petra added, "Honestly, Quip, if it is not for this phantom code ghost thing, we probably don't have time."

Quip raised his eyebrows at this and evenly replied, "We have a request that came in from our customer, Monty, er, Eric. It is one that is a bit different but important to him. I think we should do it, and perhaps give you a chance to look away from this ghost mess now and again."

Jacob said, "Focus is key on this ghost thing, Quip, and you know it. It is too intricate to stop and start activity on."

Quip grinned slightly and asked, "Are you saying you aren't capable of multi-tasking?"

Petra responded with a touch of anger, "Of course, we can both multi-task. What is it, Quip? This new request from Eric, and more importantly how soon does it need to be done?"

He touched the keyboard, and the large screen lit up with the opening slide in purple, displaying PRUDENCE PURSUIT, and surround sound music. Then for thirty seconds there was a flash of Prudence pictures that had been taken when she had visited the operations facilities during a prior effort they had engaged with her on.

Jacob looked stunned and Petra was not too far behind on the emotion scale.

Quip laughed and explained, "Eric has asked us to find the missing Prudence. She escaped her remote operations assignment through a lucky set of circumstances that she had no way of creating."

"But I thought Eric disliked this female. I know we all did, even Otto," suggested Jacob.

Petra nodded but started thumbing through the briefing material in front of her anyway. She scanned the data and even smiled a little at one point.

Quip continued, "All true, but he provided a bit of history on her we didn't know. Consider it a chapter to close. It is not a tight deadline, and I think we can treat this like a jigsaw puzzle and add pieces over many days. Let's treat it as more of a distraction during a forced lunch break daily, which none of us have been taking.

"I wanted your thoughts and buy-in before adding Wolfgang into the fun."

By this time Jacob too had scanned the information and nodded agreement, along with Petra. Quip reviewed the details, his proposed approach and the pieces of the puzzle to identify. He had set up some search programs in ICABOD with a clever way of adding puzzle pieces to form the final picture of Prudence. It resembled a picture one would find of a missing child on a carton of milk. They tossed some ideas back and forth and agreed to take at least an hour lunch each day to eat and work on the Prudence Pursuit Puzzle, nicknamed the PPP. They called Wolfgang in and actually laughed as they explained this new assignment with some enthusiasm.

Quip smiled after they left and hoped that the shift in mood would give them all a leg up on the bigger problem with the vanishing code. He returned to his office to call EZ and see where her head was at today.

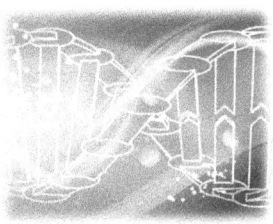

CHAPTER 36

DO NOT THINK YOU ARE ALONE IN THE DIGITAL AGE, AS SOMEONE ELSE CARES ENOUGH TO WATCH...
THE ENIGMA CHRONICLES

Zara pointedly stated, "Well, Dakota, you've been here a week now, and I've yet to see anything tangible for the hiring bonus you so expertly extracted in order to join our group. Don't make me have to agree with Dante that he was right about you being a charlatan. Tell me you have something useful and not more of your Meso-American anecdotal stories about hunting in the dark of the netherworld, exploring mystical cooking recipes using spiritual plants and grubs."

Dakota smiled, and almost chuckling, replied, "Those stories are icebreakers at dull parties and designed to get people talking about what they in fact believe. As it turns out, Dante opened up quite a bit and told me his belief in reincarnation. He was quite serious when he stated that in a previous life he rode into the Russian Steppes, the leader of his own triad, as a part of Genghis Khan's army. He waxed nostalgic when he spoke of the other two members of his triad being killed in battle, which meant he was to also forfeit his life per the harsh Mongol tradition of killing anyone who did not die with the other members of the triad. He believes that this early ancestor of his bolted from the Genghis Khan army, and then in that moment began life and lineage as a Russian."

Zara stared incredulously at Dakota for a few seconds then questioned, "He told you that bogus story? I told him not to repeat that story unless he wanted a new career as a carnival sideshow freak act! But you're right. He wholeheartedly believes it to the point his cologne is *Ode de Khan*, which even smells like horses and men racing into battle with swords and pikes.

"Tell me you have better circuitry and that I haven't wasted my time bringing you in. I already have the clown practitioner performing, and I don't want it to grow to a duet!"

Dakota chuckled and pitched a small baggie with two electronic items in it to her. He then stated, "You asked me to be your communications expert, and I said I would, madam. The first thing you do in my world is see if you are truly alone. You run a full electronic sweep to see who else is watching the private channel you are performing on. I will report to you that you were not by yourselves. Those two surveillance devices prove that someone else was watching and listening to all activities in your premises. If you think you had any secrets, please push that erroneous thought from your memory banks. Whoever it is already knows what you are doing, so all of your planning has been compromised. I suggest you rethink your future as this has probably already been planned for you. My next task is to prowl the machines here to see what was placed to record your electronic efforts and send them back to the mother ship."

Zara was stunned by the electronic eavesdropping items tossed to her. She stared at them in disbelief as she rolled them over and over in her hands. Finally she asked, "How is this possible? We are the drive-by download of payload experts, and here we are under surveillance, being monitored like children in the nursery by parents downstairs! Words fail me!"

Without turning his gaze from the computer screen, Dakota responded, "Do you have any idea who might want to be keeping tabs on you that closely? Those are pretty sophisticated electronic monitoring devices with their own on-board storage and encrypted wireless capability, so they are not cheap. From one standpoint you should consider yourself flattered they went to such an expense to study you. Is your flat bug free as well, or should we do a search and destroy there too?"

Zara was angered but suddenly felt very alone and vulnerable with these new revelations. Not being in control of her destiny was just like being back at the big house of her lost youth. It simply stole her breath to be reliving that awful point in her life. Dakota had just shown her, without being asked, that she had been exposed. But there was so much now out of balance that she could not deal with all the emotional input. She had planned, schemed, and dominated so much in her life that she had come to expect it. What she didn't expect was being man-handled and not even knowing it. But here was a man, expert in his craft, who knew where to look. So while she liked nothing in the current scenario, here was someone that she might even be able to trust.

Finally recovering some of her voice but retaining all of her anger, Zara offered, "It would seem you are well versed in your trade, Dakota. And yes, it occurs to me that there may be a secret admirer among my associates that would indeed want to know about my comings and goings. So permit me to reach a quiet area to call them to discuss their need of additional information on me."

Again without letting his gaze move from the monitor, Dakota asked, "Is that wise, Moya Dushechka? In the information business I have found that false communications can be as valuable as those that are true, under the right circumstances. I would point out that your admirer had built a one way information stream for themselves, but now you have the opportunity to turn the tables. By now they should know that their surveillance has been compromised somehow. However if you alert them of your suspicion, then their surveillance efforts will simply begin again and will be harder to find. I suggest that you let it be known that you are moving to a new facility that is more friendly to your business needs, but not mention the surveillance cameras. In this manner, they will not use extra caution but most likely extra haste to reestablish their monitoring activity. Then we will be ready to pursue the hunter."

Zara studied Dakota for a few seconds and then clarified, "You seem to be speaking from experience, and your counsel is good. I will be out for a while. When Dante returns, please give him only the bare essentials of our discussion, and let me fully brief him upon my return."

Still pouring through files on the computer, Dakota added, "I can use small words if you like or simply ignore him altogether if you prefer. I do expect it will take your presence to convey the correct message. I always seem to sense hostility when I talk with him, but he seems contained as long as you are around."

Zara smiled weakly and agreed, "I won't be gone long. When I return I can recount what I want him to know. Just leave the discussion to me for the time being."

Dakota smiled and said, "Understood, Moya Dushechka."

Zara hadn't been gone long when Dante returned to the Dteam operations area. Dante's good mood went to dark when he saw Dakota on the laptop reserved for Zara.

Trying to contain his annoyance and with no Zara to keep him in check, Dante asked, "You mind telling me why you are on Moya Dushechka's computer while she is not here to know about it? I suspected you were only looking for an opportunity to rifle through our intellectual property, ready to pirate our hard won knowledge. I told Moya Dushechka you could not be trusted, but I will fix this problem myself!"

In the small amount of time it took Dante to cross the room to accost Dakota, a time window the size of eternity opened up in front of Dakota's eyes as he opened a file under a directory called aircraft wrapper. In the file called delivery L O H R 5-6-7-8 Dakota suddenly remembered the aircraft call sign of Juan's aircraft. They were the same call sign and it was on her laptop! The Dteam, and Moya Dushechka in particular, were indeed linked to Juan's disappearance!

However, the eternity of the second was over, and Dante was now upon Dakota. Dakota barely had time to prepare for impact as he was hit hard from the side just as he turned to meet his assailant. The impact sent both of them over the chair onto the floor with Dante landing on top of Dakota.

Dante, pleased that his attack seemed to have given him the upper hand, snarled, "Now I even the score from our last encounter!"

Dante didn't have a good appreciation for a birth defect that Dakota had struggled with all his life. The underlying adrenaline leak in his system was always triggered by intense emotion or anger. Dakota was a powerful male, but when the adrenaline kicked in, nothing human could intercept, much less stop him. Before the last word was out of Dante's mouth, he was tossed like a small bag of rice launched from a large catapult. Dante's large frame was slammed into the adjacent wall upside down, which landed him on his head before he crumpled to the floor.

Dakota slammed his fists hard into Dante's kidney region twice before gathering him up by his neck and pinning him against the wall so that his feet no longer reached the floor. Dakota was about to reach over to break any flailing limbs when Zara happened into the room.

Without missing a beat, Zara smiled sweetly and crooned, "Boys! Boys! How many times have I told you not to roughhouse in the operations area?"

Dante was in pain and struggled to breathe. Dakota was focused on reeling in his hyper-powerful state. They both breathed heavily but looked at Zara.

Zara looked sternly at Dante and questioned, "You're not hurting our new team member, are you, Dante? I mean, making him hold your considerable bulk off the floor, suspended by your neck and making him only get to use one hand! Shame on you for mistreating our newest member!"

Dakota was now able to manage a small smile and let Dante down to almost be able to stand again. He conceded, "The fault is mine, Moya Dushechka. When I asked to see the style of shoe he wears, he said I was free to look at them. But my back injuries are such that I only thought to bring the shoes up to my eye level. To his credit, Dante was agreeable to my viewing request."

Zara smirked and asked, "Did you get a chance to discuss what we talked about before?"

Dakota nodded slightly and then reminded, "I seem to recall that you expressed a preference to brief him yourself. After you left, I busied myself with reviewing the Dteam machines, until Dante and I became engaged in shoe fashion, madam. May I continue with the computer review as we discussed earlier?"

Dante was now quite chastened by the fact that Zara had approved the computer scanning and was now almost trembling with thoughts that she would punish him for trying to take on Dakota again.

Zara caressed Dante's face softly and quietly ordered, "We need to move from these facilities. I am hoping you can orchestrate the relocation of our gear. I just don't trust anyone else to give it the attention and dedication required to be sure it is done promptly and efficiently. I need your masterful help in planning our move, so will you come help me, Dante? We have so much to do."

Dante, forgetting his recent failed painful attack, was now like a small puppy hoping for its next treat and responded enthusiastically, "Yes, Scheherazade, with much joy, and goodly gree! I shall make ready all for the move time you tell me!"

As Dante scampered off to make the arrangements, Zara looked at Dakota and asserted, "I don't think you will need to discuss shoe fashion for a while now that Dante has his new assignment. Let me know if you find anything else that needs our attention."

Dakota stared at Zara momentarily, recalling the call sign of Juan's aircraft on her computer, and finally replied, "Yes, of course, madam. I will let you know what I think we should do next."

Carlos said into the encrypted cell phone, "Julie, I have a little progress on our target group, but I need a little more time to stage the go forward steps...

"No, nothing I can't handle...

"Yes, the wireless cameras were a big hit with the boss lady.....

"You were right. Make sure they think they are being monitored and act like you care enough to help, worked just like you said it would.....

"How can you suggest such a thing? Come on, get your mind out of the gutter....besides I am spoken for by another. I would not trifle with those feelings....not even for a good foot massage!

"Apologies accepted. Although I know you were only teasing me, young lady....

"Take care of my niece or nephew, Julie. See you soon with the best news I can get."

CHAPTER 37

RIDDLES ARE TERRIBLY ANNOYING WHEN THE ANSWER IS ELUSIVE

After the first twelve hours, Stalker had emergency supplies airlifted to the troops on the ground on maneuvers. It was a far more expensive method, but the basics were critical. Other needed items were shipped out overland as well. The Colonel was not tickled pink with the delay but appreciated that something was being done.

The problem with the 'why' however still remained. Stalker had pulled a team of techno geeks together then tasked them with providing the forensic story on how the breach occurred. The 'why' would hopefully fall into place more readily if the 'how' was understood. This six-person team was the very best the agency had to offer and had done the technically impossible more than once. They had infiltrated other countries' systems, helped build complex programs to sift through potential threats against their country, and had even achieved success at gaining access to some terrorists' banking information. They were, in fact, highly trained, technology geniuses that could find things all over the web in some of the most unlikely places.

The team leader, Jenkins, had provided check points every four hours. The amount of information that had been gathered since Stalker had engaged the team was unbelievable, yet so far they weren't any closer to an answer. The team had access to the systems within the military network and had been performing analysis of each of the systems that were used by the supply chain operations group. The local team that ultimately had sent the supplies incorrectly had denied any issues over and over. Getting new information had been like pulling teeth. Once the team was assembled, two members had been assigned to the onsite work at that location while the rest of the team under Jenkins had worked remotely.

Stalker had summarized what was known to date for his report to Eric which was due in the morning. He wanted the more recent update from Jenkins incorporated into the report before that briefing. To help understand the entire picture, Stalker had asked that the activities for the two prior days to the maneuver be reviewed as well as all the data traffic. Military facilities were already report-driven, so the visitors, traffic, deliveries, and duty personnel, along with their assignments with status, were all known. This was simply a matter of assembling the timeline for the activities and extracting the anomalies. Odds are the anomalies were the key to the breach.

Over the three days being scrutinized, there had been eight visitors, two women and six men, who had been discounted as unrelated. None of them had been left alone or not escorted, and each had been on base less than two hours. Each person had the proper identification, was photographed, and after review didn't match to any known persons of interest. The interviews conducted with the personnel assigned to each visitor had not raised any flags or concern from those personnel. One comment that had made Stalker smile was about one female visitor who had been a real looker and was welcome to come back anytime.

There had been no events on base, so there had been no media traffic, visiting personnel from other bases, or unscheduled deliveries. There had been no foot traffic outside of the logged visitors, no family visitors, and no group events that caused busloads of base residents to exit and return.

The deliveries were all scheduled well in advance and based on requests initiated by base personnel. The delivery trucks and drivers were filmed on their way in and as they exited. The actually good delivery was filmed at the docks, and no additional people were caught on film or seen by the required observers. Not one mistake in process and protocol was observed. The base commander was apparently a stickler for rules, and no one disobeyed. The assignments of all personnel were also reviewed. There was no evidence of machine tampering with all authorization sequences having legal credentials. All of the faces stayed in their proper places, Stalker mused. This place was run by the book. Furthermore there were no complaints by base personnel.

Only two staff interviews brought any hope of finding the problem. On the day the maneuvers began, two of the computers in the supply organization area had blanked out for a few seconds. First one machine, then the other, and then they both seemed to run fine. The guys monitoring the computers both noticed and asked each other if they should reboot the systems. As the recovery seemed clean and complete, they decided not to reboot at that time. They worked through their morning orders and assignments which involved some coordination with the Colonel's troops who had left on maneuvers the previous day.

They completed the initial checks and balances to coordinate the orders for the supplies to make certain the trucks rolled by midday. Then they both went to lunch. When they returned, one of the machines had an unfamiliar screen saver with words rolling on the screen.

> *The Ghost Code exercise has completed.*
> *Thank you!*
> *Would you like your receipt emailed to you?*

When the machine was touched, the screen disappeared. Both men saw it and made note of it, but neither of the men had taken a picture. The other machine was locked and had to be unlocked. This too was noted in their logs, and that machine typically did not self-lock unless untouched for over two hours due to some special programs it launched and then received data from for efficiency analysis.

Though a case could be made that they should lock their machines when leaving for lunch, these two guys worked all day in a room with a secure door. It required fingerprint recognition for access. Based on the interviews these guys had been through so far, they were clean and had just been the targets. Stalker felt bad for them for the mark that would likely find a way onto their permanent records.

Of course, these two machines had been the main source of forensic review by Jenkins and his team. Other machines were also undergoing review, especially those that any visitors or delivery personnel might have had access to. These results were expected with the final update from Jenkins that he hoped would be coming soon. He hated unresolved problems. Unresolved problems created room for additional nonsensical rules that added even more cumbersome layers of bureaucracy. It was a never-ending circle jerk unless the root cause was located.

Stalker answered on the first ring, "Jim Hughes here. Jenkins, I hope you have a resolution for me."

Jenkins responded, "Mr. Hughes, sir, I do not. We have combed every space on the machines and found nothing of note outside of a couple of weird residual fragments in some of the hidden root directories. Nothing about them matched anything we had. The men located on-site are suggesting it was perhaps someone's game files residue that remained when the machine was reimaged and redeployed to this base. You know, sir, that with all the budget cuts, the lifetime of computer resources has been extended, and reimaging is a standard. To be certain, these files are now in the hands of the Virginia team to perhaps dig deeper, but it is doubtful at best that they will find anything.

"The machines are clean at this point, and nothing in the logs indicates otherwise. The program executed the way it was intended, and the guys seem to have entered the data correctly as they were made to repeat all of their activities for that morning. The file pointers on the receiving side simply placed the data into the wrong fields before the go command was executed. Norman, who is tracking the data and workflow, has found a few steps that could be tighter and has programmed some guardrails to insure future commands will be correctly executed by these activities.

"We tracked back all of the logon activities and authorizations and found one irregularity. One high ranking credential was used in the correct manner, but that credential cannot be tied to any of the base personnel nor to any of the lines of command at the base or with the Colonel who was impacted. It was the high clearance identification assigned to Arletta Krumhunter. Do you know why she might have logged into any of these systems?"

Stalker was dumbfounded as he thought, "What the heck was this female train-wreck doing in the middle of the maneuvers?"

Not receiving a response, Jenkins suggested, "Mr. Hughes, sir, I recognize it could be a need to know situation, and I am not one to question those situations. I just thought if we needed to look at different personnel, you might want to know who."

Stalker replied, "Jenkins, that's fine. I do happen to know that authorized user. I will do some checking from here on her. Was there anything else?"

"Yes sir! The reference to the ghost code message that the guys made in their interview appears to be legitimate. They both saw the red letter scrolling. They apologized for not picturing it, but rules clearly state that there are no fruit phone cameras or pictures allowed in high security areas. The team did some searching in our agency projects and found nothing with a code name of Ghost or any derivative. I even called my buddy over at Homeland Security, and he claimed nothing had hit them with any such name or reference or any derivative. He did say that there were some crazy Internet postings sometime back with that as a reference, but in his opinion they were from wackos. It was considered a prank by some college kids on international travel during semester breaks. You know how kids are, sir."

"I do indeed, Jenkins. Alright! I am pleased that the team was able to easily fill a possible gap and help to secure the future. Can you take a quick look at the picture I am emailing to you right now and tell me if she maps to either of the two female visitors to the base?"

"Looking now, sir. Eww, definitely not. The two females were both several pounds lighter and younger, sir. Do I need to do anything with this picture, sir?"

"I think to be safe, Jenkins, please circulate it to the base personnel, and if she was seen on base get the details. Don't let on that this is the Arletta Krumhunter you referred to as accessing the system, but remote access could have occurred."

"Will do, Mr. Hughes. I will send the written report to you within the hour and any follow up information as it is uncovered. Is that correct, sir?"

"Yes, Jenkins. Thank you for the fast work by the team."

Stalker hung up and shook his head. Some things you simply could not run away from, no matter how hard he had tried. He added some notes to his report summary and dialed his phone.

"Hey, Eric, it's me. You aren't going to believe what the team did and didn't find…"

CHAPTER 38

LOOKING FOR LOVE IN ALL THE RIGHT PLACES

Quip reviewed the current progress on Prudence Pursuit Puzzle. Another piece of her face had been added, so making a game out of finding her location seemed to be working. ICABOD estimated seventy-two percent completion of the puzzle, which was definitely progress. He wanted to review again some of the documents that Eric had provided on this assignment to expand some of the places to investigate. The webcams found some images of her trail through Europe, and any extended stops were being researched. Perhaps there had been scheduled meetings in that region that would provide additional details on not only where she landed but perhaps why.

Wolfgang had found some additional financial information that seemed to account for travel dollars. Apparently, her aunt had died a year or so before and had left her with some money in trust. Arletta had chosen not to report this alternative income source to the agency, therefore Eric's team had not yet tripped across it. Oddly enough, Wolfgang had reported that the fund was increasing with some fairly consistent by-weekly deposits. This was not usual activity for a trust, as those were typically drawn down on by the beneficiaries not increased. He was trying to get the additional information on the location of the source of the funds' transfer from point.

Quip was also doing some special reviews of selective data sources including some internal exchanges within the various governments and their agencies. One of his childhood friends worked for Interpol, so he had also asked if any information on Arletta Krumhunter was available from their sources. Granted, he could prowl around there himself, but he'd wanted to touch base with his friend Bruno so this had been a good excuse. He looked at his watch and had some time and thought perhaps he could catch EZ. He dialed her number while he glanced at the random information fragments that ICABOD displayed for more granular categorization.

EZ answered, "Well, hi there. I was just thinking about you, honey, and how much I miss you. How are you doing?"

"I am doing alright. Though I must admit I miss you as well. I liked it better when you were close by. I like holding you close. Do you want to switch to video? I would like to see you."

"Not a chance, with the way I look right now. I was outside helping with some chores on the farm. I look like, well, never mind. Just not a pretty picture that I want to expose to you unnecessarily." Then she added with that sweet southern drawl, "Suffice to say, I'm not groomed and perfumed, and I fear you'll recoil from the soil I collected doing farm chores."

He smiled and chuckled as he disagreed, "Sweetheart, you always look good to me, especially with your fiery hair all over the place. Makes me want to rip your clothes off and have my way with you. But now that I think about it, a power shower could be arranged first."

EZ laughed and said, "Alright! That's quite enough when you aren't close enough to make good on those statements, my dear. Besides I always take your clothes off first. You said you liked that about me."

He groaned, "Okay, you're right. I'll cease and desist for a bit. Things are busy here with our projects, and we picked up another one that is at least adding some variety. How is your business going?"

"With Carlos out of pocket, Andrew and I have been very busy. I know he appreciates me being here. We are busy with our regular customers. Any idea when Carlos will return? Do you think he will be able to locate Juan?"

"I think he won't stop until he finds Juan. I just hope he finds him safe and sound. We may need to ask you and Andy to help with some stuff, but I haven't finalized it yet."

"No problem, we can make it work, honey."

"Funny that you would say that, sweetheart. I want us to work. Can we do that? I promise I can come to you if you permit it."

"Quip, you know I love you very much. I am just not certain we are at a point in our lives where we can do the sort of commitment you want. Honestly, I am still thinking of the best way for us. You coming here would simply…"

Quip stopped hearing what EZ was saying as the screen caught his attention. He paused the data stream and read it closely. Then he thumbed up the information to make certain he was reading from the top of this discussion being received. It was an extensive exchange between several intermediary agents on tracking down an event that had a reference to Ghost code. So there was an event that he was certainly not going to find on the Internet. The details of the problem were vague, and there was no resolution. He packaged up as much as he could locate of the discussion and sent it over to Jacob and Petra for review. Then he had ICABOD perform a detailed search on these agents to gather any surrounding data that might also be useful. Finally, EZ's voice interrupted his activity.

"Quip, hey, are you hearing me? No response for five minutes is a sure clue that you are reading the screen. Honey, are you okay?"

"EZ, sorry. I am fine. Something did catch my eye on the screen. You know we guys do not multitask as well as you females. I was distracted when you said you were still thinking of the best way for us. I guess that means you don't want me with you yet. For the record, I want you very much, but I will be patient. You are worth the wait. Babe, I need to go, the distraction is important, and I need to follow up on it."

"No problem. I understand. We'll talk soon. I'll call you. Let me know if you need us to do any work for you. Bye, honey."

Quip trolled all the data that ICABOD had found which related to the agents and their activity. Apparently, there was a team of experts working on this classified security breach, which Quip believed was the newest ghost code attempt. He then did some other data cross-referencing for the correlations that ICABOD was tracking. ICABOD was consolidating the data at a tremendous rate into the new focus area Quip had just prescribed when Jacob came up behind him.

"I take it from your message that we have a new event to include. Do you have any more on it? Because what you sent me really doesn't have any code tracking that I saw."

"ICABOD is just summarizing selected data sources based on the new attributes I provided. We should see something soon. Is Petra joining us too?"

"Not for this, unless I call her. She is working on breaking down an encrypted file we found stored on the data I collected from Ireland. It seems she found an encasement program that wasn't used but wasn't cleared. She is hoping to open it and find either a payload inside for us to look at or a signature on the wrapper. Petra indicated that the encryption was good. We'll see. My money is on Petra breaking into it."

"Mine too. No one can best her at that." Quip whistled long then suggested, "Now, Jacob, isn't that your topless dream girl from New York?"

"Hey, I think that handle is really overstated, but, yeah, it looks like her. Zoom in on her face. Where is this from?"

"I pulled in the airport video from three days before and after from the airports in and around the base. ICABOD matched it with the facial recognition program for your original modified Petra drawing. This is from Frankfurt, to be specific."

Jacob moved to a keyboard and entered some commands. The file was pulled up and surprised both of them.

"Well, well, well. We have her departing out of Frankfurt but under a totally different name, Moya Dushechka. Same face but longer hair and lighter. She looks a little more like Petra, actually. Quip, I want to have ICABOD search for other times she has used this alias."

"Agreed, Jacob. She does seem to have some frequent flyer miles with this name as well. Let's have Wolfgang follow the money trail with this alias. I think she is perhaps a bigger player than we suspected."

"I will let Petra know what you've found on this and Julie as well. I suspect Julie will want to get this information to Carlos. Any idea on how he is doing? Have we received any good data from there, so far?"

"He is in and making friends, so it will take some time. Though knowing Carlos, he won't waste a minute."

"Alright, I am back at it. Petra and I plan on lunch around two to work on the Prudence Pursuit Puzzle, in case you want to join us. We added some pieces to her face yesterday."

"I saw. Thanks for taking the time during lunch."

"Later, man."

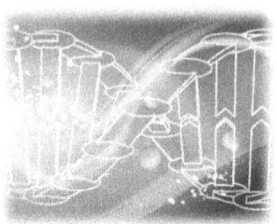

CHAPTER 39

YOU CAN RARELY TRUST ANYONE, EVEN FOR A MOMENT

Won and Ton both bowed deeply after they were ushered into Chairman Chang's lavish office by his newest office assistant. She smiled prettily as she exited and closed the door.

"Gentlemen, how delightful to see you. We have been so busy our paths have not recently crossed," Chairman warmly welcomed his nearly sons.

"Sir, it has been some time, and, might I add, you are looking quite fit. We both hope you are pleased with our recent activities?"

"Yes, of course. You always work to make certain that my wishes and desires are realized, unlike others I have on projects. If I could clone the pair of you into four," Chairman chuckled, "I would be very lucky indeed."

Both men bowed again, with the tops of Won's ears turning a bit pinkish. They moved, as if one, to the chairs adjacent to Chang's desk and simultaneously sat with lowered eyes as they awaited instructions. Both men had served Chairman Chang for a very long time and were loyal. He treated them like the sons he would never have. They were intelligent, took direction well, and did their utmost to always protect their benefactor. For them, greed and power were foreign concepts.

Chairman watched them intently for a few minutes, then asked, "How did you find working directly with the impetuous leader of the Dteam? She wishes to have a deeper commitment in this endeavor as my Callisto, yet I haven't decided if I can completely trust her."

Both men looked at each other for a few seconds, and Ton, as usual, replied, "She is a very capable female, sir. Won and I also thought she was quite pretty, though almost feral like Nikkei. She will do your bidding, provided she can make money. As long as she can make money, she can be controlled to a degree."

Won nodded with a solemn look.

After Ton's extended silence, Chairman asked, "At what point, do you both feel, can she not be controlled?"

Won and Ton looked at each other until Won nodded as if he recommended full disclosure. Ton explained, "Sir, we followed Miss Zara for many weeks before you employed her to work on your projects. With only a few minor exceptions, she has followed your instructions to the letter. We originally discovered that she had been independent for a long time. From our observations, she has an odd relationship with her employees, especially the one she calls Dante. Hence the ongoing conversation intercepts which we analyzed for your briefing.

"We think she is uncomfortable not knowing who you are. As you know, for centuries it has baffled men as to why females are so much more curious than males. In this area she is curious about how to hurt and how to control males. Not knowing you makes her somewhat more curious to find out about you."

Chairman Chang frowned slightly then stroked his chin with his fingers as if processing the information. He then asked, "Do you gentlemen feel that she could be trusted knowing my identity? Would there be any value in our meeting one another, for example?"

Both men again exchanged their thoughts with each other in silence. Ton answered, "As you mentioned early on before engaging with her, she has no misconceptions about any long term goodness in her world. As such, she expects all information to be of value to someone, regardless of the risk to her. She works hard, as she has shown even in the most recent event. But if it had failed, the end result, outside of captivity, wouldn't bother her for long. We think she would not be loyal to you. She would be loyal only to the money and the power."

"I would also have to agree with your assessment. We can work with her at arms' length for some time. This brings me to the other reason for our meeting.

"Zara has added a new member to her staff. I would like to know something about this man. From your report she seems to be almost fond of him, which is totally out of character for her. The report you provided did not go deeply into his background or describe the reason for her to hire him."

Ton looked ashamed as he admitted, "I am sorry, sir, to have not provided enough information. The time we had was too short to do more from only our conversation intercepts. We will submit to the punishment of your choice without argument."

With that they both stood and moved away from the chairs to lower themselves onto the floor in a bowed position. Neither of them moved a muscle or even looked to be breathing.

Chairman shook his head and then smiled as he soothed, "Gentlemen, rise and be seated. That comment was not a criticism of your report but agreement that the time was limited." He waited for them to return to their chairs and continued, "Your report outlined the information so that I had time to reflect on the next steps. As I said at the beginning of this discussion, I am very pleased with the results you have both delivered over recent months.

"I want some details on this new addition. This Dakota seems to be more than he appears, and I don't like surprises. Find out his background. Let's start some round-the-clock observation of him, where he goes, and who he associates with outside of Zara and her team."

Ton looked slightly relieved as he suggested, "Do you want us to confront him directly in any way, sir? Perhaps do some heavy handed persuasion to see if he breaks easily?"

Won nodded and for a brief moment seemed agreeable to that prospect.

Chairman shook his head as he clarified, "I think for right now, gentlemen, we are better served with digging into his background and then watching his actions. You both taught me a long time ago that your ability to demonstrate patience is without equal. If more is required, I know I can ask either of you to help with that aspect."

"Yes, sir. We will leave immediately and report back to you in the usual ways."

They stood and bowed as they prepared to exit. Chang sat back with a satisfied smile and a wistful thought of how nice it would be if others in his employment would be so accommodating.

Almost as an afterthought, Chairman offered, "There is a Western tradition that somehow seems oddly appropriate right now. When young people come of age, the wise parent gives them leave to use the family transportation to attend an important function with no chaperone in tow. Why don't you two take our newest aircraft in this tracking exercise? I know you were both quite pleased when you passed your small jet certification check ride, so you should consider this my congratulations gift for your professional achievement as accomplished pilots. Oh, and here is the credit card to use for fuel purchases. And as the proud parent would tell the young males upon borrowing the family car for the first time, don't forget to observe the flight regulations and be mindful of the curfews!" With that, Chairman smiled and then tossed them the keys and access codes.

Won and Ton both beamed at their graduation gift and quickly left to get on board.

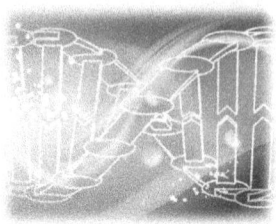

CHAPTER 40

DON'T TAKE WHAT YOU DON'T WANT

Prudence exclaimed, "I really don't understand any of this! Why the hell am I here, and now that I think of it, where is here anyway? Don't you think Chairman is going to ream you when he finds out you have abducted his precious Prudence? You're going to soil yourself again when he turns Nikkei out after dousing you with meat tenderizers and steak sauce! Just wait until I tell Chairman what you've done!"

Major Guano's smile was heavily laced with gratifying revenge as he answered, "Who do you think orchestrated this event?"

The fiery indignation quickly became fear as she asked, "Chairman is angry with me? How can that be? I've given him my agency keys to launch another attack. How can he be upset with me? You liar!"

Guano, now thoroughly enjoying his torment of the former director, gave a chilling smile as he explained, "Am I lying? Do you remember the last glass of wine he gave you so we could all toast to the next milestone of the BAI HU project? Don't you think it odd I know where we are, but you don't?

"After the drug took effect, we loaded you up in a truck for transport, which took four of us by the way, and drove you here. Before leaving, Chairman gave me back my director position. My first assignment was to take you here until he was sure there was no more need of you."

Prudence gasped and then in frightened tones asked, "How could he be displeased with me? I gave him the entrance codes for the last assault! Surely that must count for something in this part of the world?"

Major Guano sneered. "Didn't occur to you that once used it was no longer valuable? More importantly, once used in an attack on NATO, there would be people hunting the source? You're an American. Don't Americans hold a grudge and spend until they get what they want? Your user ID/password/token combination was an unmistakable beacon back to you. As such, you became a liability as soon as the operation was over! We got the needed value from you and now you are disposable goods! All that remains is the one thing I want from you in order to satisfy my maleness!"

Arletta's eyes widened, and as she backed up, she started to hyperventilate. She began to fasten up the buttons on her blouse as the leering Major moved slowly forward towards her while he started to unbutton his army tunic. Finally, with terror in her eye and her back to the wall, she grasped at her clothes to hold them from being ripped from her body. She finally locked eyes with the Major.

For a brief moment he paused as he finished undoing the last button and removed the army tunic. He threw it to her and said, "Iron this for me, bitch! I have to look good for tomorrow's meeting with Chairman. You will find everything over there."

Relieved, but oddly disappointed, Prudence scampered to meet the request and asked, "Starch too?"

To which the Major replied, "Light on the starch, servant person. And let's be clear about your role here. The guards outside have brought their laundry as well. You will service us all! Clean, iron well, and live, servant woman!"

Chairman, wanting to hear some of the gory details on Prudence's incarceration, asked Major Guano, "I trust that the new guest at our facilities was properly indoctrinated for her new role?"

"As we discussed, she began her retraining exercises and will be held until you have no further use of her."

Chairman greedily pressed for more information, "And how was the first session? Would you describe it as thoroughly satisfying, as almost a deeply religious experience for her?"

Guano now understood Chairman's need for more sordid details. He displayed a chilling smile as he explained, "She now knows that her humble station in life is to serve a man's wishes. We began breaking her offensive attitude by having her clean the dungeons as lowly washer woman and forced her to do everyone's laundry! We may even get her large size rump to slim down under the work load she is forced to do! Grinding down her pride and arrogance was most satisfying! You should have heard her wailing about sewing back on lost buttons! Supremely gratifying!"

Chairman stared momentarily, not completely understanding the Major's concept of torturing a Western female, then finally questioned, "Your idea of gratifying male revenge is to have her clean my dungeon?" He then added with a thin veil of sarcasm, "I must confess that I'm astonished at the depth of your sadistic level of cruelty, Major."

Guano, somewhat irritated, justified, "Chairman, that woman is used to having it all her way. To completely break her, she needed to do and be all the things she feels are beneath her dignity! That humbling, that crushing of her spirit, that is the gratification I sought! Once she is broken completely, then she can be disposed of like yesterday's slop bucket contents."

In his usual deadpan delivery, Chairman suggested, "So long as we don't get into putting throw pillows and flowers in to brighten up the dungeon, I guess I can live with it for now, Major.

"As a recap, she shows up complaining about being under-appreciated in her current role as a manager of a deep freeze compound that no one remembered was part of the U.S. government. She received a one way ticket to the farthest

U.S. listening post, but nobody cared what was being heard, so in effect no one was listening. Then they abandoned it but forgot to tell everyone there.

"This female supposedly wandered around for a while before approaching one of my agents offering to be of service. Presumably based on some intelligence she garnered while at the listening post. She was then brought into a top secret project as a director claiming to be able to deliver results ahead of schedule, but has the bad manners of having a concealed USB where she shouldn't.

"Did you get a chance to question her thoroughly about our suspicions, or were you too busy redecorating the dungeon to find out the information I wanted?"

The Major bristled at the comment but calmly replied, "After thirty-six straight hours of washerwoman and floor scrubber, she was quite agreeable to tell us everything we wanted to know.

"Your Prudence claimed she was not on an undercover assignment to infiltrate this project. She swears no one knows her whereabouts. In fact, no one apparently knows she is even gone, including her government. She completely broke down after several hours of interrogation, so I had her put on the drip just as we do with all our guests. I can continue the interrogation in a day or two if you like. I'll have more laundry by then."

Chairman, now more agitated with the discussion, demanded, "I sure hope my interrogation needs don't get in the way of you playing house! Run her hard at least one more time, and this time I want to know about her email login. You know, the one you haven't found yet! You didn't find anything in the one email account. Foolishly you assume that she only had the one email account, so find the others, because I don't believe we are getting all the truth.

"We don't have a lot of time before her government agency starts looking into the NATO breach and finds her user ID/password. I do not need that government to pick up a trail leading to us. Therefore, I want all loose ends accounted for. And, if I don't get what I expect, then there is someone else that will be doing laundry there! Got it?"

The Major nodded nervously, then quickly left.

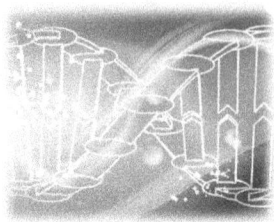

CHAPTER 41

EVEN USING THE KISS PRINCIPLE, WORTHWHILE ENDEAVORS ARE NEVER EASY

Quip, Wolfgang, Petra, and Jacob sat around the conference table in the operations center. It was the daily review session that neither Petra nor Jacob wanted to attend. They had worked practically around the clock for days to assemble this fragment and that fragment from their various sources. They had tried so many different iterations on the solution process that, had it not been for tracking them in ICABOD, they would be repeating attempts at resolution. Both of them looked exhausted. Quip and Wolfgang had found some additional details for both the Dteam and the money trail to Chairman Chang, respectively. The details were good for surround data, but that didn't make the problem of the destructive programs with disappearing code vanish.

Wolfgang offered, "Would it be helpful to begin a table by industry of the likely targets with short and long term benefits for these targets? This program has touched so many different areas we are aware of that it seems likely that the next step is precision targeting for either monetary or power gains. I have often likened Chang to a poor Hitler impersonator.

"I could work on a probability algorithm that might allow us to modify it based on time and recent events as well. With all the data that ICABOD has accumulated and the multiple methods that the data can be accessed, it makes sense that we start mining it for understanding possible future events. Big Data is nothing if it is not used, and statistical application seems relevant to our current issue."

Quip agreed, "I like it, Wolfgang. The more we can leverage the data the more we can predict possible pandemic outcomes if a solution isn't found soon. Plus, now with this captured military network invasion and the modest possibility of pinning down troops, we need to help allow for the balances to remain equal. Steps have been taken to secure the U.S. military network, but it has bigger long range ramifications, in my opinion."

Jacob flatly stated, "I think it is a wise course of action as well, Wolfgang. I feel I am letting the team down by not finding a sure method to counteract this program. Heck, I can't even determine who the programmer is.

"If Su Lin wasn't in her current diminished state of mind, I would suspect her or at least her Master Po persona. Since I know her now, as well as her true commitment to stop the use of technology for power and corruption, she is above reproach. I don't need any reminders that, because I failed to stop the grasshopper-loop, she has the mind of an adolescent instead of a brilliant renowned programmer. I have to suspect that the mastermind is using all her techniques and advanced programming language.

"We confirmed the computer power for the Chinese supercomputer, and it makes sense that one of Su Lin's protégées is making this happen, especially with Chang involved. I need to get this countermeasure developed and then tested."

Petra chimed in, "I agree. That is the key, I think, to the whole thing, a countermeasure attack. The idea of finding the program and destroying it is less likely than creating a universal solution that would fit, regardless of when and where this Ghost code is used.

"Jacob and I have bantered about the idea of doing a focused cancer type of code to attack the virus-like code structure of this Ghost Code. In that way, Jacob believes, we might be able to apply it to many systems and allow it to safely protect a given system if the Ghost Code is introduced. Jacob, you are much better at these details. Can you explain a bit further?"

"Thanks, Petra. I haven't really articulated it, even to you." Jacob rubbed his fingers through his hair and mentally assembled his words as he launched into his explanation. "The behavior that we have seen and researched from the systems

Petra and I have reviewed is behaving more like a virus than a clean executable program that a user could remove. It stores itself in various hidden folders and then evolves on different key factors. Hence it appears to evolve in the same way that a cell structure in creating a living being would evolve. I found evidence of the structure multiplying, bringing in different environmental factors that exist on a system, to determine how it should evolve and what it should become.

"This no different than how any organic life grows to maturity. They both begin with basic compounds and simply follow the instructions to complete a life form. Even a cursory inventory among the different genome structures that have been decoded show that, across all life forms, there is a ninety-eight percent commonality in cell functions and development, but the last two percent is what differentiates human beings from monkeys and so forth. What we seem to be looking at is a digital equivalent to organic growth but engineered by a computer to evolve in a computer.

"Benign code is introduced into a system with its DNA instructions and sets itself to grow into a desired evolved state, using material readily available from the host computer such as processing power and operating system code. It doesn't start off as a computer virus; it builds itself into a computer virus based on its DNA instructions. I find it curious that this digital code has its own expiration timer just like its organic counterparts.

"Since this doesn't conform to known virus signatures, we would have to look for a behavioral pattern to intercept it, which would be easier to do if we had some of the base code to match against. So with a behavioral pattern match we could launch a counter measure against this digital growth, much like an organic cancer only digital in nature. The Ghost Code does seem to fit the criteria of a living digital being, and, as such, a cancer-like counteraction, in theory, should be able to destroy it.

"I have been creating a cancer-like virus that can feed off only certain features that I have identified as present in this code. I am using the same array features that were used for finally tricking the *grasshopper-loop code* into thinking it was finished, but in a far more elaborate and destructive manner. The problem is I have no way of testing it against the source unless we can force a target to a specific machine to test the effects of my cancer program.

"Quip, I know you have repeatedly tried to access the Chinese supercomputer with no success to date. I think that it is perhaps used to test different strains of the Ghost Code, as it were, but may not house the actual programs or viruses. I think the source of those is someplace else, hidden and restricted for the programmer's use only. If I created something as spectacularly destructive as this, I wouldn't want anyone to know where the source was or I would become unnecessary.

"As the creator, I would have my own agenda for what I wanted the code to do. If I were the creator, and considering what has occurred so far, I would not be finished until I could control the entire cycle. I think that is what is helping us. If we are still finding fragments, we are somewhat safe from a massive release of it. The entire cycle goal, I believe, is to have it create itself, destroy its target and then vanish in total. The code creator would be unsatisfied with anything less, especially if they were trained by Master Po."

Everyone looked at Jacob with new appreciation, including Petra. This was the first time Jacob had articulated it from end-to-end. It made sense out of the random madness they had seen. It also reaffirmed the testing approach in an effort to resolve the entire cycle.

Quip said, "So if that is true, and to be honest, Jacob, it totally makes sense to me, then we need to discover not only the matrix of targets as Wolfgang suggested, but also how we can get a targeted test aimed where we need it to be aimed.

"I need to continue to look at entry into the supercomputer as well as renewed access into the Cyber-Warfare College network and discover any new devices for monitoring."

Petra added, "I think we might be able to leverage some of the intel that Carlos may find to help that process along. I will update Julie on the current focus and have her convey some of the needed data we are seeking to Carlos.

"Jacob, how soon can your construction of the cancer be ready to use? And do you still want it encrypted for distribution?"

Jacob replied with some renewed enthusiasm, "I think I could finish the programing aspects by tomorrow, and then we can work on the encryption provision. If it works, the next step would be the Nebelwerfer Mechanism for delivery."

Wolfgang suggested, "I think the other piece of business we need to keep in mind is to find the source and plant a cancer to destroy this code at its source, while convincing the creator, if we can identify him or her, that the program ate itself and is a useless endeavor. I think this will be the bigger challenge to this team. In other words, kill it at its source rather than trying to cure the havoc it will create."

Quip agreed, "I think the plans overall are good. Let's get to work and plan for an update status tomorrow afternoon. I want to make certain we have enough time to complete our tasks. For the first time since we began this project, it would seem we have an end in sight. Thanks all."

Petra returned to her office and phoned Julie. She updated Julie on the targeted items that Carlos might keep an eye out for, while inside the Dteam operations center. Julie was anxious that communications with Carlos were inconsistent, and she worried, if he located something, he might take action without any backup or making her aware of the problem.

"Julie, I am not certain what exactly I can do to help with that. It is not an area of my expertise. I will ask the team if they have some ideas for that and have Quip get back with you at some point soon."

"Thank you, Petra."

"Now onto to more important things. How are you feeling? Are you taking your vitamins and making the scheduled doctor appointments?"

Julie laughed then added with a chuckle, "Yes, of course. Are you and Mom ganging up on me? She asked me that yesterday too. I am a big girl, and I have a great doctor. Things are good."

"Oops! Sorry, sweetie. I haven't spoken to Mom in a while, but I should have figured she'd be all over it. I won't ask again. Just want to know you are feeling okay."

"I know, Pet. I am feeling good. My clothes are starting to get a little tight though, so changing out some items seems next on my agenda. Soon I will look like a walrus, I guess. It is all worth it though. No kicking yet but soon said the doctor if I am paying attention. I am so focused on Carlos and locating Juan, that I am doing the healthy part but sort of ignoring the rest. Do you think I am wrong to want Juan to share that with me?"

"No, I think you are right, Julie. I also think you need to experience it all so that when you find Juan you can tell him about the points he missed."

Tears welled into Julie's eyes, but she kept them at bay. She caught her breath and swallowed before she replied, "You're right. I will start a journal. Gotta go, love you."

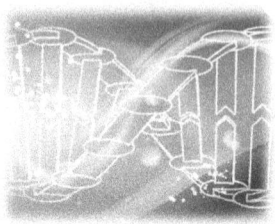

CHAPTER 42

DON'T SAY WHAT I DID AND I'LL DO WHAT YOU SAY

Quip said, "Yes, Julie, I understand. But we really don't have the kind of communications monitoring expertise that Carlos has, so I'm not really in a position to…

"Yes, of course I'm interested in helping find Juan, so it follows that I'm interested in helping Carlos…

"Now, sweetie, listen, without top notch communications tracking ability, all you'll do is bollix up things for…

"There is no need to use that kind of tone with me in this conversation. Geez, your hormones must really be out of whack due to your pregnancy for you to accuse me of not caring…

"Julie, I'm sure I would never ask to have a cubic meter of sand forced up my…

"Alright, alright." Quip sighed and rolled his eyes, exacerbated, as he placated, "I've got another idea if you'll just listen!

"Finally, that's better! Let me engage Andy and EZ to see what they can do about discreetly monitoring for Carlos…Uh yeah, right, Dakota, that's what I meant. Monitoring for Dakota alerts, and keep you in the loop. Got it.

"Sweetie, we are not going to abandon, uh, Dakota, but the last thing he needs is something sloppy that gums up his cover and puts him at risk…

"Oh, now that makes sense, once I promised to bring in Andy and EZ to help. Huh?

"Does your mother know you use those kind of words with the other children, young lady? I have a good mind to tell her about this conversation and…"

"Uh, Julie, I mean really now. Does anyone need to hear that sordid episode of mine? After all it has been quite some time, and the community services I did should have…"

"No, Julie. I really don't want to see it published on the Internet…"

"You know, sweetie, I'm feeling pretty good about this conversation, so let me let you go so I can start things rolling with Andy and EZ…"

"…And we don't need to bring that subject up again, yes? Thank you for your discretion on my indiscretion. So we are even then?"

After Quip hung up the phone, he said to no one in particular, "I don't know why she can't forget that incident or at least stop blackmailing me with it. Rotten girl! Actually they are all rotten! Sure do love all those rotten girls though," he added with a wistful smile.

Andy answered the call, "Hello there, young feller! It's been a while since we talked. I was beginning to think you were upset with me."

Quip replied, "Andy, this is a business call, and I am hoping to get both you and Eilla-Zan working on an activity as quickly as possible. Is she handy and could she join this call?"

Andy said, "She is around here somewhere. Do I need to fetch her, or can I just brief her when she gets back? I think she is working with our friend Su Lin, but if it is really important…."

Quip flashed back to the scene where they had all watched Su Lin crumble and almost die a few months earlier and said, "No, no, that's fine. Let her work with Su Lin and brief her after the fact. Andy, we have a situation where we need to listen for and get communications to, if need be, a person now operating under the pseudonym Dakota. We need to do that in such a way that no one else knows they are being monitored."

Andy's brow wrinkled as he asked, "I don't believe I know anyone named Dakota."

Quip responded, "Dakota is the undercover identity being used by your out-on-leave-staff, Carlos."

Andy nodded and said, "So that's why I haven't been able to reach him. He's doing some *cloak and dagger stuff* for y'all."

Quip now wondered if this was such a good idea after all, clucked his tongue and clarified, "There's more to it than that, Andy. Just for the record, this was his idea not ours. His brother, Juan, vanished without a trace. Carlos swore to find the perpetrators just before Juan went off the air.

"Now you know Carlos well enough to know this is an extreme point of honor, and there was no holding him back. I am not really surprised he didn't tell you. Now here's the issue. He has been working on a lead so we have to wait until he reaches out to us, but if something goes wrong we won't know until it's too late.

"My team doesn't have the communications expertise to find or track him while he is in this stealth mode. With what you and EZ have learned from Carlos, I'm hoping you can help locate him and create an *Information Halo* around him so that anything approaching or anything intersecting Dakota can be relayed to us for further analysis. I am classifying this as sub-contract activity and as such the usual fees to your team apply, and I would like to have you start immediately. Will that be alright?"

Andy, now a little indignant, harrumphed and responded, "Now, y'all just wait a minute, young feller! There's good folk hunting missing family and you expect I'm holding out for a contracting fee? You keep up that kind of jaw-boning and I'll box your ears! Now why didn't you just say that Carlos and Juan are in trouble in the first place! This isn't the time for paycheck discussions. This is the time for finding and helping family, young man!

"So you just tell me all I need, then step aside while me and EZ start combing the planet! Does that sound like we are committed to help, or do I need to put it straighter for you?"

An emotional wave welled up in Quip, who then smiled and conveyed, "Andy, I don't know how I ever thought that this would be a hard sell to you. I am glad for your help in this. We have so many intersect points beginning to converge, and most of them seem to point to where Dakota is now hunting.

"Our fear is that he will get in too deep, and we won't be able to retrieve him. We need to know what is going on and how we can help without *mucking it up*, as the Brits would say."

Andy said with a twinkle in his eye, "I understand completely, young feller! EZ just got back so let me brief her, and we will get to work. You know Carlos left all his communications hacking tools here and gave us a pretty good tutorial on how to use them before he took off. Looks like a good time for the student to go to work with the instructor's toolkit."

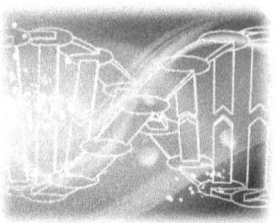

CHAPTER 43

TO SEE ALL THE ACTION UP CLOSE, ALWAYS TAKE THE FRONT ROW SEATS...
THE ENIGMA CHRONICLES

Julie answered the call as soon as she saw the caller ID. "Dakota, I'm glad you called back. I spoke to a mutual acquaintance of ours, and he has agreed to monitor any real time communications that you might make and setup an Information Halo around you. This might provide us heads-up on any incoming attack vectors. And, before you start complaining about being deep and cloaked, they will not be noticeable to those around you. So that is my news. What have you learned?"

Dakota accepted the help gracefully and replied, "Thanks, Julie. Just don't let them gum up my game, and we should be good. Right now we are highly mobile due to a relocation decision made by Moya Dushechka, so we are in an unpredictable mode right now. The good news is it gives me confusion to work under cover, but the bad news is I cannot depend upon their routines to help predict snooping time.

"I found one piece of evidence that may have linked these people to Juan's disappearance, but I need more time and better qualifiers. I can tell you I'm hunting in the right part of the forest."

Julie, now excited that Dakota had some piece of evidence, asked, "So do you know where he is and what happened to him? Tell me what you found, please!"

Dakota swallowed hard and chided himself for having even mentioned the small piece of evidence as he clarified, "Julie, it is too soon to over amp on a single piece of information when it could also mean nothing. I need more recon on this bunch, and right now the chaos is giving me cover. It is also a time where I can make a mistake. Please reel in the emotions, and let me work it so I don't blow my cover, okay?"

Before Julie could respond, Dakota quickly finished, "I need to go now! Bye, kiddo!"

Julie felt elated and let down at the same time by Dakota's comments but refused to give up believing Juan would be found and returned home.

Moya Dushechka sized up Dakota and questioned, "Bronze one, who were you speaking with so intently?"

A rather sullen Dakota responded, "She simply won't go out with me and will not take me seriously! She believes I'm too scruffy of a male for her to consider me suitable material for a long term relationship.

"Sorry, Moya Dushechka, I'm sure you don't care about my romantic wins and losses, mostly losses since coming to this wretched city. But enough of that. Do we have new tasks or marching orders that this emotionally bruised male can work on for you?"

Dante had come into the room as well and smirked as he suggested, "So in a city of eight million people with fifty percent of them female, you cannot get a date? Har! Har! Perhaps one of those Internet dating services would be able to, how do the Americans say, *hook you up* with your dream female? Uh, for a fee of course.

"However, before you put your credit card number in, ask me if it is one of the sites we have compromised first! There is something very gratifying about lifting a credit card number from a lonely heart to add fraudulent charges to on top of their emotional state. I just love finding someone down and kicking them to boot. Ha! Get it, to boot? I am making humor too now!"

In keeping with his typical deadpan delivery, Dakota said, "Gee thanks, AnDante. That really cheered me up. Oh, and this is me laughing uproariously at your grade school humor attempt."

Moya Dushechka chuckled at the antics of the two and, while smoothing out Dakota's hair, said, "It is just as well, my bronze beauty. I'm not one to let my stallions out of the stable to look for unchaperoned romantic interludes with my potential rivals for your affection. So perhaps we should…"

Moya Dushechka became quickly distracted by an incoming text message which completely stopped her toying gestures with Dakota. After she read the text she announced, "I have an urgent call I must take, so I will leave you gentlemen to continue with operations. I will return shortly."

She promptly departed, leaving the males behind with Dante clearly annoyed that Moya Dushechka had yet again shown Dakota the almost genuine affection that he desperately craved.

Dakota did not want to let her get out of his sight and moved to follow her under the pretext of calling a girlfriend wanna-be back.

Dante placed his heavy hand on Dakota's shoulder and insisted, "Did you not hear her, Dakota? We are to remain here so she can have a private conversation, you toad! Besides that, I need to see work from you for a change. All this time you are here, all I see is flirting with Moya Dushechka but no useful keystrokes to add monies to the coffers. So, now you work!"

In one swift move Dakota drove back his elbow straight into Dante's chest. Although he missed the solar plexus, it was still enough to cause Dante to double over. Dakota turned, in a hurry to tail Moya Dushechka, tried to get out of the door, but Dante was all over him roaring even though he couldn't fully breathe.

Carlos was not as accomplished in martial arts as Juan, but he was an excellent street fighter which, when coupled with his adrenalin leak, almost made him unstoppable. Dante's blind attack flamed Dakota's anger which pumped adrenalin into his system and launched him into overdrive. The frustration of losing his tail of Moya Dushechka, Juan's information on the Dteam's computers, and the savage attack of Dante, meant that Carlos had been pushed into lethal mode. Even though Dante was a big man as well, he really had little chance of survival, let alone winning the contest. Dakota landed sledgehammer-like fist blows down Dante's face and across his rib cage, either breaking or at least cracking most of the ribs. Dante's troubling return punches got one hand crushed and the other forearm snapped, rendering Dante incapable of further resistance. The final punishing blow to the stomach began internal hemorrhaging whereupon Dante sank to the floor unconscious.

Carlos staggered back as he tried to calm himself to bring the anger and adrenalin leak under control. After a few minutes of concentrated focus, he was able to bring his breathing and heart rate under control, then began assessing the situation. Carlos was dismayed by what he saw around him and the lifeless hulk of Dante on the floor. He then inspected himself to see if he had sustained any damage, only to find several fingers inoperative and bleeding from the pounding he delivered to Dante.

He was furious with himself at having lost the opportunity to tail Moya Dushechka and having destroyed Dante. He also was now aware of a painful limp in his right leg and his own troubled breathing which suggested that he too might have some cracked ribs. Carlos then discovered that at some point during the fight Dante had sliced him somewhat across his upper chest but not very deeply.

As much as he wanted to follow Moya Dushechka, he knew that he needed to fix this situation. He had to do something with Dante and create a believable story for Zara so he could continue to probe for information. Of course all of these immediate needs seemed colossal, given the time constraints and his own growing pain. An increased sense of fear and defeat almost overtook Carlos until he pulled out his phone and punched in an outbound call.

A voice answered, "Well hi! I didn't expect to hear from you so soon. What's up?"

Carlos, as he reeled from pain, insisted, "You remember that offer of yours to help that you made to me? Well, help."

Julie, now alarmed, responded, "What?"

Carlos continued with a weakened voice, "And that first aid kit we discussed? You know the one with the cute funny animal bandages and the Dammit-All pain killer? Will you bring that too, please? Oh yes, and a bottle of cheap tequila would be nice as well."

Julie was half way out the door in full stride as she said, "On my way, Carlos! I am following the signal and should be there in eight minutes."

Carlos, now woozy from the pain, said, "So today's lecture is going to be on what to do with dead bodies on the spur of the moment, field dressing wounds and broken ribs, work area clean up, concocting a believable cover story, and of course anger management. The guest speaker that will probably be in attendance promises a pop quiz. However, no cause for alarm since it will be open book, and free form discussion is the venue."

Julie, now really concerned over Carlos's ramblings, pleaded, "Carlos, hold on! I'll be right there! We will work through this, but let me do the talking. Got it?"

Carlos could only nod and, resting against the wall, allowed himself to slide down to a sitting position, now having almost no energy left at all to respond. Julie called out his name again, but Carlos could only nod with no power left to speak.

Julie, now frightened by the silence, demanded, "I'm almost there, my brother! Hang on! I couldn't bear losing you too! Hang on….."

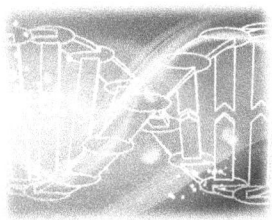

CHAPTER 44

LOCATING THE PRIZE IS LESS FUN THAN ASSEMBLING THE CLUES

Jacob absentmindedly munched on his sandwich while working through some additional elements on the Prudence Pursuit Puzzle. One more piece was required to complete the picture. The woman had traveled through so many different countries very randomly. She had used her identification at the various check points. Outside of her initial withdrawal from her bank account, she had not used any credit cards during her travel, so it was very challenging to determine where she stayed, or ate, or even the travel modes used.

There had been some conflicts as well with time and dates of various border crossings through some of the smaller European countries. Between searching the various customs databases, some video footage from a few major cities over the entire data range, and persistence by the team, the rough travels of the woman were mapped. If it weren't for ICABOD's facial recognition programs, it would have taken far longer to complete the process even though Prudence's distinctive, though decidedly unattractive, physical characteristics made the search easier.

Jacob had swallowed his last bite of sandwich as he watched the screen display a wavy gravy distortion as a dirge melody sifted through the speakers. The entire image congealed into the female being tracked then disappeared into the map of her adventure. Along the bottom was a ticker tape that flickered congratulations on completing the quest which made Jacob stand and add in a faux happy dance with a huge shout. Concerned with the shouting, Quip and Petra both rushed into the area and then smiled.

Jacob announced, "Okay, now we have a lead on the elusive Prudence. She appears to have entered China at the Shanghai Pudong International Airport, which was confirmed by the customs information. A video capture shows her in the airport with two men with nondescript features meeting her and escorting her to an area for smaller private planes where the images ended as the trio exited toward the private plane boarding areas. That was many weeks ago and there is no other record of her leaving. I think she is still there, and based on some prior history I think we can agree who she is aligned with."

Petra asked, "Can you show me the film with the three of them, please?"

As Jacob pulled up the clip, all eyes watched the busy scene at the airport as Prudence exited the customs area. The two men were obviously Asian, but no other clarification of the features could be found during the length of the video.

"The only thing I can suggest," Quip indicated after the third viewing, "is that the men appear to be fairly identical. Let me see if ICABOD can extend his comparison of features to entire body types with this video. We are lucky as the quality of this video is pretty good."

As they waited for the modification of the program to occur, Jacob started listing reasons for Prudence being in China and not leaving. She wasn't one to simply travel and see the sights, nor was she likely to be having a romantic interlude after being met by two men. The United States certainly was aware of the supercomputer in China, so she could have been sent to investigate it. But Eric would have likely known if that was the case. Jacob added and deleted items until beeping indicated ICABOD had some information available.

Petra was astonished as she read the screen then vocalized, "I would not have thought to do that comparison. Should we discount it as the match is only indicating seventy-three percent? This really puts a different light on some of the involvement."

Quip indicated, "If we look at the matched areas the program identified as well as the related incidents that ICABOD pulled up, I think our confidence level can increase."

"I have to agree," stated Jacob. "None of us believe in coincidences, but let's get Wolfgang on board as well. His viewpoint, I think, would be quite valuable."

They agreed and asked Wolfgang to come down to discuss. After they updated him on the program and the review of the path Prudence had taken, he pulled up some of the financial information that he had been tracking and started some of those correlations. After the lengthy discussion and other proof points from the older video films at U.S. airports, they all agreed they had confirmation as to where to look.

Quip and Jacob went to the small conference room to provide the update to Eric. Quip set up the recording program and all the masking for tracking call origination and dialed. The call was immediately answered.

"Hello, Quip, I presume you have some news for me," began Eric.

"Yes sir. We have a good idea on where your missing lady is currently."

Eric laughed, "Arletta is a lot of things, but I would beg to differ that she is a lady. A viper perhaps, but I digress. What have you found?"

"We were able to track her across Europe and finally found her entry into China. We have some compelling evidence to suggest that she is currently with Chairman Chang, with whom your team is already familiar. She has been there for many weeks. We found that some funds were transferred to her private account in the Caymans which would suggest she is being paid for some services."

Eric was silent, then asked, "Should I ask how you are able to track some funds into areas that we have limited views on, or just take your word for it?"

Quip said, "Eric, we have a fairly transparent relationship. I would simply take it as part of our extended service to you."

Eric chuckled then said, "Okay, though that is only on some limited levels. So she is working with Chang and getting paid. Damn-it, that means we need to retrieve her to protect ourselves. I hate wasting resources, but I think we will take it from here. Thanks, Quip, to you and your team for the efforts. Send me your bill."

"Eric, thank you. If you require anything else on her, please let me know."

After Eric disconnected, Jacob shook his head in disbelief then suggested, "Quip, if she is with Chang, then he could have access into some things he has no business poking into."

"I agree, which is why we needed to provide Eric with the information on the funds transfer. He is very astute. No portion of her access will be accepted anywhere on the planet as of right now, I suspect. Thanks for listening to the call. Let's go back to work. We have a ghost to catch."

Jacob laughed then said, "Yeah or at least kill the specter."

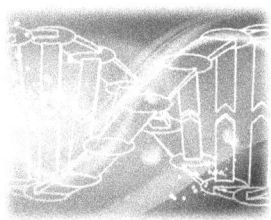

CHAPTER 45

TIME – OUT OF MIND

The radio crackled in the headsets of Won and Ton as the voice insisted, "International private jet, signature ID Whiskey Tango Foxtrot 7-8-9, you are on a collision vector with a DC-80 commercial airliner that is approaching from your seven o'clock position. Acknowledge! Over!"

Won and Ton looked anxiously at each other and Ton replied, "Air traffic Control, we are wearing digital watches! Please give another clue! Over!"

The air traffic controller, now thinking he was dealing with a couple of smart-asses, then replied, "Whiskey Tango Foxtrot 7-8-9, please execute a 370 degree maneuver to avoid an unnecessary *air-discussion* with the DC-80 bearing down on you. Over!"

Now Won and Ton were really becoming alarmed and quickly forgot pieces of their training.

Ton was unable to disguise the fear in his voice and said, "Traffic Control, we can't find a 370 degree setting in our instruments. Have you got another suggestion? Over!"

It took a second for the air traffic controller to come back, and barely able to cover the disgust in his voice, he said, "Whiskey Tango Foxtrot 7-8-9, please signal the other aircraft in the area that you are executing a fast climbing right turn by sticking your arm out of the cockpit window to indicate that you are moving out of the way! Please continue a ten degree right turn and climb two thousand feet, practicing good noise abatement procedures! Over!"

Again Won and Ton both looked at each other in wonderment and confusion.

Ton responded, "Uh, tower flight control, we are at eighteen thousand feet already, so why would noise abatement procedures be of any value? Over!"

The tower flight controller smirked and said, "Whiskey Tango Foxtrot 7-8-9, the noise abatement procedures would be for your benefit since the DC-80 aircraft would avoid slamming into your aimless flight wanderings, thus saving your ears from the loud noise of a mid-air crash. Additionally, may I recommend that you refile your flight plan and land at a regional airport that doesn't have as much commercial traffic as this International airport? Over!"

A very sullen Won and Ton precisely executed the tower instructions and went on to land at a smaller airport without further incident.

EZ exclaimed, "Wow, this is kind of cool! This program of Carlos's not only tracks but allows you to listen in on radio communications! Ha! You should hear what is going on between an aircraft and the New York control tower! Talk about a couple of newbie pilots with a classic rectal/cranial inversion affliction! I could launch and host my own radio talk show with regular material like this!"

Andy frowned as he asked, "Eilla-Zan, how many times do I need to remind you to curb your vulgarities, young lady?"

EZ sheepishly smiled, then dissolved into a puzzled look as she stared into the three dimensional image being delivered by Quip's smart program to her big flat screen.

Fully engaged in the ground and satellite telemetry being served up to her display, EZ said, "Andy, this seems rather odd. Quip's smart program is taking our real time information feeds and combining them with its huge database store. There is a cross reference intersection pointing out that these two under-achiever pilots actually have another aircraft identity beacon broadcasting on a different phase sequence.

"So what I'm seeing here is that this aircraft of foreign origin has not just one but two signature ID beacons and........"

Andy moved over to get a closer look and saw what EZ had discovered, then finished her sentence, "And it's Juan's plane beacon ID L O H R 5-6-7-8, as well as the primary call sign Whiskey Tango Foxtrot 7-8-9. So what is this program saying about that piece of information?"

EZ replied, "Quip's program is suggesting that this aircraft has been refurbished with a new signature beacon ID, but the owners failed to find and reprogram the secondary fail-safe transponder in the aircraft. The preliminary conclusion is that Juan's aircraft is still fully operational and presently on the ground in the eastern United States!"

Andy nodded and agreed, "Then it follows we should work backwards on the plane's acquisition and find out who the two almost pilots, Bubba and Cooter with the rectal/cranial inversion, are to see where that piece of information leads!"

EZ grinned mischievously as she raised an eyebrow and questioned, "Oh, Poppa, have you always been so vulgar around the ladies?"

Andy grinned as well and said with a wink, "We need to alert the Quipster of this potential lead. Uh, do you want me to do that, or you want that task?"

Smiling, EZ scampered off to make the call to Quip and visit with him in private.

Quip answered his cell phone, "Hi babe, how is it going? Is this a business call or personal?"

EZ responded, "Both! So which do you want to do first? If we do work first then the personal stuff, will we even remember the business discussion? But if we start with the personal, will we ever get to the business topic?"

Quip grinned then said, "Oh, ye of little faith! Let's do the business first then discuss personal. So let's begin. Remember you only have sixty seconds, then we move on, got it?"

EZ provided what they had learned so far and then suggested, "Okay, I gave you the briefing with fifteen seconds to spare. Good stuff, yes? Now let's talk about us!"

Quip smiled but deflected, "I'd love to, babe, but let me alert our people on the ground and call you right back, okay?"

EZ pouted and replied with disappointment evident in her voice, "Alright. But when you call back, I had better get some juicy naughty talk from you! Okay?"

Quip reassured, "Yes, of course. When I call you back, remind me to tell you about my dream about us and elevator sex!"

EZ furrowed her brow in puzzlement but responded, "You dreamed about being elevated in an elevator by EZ? Oh, I do want to hear about that!"

A dejected Quip replied, "You were right. We should have done the personal first."

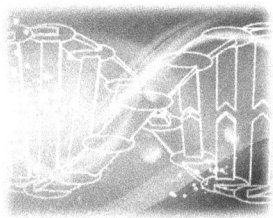

CHAPTER 46

PUT ME IN COACH!

Eric thought about all the reasons he really didn't want Arletta found. However, the issues which resulted by her being loose, wreaking havoc with her self-centered agenda, more than outweighed these. He just didn't like her, but she needed to be dealt with and soon. He picked up his phone and toyed with the handset for a minute before he placed the call.

"Do you have any further updates for me, Stalker, on Arletta's identification being used? Also, I have disabled every other access she has ever had."

"Eric, I can't find any other trace of her identification being used and really nothing before this incident. The guys on my team are still trying to piece together how this could have occurred, but not with any real progress.

"It is much more like a once-and-done action. It oddly reminds me of a drive-by shooting. All of the personnel on the base are checking out completely clean. None of the staff are involved. It must be the visitors or contractors. They have tightened security, and if any of the visitors in the days before the incident return, they will be apprehended for questioning. That's about all I can do for now. I know you wanted more."

"Stalker, if there is nothing more to be done on the base incident, then I am going to ask that you renew your efforts to find our missing Arletta, the Destructive."

Stalker chuckled but asked, "Hmm, what has the female done that I hadn't uncovered with my investigation?"

Eric sighed then replied, "I had the team we contracted with try to find a lead. The resourcefulness of this team does amaze me at times. One of these days I'll introduce you. Anyway, I now have a trail that Arletta appears to have taken that I need you to validate. I think she really went off the deep end this time."

"So this is not a simple copy machine prank?"

Now Eric laughed. "Not even close, but that subject really needs to go away, buddy. No, this is really now a breach to national security. We need her brought back in chains for trial. I need to figure out how to break it to her parents."

Stalker paused then solemnly questioned, "Would it be better to simply have her caught in some strange crossfire incident, rather than force her family to live with what sounds like insurmountable shame? Not that she doesn't probably deserve the shame of a trial like that."

"As tempting as that sounds, she needs to face the results of her actions. I am sorry for her folks, but …."

"Alright, Eric. Where is she supposed to be, and I will send a team in for retrieval."

"Well, that's just it, Stalker. This is a one man operation, and you're nominated."

Stalker looked up toward the ceiling and shook his head as he asked, "Why me, other than punishing me for teasing you about the event? I promise, I won't ever mention it again. I have staff I can call upon all over Europe that we can use."

"I know you do. Europe is not likely where she is, though I know that is where you tracked her. She seems to have made it a bit further and acquired some new relationships in her travels."

Stalker closed his eyes and groaned, "Okay, where is the bitch?"

"She seems to be sleeping with an old enemy of yours, which is why I want you to retrieve her alone. That almost gentlemen in China, with the tiger, seems to be where she connected the dots. Her motives are still foggy, but there is the Chinese supercomputer and Chairman Chang's untouchable attitude."

Stalker shook his head and responded after a minute or two, "I would like to say I am surprised. However, the extent of her messing around in areas outside of her purview is a repeating theme. She has never demonstrated self-control.

"There are so many ways that the Chinese are trying to optimize their position as a world power. I can just see her selling her information to these guys. The intel being accumulated to understand the steps that they may take to fully control the dollar, along with their technology advancements, is something we need to remain vigilant on. To think that they would infiltrate our military bases electronically cannot be tolerated."

Eric agreed, "That is my whole point in wanting you to extract her from her location which is thought to be Chang's compound or the operations area within their Cyber-Warfare University. The first you have already been to, and the other I can provide good location information to you."

"You realize that it will take me several days to even get into position to locate her. Extracting her, if she is protected by Chang, will be even more challenging. I mean, it's not like checking out a library book with these people," suggested Stalker even while his mind started assembling the details of his plan.

"I do, and you will need to keep in contact. This is obviously an operation that we will need to handle with minimal State Department involvement, though I have agreement at the highest levels that she needs to be brought out. Preferably breathing."

Stalker chuckled again as he agreed, "Well, since you asked so nicely, of course that is the goal. I would prefer making it home breathing as well.

"I will get the logistics, any identity papers for the extraction, and the contingencies to you by end of day. Will that suffice, boss?"

"Yes. And, Stalker, I do want you to return intact."

"Me, too! I will call you later."

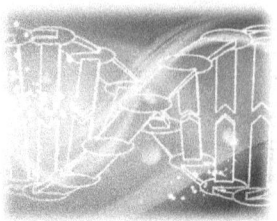

CHAPTER 47

WHOEVER SAID FOLLOW YOUR DREAMS, DIDN'T REALIZE DREAMS SOMETIMES TURN INTO NIGHTMARES...
THE ENIGMA CHRONICLES

Zara confidently dialed the number and announced, "Mephisto, your request seemed urgent with much importance attached to it. So here is your Callisto. How may the contractor serve you now?"

Mephisto chuckled then suggested, "Any other time we visit you always begin with, 'is this a partner or contractor servant conversation?' The one time I'm ready to discuss partner status you act like it's no longer top of mind. Curious, isn't it, my Callisto?"

Zara's heart skipped a beat when the topic was broached. She tried to keep calmness in her voice as she asked, "Mephisto, are we to have such a conversation, or are you just making idle chat before changing the subject?"

Mephisto replied, "I find that I have enough employees and contractors, but what I seem to be lacking are properly motivated equity partners. I grow tired of employees waiting to be told what to do and then performing my careful instructions so poorly that I am required to repair the situation. I need partners who will understand our needs and not stop until those needs are filled, with no blow-back on us. Thus yes, the first part of the conversation is, are you prepared to be a partner?"

Zara now beamed at the offer and struggled to sound calm as she evenly said, "I have stated my intentions previously, and they have not changed. I am prepared to be an equity partner with you."

"Excellent! Now for the next part of the discussion, and this is where most people turn to cheese. How much of an equity partnership are you willing to take on, and how much do you have to invest for an equity stake?"

Zara was crestfallen at the request for funding of her equity position. She had not realized that partners invested money in an operation to make money. She meekly responded, "Mephisto, I don't have…..I was expecting to be your partner by leveraging sweat equity."

Mephisto laughed uproariously then finally stated, "Ah, I see all now, my Callisto! You want all the upside but none of the downside. Oh, and let me guess, you want a salary as well to cover your living expenses! Tell me, do we need to discuss vacation, day care, and a health care plan as well? So let me turn this around so you can see how it sounds.

"Callisto, let me come to work for you, but let me share in your future profits with no investment capital. I promise to work hard if you will pay me wages so I can live comfortably in the interim period. Just like that Dakota you put on your payroll not long ago. Tell me, how generous were you with his equity position in your organization?"

Zara was stunned by the casual reference to Dakota and crushed by the comparison between the two of them. She was also bitterly disappointed in how Mephisto belittled her very naïve approach to being an equity partner. She couldn't even respond.

Mephisto chuckled again and asked, "Callisto, are you still there? So tell me, has what I said given you reason to doubt your request of me? If you would not do it for someone, then why would anyone do it for you?"

Zara was feeling so low that she had trouble as she responded, "Mephisto, you've…you've made your point. How can the lowly contractor be of service to the powerful lord and master?"

Mephisto reigned in his crushing sarcasm and kindly suggested, "Callisto, I haven't discounted your offer yet! I am actually interested in having a trusted partner, but we are still negotiating the price. Do not be so despondent! So here is the price tag to buy in at a ten percent equity position. I need five million Euros from you for an equity position in my operations. That will entitle you to ten percent of the hundred million I expect to net from this project. That means you would double your investment if we win but lose everything if we miss. This was the discussion I wanted to have before our next phase begins. You need to consider if you want in as an equity partner or continue as a contractor. I don't expect an answer right this minute, but don't take too long to respond. Shall we say in two days we can speak again, yes?"

Zara swallowed hard before she evenly said, "Mephisto, it occurs to me that since you know everything about me and my business, you must know I don't have that kind of money. That makes it a moot point then for me to buy into your operations. Why taunt me with the offer?"

"Your history, my dear Callisto, always shows you were more resourceful than you gave yourself credit for. I am willing to make that same bet. Give the offer some thought before you say no or give up, as I expect something will occur to you. Until the next discussion, my Callisto."

Zara felt beaten and angry at having been run around the block by Mephisto with no leverage on him. She resented that he knew everything about her, but she didn't even know his real name. She swore to herself that this fact would change, and she would be dictating terms to Mephisto and soon. The thought of turning five million into ten million was extremely appealing, and she felt mesmerized by the potential he'd suggested.

As she pondered all that had been discussed, only one thing came to the forefront. Where was she going to get five million Euros for the buy-in?

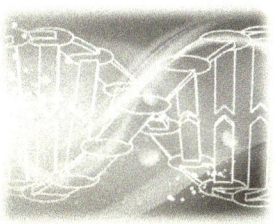

CHAPTER 48

SHOTGUN SOLUTIONS ARE RISKY YET SOMETIMES EFFECTIVE

Julie arrived at her destination. She parked her car down the block and followed the evening shadows of the quiet street to the doorway. She wasn't sure what she'd find but was certain it would be ugly. She prayed that Carlos, or Dakota as she reminded herself, would still be alive. He had sounded so awful before he'd presumably passed out. She opened the door and walked down the hallway, grateful that no one challenged her. Every fiber of her being was in ready mode to whatever occurred. Julie heard a slight moan from the open door to her right and entered.

The place was a mess. A man was crumbled up against a wall. Julie knelt down and felt for a pulse. She grabbed the knife that lay near his hand and stuffed it into her coat pocket. His breathing was shallow, and he had a slight pulse, though he was totally unconscious. She stood and looked around until she located Dakota, who was leaned up against a desk. His eyes were almost open, his face was battered, there was blood on his chest, and his breathing was labored. As she moved to his side to assess his injuries, she decided to break an ammonia capsule under his nose to raise his level of awareness. His eyes opened.

Julie quietly asked even as she felt and prodded at him, "You crazy man. What happened? Is anything broken?"

Dakota whispered back, "JAC, everything is broken. I killed him. I so messed up. I have more things to search…"

His voice trailed off even as Julie observed him gaining in some level of awareness.

Julie whispered, "He's not dead. Out like a light, but alive. I would bet a severe concussion or borderline coma, but I'm not certain. Can you walk? I can help get you out of here."

Dakota opened his eyes as he mumbled, "Not leaving. I need to find Juan. I need to follow the leads.

"It hurts to breathe. I must have busted a rib or two. Need to lay down for a minute."

Julie helped him lie down and grabbed his jacket to put under his head. She took out the kid motif Band-Aids and applied them after swabbing each cut on his face with peroxide wipes. None of the cuts were too deep so far. He opened his eyes a bit and winced when she pressed too hard.

"You are so lucky it isn't worse," she admonished. "How could you hope to accomplish your goals, fighting with him?"

Dakota clarified, "I needed to follow and listen to Zara's conversation. It seemed like a good lead, only Iron Man over there is just way too possessive."

Julie worked quickly and ignored the tears that started to trail down her cheeks, but quietly agreed, "I know what it is to be around possessive males. It is such a shame. I am so sorry…"

"Sorry about what?" a female voice intruded over Julie's shoulder. "What happened here to my workers? Who are you, and why are you saying sorry to him?"

Dakota closed his eyes as he felt Julie slightly react. He hoped that Julie was ready to take on Zara. He tried to garner all his strength in case he need to help Julie. In his current condition he would be of little value, so playing possum for the time being seemed the most prudent.

"Ahh!" Julie exclaimed, as she turned her head to face the voice. "You scared me to death. I thought they had come back. I am trying to dress some of these wounds, and then I will go back and look at the other man who is unconscious. What a mess this is. I am so sorry."

The female remained close and loudly repeated, "Who are you and why are you sorry?"

Julie replied with a fear laced voice, as she continued working Dakota's wounds, "My brother and his friend came. They did this!" She swept one arm around the area. "They attacked your, umm, workers on my behalf. Unjustly, I might add. Oh, my name is JAC. Who are you?"

Zara smiled a bit at the fumbling, fearful female as she personally assessed the situation. This JAC looked a bit on the plump side, with wide lips, and tangled hair and a boy's name. How ordinary. Zara felt no threat from this woman but still wondered why she was attending Dakota.

Zara stated, "My name is Zara, and these men work for me. How is the other one?"

Julie said, "I checked him first. His pulse is weak but steady. He appears to have a concussion and needs to go to the hospital. I am in nursing school, but not far enough into my studies to tell you much more.

"Dakota was groaning rather loudly. I came to help lessen his pain. I also am trying to determine if he needs hospitalization as well. I brought the first-aid kit I keep in my car and have been cleaning wounds and taping where I can. His laceration doesn't appear to need stitches. You could help by calling for an ambulance."

Zara went and felt Dante's pulse and lifted his eye lids. No movement whatsoever. Expert medical treatment would be good. She just didn't want strangers marching all over the place or that sort of question and answer session. She was grateful the other workers had not yet started at this new location. This was so inconvenient a time for this disruption in standard Dteam business, now that Zara had other problems to solve. Dante would be of no use, and Dakota seemed too new to trust. She needed to think about that as a real possibility if she wanted to achieve her other goal which Mephisto had just dangled.

Zara said, "No, I think we will wait to make that call. You tell me more about what happened, and why I leave with everyone working and making my deadlines for moving in, only to return to a mess that you seem to know something about."

Julie drew in a breath and collected her thoughts even while she kept administering first-aid, then explained, "The whole thing is so outrageous, you'll never believe me, but you deserve the truth, Miss Zara. I will give you the shortened version of a long tedious story.

"My brother, Andrew, has a need to totally control me, and he has driven me nuts my entire life. He tracks me everywhere I go. He makes certain that he can reach me within minutes. It is like having an extra shadow. Even though I am old enough to date who I want and even have sex, he simply doesn't want me to go anywhere, do anything, or make my own decisions. Every now and again I have escaped and had a date. Do you know what it is like to want to escape, Miss Zara?"

Zara nodded and acquiesced, "Yes. I escaped a life I didn't want, and I control my destiny. Please continue, JAC. How did it get to my doorstep?"

JAC shrugged her shoulders slowly as she continued, "From the first time I was allowed to go out and go to a party, he has shown up and behaved like a barbarian to anyone he thinks I'm with. After our parents died, he became worse. He wanted me to stay in the house, period, so I ran away.

"I moved to a different apartment several months ago, started nursing school, and thought I was under his radar. Then he located me and started with his stalking, his threats, and badgering. My apartment landlord was threatened just yesterday if he didn't describe the men that had visited me. He caved after some forceful persuasion."

Julie stopped her treatment and stopped talking as if totally undone, and tears streamed down her face. Then she looked up at Zara and exclaimed, "You're beautiful and you look confident. You'd never let someone take advantage of you. I'm just not strong like that."

Zara nodded her agreement because she knew only too well how bad the situation could have been. Then she softened to a degree and allowed, "I can understand having a stupid pig of a man try to control you, but why Dakota here. Is he your boyfriend?"

Julie swallowed, shook her head, and then continued, "No. Not at all. He just happened to be in a bar I was at a couple of nights ago and came to my rescue. Andrew decided to show up and pushed me. Dakota stood in and well, um, sort of defended me."

Zara raised her eyebrows a bit then asked, "Then is your brother stupid?"

Julie blushed a bit then added, "No and yes. He found out that I am well, ummm, pregnant and was looking for the man responsible to force him to marry me."

Zara masked her disappointment as she asked, "Is Dakota then the father of your child?"

Julie rolled her eyes for effect and said, "Heck no. We aren't an item. He did give me his number and said I could call if Andrew threatened me, and he'd speak to him. Which I thought was very nice."

"And who is the father then, if not Dakota? Certainly it is not my other worker, lying in a heap."

"I'm not sure I want to know you or want you to know my business. But since this is my fault, I will tell you. The father is a lovely man that I picked up in a bar so I could have a baby. I have no plans to marry him or even see him again. He doesn't know how happy he made me, making me pregnant."

Zara looked almost disgusted at the stupidity of the woman. Why would anyone make herself so vulnerable as to have a child on purpose with an unknown man? She had fortunately avoided that mistake.

Julie glanced down at the same time to catch a hint of a smile flicker across Dakota's mouth. She then stood up and faced Zara as she said, "The truth is my brother followed your Dakota. He is convinced that Dakota is the father. He came to my apartment to tell me off. Then he called his friend from the living room when he thought I was sleeping. I overheard him saying that he had a line on the guy who did me and wanted to meet here and stated a time.

"I called Dakota to tell him, but we didn't finish our conversation before he hung up. Since I hadn't finished warning him, I rushed over as Andrew and his friend EZ were getting down to business. I yelled and told them I was calling 9-1-1 as I backed out of the door. They rushed out and took off down the street. Then I came in to see if I could help."

Julie stopped speaking and nearly held her breath as she looked Zara in the eye. Zara seemed to replay the explanation and then smiled slightly. Zara moved toward Dakota who now seemed to have his eyes open.

Zara soothed, "My bronze one, are you back with me now?"

Dakota grimaced but replied, "I think I am, Moya Dushechka. I feel like I was steam rolled. What happened? Where is AnDante?"

Zara replied, "He is worse off than you are. Do you recall this woman's brother and his friend coming in here?"

Dakota cocked his head to one side as if gathering his thoughts and slowly replied, "I recall two guys, yes. Dante tried to prevent their entry. He helped alert me."

Julie reached to help Zara as they steadied Dakota into a chair.

He peered over at Julie, offered a slight wink, then said, "The girl from the bar. Oh wow, was that your brother?"

Julie nodded and then looked away as she headed back toward Dante. She checked his pulse, but he was unresponsive.

"Madam, your other guy here isn't going to wake up like Dakota. Can I call that ambulance or will you?"

Zara stated, "It seems pointless to involve the authorities. Do you perhaps have a car that you might use to take him to the hospital? You studying to be a nurse might get him help faster than I could."

Julie weighed the options and suggested, "I don't mind driving him there, but I cannot lift the dead weight of a man in my condition."

Dakota shifted as if he would try to stand to help, but Zara rested a hand on his shoulder, keeping him in place. "I think that I can help, and I have a two-wheeler used to move the equipment and furniture in here. Let us see what we can do."

"Miss Zara, I can go get my car and then I can help you wheel him. I just won't lift him. It would be too dangerous."

Dakota looked at Julie and pleaded wordlessly that she take care of his niece or nephew. He would get up if he had to, but Zara's idea with the two-wheeler could work.

Zara moved toward JAC, looked at Dante, and then said, "It would seem better to get him help sooner. You go get your car. The hospital is fairly close. I will write directions for you."

Julie gathered her things up and walked toward the door without so much as a glance back. She walked to her car and threw the items into the trunk. She sat thinking about the steps that needed to be taken, such as whether Dakota should leave with her. At least she knew that Andy and EZ were tracking signals.

After JAC walked out, Dakota insisted, "Don't worry, Moya Dushechka, I will be fine in a day or two. I will help you. Dante, I am sure, will be okay. I know how much he supports this business."

"I am sure you will. I am so glad you are alright, my bronze one. Dante is going to be out of commission for some time, I suspect. I will help this JAC get Dante loaded, and then we will talk. I have much to do."

She carefully loaded Dante onto the two-wheeler and leveraged it into position to roll. Slowly Zara navigated it toward the door just as JAC opened it. JAC helped guide the two-wheeler out to the curb, and together they wrestled him into the front seat. Zara kissed his cheek and patted his arm.

Zara turned to JAC and said, "Thank you for telling me your story, JAC. So few people tell the truth. Good luck to you.

"Take him to the hospital, and I will check on him tomorrow. I stuffed his identification into his coat, so the doctors will find it and you won't have to stay with him. Just leave him for the doctors to handle. I trust we will never meet again."

Julie added, "I will take care of this and keep Andrew away. Tell Dakota, I hope he recovers quickly."

Julie followed the instructions and pulled up to the hospital's emergency doors. She went in and asked for help and a wheel chair. A nurse came around and joined her with the wheel chair. Together they extracted Dante.

Julie said, "I found this man. I think he's been mugged. I don't want to be involved, but I couldn't just leave him on the street."

The nurse looked quizzically at Julie, then seemed to recognize some element of truth and replied, "I guess you are a good citizen. Obviously you're not from around here. We'll take care of him."

As Julie drove away, she started to shake as she dialed the familiar number. When he answered, she stated, "Hey, it's me. This is going to sound like one of your stories, but I need some support…"

CHAPTER 49

IF ONLY ALL THE PSYCHOTICS COULD BE COMMITTED

When Eilla-Zan answered, Quip said, "Alright, beautiful, where were we?" She laughed and asked, "My goodness, Quip, what time is it in your world? I'm snuggled in bed with nothing on!"

"Just the way I like you, babe. Well good, I can tell you a bedtime story and let you go back to sleep. I just woke up and wanted to hear your voice."

"I was sorry our other conversation was cut short. It sounded like it was important, though, with what we grabbed in the transmission. Did it work out for you? We continued to monitor stuff, including some additional activity with Carlos."

She yawned then continued, "He seems to have been injured in some way, and Julie was giving first-aid. She kept a line open during this bizarre conversation where she mentioned us like she wanted to insure we would stay tuned. Which of course we did. It was continuously uploading to your program when Andy sent me to get some rest a while ago. He felt it was escalating and wanted me to get a little rest and relieve him in a couple of hours."

Quip was frustrated as he asked, "Honey, are we talking about work first, again? How am I ever going to get time to tell you my dream about you if you keep giving me work updates? Argh, let me go to my laptop and see the updates you made."

EZ murmured, "While you are talking with me, I'll tell you some things. I've been thinking about the time we should spend together. I miss having you with me in the beginning, middle and end of the night. We are very good together, Quip. I would like to consider your offer of more permanence, sooner rather than later."

Quip groaned at both reading the results of the program and ICABOD's projections. "Honey, I think I am hearing some very good news from you, but I have to review this great information you and Andy provided. Umm, err. Can I call you back, babe?"

EZ regrettably replied, "Yes, honey. You go take care of what you need to. Next time, start your story about the elevator sex, and I'll keep my big mouth shut while I listen and fanaticize."

"Okay, babe. I did hear you and I love you, Eilla-Zan. I'll call you back soon."

Quip went downstairs to the operations center. He was actually glad he had stayed last night instead of going to Wolfgang's with the others. After he sent messages off to Petra and to Jacob, he woke up the computers. It was close to midnight in New York, and he thought about calling Julie, though until he reviewed the information it seemed imprudent to do so. Jacob had texted back that they were up and would arrive shortly with some breakfast. He was reviewing all the data when the phone rang.

"Okay, so tell me, Julie, what is going on? Is Carlos safe? Are you alright? How is the baby?"

"I think he is okay, but he wouldn't let me take him for medical attention. Do you know if Andy and EZ were able to monitor the conversation? It should have been alright as long as the cell phone battery held out."

"Yes, I have part of the transcript here and am reviewing it actually. Are you nuts trying to lift a man in your condition? If anything happens to you, your folks would kill me."

Julie laughed, "No, I am fine, and the baby is fine."

Julie masked some of her emotions as she related the events of the evening in great detail. She provided filler to the information Quip had read, which improved his view on the entire situation. As usual she had taken all the right steps, and he chuckled at her on-the-fly story which he almost believed, so he knew this Zara would have bought it for the time being. He sent an instant message to Andy and received a confirmation that Carlos' signal was still working though the conversation had ceased.

Julie continued, "Quip, my biggest concern at this point is this Dante fellow. I left him at the hospital, and I think he is close to coma, but it would really be problematic if he showed back up at work and told his view of the story. I need some help to make this not a possible problem. Any ideas?"

"I agree, sweetie. That is the one loose element for now. Let me see if I have earned any favors this week and see what I can do. I will text you the status after I make a call. You go back to your place, get some rest and wait for Dakota to contact you. He is one tough male, and I doubt a beating will keep him from finding out the information he is seeking."

"Okay, I am a bit tired. Would you tell Petra I'll call later on? I know she will worry too. Thanks, Quip."

Quip rubbed his hands over his eyes and thought about how he might approach this. Then he decided that straight ahead was the most efficient. He dialed the phone and hoped for an immediate answer. He was not disappointed.

"Hello."

"Hey, Eric, Quip here. Sorry to call so late, but I have a favor to ask."

"Quip, give me a second. I am surprised. What can I do for you and at this hour?"

"Yeah, well, I am sorry for the hour, but this is a bit odd. Do you still have some resources in the medical field in New York City?"

"Of course. Why do you ask?"

Quip explained to a minimal degree about this man that was in the Manhattan hospital. He explained that this man was part of a covert operations group backed by the Russian Mafia. He made it a quick and succinct description with no mention of Carlos or any other part of their operation. He knew if he pulled this off he would owe Eric big time.

"So, Quip, are you asking me to make certain this guy is put on ice for a while, really?"

"Eric, I don't want him hurt, just a captive. If you can do it medically then he can't lawyer up and get released on bail or be out roaming around doing something even, until we get a better line on the operation he is involved with. And I will share the results with you if it has any benefit to your government."

"If we get him locked up in the psych ward at the hospital for a month or so, would that take care of your problem?"

"That would do it, Eric. Can you do that?"

"Yes, I think I can help with this with your rapid response to my previous request. Does this get the bill reduced, since I hadn't seen it yet?"

"Oh, I think you can count on it, Eric. Thanks, man."

"Alright, Quip, consider it done!"

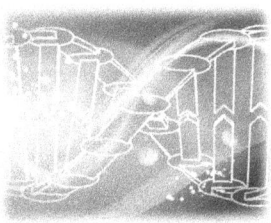

CHAPTER 50

MONEY IS NOTHING WITHOUT PEOPLE YOU CAN TRUST

Zara gazed intently at Dakota while he seemed to work his assignments. She noticed he moved stiffly and not all his fingers were operational when he used the keyboard. Zara felt somewhat envious of the plump JAC who had helped Dakota after her brother had assaulted him and Dante. She even felt a little shame at not having gone to see how Dante was or even called to check his status. But he knew where she was located if he needed her.

With all these feelings swirling around in her head, she didn't hear Dakota the first time. Dakota repeated, "You must be deep in troubled thought not to hear me even though you were staring right at me, Moya Dushechka. So let me ask again. Was the Zara name you used with JAC an alias or your real name? If it is your real name, I would prefer to call you that rather than Moya Dushechka, as that seems more fitting for Dante to call you by that name."

Zara was more than a little wistful when she replied, "My name is Zara, but I find it odd that I would prefer you call me by my Internet handle. Moya Dushechka is a term of affection where I come from, and my real name seems somehow too formal when you say it."

Dakota smiled slightly and said, "I can see Dante getting to use Moya Dushechka when speaking to you or about you, since he obviously has a crush on you. My feeling is that I have not yet earned the same right, so if you will permit me, I will call you by your real name Zara to keep our interaction all business."

Zara was a little let down that instead of Dakota becoming more familiar with her, he actually placed more emotional barriers. After she studied him for a few seconds more, she stated, "Does this mean you would never come to my rescue in a bar if I was being accosted by a belligerent male that was shoving me around? How does a female get to have the protection of someone like you, my bronze warrior?"

Dakota suppressed a smile, knowing Zara was miffed and believed that he had defended JAC's honor. He didn't want to alienate Zara, nor did he want to play the suitor for her female ego since that might lead to him being compromised at her whim. It occurred to him that females like her were how the legend of Medusa came to be. Part of him even laughed at the thought of preserving his chastity from this attractive but fearsome female.

Dakota chose his words carefully as he placated, "Zara, you are not a female who needs a male champion to defend you because you are not weak. You are an Amazon Warrior class female that would only have a male champion if you could have him fight alongside you against all assailants.

"I judged the lady JAC to be at risk and unable to defend herself against a bully. I stepped in with no ulterior motive than to defend a female in trouble. She was quite clear in her statement that her future was not going to include me, but thanked me just the same. I sometimes do things that even I don't quite understand. As you have seen, in the world of Dakota, no good deed goes unpunished."

Zara smirked but beamed at being likened to an Amazon Warrior in Dakota's musings. Zara affirmed, "Then can we agree for the time being that you call me Zara until I need that champion?"

Dakota smiled and agreed, "Until the time that you need a champion, Zara."

Zara smiled at Dakota like he was her first date as she continued, "So now that we understand each other a little better, I need to see your communication tracking skills function on a high profile job that no one can know about, and we dare not be caught doing.

"I have a call coming up with someone that I need more information on, and I want you to help me get it. If you are caught in this activity I will, how do the Westerners say, *throw you under the bus* with little hesitation and no remorse. All I have is his call sign name of Mephisto, and I am reasonably sure all of our conversations, thus far, have been encrypted. So the next time I excuse myself to make or take a mysterious phone call, you should assume it to be Mephisto, and I want you to trap the conversation and work backwards on the caller. After you found those hidden cameras, assume that I am being watched somehow, so keep your distance. Do not get caught and tell no one! Understood?"

Dakota grinned and said, "Understood, Zara!"

Zara sat and fumbled with her phone while she waited for Mephisto to call her. The two days' think time had been extended with a text message that simply said, make it four days. She had only half-heartedly looked for funding sources, but none of them were any use. To achieve the needed five million Euros for funding her equity buy-in position would have meant she would have to have ten million friends as well funded as the ones she had actually asked. She shrugged her shoulders and mentally dismissed the equity position as unobtainable when the expected call arrived.

Zara answered, "Good morning, Mephisto. I trust that deferring our call by two more days was a good omen with no additional burdens?"

Mephisto smiled and replied, "Ah, my Callisto, how good it is to hear your voice. In answer to your query, yes, my project is progressing as desired and now gives me time to re-open our equity discussion talks. What news do you have for me, my Callisto?"

With a fatalistic smile Zara calmly responded, "Mephisto, I have explored all my useful options and can readily admit that I have no funding resources to buy my way into the partnership offer you made to me. I am resigned to my fate of being your contractor with little hope of being more. I trust you will want to continue our relationship as I have come to enjoy our arrangement, but I understand if you feel I offer no more value."

Somewhat surprised at the soft answer, Mephisto offered, "My Callisto, you are still so despondent and gloomy in your outlook of the future!

"But come now, I knew the five million Euros would be a formidable obstacle. I wanted to see how honest or how resourceful you could be. As it turns out, it was your honesty that I was most interested in securing, not the resources. Money is nothing without people you can trust. You proved I can trust you, and that has value in my organization. I want to suggest a different way to approach the equity partnership.

"I need a payload launched, that incorporates all of my code, at a wealthy organization we will talk about later, and I have included a method to collect a ransom. I need someone I can trust to deliver and launch it at the intended targets. For that, I am willing to grant you a one percent equity stake upon completion of the exercise which should be worth one million Euros to you. In exchange, you forfeit the last one hundred thousand Euros bonus and cover your own expenses to see the payload launched and the target hit.

"This then will be your sweat-equity offering that I am willing to accept. Does that help the despondency and improve your mental outlook? What say you, my Callisto? Do we have a deal?"

Zara couldn't believe the words she heard and almost cried out with a shout of joy. She struggled to reel in her emotional high until she replied, "Mephisto, I….I don't know what to say! Your terms are quite generous and indeed, yes, we have a deal! When do I get to meet my new partner and take delivery of your code to be launched?"

Mephisto chuckled and clarified, "Still anxious to see the man behind the curtain, I see. We will continue to work through intermediaries for the time being, but don't despair. We will meet soon enough. Time is not our friend at this juncture. Have patience, do as we have agreed, and we will both profit nicely. Agreed?"

Zara nodded her head and, still smiling, said, "Agreed, Mephisto! Thank you for your trust."

CHAPTER 51

TWO SOULS CAN BE MOLDED INTO ONE

Carlos had only worked a part of the day. His wounds were slowly healing, but he moved slowly and had developed an annoying limp, which Zara had noticed. She also asked him to think about some additional work that involved his working with her to develop complex information transmissions, though the details of the why and the targets were not revealed. She had stepped out briefly for an errand, and he had continued searching her machine but had stopped to complete his assigned tasks. He noticed some additional documents that seemed related to Juan's aircraft, but he had only caught a glimpse of them. He needed more time for his focused Juan research, but Zara had returned and sent him home.

Once he had returned home, Carlos called Julie and chatted briefly about the information he had found and the additional systems that he had set up for monitoring. They had exchanged some pleasantries. Julie indicated she was still feeling great and had started to gain a few pounds, but some limitations had been placed on her activities. Carlos admitted he was healing, yet moving slowly. Zara had not indicated that she'd heard from Dante at all, which relieved Julie.

Julie offered again to pick him up and take him to the doctor, which he quickly declined. He figured her hormones must be totally out of control as she then launched into a tirade and listed his numerous indiscretions. Not only did he place himself at risk, but he didn't do so well on the calling people and updating them or just saying hello. When was the last time he had called his boss, Andrew, and told him what was going on? Then of course there was his love interest with Lara. When did he last speak to her? If he didn't want to share what was going on with him regarding Juan, then he certainly could ask Lara about what was happening in her life, or tell her to go date someone else.

Julie's tirade concerning Lara had really gotten to him. He had totally avoided contact with Lara on purpose. If he told her how much he missed her, he'd be out of New York and on his way to Sao Paulo or someplace in between. Just the thoughts of her smile, warmth, and charming laughter altered his mind, and he pressed her number. While it connected, he closed his eyes and pictured her mahogany hair, tanned skin, and supple female-endowed body.

"My prince, I am so glad you called. I miss you so much," Lara exclaimed.

"It is good to hear your voice, sweetheart. Are you home or on location doing your wonderful fashion thing?" he asked as he hoped she wouldn't ask him about his work.

She laughed a bit and explained, "I am home. We completed a great session in Jamaica, and I have been culling through the shots trying to select the ones for the catalog and others for the advertising inputs in the various women magazines. I can hardly wait to show them to you. Julie was simply great at the shoot. She is so pretty, don't you think?"

Carlos remained with his eyes closed as if trying to shut out the rest of the world. "Yes, my love, she is very pretty and smart. I am so glad she is taking care of my niece or nephew. Has she told you if she knows the gender yet?"

"Funny you should ask that, but, no, she hasn't, and I asked her last time we spoke. She only told me she was staying up with the doctor appointments, working some, and gaining a lot of weight. She asked me when I was going to start getting a maternity clothes line in place, and that she would be my first customer. She is always in such good shape that it is hard to imagine her as anything other than a pretty fit female with a bump straight out front. Of course I haven't seen her in several weeks now."

"I am glad you two are keeping in touch. Sweetheart, you know I love you and miss you, and if not I promise I do. I just need to sort this out and see if I can put the pieces all together, so try not to be mad, please."

"I don't believe that anywhere in this conversation I have questioned your actions or behavior. My prince, I am always here for you, no matter what, and hearing your voice makes me very happy. When you get things worked out, we will get together somewhere, just like always. I love being with you, but I won't bother you or cause you worry when I know you have to do what you think is right. Does that make sense?"

Carlos opened his eyes and gazed out of the window as he felt some weight lift off his frame. He felt better and less burdened than he had in weeks. His wounds still hurt, but her faith in him was what he had almost lost sight of and was grateful of her reminder.

"Lara, I think that you are an amazing woman. I am so glad we met and joined together as one soul. You're right! When I finish up here we will meet, and I will explain it all, I promise."

Lara purred, "I look forward to that time. I want to show you all the progress I am making with the business. I think you will like it, and maybe I can go forward with a maternity clothes line, what do you think?"

Suddenly side tracked by where his mind wandered, he was about to state a long term commitment when Carlos heard an insistent knock at his door.

"Ah, honey, umm..., hold that thought. I need to go now. I love you, sweetheart. I will call as soon as I can."

Lara looked at the disconnected phone in her hands, and smiled as the tears started to leak from her eyes and down her pretty cheeks.

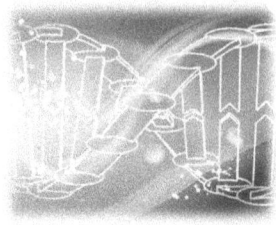

CHAPTER 52

THERE IS SO MUCH TO SEE WHEN YOU CLOSE YOUR EYES

Carlos smiled as Julie answered. With some effort he said, "Madam, how are you this fine day?"

Julie sensed something was amiss so she cautiously responded, "Dakota, what's up? The last time a conversation between us started like this you needed *air cover* and lots of it. Please tell me you are bored, or calling me from a bar because you are simply lonely."

Carlos shook his head and replied, "Now you are being unfair. No, I'm not calling from a bar because I'm lonely. I will admit to slugging down some very under-whelming tequila to improve my mood. Besides that, I promised you I would not get into a fight with another clown like Dante, and I always try to keep my word, little sister."

Julie heard Carlos swig down another drink from a bottle of something and bring it to rest again, on what sounded like an uncarpeted floor.

Suspicious, Julie asked, "Dakota, why does it sound like I'm not getting the entire story? What's wrong?"

Carlos put down the phone to take another swig and then retrieved the phone and wondered, "Did I ever tell you about my apprenticeship to an old Yaqui Indian who was a master of mystics? Boy, talk about a hoot! Juan thought I had lost it big time, living in the Chihuahuan Desert running around in a loin cloth.

"That mystic master taught me how to track in pitch dark. I thought that was a far-out skill. Running in pitch dark is like running with your eyes closed. Yes, I tripped over anything and everything until he taught me to not use my eyes."

Carlos put down the cell phone onto the surface that resulted in a slight echo sound over the phone. With his good arm, he swigged down another drink, exchanged the bottle for the phone, and resumed his story.

"You know, Julie, as crazy as it sounds, tracking using your senses and not your eyes is not only possible but the best way to stalk. It is also the only way to experience the spirit world that old Yaqui mystic knew so well. There is so much to see when you close your eyes. I can't even really explain it, so you will have to take my word for it."

Julie was now frightened that something was desperately wrong, which was the cause of Carlos' rambling speech.

"Dakota, why does it sound like you're in pain and now self-administering your own pain relief medicine?"

Carlos was comfortably numb to the pain and wanted to continue with his ramblings, so he ignored her question and continued, "Well, the old master taught me how to not really run in the dark but glide effortlessly among the rocks, bushes, and trees. Then I started to see, in a metaphorical sense, spirits moving between worlds. Sort of like being at a park with other joggers, but not really.

"Anyway the mystical life wasn't really for me. My old master Yaqui Indian got furious with me, because, in a moment of weakness, I had to have a cheeseburger after living off the land for eight weeks. He said I would never become a true Yaqui Mystic and that I should go back to my spiritually-crippled urbanized world. He may have been right about me returning to civilization, but I never forgot how to track without using my eyes."

Carlos now breathed hard and grimaced as he tried to sit up straighter. He rested against the wall. He let out a small whelp of pain that clearly signaled his probable condition.

"Dakota, where are you? You sound like you hurt a lot! Let me come help you!"

Carlos smiled weakly and after another quick shot of tequila continued, "You know how sometimes you have things work against you, then other times providence simply grabs at you from a second hand store? From the second hand store, the owner says, 'Son, I couldn't help but notice your limp, and I've got just the thing for you! Look at this walking cane! Now this is not just any old walking cane, but in fact, a highly styled, well finished piece of wood that was lovingly hand crafted from the same wood used to build a Louisville Slugger! This excellent piece of hand crafted wood could not only function as a walking stick for that hurt leg, but also as a fine weapon in times of peril. I can let you have it at a discount because I like you. And, heck, I'll make a deal with you. If you buy it now for your limp and my peace of mind, I'll buy it back from you once your limp is gone.

'My name is Leroy, and I just inherited this second hand store from my dearly departed uncle. Well sir, I'm trying to build up some trade now that I am the sole proprietor. The ways I sees it, you gotta care about your customer if you are gonna make a go of it in business. How about that offer, sir?'

Julie was only partially listening while she was also trying to geo-locate Carlos through his cell phone. She fired off a couple of text messages for assistance.

"Uh, that was nice of him, Dakota. But, dear brother, why won't you tell me how I can help you? I know that tone in your voice, and you are scaring me as well as the baby. You know Juan would not approve."

Carlos grinned at Julie's minor manipulation. "You know, I usually don't fold up like a cheap lawn chair when being hustled, but something about that Leroy with his gold tooth grin, trying to sell me that Louisville Slugger cane, made me remember that the Yaqui spirits sometimes approach you during the day. I bought that cane from him, and we shook hands like we'd always been friends."

Julie now had Andy, EZ, and Quip listening to the transmission of Carlos's ramblings real-time, after they had homed in on his location.

"Umm, that was a nice thing for Leroy to do. What happened next, since you won't tell me where you are?"

Carlos suddenly felt very cold as he shivered, then replied, "I sure wish I had a blanket. I just got very cold.

"I left and was limping back toward work with my new cane, trying to figure out my next move with Zara, when I saw them.

"Actually, I didn't see them at first, but more felt them. The Yaqui tracker in me welled up so quickly that I was moving into the shadows before I noticed it myself. I got back to the offices, but before I stepped across the street, I automatically pushed deeper into the shadows when I saw them out front talking to Zara. I had felt their presence and had seen them before they saw me. The Yaqui mystic would have been proud of me even after my cheeseburger indiscretion. I couldn't hear what they were saying at that distance, but the Yaqui spirits warned of danger."

Julie, now totally reengaged with the story, asked, "Warned you of who? Who did you think these men were, Dakota?"

A very somber and focused Carlos replied, "In a previous life, of which I hope you have not been made aware of, I think I dealt with these two men for their identity laundering expertise. They would have known who I was on sight. It would have ruined my cover with Zara. I only know them as the Asian twins, Won and Ton. Never learned why the scarred one never spoke, but I do know they like buying stolen aircraft.

"As soon as I saw them, I had two ideas race through my mind. The first was they would blow my cover story with Zara so I couldn't let them see me coming in. The second was that Zara had Juan's aircraft call sign on her computer, and these two aircraft pirates were talking to her.

"I thought there were more details I could learn from the files on her computer. I quickly gimped around to the back entrance and snuck into the work space to copy some files off her machine just in case, which I have on a thumb drive. When I returned to my original observation point, she was shaking her head and pointed them away and went into the offices. Then I followed them and, well, one out of two isn't bad for someone with a hurt leg."

Julie was both alarmed and elated as she asked, "You found a lead on Juan's plane on Zara's computer, and you saw her talking to the aircraft buyers that Juan told me were picked up by the federales several months ago with their stolen aircraft?"

"Well, I knew this conversation might help fill in some pieces of the puzzle. I didn't get everything I wanted off the computer. I did get more than I bargained for from the twins.

"I followed them as they headed toward my place, which you know is in a fairly quiet neighborhood with a couple of abandoned buildings. They vanished into the shadows of one of the abandoned buildings, and I, of course, followed. As it turns out, they are pretty good at the martial arts thing, and got a couple good licks on me. But Leroy's Louisville Slugger evened things up with two solid base hits and two strike outs on the floor.

"Now that I got all that out and you have done as I think you have, can you come and help me out here? It would help if you put these two on ice while we run down the info I scammed. I'm kind of cold and tired now."

She wiped the tears from her cheeks, grinned, and then commented, "On my way! You can go ahead and rest for a while."

Quip reached for another phone and hit a familiar speed dial button. As soon as he reached the call party, he greeted, "Ah, Eric, it's been ages since we last visited!"

Eric raised an eyebrow but replied, "Uh, Quip, we spoke yesterday, so I gather that the reason for this call is that you need another favor judging from the tone of your greeting. What is it now?"

Quip was now taken aback by the comment as he continued, "Eric, you wound me, sir! Can't I call and chat with a friend?

"However, since you bring it up, I do need a modest favor for someone I have on the ground in New York City, quite literally. I have a downed team member who needs some very discreet medical attention that doesn't involve questions being asked of him, and two more folks secured and held until we can arrange some transport and drop off point. I think that's all. So how is the rest of your day going, my friend?"

THE ENIGMA WRAITH

Eric stared dumbfounded then finally responded, "Quip, my day was fine until I got my first call of the morning, this call actually. I was dreading the root canal I have scheduled for this afternoon, but after hearing your request, I am now actually looking forward to the root canal!

"Geez, Quip, when did I start working for you? I and this agency have more important things to do than pickup and deliver your dirty laundry! Tell me why I shouldn't just hang up on you, and let you go through normal channels?"

A humbled Quip quietly responded, "Gee, Eric, you make it sound like we don't help one another, like with finding Prudence or willing to step in if your team cannot locate her since we have experience in that part of the world. Alright, alright, I withdraw the request, and I'll work with a couple of contractors. Thanks for taking my call, and we'll talk some other time. Good day, sir!"

Before Quip hung up, Eric interrupted, "Wait! Wait! You know something more about Prudence…I mean Arletta Krumhunter? You need to learn to sell better by first stating what I want and then ask for the resources required to get me what I want! Tell your people to greet the next visitor team with the question, *'who are you and why are you at my sand lot?'* He will respond with *'I am the Beach-Master,'* and his team will go to work. I think I can have them there in forty minutes. Now tell me the additional information about Arletta."

Quip grinned and replied, "You're a good man, Eric! I can't tell you anything additional about where she is until I get the additional information on the ground in New York, so I am glad that you offered to help. Helping us means that we can now help you, kind sir. I will prep our people in New York on the protocol they need to observe. Must dash! Talk later."

Eric said to no one in particular as he sent a status note request to Stalker, "It looks like he got everything he wanted, including transportation, and I am still staring down a dark elevator tunnel, serving up endless solutions. In other words, he got the craft, and I got the shaft. Again. Just like working with Otto. Dammit!"

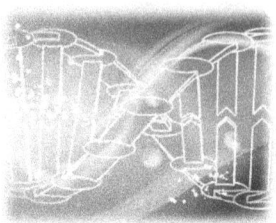

CHAPTER 53

DID YOU WANT THAT HERO-SIZED?

As she stared intently at Jacob, Petra asked, "Where were you last night? You didn't come to bed, and this place looks like it was *binged* by a horde of computer coding addicts. There is take-out delivery food and energy drink cans all over the place! You've been at for thirty-six hours straight, honey, and I'm worried. I even heard Quip joke that you two were looking to score some illicit body stimulants from the local drug dealer in order to carry on! That's not even funny, and this coding-binge has to end. And I mean right now!"

Jacob was weaving back and forth in his chair, practically not hearing anything of Petra's rant. A slow smile formed on Jacob's face, and without turning his glazed stare from the computer screen, he asked in an extremely tired voice that spoke to his near exhausted mental state, "Dr. Quip, you wants to show her what we gots?"

Quip was slumped forward in his chair while his head rested on his forearms. He slowly rolled his head to the right to see left but still had his eyes closed as he said, "I'm not showing her mine, that's your job! But okay, if you show her yours, then I guess I can show her mine. Now if I do show her mine, I don't want any complaints from you about her comparisons, got it?"

Jacob was so tired that the old gag produced only a slight chuckle, and still staring at the computer screen, he replied, "I'll admit that your 3-D project computer screen is larger than my regular flat screen. However, if we are talking the male goods, I'll have you know that I have to wear shorts that come down to my knees so I don't get arrested for indecent exposure while in public!"

Quip managed a feeble grin and responded, "Hah! Is that the best you can do? My boy, I can wear regular shorts in public because I wear *Big Jim* wrapped around my waist a couple of times! Boy, talk about your amateurs!"

Jacob, now chuckling a little harder, retorted, "Oh yeah, well, the only reason I get away with shorts down to my knees is that I have to fold the beast in half! Do you know what it's like not being able to wear a kilt because every time you cross a bridge some smart-aleck female has to call out, *'hey, can you tell if the water is cold? And while you're at it, can you tell me how deep it is?'* It's almost more than a person can bear sometimes."

Petra, turned livid at the two males who had devolved into adolescent male boasting rights, practically shouted, "Alright, that's enough of that, boys! Both of you out of here. Go get some rest so you can make some sense again!"

Quip was still giggling when Jacob regained some of his cognizant abilities and suggested, "Quip, bring it up on the big screen so we can show Petra what we did accomplish."

Quip launched the 3-D image and Jacob explained, "Petra, the behavioral pattern approach to building a digital cancer for our ghost code has yielded some very good results. The image on the screen is actually a synthesis of logging activity, code changes going on under the notice of the virus scanning software, and the pirating of virus-building code from other programs.

"Quip thought it might be more useful to visualize the activity on screen, so we let ICABOD paint the activity in this 3-D image, allowing us to see in real-time what's going on.

"Watch how our version of the ghost code builds itself along with the behavioral patterns that we extracted from the various target sites that were hit. The material that we received from Carlos yielded the most useful patterns because it showed us the most subdirectories out of all of our research. Every one of our inspected ghost code sites had some of these subdirectory structures, but he found the most. Realizing that the creator was anxious to completely erase his subdirectories, used to store pirated code, meant that he was not changing it from one version to the next."

Quip sat up straighter and seemed somewhat coherent again, as he added, "With known file and directory storage usage, we surmised that whenever this behavior was detected it would indicate that the ghost code was present and beginning to assemble the digital virus. This is key to us, because we want to launch our attack on the ghost code and not against normal code. Once we have the pattern of creating subdirectories, copying code snippets, and file size increases that go unreported to the operating system log files or the anti-virus software, we have our pattern. More importantly we have our target vector."

Jacob picked up the explanation thread as he continued, "You can see in real time on the 3-D screen the normal operations of a computer operating system with the ebb and flow of digital activity. Now, Quip, launch our ghost-wannabe program and observe how it behaves."

"The virus I built operates so fast, I had to put in some timer code to slow it down so we could observe the growth characteristics. Understand our goal was not to build a competitor virus but build a target. This is much like shooting skeet where we have a target thrown in a predictable way so we can learn to shoot it with enough lead."

Petra's anger disappeared as she watched the 3-D image move almost like a series of clouds in a dance arrangement. She witnessed as the image developed a pod on one side of the larger cloud while quick light flashes emanating from it suggested that snippets of code had been snatched. She was witnessing the growth of a computer-generated digital life. It was breathtakingly beautiful but recognizable as potentially deadly.

Quip said, "See how fast it can find and collect usable code material to assemble itself? I'm quite glad that we have old Jacob boy on our side. Okay, Jacob, launch the cancer."

With a few keystrokes, Jacob launched the cancer into the fray, and in moments the digital growth started to shrink and finally was gone. Jacob sat and smiled with a hint of self-congratulation.

"How many is that now, Quip? I've lost track."

Quip grinned and replied, "You just like hearing me say gobs! You're not fooling anybody, *Mister water-temperature-reporter-and-depth-finder-from-a-bridge-in-a-kilt-with-no-hands*! You are so bogus with that claim!"

Petra looked puzzled as she asked, "What do you mean, how many times? It is just the same test repeated over and over, right?"

Jacob looked thoughtfully at the 3-D display then clarified, "Nope. We incorporated an obfuscation algorithm so the virus would try to build itself in a myriad of ways with different build approaches that could match infinite end states. I wanted to make sure that we could spot the ghost code no matter how he tried to grow himself."

Petra was just realizing the depth of the accomplishment. With a hint of awe, she indicated, "I can see how the trigger works to launch it, but how does the cancer work to kill the ghost code? How does it assassinate the ghost code?"

Jacob breathed a heavy sigh as he explained, "I used the *grasshopper-loop* with its kill switch as the main attack logic. I introduced the notion of behavior patterns into it so when it recognizes the pattern, it simply shows up to be incorporated into the ghost code but continues to add programming logic into the virus that makes the ghost code consume itself much like an organic cancer would do. Su Lin would be pleased, I think, with how her logic is going to be used."

Quip grinned and added, "A fitting legacy to a brilliant programmer. Oh, and I think you deserve some small amount of credit too, Jacob, with over a hundred completed scenarios without a miss."

Jacob's look of annoyance was unmistakable as he said, "Why, thank you, *Mister I-don't-have-a-spare-tire-but-an-anaconda-wrapped-around-my-waist*! Brother! You do realize that you are a legend in your own mind, right?"

Petra now understood why they wouldn't stop but insisted, "Alright, let's have everyone power down and get some rest. You gentlemen have had a busy day, and a long one at that."

Then as she linked arms with Jacob to lead him out, she looked over her shoulder with a wink and a smile as she purred, "Oh, just so you know, Quip, Jacob isn't exaggerating."

Looking longingly at Jacob, Petra murmured, "Honey, let's go to bed."

Petra winked again at Quip as they left. Quip's eyebrows were fully raised.

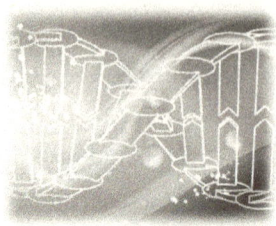

CHAPTER 54

GIVING UP IS NOT AN OPTION, BUT GIVING IN CAN BE CONSIDERED

After several transport changes, with limited sleep while doing several days of stake out in what he considered unfriendly territory, Stalker was ready to return home. He couldn't shake the facts that he had been working from. Arletta had been in the areas he staked out. Several interviews with locals had proven that, as well as the general comments regarding the rude American female. Even the old photo he'd used during these interviews, along with the looking for his sister cover, had confirmed it. She hadn't been seen for some time, and the last time she had been seen was correlated back to the few days subsequent to the breach at the base. He had returned to the common tourist hotel in town, set up his security jamming signals to defeat the bugs, and placed his call.

"Hey, it's me, do you have a few minutes for an update?"

"About time you checked in! Are you headed back with a reluctant Arletta?"

"No, Eric. I was able to confirm she was here and making herself quite at home. I discovered where she had stayed and found her things stored by the hotel where she rented by the month. She hasn't returned for some time. It was hard to even get that much detail, and you will reimburse me."

Eric chuckled, "And just when have I failed to approve your expenses? Where is she then? Did you check out both the locations I provided? There are multiple buildings at both of those complexes, as I recall."

With almost a defeated tone, Stalker confirmed, "Of course I checked out all the buildings, and I can account for the traffic and people at both places. I even followed Chang and a Major Guano whom I identified as his number two. Nothing. Flat nothing on Arletta."

Eric pondered for a minute and then conveyed, "I will not call her Congressman father and say that she is missing in China and I have no idea why. That simply won't work. I know how thorough you are, but I would rather not have you come back and then get another lead and send you right back."

"I agree, Eric, that would be nuts. I did search thoroughly for the target sites provided. Can you reach out again and see if there are any other places in and around this area that would be worth checking?"

"Exactly what I was thinking. Let me place a couple of calls, and I'll be back with you as soon as I can. Go sight see or something for a few hours."

Stalker chuckled, "No really, boss, I have done all the sightseeing here that I can stand. The food here stinks, and everything is too short for this six foot six frame. Worse than Japan in that regard."

They disconnected, and Eric thought about how he could approach this request as he replayed the last exchange with Quip, as he placed the call.

Quip immediately answered, "Hello, Monty, er, Eric, what a pleasant surprise. Thanks again for helping with that situation in New York. I promise that more than took care of the charges for our research effort. What's up and how can we be of service? My staff is close to finishing up a project, and I was wondering what might be on the horizon."

Eric said, "Quip, I think you may as well consider this, not a new project, but warranty work. Your last bit of information has not provided the intended result. Arletta isn't at either of the suggested locations."

"Hmmm. Give me a minute, Eric, and let me see if something else may have surfaced."

Quip accessed the information from the PPP, and there were no additional signs of Arletta exiting that region of the world. She simply had to be there. He sat back and thought about all the other possibilities, and then he recalled that one very remote outpost that Otto had located. He couldn't recall if a map had been constructed or not. The access was very limited as he recalled.

"Sorry, Eric. There is another place in the region that might be possible if Arletta has fallen out of favor but is still alive. The problem is that I can't direct you to it. It is a place that one person on my team can reach, but I hesitate to let my team go there right now as they are on another assignment."

"Can you get me close at all, and I'll get my local person to go the distance?"

"I wish I could, but it is off a narrowed portion of the Yanzi. I gather you don't want to just leave her fending for herself?"

"Quip, as tempting as that is, it would be a political nightmare and could expose some security breaches that I think she is at the bottom of. If she is alive, I need her back if for no other reason than to determine what she said to whom."

"Alright, Eric. I understand. Let me reach out to my resource and get back with you."

Eric sighed and replied, "Thank you. I sense that this is a bigger favor than just warranty work. If it works out, you can bill me double and I'll still owe you."

Quip laughed, "Ah, music to my ears. I'll call you back."

Quip called the team and took their inputs on the subject. He hated to ask Julie to place herself into any possible danger. Wolfgang was the first to agree that it needed to be avoided but then countered with 'we need to do what is best in the long run.' Petra said Julie was in great health with the baby and wouldn't be slowed down. They discussed several different avenues and kept returning to the same option. Quip called Julie from the speaker phone in the conference room.

"Hey, Julie, how are you feeling today?"

"Things are good, Quip. Carlos seems to be on the mend, and he continues to poke around in the Dteam systems. Busy boy, who has promised no more cowboy actions. I presume your flame, EZ, is still monitoring conversations."

Quip grinned at the thought of EZ's fiery hair and replied, "With all that red hair, how could I not adore her? She is the one for me; she just doesn't realize it yet.

"I digress though. Sweetie, I had another reason for calling you. Do you recall that trip you took to fetch Master Po from captivity?"

Julie shivered slightly as the image of that place and Master Po slipped into her memory. It had been an arduous trip, but defeating the security system so deftly was an activity that pleased her. She had not documented any of the location trails nor the counter security methods she had used, as Otto hadn't wanted the information stored anywhere but her brain.

"I do. Why would you ask that now?"

Quip and Jacob joined together to explain their side job of hunting for Arletta and the current results of the search. Petra reminded Julie of how closely Otto had worked with Julie on the extraction of Master Po. Julie explained that she had promised not to give up the details of the place. No matter how much the three of them grilled her, she refused. Even Wolfgang could not convince her it was alright to break her promise, and he respected her decision.

Quip threatened, "Julie, we need to see if this is a plausible location for a United States citizen that Eric insists needs to be recovered, if she is still alive. If you won't provide the specifics, then I have to ask you to go."

Julie agreed, "Quip, I will go, just as soon as Carlos finishes finding all the information he can."

"Julie, that presents a problem. Honey, if she is still alive she may not have much longer if she has run out of valuable information to share."

"Quip, I need to wait until Carlos finds everything he can."

Petra interjected, "Carlos is being monitored continuously along with communications being recorded. He has done an amazing job, but it will still take some time to get all the information. That was what you related to me last night."

"Julie, how long would it take you to get there and back?"

"Pet, with the right resources, maybe three days, four at the outside. I would need an aircraft and some support for manning the boat as well if I locate her. I also need the drugs in case she has had the same interrogation methods used on Master Po."

Quip stated, "If I can get all of that, can you leave tomorrow?"

Julie smiled, knowing there was no way he could accommodate her list of items in under a week, which is what it had taken the last time. "Tell you what, Quip. If you can get this all together and in New York by tomorrow, say noontime, then I will do it. Otherwise, it waits until Carlos is finished, and you stop asking."

"On your word, Julie. You will be contacted in the morning with meet up points. You will be careful and check in with me every day, right?"

Julie laughed and confidently replied, "Quip, by tomorrow noon."

"Yes! Be safe!" Quip said as he disconnected.

He dialed Eric back, and as the call connected, Quip said, "Eric, okay, we have a deal if you can line up everything that I have on the list I am sending via our secure email in the next few minutes."

"Works for me. Will it include the information on contacting your team member?"

"Yes, sir. JAC needs to go along as she will not reveal the details. Your man on that end must agree to follow her every instruction, which could include blindfolding. It is her call."

"Alright, I'm sure she is a professional."

"Eric, she is not only a professional but part of my team, and you will insure her total safety and return with all parts intact, got it?!"

"Agreed, Quip. And thanks for the extra effort from your team on this."

"No problem, it is all business. The details have been sent. Can you grab them and let me know if you have any questions?"

"Sure. Just a few minutes." Eric retrieved the file and unencrypted it. He reread it three times and shook his head. "Quip, are you serious about this?"

"Yes, sir. Consider it part of the deal."

"Why now rather than when we first took possession of them?"

"I figure it will be a fair exchange for your Prudence, Eric."

Julie answered the door after she recognized the man on the other side, though seeing him there surprised her.

"Hello, Beach-Master. Why are you here, and, more importantly, how did you find me?"

"Hello again, JAC. It seems our paths are simply meant to cross. You need to call me Commander though, madam. I thought we agreed on that."

It dawned on her that Quip had won, so JAC flashed her brilliant megawatt smile as she replied, "Commander, of course I do recall. Come in for a few minutes and have some coffee while I get ready, and then we can go."

"Thank you. You look a bit different from the last time we met, though I brought along a reminder from that event that is supposed to go with us."

JAC replied as she headed to the bathroom with her clothes, just before she closed the door. "Really? What is that?"

Commander said to the door in a loud enough voice to carry through, "Well, JAC, they're not really a what, but who. I believe you called them the *ATM, or Asian Twin Men*."

JAC jerked open the bathroom door and barreled out with a confused expression. She asked, "Commander, just why would you bring those two men with you? They are dangerous, and I thought you were keeping them on ice."

"I was told to bring them as they would be left at the drop site if the target was located. I'm just doing as ordered, JAC."

JAC recovered then returned to the bathroom to finish changing and reminded herself she would be telling Quip off in the very near future. This was crazy, just crazy.

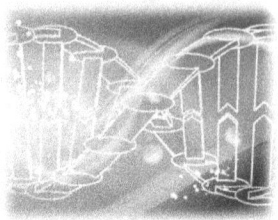

CHAPTER 55

WHEN YOU DANCE WITH THE DEVIL, NEVER STEP ON HIS TAIL

Callisto was dumbfounded by the accusation but responded, "What do you mean the last payload didn't launch? I personally delivered it from my personal laptop as we discussed, so I know it was uploaded to the target just like the others. I haven't deviated from the routine in multiple deliveries that have performed as required. Are you confident that the code you gave me to upload is the correct code? I mean, is it possible that….."

Mephisto cut her words off with a terse comment, "Who do you think you're talking to? I'm not some retailer that got my overnight package of flowers delivered to the wrong address! These codes are carefully crafted the same way, from the same computer, that is only run by one programmer! This is the final code load we were going to market with, on our last trial run. Our mission and money were in your hands, but you had buttery-fingers? Reread the instructions to me over the phone and tell me yes or no if they were completed!"

Callisto swallowed hard and stepped through each of the instruction lines with Mephisto to confirm every step was dutifully followed. Mephisto was seething with anger, but it was plain Callisto had followed every step flawlessly.

After a long pause, Mephisto admitted, "Alright, something is wrong, but where is the issue? It is obvious you followed the instructions, so that either leaves the target was not susceptible to our delivery or the source product was damaged in its creation. Since no one has been capable of stopping our code once introduced, it suggests that the package I gave you was damaged somehow or …"

Callisto didn't dare suggest what she was thinking, but then Mephisto added, "….or the programmer mucked up the code with a final set of tweaks. Let me run with this, Callisto, for now. I have some people to talk to before our next step. Stand by for new instructions and another package. There could have been a fluke event that interrupted our final test, but something doesn't seem quite right and now I want answers."

After disconnecting, Callisto shivered and struggled to get her breathing back under control. She reminded herself that when you dance with the devil, you should never step on his tail.

Quip said, "Whew! I'd wager old Mephisto is really ticked off! Andy and EZ, thanks for getting me a muted linked-listen-in on that conversation. How long before you can get me a geo-location of Mephisto?"

"EZ is shipping you the coordinates in an encrypted email that should be there in two shakes of a lamb's tail." Andy continued, "This scenario you just pulled off reminds me of an old 1941 musical tune that goes almost like this; ▨ Pardon me boy, did we just derail your little choo choo train? ▨ Har! Har!"

Everyone chuckled for a few moments.

"Thanks again to you both! I'll be dropping the call now, but please keep an eye open for any more muted listen-in opportunities on Callisto."

After disconnecting the conference bridge, Quip finished his previous sentence, "When she is speaking with Mephisto, commonly referred to as Chairman Chang."

Petra and Jacob both looked at each other quizzically, and Quip, seeing their unspoken question, offered, "I've been on conference calls with Otto when he was speaking to Chairman. He has a very deep resonant voice and a distinct dialect that is easy to remember. Particularly when he loses his temper.

"Well team, Carlos's undercover intelligence has paid off nicely. He gave us enough to deduce most of what the ghost code can do. With the clandestine planting of Jacob's cancer code on Callisto's delivery laptop, we got almost everything we needed when she tried to deliver another payload. As a big bonus, your cancer virus disinfected the ghost code before it could launch, thus proving your programming logic was sound.

"Well done on launching a parallel mirror recorder program that was interleaving transmissions to us at the same time the code was trying to execute. Getting a program onto Callisto's machine to relay all programmatic activity almost as fast as the program runs, means that we don't have to try to physically retrieve the desired files."

Jacob grinned and said, "Oh, but I did that too, Quip. I figured that if the machine lost connectivity, we could still retrieve the program activity should the need occur. Also I figured that if Mephisto, aka Chairman, got suspicious of Callisto and scanned her machine deep enough, he would find incriminating evidence that pointed to her trying to debug his code."

Quip sat and blinked a few seconds and then said, "I am ashamed that you thought of that angle before me. Poop!" Then a bit chastened, he added, "I'm… I'm sorry you had to hear that!"

Petra offered, "Now we have an almost complete digital fingerprint to work against, and we know who is behind the ghost code. However, we don't yet understand the end game Chairman has in mind. On the call he indicated that this was the final version which suggests that he is ready to, as they say in advertising, begin the market launch. We still don't know the intended target or targets."

Jacob thoughtfully asked, "What is it they teach in military academies? The best form of defense is attack? If I morph the phrase a little bit for our circumstances, I would suggest 'when you don't know your cyber adversary's intended victim, make your cyber adversary the target'."

Quip sat quietly for a few seconds then agreed, "As much as I hate having Jacob deliver all the best lines in this meeting, I have to agree with the approach. Team, we have our target vector, and we need a little finesse to arrange our own calling card."

Petra mused aloud, "Jacob, if I understand your open ended comment, you are suggesting we launch a preemptive strike against the Chairman rather than waiting to see his next attack unfold."

Jacob nodded agreement then thoughtfully added, "If we were to disinfect his organization first and leave a threatening calling card, to use Quip's trite phrase, he would certainly understand we hold the upper hand in this digital warfare game. We want to sink his digital battleships before he can launch his attack."

Petra said, "We now know that there is only one programmer, and the ghost code is built on only one machine. I know it's only one machine, but it's still a substantial haystack to be sifting through. Our only problem is we haven't found a way into their computer network to harvest their work. Any ideas about how we can get in and retrieve it?"

Jacob mused aloud, "I think we can safely assume that their ghost code incubator machine is not attached to the Internet for security purposes. I would expect that the programmer is manually delivering the product to Chairman with the detonator device that gives the ghost code its launch sequence and life evolution timer. The instructions Callisto read back to Mephisto strongly suggest two pieces of code that, when combined, give the ghost code its abilities and defines its lifespan."

With a distinct pout on his face, Quip whined, "Petra! Jacob is making all the important observations again! Make him stop so I can say cool stuff, too!"

Shaking her head with a half-focused look in her eyes that could only be interpreted as a *why me look,* Petra sighed and insisted, "Children, it's time for your nap because mother is tired of you again!"

Jacob smirked a little as he ignored the suggestion and added, "You're probably deflecting, Quip, since we haven't been able to penetrate the digital Chinese wall defending the ghost code incubator machine. Perhaps breaching their defenses is beyond our reach."

Quip, now thoroughly indignant, argued, "You make it sound like it's impossible to get past the Chinese cyber defenses! Nothing is impossible with the Quipster on the job, boys and girls! I said I've only been poking around their defenses, not conducting a full scale breach with ICABOD!

"Who do you think got us past the Cyber Warfare College air-gapped defenses the first time? Remember who it was that helped deliver that poisoned firmware code to the Iranian nuclear plant that crippled their systems for at least ten years? If you think this is something new or that I can't do it, let me tell you, I can deliver. Stand back and let Doctor Quip do his surgery magic! I'm on it, and believe you-me, I'm gonna kick some digital butt!"

Quip made a beeline to his machine to begin his digital onslaught to find the machine which was home to the ghost code. As he issued commands to ICABOD, he was oblivious to the rest of the operations center.

Petra and Jacob looked at each other intently for a few seconds until Petra said, "You really shouldn't bait him like that, Jacob."

Jacob smiled and suggested, "It worked, didn't it?"

CHAPTER 56

WHEN TRAVELING, CARRY MINIMUM AMOUNTS OF BAGGAGE

JAC and Commander had travelled to the other side of the world with first class equipment. Direct flights were definitely the way to go. They had entered China with flawless papers. She appreciated what it took to make those sorts of identity papers and, within the timeline they were completed, it was phenomenal. Commander had everything that was on the list and a few extra items she was certain would be used.

During the flight, she'd phoned Quip to read him the riot act about the entire situation. He of course reminded her of her promise. He also reassured her that if anything relevant was revealed from Carlos's activities, he would let her know. As far as taking the *ATM* along, Quip had explained that he had no desire to let them stay on ice and support them when they could transport them far, far away. That was not the business the R-Group was in and so forth. JAC couldn't argue the point. For the boat trip and hike in they would remain mostly in silence.

"JAC, are you feeling alright? You don't seem to be eating or drinking a great deal."

"Commander, I am just fine. I don't like to eat a lot before this type of activity. My insides get a little queasy these days anyway."

Commander raised an eyebrow and cocked his head as he thoughtfully looked at her, then probed, "I thought something looked different from the last time I saw you. You still look fit as anyone on my team, but something has changed." He paused and examined her from head to toe, then said, "No insult, madam, but are you gaining weight?"

JAC flashed a smile and explained, "I am, and for all the right reasons."

Commander was flabbergasted and insisted, "JAC, you can simply tell me what to do and stay at the base camp. You don't need to risk yourself, much less a baby, for anyone. If you were my woman, I wouldn't permit it."

JAC laughed then chuckled as she stated, "This is my job, Commander. I am just fine, and I am in charge of me, not you. Got it! I might have gained a little weight, but I bet I can still kick some ass, so knock it off. I will, however, defer to you for the lifting portion of this adventure." She turned away for a moment as she chuckled again.

Then she turned back, looked him straight in the eyes, and seriously conveyed, "I might also suggest that any woman that would put up with you wouldn't wait for permission."

With nothing more to be said, the reprieve came to both their ear buds that the rendezvous point was within a thousand meters.

A man walked out of the shadows toward them and said, "Commander, how good of you to meet me. Madam, thank you for joining this little party."

"Stalker, this is JAC. She is very good at what she does, and we do the heavy lifting, she does the guiding."

"Hello, Miss JAC. What is your plan?"

"Stalker, what an interesting name. I suspect that whole name thing would make a great story. We need to get the men loaded onto the boat and in the water. We have some distance to travel, and I want to get back home soon."

JAC conveyed the details of her plan that required some floating and then some hiking. She also explained the security system at their destination as she recalled it. Stalker and Commander both agreed to her approach and looked at her with professional admiration. The boat was loaded with Won and Ton who were drugged with no idea how far they had traveled or where they were. Each of them took supplies in their backpacks and boarded.

Stalker and Commander poled the boat silently down the river. A few night creature noises and the water lapping at the sides of the boat were all that was heard. JAC worked on her fruit phone with creating the disrupter she planned to use on the first line of security defense. She signaled that they were close and indicated where they could beach the craft. Then she injected Won and Ton with a bit more of the drugs. It would make them heavier to carry but infinitely more manageable as they approached the site. Besides, she wasn't carrying them.

They beached the craft and secured it well. JAC figured the round trip to be two hours. With the non-descript boat in this isolated location, she was confident it would be there when they returned with Arletta. What a shame, she thought, after Quip had regaled her with some of this woman's devious activities, to rescue her at all. Still, everyone deserved their day in court.

Commander and Stalker each hoisted a man over their shoulder. These two were lethal but relatively small and light-weight. JAC lead the way to the location. When they arrived at the perimeter fence, everything was quiet. No lights or movement anywhere. Even the night creatures were silent in this area. JAC used the first jammer and entered the compound while she motioned for them to stay in place and wait for her signal. On the far side of the same building where she'd located Master Po, the bluish light showed through the one small window. Holding up her fruit phone, she stood motionless and recorded for almost ten minutes. As she played it back, it was clear that a woman was inside.

She signaled to the guys, and they made their way to her location right as she finished uploading the recording for the continuous feed on the video. They quietly set down the drugged men. They would be able to speak inside the building but needed to make it only necessary conversation. Commander exited to see if anyone was about and essentially secure the area, while Stalker approached the woman on the table after dropping his two bundles up against the wall. JAC was next to him a moment later with the hypodermic filled with the mixture of B-complex and an adrenaline boost as a chaser that she felt was sized to the estimated weight of the woman.

"It is Arletta, right?" asked JAC.

"Yes, though she looks like half the size of before. They must be rather hard on her in addition to starving her. Look at how sunken her eye sockets are. I doubt even with your concoction she'll be able to walk out."

"This is an amazing mix, Stalker. It would make almost anyone temporarily feel like they could climb a mountain for a short time."

"Oh, I understand. But her muscle tone was never good, and now it looks like it is merely flab. Unless this hypodermic cocktail can grow muscle tissue where it didn't exist before, I'm afraid we are going to be dragging Arletta. That brings to mind this horrible image of something pulled from… argh, I can't even say it!"

"I see what you are saying." JAC chuckled, "You may be right. The last time I used this drug the person was a reasonably fit person before they were taken."

"Before you inject her, let's take a look at the guy in the corner and see if we can identify him as at least a Westerner that needs rescuing."

JAC looked around, astounded, as she had only focused on the woman on the table. She moved quickly to the unconscious man and said, "I had no idea there was anyone else. We could be really good Samaritans today then, to make up for this poor excuse for a woman."

As they reached him, Stalker helped turn the man over toward the bluish light.

As the shadows cleared, JAC gasped and almost forgot all her training in a single heartbeat. A thousand thoughts and emotions swirled through her, leaving her unable to even breathe. After an eternity of only a few seconds, JAC exclaimed, "Juan, Juan, honey, is that you? Why are you here? How did you get here?"

Stalker looked at JAC then questioned, "You know this guy?"

The tears started running down JAC's face as she whispered, "He was gone, lost, and supposedly dead."

Then she got mad, as she instinctively injected Juan with all the contents, and handed the needle to Stalker. She grabbed him by the shoulders and pulled him part way up and demanded, "You wake up right this minute, Juan. I need you. You need to get up now, mister."

Juan's eyes fluttered a bit as he tried to focus and whispered, "Julie, my love, are you here again to help me while they torture me one more time? I love you, honey. Thank you for being with me. I won't let them find you, honey."

JAC shook him and said, "Juan, no one will torture you right now. But get up, we gotta go now!" She added a slap to the face to get his attention, and his eyes cleared.

Stalker was totally confused but refilled the needle and injected Arletta, knowing he'd have to carry her for a while, and sarcastically groused, "Well, it's a good thing we brought more than a single dose to this secure compound and bus stop."

Commander entered and with a show of hand indicated all was clear outside. They all knew it was time to go. It would take some time to extract two people rather than the one they had planned. Stalker knew, without a doubt, that finding this man held captive here was so far out of anyone's plan, and that JAC would protect this man no matter what.

Juan focused a bit more but was still confused as he questioned, "Why are you here? How did you find me?

"You know these people have the oddest notion of hospitality. They kept coming in and beating me, but then couldn't understand why my morale was so low. I think though, we should have them over for dinner real soon. It is so hard to make friends in this part of the world. It would be a shame if I didn't reciprocate. Don't you agree? Can you help me find something heavy to invite them with?"

JAC shook Juan and sternly demanded, "Juan, snap out of it! I need you to stand, put one foot in front of the other, and leave with us now. I need you to focus so we can get out. If you won't stand on your own, I will have Commander here fireman-carry you, and tell Carlos. Just how are you going to explain that to him?"

"Alright, sweetheart, don't tell him you found me down again." Juan's thinking began to clear as he recalled their prior conversation and asked, "How is our baby?"

JAC smiled as she helped him rise and added, "Finally, I can tell you. I have waited so long, it seems, to tell you. Juan, our babies are doing fine. Now let's go home!"

Commander helped Stalker hoist up Arletta and turned to assist JAC as he asked, "You're out here doing this and having twins? Madam, I might as well say it. You've got more guts than a government-monitored slaughter house."

Sizing up Juan and helping to keep them all moving, the Commander offered, "Buddy, you better listen up and follow her orders, or she will kick your ass! And if you don't appreciate this amazon warrior coming to your rescue, I'll kick your ass!"

Stalker added, "Folks, if you don't move faster, the guards are going to give us the promised whipping! We need faster and quieter!"

Picking up their pace, the team moved silently and boarded the craft once back in the water.

Juan became steadier as he moved. Once settled in the boat, he looked at JAC and questioned, "We're having twins? Really? Or are you just yanking my chain for being away? It wasn't my fault by the way."

JAC flashed him the best of her smiles as she reassured, "Honey, the doctor showed me the sonogram and confirmed twins. No one knows but you. Well, I guess Commander here."

Stalker whispered, "I guess I don't count. Twins, really?"

JAC smiled as she helped Juan onto his side and leaned him against her, then whispered, "Honey, can we discuss this later?"

As the faint light from the dawning sky revealed Juan, he winked at her and vowed, "Oh, I promise we will."

CHAPTER 57

CAUGHT IN A COMPLEX LABYRINTH WITHOUT THE KEY

Carlos still had trouble sleeping at night. The two heavy fight incidents with all the injuries he had sustained, plus the pain medication, gave him fitful sleep when he did drift off. This night's sleep wasn't any better than the last few weeks, but tonight something else seemed wrong. Carlos woke with a start just before his cell phone chirped that it had received a SMS message. He didn't reach for the phone right away because in the faint night light of his room he could just barely make out someone sitting in the chair across from the bed, staring at him.

The imagery of running with the desert specters flashed through his mind, and he had to fight against being seized by fear. He resisted the urge to call out to the penetrating eyes that looked at him with such malevolence. The figure moved ever so slightly. Then he noticed the glint of a gun barrel pointed at him.

Finally after several seconds of staring into the dark, the mouth that went with the eyes spoke to Carlos angrily, "I see that you don't sleep very well after your personal combat episodes. To think I was actually worried about your well-being for a brief time. I will never let those feelings loose again, particularly for someone as treacherous as you, Dakota! Or whoever the hell you are!"

Somewhat rattled, Carlos managed to respond, "Zara, how nice of you to check in on me. Does this mean I get breakfast in bed, too? I've had a craving for waffles here of late."

Zara mused out loud, "I was so close! So close to having everything that I worked so hard for! No more taking orders from a male. No more bowing and scraping to their paid-for delights. This go-round maybe even a worthy male that actually could have been my prince! You cost me everything!"

Carlos realized that his cover was blown, and Zara was here to kill him. He glanced down at the cell phone again when the second SMS text message arrived. The message was the same as the first message:

> *Run Dakota!*

Carlos tried to buy some time to see if he could find a way to get out of this jam. He demanded, "What did you do with my brother? You know, the one whose plane you sabotaged with the ghost code crap of yours!"

Zara smiled faintly and replied, "Why I didn't do anything with him. We delivered the code into his aircraft and simply walked away. My payment terms were very specifically to deliver and not look back or ask questions. My paydays were built by following instructions from Mephisto. I almost had him believing that it was his programmer that screwed up the last product launch, until I got a phone call that changed everything."

Carlos was now hyper-alert and looked around for anything that could help his situation as he goaded, "Well, I'm pretty sure it wasn't a call telling you that you won big in the lottery."

Zara stated, "Actually, it was a call that told me we had hit it big time. Dante conned a ward orderly to let him use a phone to call me.

"Say what you want about him, but his social engineering skills are still extraordinary. There he is, trapped in a hospital mental ward, and his only thought is to call and warn me about you rifling my personal computer. The one I use to deliver all the payloads, but now mysteriously doesn't do that anymore. What is even worse is that Mephisto found a bunch of fragmented code on my machine that makes it look like it was me hacking his code. You robbed me of my payday, you bastard!"

Carlos's cell phone started playing a cheery tune indicating that he had an incoming phone call. Carlos looked in Zara's direction.

Zara shook her head and indicated, "No, I don't want you to answer it. Let it roll to voice mail. I am busy enjoying my revenge, you bronze weasel."

Once the ringing subsided, the phone chirped one more time but showed a small connected indicator at the bottom that meant Carlos was on open mike. Carlos noticed the muted call monitoring, smiled and asked, "So, Zara, does this mean our date tonight is off? I mean, you seem pretty upset what with me asking if we could go Dutch treat and all."

Zara smirked a little and replied, "Yes, the date is canceled, because that is your fate as well. And since you robbed me of my payday and because you're male, guess where you get the first bullet? It will please me to see you suffer totally before I leave."

She raised the gun and leveled it between his legs as she whispered, "Say goodbye, Dakota!"

A heavy hand pounded on the door to the apartment at the same time that the cell phone started coughing. These two distractions were enough to allow a pillow to go sailing in Zara's direction and for Carlos to roll out of bed as Zara squeezed off two rounds into the mattress where he had been sitting. The door flew open, and through it came four of Commander's team members ready for a breaching assault in a hostile situation.

Unable to get a fix on her assailants coming at her from both directions, Zara put the gun in her mouth and pulled the trigger. She was dismayed when the German Lugar from World War II apparently jammed. Carlos and the Commander's team quickly had Zara on her stomach on the floor and soon had her nicely bound with heavy cable tie wraps.

Carlos was still breathing heavily when he grabbed up the cell phone and conveyed, "Thanks, guys, for saving my bacon again!"

He turned to the assault team lead and, as he shook her hand, said, "And a very large thank you to you as well, madam. Your timing is impeccable, but I'm afraid the mattress will never be the same."

Zara was now completely subdued but continued to swear at her captors in Russian and struggled to get free.

Carlos looked down at Zara and said, "Well, honey, I'm sorry about our date, but you're all tied up tonight."

Looking then at the assault team lead, Carlos quipped, "Cable tie wraps, not just for the computer room anymore."

Everyone grinned except Zara as the team removed her.

Carlos went into the bathroom and washed his face as he assessed his wounds. He felt a bit better but totally annoyed that he hadn't discovered the details of who Zara had sabotaged the plane for. He ran his fingers through his hair as he noticed the cell phone showed another text message was saved. He must have missed it while he was dealing with his visitors.

> *Carlos I found Juan. He is alive and we are headed to Bethesda Hospital. Meet us there. I will call when we land. JAC*

Suddenly Carlos had no pain as the elephant on his back had vanished.

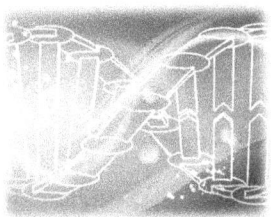

CHAPTER 58

AT TIMES IT IS NOT WORTH PUTTING THE PIECES BACK TOGETHER

Stalker slumped into the first chair at the small conference table at the far end of Eric's office. The receptionist had suggested he wait in the office as Eric was expected shortly. The office had no decorations outside of the normal government issued items equivalent to Eric's grade level. No family photos or other personal items were present which made the office fairly unremarkable with typical bulk purchased furniture. Stalker knew this chair he had chosen was resisted by most people as it was referred to as the hot seat, so it was the most comfortable.

He leaned back to wait for Eric and replayed the mission to China in his head. It had been a very surprising mission in many ways, as well as disconcerting to others. Eric would have to make some tough decisions. Stalker must have dozed slightly as Eric reached the table and sat in the chair next to him before he noticed. His years of training prevented him from flinching, but he knew that in other circumstances that lack of awareness could have killed him.

Eric looked at his friend, Jim Hughes, commonly known as Stalker, and sensed the man needed a vacation. Trying to insert some levity, he dryly asked, "Have you showered or changed at all since China? No wonder my assistant sent you inside to wait."

Stalker opened his eyes and replied, "Sure. I used the office showers and even had a change of clothes right after we landed. Then, of course, I spent an additional twenty hours questioning Arletta at the hospital. Along with everything those guards did trying to extract information, they also messed up her digestive system. She can't keep anything down. Okay, to be honest, I don't move as fast when I think I am in friendly territory like a hospital. I was a little slow and had no other clean clothes in my locker."

"Do you have any idea what information she gave to them? How far-reaching are her treasonous activities?"

"Eric, during her lucid moments, she admitted to giving them her codes and access sequences to the military base systems and some overrides. Her clearance level and codes fortunately do not extend to nuclear missiles or presidential security, or she would have provided those to these guys. Overall, fairly extensive acts of treason.

"Everything she ever had clearance for or access into has been scrubbed. I have the team reviewing every personal account she has ever used with a fine tooth comb to gather evidence."

"Have her parents been notified of her whereabouts or condition?"

"As we discussed, Eric," replied Stalker with annoyance, "no one outside of your little circle has been told. You said you wanted to deal with the information distribution, and believe me, it is all yours.

"You need to understand, Eric, Arletta is flat broken. She may have some moments of clarity, but I suspect they will be less and less over time."

"I believe you just confirmed that she shared confidential information outside of our government. To a country, by the way, that some folks see as not friendly to the interests of the United States. I think I need more details if you are suggesting she has few moments of clarity. That sounds like a mentally incompetent defense in the making, which, from this female, wouldn't surprise me in the least."

"Eric, I don't think so. When we pulled her from that camp, which I would have never found without your contractor, she remained fairly lucid up to an hour into the return flight. The injection that your contractor brought with her did the trick, but it didn't last. I questioned her during the boat ride down the

Yangzi as well as during the flight. Then she went into what I can only term a downward spiral.

"It was kind of sad, really. She switched between begging for mercy, wringing her hands and weeping, asking for some food then throwing it up, and calling for someone named Nikkei. It was frankly creepy because I think the Nikkei is a tiger that she rides away on into the sunset or some such nonsense.

"I spoke to the doctors at length as they plied her with various drugs. One of the doctors believed she was poisoned over time which is why her system is so dicey. They have decided to keep her on intravenous for several days while they flush her system. Her skin is sagging everywhere. I bet she has lost well over a hundred pounds, but not on the kind of diet we would recommend to anyone.

"At one point a few hours ago, she started screaming and crying about doing laundry and using what I think she referred to as a washboard. When one of the doctors heard this particular tirade, he said it explained her raw hands and perhaps why her hair was falling out from possibly a use of lye soaps. Heck, Eric, even her hair is falling out, and that was one of her few redeeming features."

"Wow, it does sound like she had a very hard time, Jim. That doesn't excuse the path she started down, only that the results were likely far more extreme than she envisioned. She has never been able to plan accurately, part of her many professional issues. Consider this my condolences look."

Eric's facial features moved not at all, until Stalker finally broke the silence with a chortle. Then they both started to laugh mindlessly at a situation that no one could have predicted. The entire affair had worn them down to the point of feeling like they were at the back of the movie theater watching someone else's life. They stopped laughing when the intercom on Eric's phone opened, and a sweet female voice announced the next appointment had arrived. They both immediately sobered up.

Eric loudly announced, "Give us ten more minutes, please. Thanks.

"What are your recommendations, Jim? Do we keep her on ice, tell her parents, or what?"

"Eric, I think for right now you do a court order to commit her for a six month physical and mental evaluation at our military facility here in Washington. Her parents can visit her."

"Okay, that makes sense. With the full evaluation over that period of time, the doctors can determine if she can stand trial. I will tell her Congressman father everything in the hopes that he won't pressure for her release, knowing that if he tries it we will arrest her for treason.

"Thanks for taking this mission on. I know it was not desired, but as usual you got results."

"No problem. It gave me a chance to meet a remarkable female and, I guess, field agent."

"Who was that?"

"Your contractor, the one called JAC."

"JAC is a female? Oh brother, does that explain some of the arm twisting when I requested help. But, why remarkable? You've worked with women before with no issues."

Stalker laughed as he explained with a touch of admiration, "Yeah, I have, and I have appreciated those that are great field agents. This one, however, is apparently having twins, so you might want to get a gift."

Eric's look of shock was priceless. Rarely had Stalker totally surprised Eric. He stood, with Eric not moving and not talking, and made his way to the door and opened it. Just before he closed it on his way out, he turned back and said, "Got you to look."

CHAPTER 59

LET'S CHANGE THE GAME TO 'ROLL OVER AND LIVE'

Juan's eyes fluttered a little, and he rolled his head to the left to find his brother Carlos gazing at him with a gratified smile on his face. Juan managed a weak smile by way of return. Juan seemed under-powered and pale in the hospital bed as he unsuccessfully tried a couple of times to sit up. Finally Carlos helped him to a more comfortable position.

After a few seconds, Carlos spoke in a cheery though greatly exaggerated gay manner, "So how was your day? Tell me about the vacation! Your tan looks so good. I'm so envious! My goodness you've lost weight! Tell me, what exercise and diet did you do to get that *to die for figure*, hmmm? Details, details! And the big question is, how is your romance going?"

Juan managed several chuckles before he groaned then said, "Alright! Stop it! That hurts! Don't make me laugh when I hurt!"

Carlos began to laugh but stopped short as he groaned, "Ow! That hurts too! I guess my ribs aren't any better than yours! Here we are, ready to tell jokes and do our best comedy routines but can't enjoy the other's mirthful pain because we are both on the mend! You'd think we were kids again who had just fallen out of our favorite climbing tree."

Juan studied Carlos for a few seconds and agreed, "You do look a little worse for wear too. In fact, it looks like you fell down six flights of stairs in a one story building. What is with the cane? And now that I think of it, where is Julie?"

Carlos replied, "I sent her home to get some rest. It is my watch now."

After a few minutes companionable silence while the pain lessened, Carlos softly added, "It is good to have you back, little brother. I am so pleased that you are all in one piece, with some animation to your being. Everyone connected with your Julie helped look for you. I understand that finding you was more luck than anything."

Juan grinned as he responded, "You remember what our Uncle Jesus used to always tell us, don't you? Never admit that luck had anything to do with it. Always maintain that it was superior skill and cunning that saw the day through! I wonder how that old bastard is doing these days."

Then in a sober moment, Carlos asked, "You feel like telling me about it? You were there over the air and then nothing…..not even goodbye. I can't speak for how the others felt, but you are all I have left of our core family, and, well, I would like closure to this story from your side.

"I have felt so hollow and alone these past weeks that…it would please me to just hear your voice, if you have the strength."

Juan nodded a little and with a pleased look on his face began, "I sure hope I never have to stare down that kind of mess again.

"As you may recall, I was talking to Julie with you and Lara conferenced in, riding an aircraft that was destined for the ocean, with my cell phone battery dying, too. I had just about given up and planned to say goodbye, when I noticed the on-board computer re-initializing. As it flickered to life, it displayed a message that is forever imprinted in my brain."

> *This concludes our test of the emergency broadcast system. Had this been a real emergency you would have been instructed where to tune in your area. We now return you to your regularly scheduled program.*

"You know, Carlos, it was the first time I was really scared. So frozen for a few seconds that I dropped the phone. I grabbed at the controls, thinking I could finally get the aircraft out of our jam, but nothing responded in the ailerons or the rudder. I mean nothing made any difference in my trajectory. Then something weird happened."

Carlos looked incredulously at Juan and asked, "You mean what had already happened wasn't weird enough? You're just now getting to the weird part?"

Juan, in all seriousness, replied, "Yeah, it got weird then. This voice crackled over the radio and asked if I could save the aircraft from auguring in. The voice said if I could beat the Mach Tuck destruct sequence, my reward would be all I could ever hope for."

Carlos looked ashen, still in disbelief, but interjected, "You're in a death ride heading for ground zero. You have no way to slow down or control the aircraft, and they want to play a game of *Have I got a deal for you*? Well, that's especially different and sweet of them too!"

Juan recalled his thoughts from that time and related, "Yeah, I know. But the bargaining chips seemed to all be in their favor, so times being what they were, I took the deal. Not, however, before insisting on upping the ante with some gum, candy, balloons, and party hats for all my friends. Uh.., they didn't find any of that when they rescued me, did they?"

Carlos winced a little as he chuckled but answered, "No, little brother, no party favors were located."

"Anyway, I recalled one time, from my flight training days, that we talked about defeating this Mach Tuck scenario by slowing the aircraft enough so that the ailerons would give you control again. So with the computers back up and hydraulics available, I overrode the main program and dropped the gear in midflight. You should know that the alarm sirens work perfectly when you do that.

"Boy, she wailed and bucked when the gear dropped. Well, it was just enough, and I mean barely enough, to regain some control of the aircraft, so I rolled her up on her back, and her nose went up to the moon from the air drag on the landing gear, and with gravity working in my favor, that did the trick. I slowed down enough that all surface controls now gave me full operational control. I put the gear back up and leveled out."

Carlos looked terribly puzzled as he questioned, "So the aircraft slowed enough, and you regained control but then...?"

Juan wrinkled his nose and replied, "Yeah, I know what you're thinking. Why didn't you just return to base and get a job as a cab driver or use the radio for contact to anyone.

"Well, it turned out that they needed me to save the plane. Soon as that was done, they took control of the aircraft and piloted it remotely to where they were waiting. When I got on the ground, they were ready for me. I was pretty mad and ready to wax these Asian dudes that greeted me, but I must have been darted or something because I never got to land a punch or rip out their larynxes. The next thing I knew, I was a long term guest of hotel house of horrors and pain-o-plenty day spa that had these characters that kept coming in asking me where my ticket was. When I said I didn't have one, they lowered the boom on me."

Juan sat looking like a man recovered from a bad dream with a dopey smile plastered on his face as he continued, "And then, there she was! She gave me great, non-prescription meds and demanded I get up and walk to the nearest exit.

"Did I ever tell you, Carlos, how much I love that lady?"

Carlos swallowed hard to lower his emotional tidal wave and said, "Now that you mention it, no. I'll bet it's a great sell to her when it's her watch again. Just my opinion, for what it's worth.

"You should also know that she was instrumental in helping me keep my bacon out of the fire while I hunted for you. Lara has my heart and will always be first, but I will tell you that I love your little lady almost as much as you do. I hope you plan to make her a real little sister to me.

"Why don't you rest a while now? There is much to do and see when we are both better. Agreed?"

Juan smiled as he responded with his eyes already closed, "Agreed. I think my romance will be fine when I ask her to marry me again."

A little misty eyed, Carlos said "I am so glad you're home. I was so worried that I would never see you again, Juan."

Grinning, Juan said, "Ahh, when you've seen Juan you've seen them all!"

They both chuckled while each man held their sore ribs.

CHAPTER 60

TRUST IS BEST WHEN IT IS DEEP AND WIDE

After several nights of solid rest, followed by a few days of other tests on the Ghost Obliteration Binary Solution, or GOBS program as he'd coined it, Jacob was ready with a utility version of the software. The team planned to provide this to a select group of targets while working toward the final destruction of the creator system. The back and forth discussion regarding using a utility program for targets was specifically on the off chance that some other time release program was present on a computer with an unknown location. Jacob had successfully argued it was far better to spend the time to create a utility to be safe rather than sorry.

The evening before, while the team had been relaxing after dinner, the call from Julie had put them all over the top. Her excitement and pleasure was palatable over the phone. Juan was located and alive. The unbelievable coincidence of finding Juan in Arletta's location made her forever grateful to Quip for sending her in to help locate Arletta. Quip's head swelled to the point that Wolfgang made snide comments about Quip safely exiting the library without his ears rubbing off on the door jam.

Juan had been rushed to a hospital in Bethesda for treatment and observation along with Arletta. Julie joked that Arletta would likely never be the same and also possibly imprisoned. Julie had explained she had left a text message for Carlos but expected him to be in Bethesda soon. Julie planned to remain with Juan until he was released. Julie asked Quip to please follow up with Andy to make certain that Carlos was successfully being tracked and that he was safe. Petra was asked to convey the information to Lara. It was all good. Jacob had picked up Petra after the call, spun her around the room, then kissed her so fast that they had made their excuses and raced off to bed for hours of making love.

Here he was working on the final tweaks for GOBS along with the encryption wrapper that Petra had built. The very sophisticated encryption key that would be used was delivered in three pieces through different delivery methods. Together they had a great product to deliver. Jacob enjoyed working with this team. He hadn't felt this good since, well, he couldn't remember when.

He reviewed the rehearsed story one more time to make sure he could convince John C that loading this code was totally necessary. There were some parts of the 'why' that he wouldn't share. Jacob knew their relationship was one of trust, but loading up financial systems with unknown code would take a huge leap of faith.

John C answered on the first ring, "Jacob, my man, how are you, lad? Still chasing ghosts, are ye?"

"Not any more, John C. Are you interested in getting the cure for the common wraith?"

"Of course I am, but I would enjoy the details that you have apparently gathered if you have a cure, as you say. I have continued, on and off, prying into various things but have discovered next to nothing."

"John C, as much as I would like to give you additional details, in this case that is just not possible. It is unlikely that any of the rest of your machines are currently infested. I believe there exists the possibility that the ghost code could still be there in a dormant state, waiting to be triggered. Therefore I would like to give you the utility that cures the common wraith or ghost. No charge. I personally would recommend you apply it to all systems in your institution, including smart devices and cell phones.

"Speaking of cell phones, how is your VP? Does he still have a job?"

John C chortled and said, "He has a job, but it is over the office workers and no longer the IT department. I was offered his job, but it is too constrictive to me. I did get to interview the new VP, and she is totally wonderful. We have a great relationship, and I have her ear, sometimes between my teeth."

Jacob laughed a bit and asked, "Really. So you're mixing it up with management now? I wouldn't have thought you would ever do that, but I guess for a pretty face you just might."

"No, not really, but I couldn't resist teasing you, lad. Does your utility come with any instructions, or is this a load and forget thing? I do need to document changes I make, just in case, though I have no problem backing your recommendations. You are fairly well known here, especially since you cavort with tattoo artists that do great work."

Jacob was surprised by the statement but responded, "The encryption key will be sent in three pieces, and the last one will include the sequence of use. The utility and the encryption key are loaded in order, and the rest just happens. The only trick is that you need to have a central machine that all the bank's devices can point to. All new devices deployed should have this loaded as part of the standard load. There will be no disruption to any other program at any time. Frankly, in the ten seconds it takes to load, it will disappear before you can see it. That is the part that might be unnerving, but I promise it will work now and if anything of the same sort arrives in the future. Long-term protection and no charge as you helped my team discuss how to defeat it. Yours was not the only system infected."

"Alright, Jacob-lad, I will do as you ask so send along all the pieces. I will try it on my laptop for three days and then roll it out if I have no incident. Fair enough?"

"More than fair," agreed Jacob. "Now what about this tattoo stuff? Did you get one that you can live with?"

John C explained, "I did and I get requested to show it off all the time. It is a castle scene with soldiers in the turrets and a dragon in the mote. The colors are beautiful. Your friend, Gentleman Josh, couldn't finish it while he was here, but we agreed to hook up in the States in a month or two and finish it.

"How about you, did you ask your lady for permission and perhaps get her interested in exploring one herself?"

Jacob replied with a grin, "I didn't even remember to do that since we've been so busy, but I will tonight. Thank you for the reminder. I will let you know what we decide.

"I am sending all the parts, of which there are three. The final one will be via express delivery with your signature required. Thanks, John C, and call me if there are any issues."

"Will do, cheers!"

Jacob asked Quip, "Any idea why ICABOD postulated the future threat from dormant ghost code? I mean, I didn't make the request from it."

Quip seemed a little unsettled and said, "Yes, it was odd. Just out of the blue he started sending me these little snippets that seem to have no basis in a standard request. After things settle down a little bit, I need to run some diagnostics on ICABOD and just groom him programmatically. We have been pushing him a lot and having him access more data sources all the time, so he probably needs a health check. I better make myself a note now in my calendar……that's funny, there is already a meeting minder in there for that activity that has been there for two days. I must have put it there absentmindedly while talking on the phone to EZ."

Quip grinned at Jacob and said, "Come on, lad, let's go to dinner where you can regale me of my recent exploits!"

Jacob looked at Quip with some disdain and said, "You mean you're not tired of hearing how you catch bullets with your teeth or leap moderate buildings with a great deal of effort?"

Quip grinned and suggested, "Tell me more about my admirable qualities!"

CHAPTER 61

FEMALES ARE A FAVORED DELIVERY METHOD FOR RAPID INFORMATION SPREADING

Petra danced into the operations center totally ecstatic. Not only did Julie get her man, quite literally, but Petra found herself more in love with Jacob than ever. After they delivered the code, she wanted to insist that they take a vacation. Petra wanted to show Jacob the lovely winery she had visited and just relax. Perhaps, if they combined the last delivery of the GOBS along with the visit, that would work.

Julie had called and talked for a good thirty minutes after arriving at the hospital in the United States. She sounded deliriously happy and indicated that she had checked out fine by the doctors there. Commander had insisted she be checked out after the extended trip. Julie had confided that she was having twins and apologized at not sharing sooner as she wanted to keep the news for Juan as long as possible.

Petra was requested not to share the information with anyone yet, outside of Jacob. Julie indicated her weight gain was still modest, and the doctor said it was all babies and no excess weight to speak of. Clothing was becoming a problem though, so Julie agreed that, yes, Lara could also be told, but only if she could provide stylish maternity clothes and ship them over. They had discussed the maternity line during the shoot in Jamaica, so it was not an outlandish request.

Petra had called Lara and updated her on all the news. When she learned that Carlos had been informed, her relief was quite palatable even over the phone. Lara laughed at the request of clothes for Julie and indicated the first sample clothes were in fact ready. Petra provided the address of the hotel adjacent to the hospital where Julie had a room. Lara was so relieved for all of them that she had gone on and on. Petra suggested that Lara call Julie later in the day to get additional information first hand. Julie would undoubtedly be happy to hear from Lara and even provide some additional details. Petra had confirmed that no future plans were to be discussed until Juan was released from the hospital. Until then, they agreed to share all the information they each learned from their conversations with Julie and talk more frequently.

Petra then called Thiago and explained to him what had been discovered. She provided some recommendations that would apply to the hydroelectric plant she had visited as well as some other plants in the region. Thiago basically gave her the green light to do as she deemed best for the hydroelectric plants, and he would make certain the right funding arms were available to each of the plants in the region. Thiago indicated if she had any issues with Javier to make certain to let him know.

Petra reviewed the details of how the utility and encryption key were to be sent. Though she and Jacob had walked through it, she wanted to be certain she conveyed it correctly to the weasel Javier. Ideally, he would allow her remote access to the primary machine, and it could be distributed from there. She shuddered with the memory of his slimy demeanor, but then he was far, far away from her. She closed her eyes and dialed his number.

"Hello?"

The voice that answered did not equate to Javier, so she formally responded, "My name is Petra Rancowski. Who is this, please?"

"Hi, Petra, this is Pavan. How nice to hear from you. To what do I owe the pleasure of your call, madam?"

"Pavan, I am so sorry. I meant to call your supervisor. I must have mixed up the phone numbers in my notes."

Pavan's voice was happy as he declared, "No, you didn't. This was and is the supervisor's phone number. I am now the supervisor. Thanks to your visit and a few other items, it was decided that I was more suited to run the plant than Javier. I have been training someone for my former role."

Petra smiled at what would undoubtedly now be far easier than she expected as she relayed, "My congratulations, young man. I am sure you are ready for such large responsibilities. I liked the ideas you had when we visited, which brings me to what I wanted to accomplish with this call.

"I have some formal recommendations that I would like to send to you, along with some safeguard programs I would like your permission to install on your primary system. Do you have some time to discuss now, or should I call back at a better time?"

Pavan said, "Now is quite good. I am certain whatever you suggest will align with the changes I have been making and proposing."

Petra grinned then suggested, "I am quite certain many of our thoughts will overlap. Let's get started, shall we?"

Petra was provided with temporary secured access to their main system. She connected, while he observed from his side, and applied GOBS in total. It was so fast even she was surprised. She then went through each of the items that were included in her written report. As a reminder, she told Pavan that the energy board would be receiving a copy, and she had already gained approval from one of the high ranking officials.

Together they observed the auto download of GOBS to two other devices. Petra explained how all new devices, including laptops and smart phones, should be connected to the main server, and she gave him the commands to use for the download to be completed. She explained that it needed to be a part of the long term procedures.

"Petra, I must say that what you suggest is totally awesome. It is the most secure approach I have seen. I thought I was thorough, but apparently I have a lot more to learn."

"Pavan, we can all learn, and technology changes so quickly we all need to keep an open mind. You will do fine, Mr. Supervisor."

"Petra, do you think if I put into my plan a semi-annual review by your firm that it would be accepted? I mean, you are a legitimate security organization, right?"

Petra chuckled at the thought that all of this had now resulted in new business for the team, as she affirmed, "Yes, Pavan, the R-Group can perform these types of reviews as we do for many organizations all over the world. We can also, if needed, bring our credentials to your board of directors. With a regional utility such as yours, it may be necessary. We only ask that our clients keep our information confidential. We don't require customer references, so we don't have a marketing team that will pester your organization. No blogging or tweeting us though, agreed?"

Pavan laughed uproariously and finally, when he regained his breath, replied, "No problem, I enjoy not getting bothered by those dialing-for-dollars-callers."

"Then I suspect we will be in touch now and again, Pavan. I wish you the very best as your career broadens, sir."

"Thank you, Petra. Have a nice day!"

Petra smiled as she disconnected. Quip would be pleased with a new client.

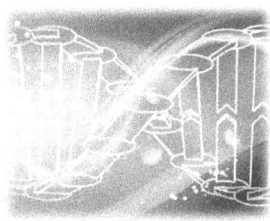

CHAPTER 62

I CAN'T TELL WHAT YOU'VE DONE, SO CAN YOU TELL ME WHAT I'M GOING TO DO?

Eric answered the phone, "Okay, Quip, what is it this time?"

Quip feigned a hurt look as he responded, "Eric, I fear our relationship has deteriorated into us being an old married couple constantly agitating each other as a form of entertainment! Can't I call to discuss our successes without your suspicions of my motivation? I know you are in the lack-of-trust business, but surely we could exchange a few more pleasantries before getting down to business."

Eric agreed, "I suppose you've got a point. Just a lot going on. How are you doing, Quip?"

Quip chuckled and said, "Now see, wasn't that easy? As a matter of interest, I wasn't calling to ask for anything. I wanted to show you how good it is to be working together with your team, by helping you disarm the untidy set of circumstances left open by the data system breach that occurred at your NATO base in Germany."

Eric stared intently and, with an agitated edge to his voice, questioned, "So your sources picked up on that event as well, huh? If you are calling to gloat about it, I can't comment, and if you are calling to offer help, the case is closed."

Quip continued, "Yes, we heard about it. For the record, I am not calling to gloat. I was calling to help you do something about it."

Eric thought for a second and then asked, "Are you calling about that encrypted email you sent that talks about a program called GOBS? Frankly, I haven't looked at it yet because the name sounded so bogus that I thought it was another one of your gags. Right now I am too busy to waste time with gags."

Quip was stunned with the revelation that the GOBS information had already been sent and that it had been done with his encrypted email process that no one else knew or used. After trying to make sense of the event for a few seconds, Quip finally innocently asked, "Uh, you mean you haven't looked at it yet? So how long have you looked past it without being interested in the contents? You could have called for clarification, you know. We are all busy, and not hearing from you caused me to stop to follow-up."

Eric relented, "It's only been a day, and so would you mind telling me what the damn thing is and what this is all about? You almost act like you don't know when you sent it to me. I mean, without a phone call to discuss your intentions, for all I know it's a computer virus in your encrypted wrapper."

Quip was trying to hide being flustered as he continued, "I wanted to get this computer virus cure called GOBS out to all the known targets of the ghost code for their defensive protection. I wanted to try my hand at being proactive.

"I am sorry I didn't call you right away to give a more formal explanation, but I expected you to call me. We have a lot going on here, not the least of which is the return of a missing person who was among the first to get whacked by the damn ghost code! So let me make my intentions clear on this topic. This GOBS ghost code killer does exactly what I just called it; it kills the ghost code and I, representing the R-Group, want to make it available to you as a thank you for our recent interactions.

"You told me once to give you something you needed first and then make follow-on requests for favors after the fact. As it turns out, we don't have any requests at this time to make, Eric. Please carefully read the installation instructions and have your computer security folks enjoy the fruits of our labors being delivered because of our long standing relationship, kind sir."

Eric, now quite chastened, apologized, "I'm sorry, Quip, to have been so unmindful of the gift and so cynical about your intentions. Yes, I do need closure on the data center breach, and now that I know this is a legitimate offer of something we really do need, I wish to apologize for discounting your organization's generosity. Thank you, Quip. I will get this code into my people's hands as soon as I hang up here."

Before Eric could disconnect, Quip said, "Actually, Eric, there is one thing you could do for us. That corporate jet that you seized from the Asian twins, Won and Ton: may we have it, please? It belongs to one of our customers out of Brazil and was captured in one of the other ghost code events. I would like to get it returned to the rightful owners."

Eric sat and looked quizzically into space for a few seconds, then thoughtfully replied, "Quip, per your email instructions, we had it delivered to Lara Bernardes, owner of Destiny Fashions of Brazil, last week. It was an easy transaction since they had their people come get it, and all we had to do was release it to them. Don't tell me you forgot that email as well? Now should I be concerned for your health? Perhaps you should follow Otto's example and take some time off."

Quip took a deep breath and calmly replied, "As I indicated, a lot has been going on here of late. Best wishes, Eric. Speak to you soon."

Quip walked over to the audio/visual terminal that he always used when working with ICABOD and began running some extensive diagnostics. The results were good.

Quip verbalized, "ICABOD, I appreciate your attention to detail in all matters. I need you to at least copy me on my own emails so I know what has been overlooked. If you do something that I don't know about or initiate an action that didn't come from me, it makes it appear that I'm either absentminded or incompetent. I'd rather not give anyone that impression, ever. Understood? I mean, you're getting better at being me than me!"

The printed response was displayed in the 3-D monitor and showed, "Acknowledged and understood, Dr. Quip. Your instructions are to leave no loose ends in the R-group activities. Is there further dissatisfaction with this computer's performance?"

Quip, now a little chastened, replied, "I am not dissatisfied with your performance, but sometimes even I am amazed. Thank you, ICABOD."

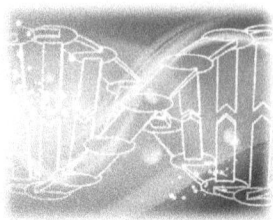

CHAPTER 63

LIFE IS TRULY A MERRY-GO-ROUND THAT SOMETIMES STOPS IN STRANGE PLACES

Julie and Carlos had taken Juan by car to the company apartment in New York City where she had stayed while tracking Carlos. Though Juan had been released, he was to maintain a minimum activity level for a few weeks as he slowly regained his strength. He was also limited on flying, especially for any overseas trips until the doctor released him. Carlos planned to stay in the apartment to help out with Juan's therapy and to be reassured that Juan was alive and well. Carlos had alerted Lara and invited her to join him for a few days, which had put her on a commercial flight due to arrive later in the day.

Juan's attitude was great. As he slept less, his bantering with both Julie and Carlos increased. After a mere three days out of the hospital, it looked as if recovery was eminent. The day before, Juan and Carlos had actually taken a walk outside for several hours. After a nice supper, which Julie had prepared in the well-appointed kitchen, Juan had laughed at a few jokes, told a few stories and retired early. Julie had cleaned up from their meal and gone to bed, hoping to find Juan awake, but he hadn't moved.

Though Juan was attentive to Julie and held her a lot, he avoided any sort of lovemaking, which was really beginning to worry her. Their physical relationship had always been exciting, voracious, and typically without restraint by either of them. Now, however, Juan made no overt moves toward her and even avoided her moves in that direction. Julie had awakened early and motionlessly watched Juan sleeping. He hadn't had any nightmares or sleeplessness, but he also hadn't seemed to even want to make love to her. She had decided he simply didn't want her or the babies any more. Two babies were more than he'd bargained for, she'd concluded, as the tears leaked from her eyes as she squeezed them shut.

Juan peeled open one eye and observed the tears and pulled her close as he asked, "Sweetheart, what is the matter? Why are you crying?"

Her eyes remained closed as she whispered, "I'm just sad 'cause you don't want me anymore."

Juan was totally surprised by this response and gathered her even closer as he reached toward her slightly rounded abdomen and stated with conviction, "Of course I want you. I love you, Julie. Thoughts of you kept me alive. That, and thoughts of our baby, were what I held onto. Please tell me I can stay."

"You can stay if you want to, but you don't have to just because of the babies. I have no right to tie you down. This was all unplanned."

"True enough. It is an unplanned miracle that I more than want to stay and enjoy. Why are you going down this path and being so sad, sweetheart?"

Julie held her breath while she gathered her courage then replied, "Juan honey, you obviously don't really feel that way. We have been together for three days, going on four, and you are obviously feeling much improved. And…"

Juan was desperately confused as he searched to discover how this was his fault as he quietly waited for her to finish. When he couldn't stand it any longer, he prompted, "And what, honey."

"And you don't want to make love to me. Every single time I have tried to approach you to kiss you or stroke your skin you have countered, avoided, or walked away. I knew I was getting fat, but I am doing all the exercises the doctor allows at this point. I am not gaining a lot of weight, things are just shifting."

Juan looked Julie in the eyes and solemnly replied, "Sweetheart, since the moment I woke up in the hospital, I have wanted to make love to you, repeatedly too. I asked my doctor, and he suggested that with having twins and the angst of being separated, it might hurt you or the babies and to just wait until I could go with you to see your doctor and ask him. Frankly, the waiting for your doctor appointment is really frustrating me."

Julie pushed him over in one swift move, moved on top of him and announced, "Oh heck, what a lot of time we've wasted."

She kissed him with such passion that his body had no choice but to respond. All the pent up emotions and passions burst around them as they touched and tasted each other. Their hands stroked and explored all the places they had missed. Juan was careful but moved her to the bottom as he tasted her mouth and continued to move down tasting everything on the delightful journey. As he touched and licked her most feminine area, she exploded into a release that reminded him how much he loved to please her. Her body responded in rapid succession to two additional releases until she begged him to enter her.

Time ceased as he continued to stroke in and out in their love dance. He continued long past his normal endurance as he simply wanted to continue to feel her hot moist sleeve that grew tighter and tighter around him. She pulled him in close and then closer with each subsequent stroke. He found himself losing control until he finally released at the same time she climaxed yet again. He pulled her near as he rolled them to the side, and they breathed in unison. As they slowly recovered, time seemed to start up as more color was visible in the room and sounds waffled through the walls. Carlos was up and fixing coffee and, with any luck, breakfast.

Juan asked, after they shifted the pillows and Julie nestled onto his shoulder, "So that seems to have answered a lot of both our questions. As long as you are feeling good and that responsive, I will make love to you all day long if you want. I missed you and I want you."

"Back at you, honey. I want you to want me and be happy about bringing two new lives into the world."

"Sweetheart, I am so delighted that we are having twins, I can't explain the depth of my feelings." Juan reached over the side of the bed without letting go of her and then backed up.

"Honey, are you okay? Am I squishing your shoulder?" Julie asked.

"I am just fine. You aren't and probably couldn't crush me even at full term. However, if you will open your eyes and say you will marry me, I would be the happiest man in the world."

Julie jerked up into a sitting position as she looked at Juan in utter astonishment. Then she caught sight of the glittering object in his fingers. A combination of diamonds and sapphires in a gold setting with woven golden leaves seemed to wink at her. She blinked several times as she inhaled. Juan, not one for halfway measures, reached for her left hand and slipped the beautiful ring onto her finger and smiled, as he had just won the race of a lifetime.

"Julie, marry me and make an honest man of me. Please, will you say yes?"

Julie glanced at the ring and looked at Juan and threw her arms around him as she repeated, "Yes, yes, yes!"

Then she kissed him again and begged for more. Juan found several ways to please his Julie, and she returned the passion in equal measure. After extended lovemaking and a short nap, she woke up suddenly ravenous.

"I'm up for a shower and then some breakfast. Care to join me?"

Juan smiled as he replied, "Of course. Then we will start telling the world. I want to get married as quickly as possible. We have wasted too much time already."

After they showered and dressed, breakfast was served by Carlos who obviously knew of his brother's intentions. They had ventured out to the jewelry store together when Juan had selected the ring. Juan even offered to let her change the ring for something better, but her megawatt smile revealed that would not be the case. Carlos hugged her and told her that now she would really be his sister as he congratulated them both.

Julie called everyone in the family to alert them that they were now on detonation for a rapid wedding, the where to be determined. Petra, Eilla-Zan, Haddy, and, she hoped, Lara, when Lara landed in New York later today, would help with the wedding plans. Haddy had promised that she would do the bridal shower in New York on Sunday and wouldn't take no for an answer. Julie laughed and cried at the support she received.

Later Julie picked up Lara at the airport while Carlos and Juan went to the Mexican Embassy to check on the marriage license requirements.

Juan wanted to move forward quickly but wanted the legalities understood, especially if they married in the United States. Once Haddy arrived, Juan felt certain that the mother of the bride would set him straight on all the details, and he would nod his head. Julie had laughed when they had discussed it, but as he had not met her parents he suspected the worst. No matter what, he would marry Julie and soon.

After they completed their respective chores, they planned to meet at a lovely Italian restaurant to celebrate. Carlos wanted to see Lara and wanted to make it a memorable dinner as he had some private celebration planned with his love.

CHAPTER 64

DEMONSTRATING A GREAT SENSE OF HUMOR MEANS APPRECIATING THE JOKE PLAYED ON YOU ...
THE ENIGMA CHRONICLES

Professor Lin and Major Guano rushed anxiously to greet Chairman Chang as he entered the facility. Before they even sat down at the conference table, they both talked at once, trying to describe the events prior to Chairman's arrival. Chairman calmly selected a comfortable chair in the conference room and waved his hand to stop their verbal ramblings and apologies.

Finally after a few seconds of quiet, Chairman smiled and said, "Let me tell you a story, gentlemen. It is a tale told with a purpose that contains an important lesson at the end.

"One of my associates no longer has the ability to speak based on his lack of good judgment while transporting my white tiger, Nikkei. He had the bad manners to aggravate the animal and then range too close to her cage, while sticking his tongue out to show his defiance and contempt for the caged animal. Nikkei's big, powerful and quick paw shot out between the bars to rake her antagonist. As she did so, the trip claw on the tiger's paw hooked itself deep into my associate's tongue, which was torn from its normal resting place. The animal continued to draw down its large paw until finishing the mauling.

"We assumed that the animal consumed the fresh meat since there was no trace of it after he was bandaged up. You should know, by way of this story, that a tradition was established that anyone caught lying or distorting the truth, in an effort to deceive me, gets their tongue fed to Nikkei. My feeling is, if you can't speak wisely then Nikkei gets what has become a favorite delicacy of hers.

"Now thorough incompetence or out-and-out sabotage will earn the individual a rebranding of their chosen vocation into a new play toy for Nikkei. This involves being tied up and suspended upside down in Nikkei's cage with lots of little dingle bells attached, so when she bats her new toy around, it will make lots of jingly sounds, thus improving her enjoyment. My observation has been that felines can bat a new toy around for hours."

Chairman continued after a few moments of silence to let the story's significance sink in and then said, "But enough of these quaint stories, gentlemen. I am really here to listen to what has happened to my important project and why it is now hopelessly crippled. So given my preference for the truth and accuracy in our discussions, would you please tell me, in your own words, what happened? I recommend you start at the beginning."

Perspiring and breathing hard, Professor Lin and Major Guano both swallowed, but it was the Major who spoke first and said, "Chairman, after your call I raced over to the facilities to retrace my steps, looking for any irregularities in the process. Things appeared to be back to normal after the outage earlier this week, but some activities were still in process for some of the lesser technical appliances. I could not find anything wrong with our handover or delivery process since Professor Lin always pushes the package to the terminal. The wrappers are sealed with it in a compressed and encrypted file. The file is then loaded onto a portable Terabit drive for transport to the drop off point. It is as it has been the same for all the packages, Chairman Chang."

After a brief period of silence, all eyes leveled on Professor Lin, who nervously confirmed, "It is just as the Major stated. The supercomputer, IQ 5678, takes the input parameters as designated for the intended target and builds the package. It is then pushed to the transfer terminal where final processing is completed. No deviation to the process has been introduced anywhere. Since Arletta's departure, it has only been myself and Major Guano handling the process."

Chairman tilted his head to one side and, with a thoughtful look, asked, "Outage? What outage?"

Professor Lin again nervously replied, "We had a power outage earlier in the week that lasted for several hours. We were frantically trying to properly close down all servers, appliances, and of course the IQ 5678 before the battery backups were exhausted."

Chairman Chang, now puzzled, reasoned, "The battery backups are only good for twenty minutes, but that is more than enough time for the diesel generators to kick in. They are designed to run the whole facility. Did they not function as expected?"

Now trying to compensate for a dry mouth from excessive swallowing, Professor Lin hesitatingly explained, "The diesel generators had no fuel in the tanks due to misplaced paperwork requesting that a tanker of diesel be sent to the facilities. The ministry of energy clerk thought the request was in error since this was a computer facility, not a truck stop. The error was only uncovered after the diesel generators would not fire up and come on-line. That situation is still not resolved."

Chairman was now irritated by the oversight but then asked, "And what do you mean the power went out? This facility was built at great expense. I might also add that there are no less than six, count them six, power feeds coming into all areas of the building to defeat just such a problem so as not to have a single point of failure! How is it possible that all six power feeds got knocked out at once?"

As Professor Lin was unable to speak any longer, Major Guano continued, "Chairman, what has been discovered is that all six different power feeds came through one power switching station which was affected by a computer malfunction. Instead of power being evenly distributed to its area of grid responsibilities, it simply did nothing for five hours. It had to be reloaded from scratch and reprogrammed since its backups were, in fact, one backup. All the backups had been copied to the same tape library since the station was brought on-line which ruined the media. I believe they call it *'Denial of Electrical Service Keeping Important Machinery Offline'* or DESKIMO, if you will."

After he retrieved some water for his parched condition, the Professor rejoined the conversation as he explained, "Once the power came back on, I began the initial program load on IQ 5678 so it could load the operating system and all of its device drivers. However, with every computer device in the data center doing the same thing, we had wide power fluctuations, and some equipment had to be rebooted several times before it correctly initialized. I actually had to restart IQ 5678 twice before it came back on-line. We still have some peripheral equipment that has been unable to come back up yet.

"I noticed that the supercomputer began to behave sluggishly and even peculiarly during the boot sequence, but I assumed that it was because of all the power demands on the data center. I raced to input all the parameters for the last package and finally was able to push the code to the edge terminal."

Guano then offered, "I knew we were running behind schedule, so we got a little wireless hub to connect my PC so we could transfer your package directly to the pickup point rather than use the Terabit drive to transport to another location."

Barely able to control his anger and his flaring nostrils, Chairman admonished, "You hooked up a wireless hub router to the gateway machine? Is that what I'm hearing? You hooked up a gateway hub to our carefully isolated supercomputer so it could transmit faster outbound! Oh, and by the way, take incoming traffic, as well? Is that what you two did?"

While the professor cowered, the Major stiffened as he defended, "No, sir! We did not connect the edge terminal to the wireless device. We have always shuttled files back and forth using the Terabit drive. We merely used the Terabit drive to move files from and to the edge terminal."

Chairman calmed down a little after the statement but insisted, "Show me the terminal process. Build a new package now and walk me through it so I can see how this is supposed to flow."

Guano and Lin collided with each other trying to get out to do the Chairman's bidding. Chairman had to supervise them so the Professor worked the terminal and the Major shuttled the Terabit drive to demonstrate the process. The Professor launched the package sequence, and almost immediately they were all confronted with an unfriendly screen greeting and a question posed:

> *Do you know the definition of insanity?*
> *The answer is, doing the same thing over and over again expecting different results.*
> *The point of this message is to tell you that there will be no different results, other than this one, for this poisonous code you constructed.*
> *Ghost Code-Patent denied.*

Professor Lin and the Major both turned white as a ghost at the sight of the message, and the professor would have passed out if he hadn't already been sitting down. Chairman sat and stared blankly at the screen, watching as it cleared itself back to a data entry screen.

After a few seconds of uncomfortable silence, Chairman calmly asked, "You both understand what has happened, don't you?"

They both looked at the Chairman with terror in their eyes, but neither could speak.

Chairman rocked his head to one side as he continued, "They knocked down the power feeding into the data center with an excellent computer hack on a key power switching station. Then they primed a data center breaching exercise timed to hit a system just as it is coming up and on-line, which is also when any system is most vulnerable. They must have surmised that since the system was 'air-gapped' from the Internet there would be no firewall or Intrusion Protection appliance standing guard. All they needed was someone or something to move their attack code to the IQ 5678 supercomputer, and the Terabit drive was cleverly used as the transport mechanism."

The calm quiet demeanor of the Chairman had both the professor and the major reeling from anxiety attacks of what they believed was going to happen to them. Major Guano imagined he heard dingle balls jingling and snapped his head around to look, based on the Chairman's earlier story. The Professor was hyperventilating.

Chairman lamented, "So the IQ 5678 was attacked and obviously infected at exactly the right time in the Initial Program Load. Based on the message we have just seen, we can reasonably assume that the supercomputer is thoroughly compromised."

Chairman then studied both men, who were close to collapse emotionally and psychologically, but thoughtfully said, "You both know I absolutely hate being bested, but I have to admit to a small amount of admiration for the computer magicians who simply out-thought all of our careful preparations and planning. So, gentlemen, how long to restore IQ 5678 from backup? We may have to go back a ways to find a clean environment which means there will be some lost work, but we should be able to clean the parasite out and resume our project."

Fresh terror gripped the two as they look horrified at each other and then turned back to the Chairman. Only Major Guano showed any courage as he said, "Uh, Chairman, one of the systems that cannot be brought back up and on-line is the backup tape libraries. The preliminary reports are whatever destroyed the tape backups at the power relay station were also leveled at the internal systems here. There are no backups. There is no telemetry to restore from. What we are looking at is starting from scratch after we re-format all the drives with a destructive cleansing process."

The silence lasted so long that both men are about to soil their britches when the Chairman started to chuckle. They both looked at each other in wonderment as the chuckle turned into howls of laughter. The two men stared incredulously at Chairman as he rose and continued to laugh as he walked out of the building.

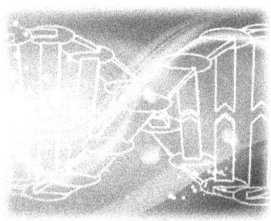

CHAPTER 65

LITTLE GIRLS GROW UP INTO LOVELY LADIES, BUT THEY STILL GIGGLE

Haddy and Petra arrived in New York on Wednesday morning and were met outside of the airport security by Julie and Lara. After the luggage was retrieved and stored in the rented limo, the ladies were taken to the other New York airport where they waited for Eilla-Zan's flight to land. Julie looked so pretty and happy, exactly like a bride-to-be should look. The conversation covered everything from the upcoming shower, the possible dates for the wedding, Juan's current health and travel limitations and everything in between.

EZ strutted through the security doors into the baggage claim area with Su Lin, who was essentially a ward of Andrew, EZ's father. The squeals of recognition and delight raised the eyebrows of airport security. They looked as if they would step into the fray until they realized this was not a security breach in the making.

EZ identified three bags that were collected from the conveyer belt, then these were loaded into the limo by the driver. Haddy had insisted on hotel rooms for EZ, Su Lin, Petra, and herself so as not to crowd the two couples in the corporate apartment.

After they checked in and arranged for the bags to be delivered to their rooms, they all decided a late lunch and discussion were needed. The hotel offered a lovely area that could easily accommodate the six of them. After the drinks and appetizers arrived, Haddy started the conversation regarding the shower.

"Julie, I have arranged for a delightful shower for Sunday. I am so excited that I fear I have gone way overboard, but, my darling daughter, you are so worth it."

"Mom, I am just so happy with getting Juan back, that anything you and the others decide is okay with me. I really appreciate all of you coming here for the celebration. Juan will only be able to fly for short hops, and that sadly doesn't include any transatlantic by air right now.

"I cannot wait for you all to see him when we get to dinner later tonight. He looks so wonderful, and you can hardly tell that he had such a horrible experience. He is gaining back his strength rapidly, and Carlos has been working with him as well since I can't spar right now."

Petra smiled and asked, "How are the babies doing? I was so surprised when you said that twins had been confirmed. I am so excited. Now I get to spoil two at once. Do you know their gender yet?"

Julie flashed her trademark smile and excitedly replied, "I am getting one of each. At least that is what the sonogram indicated. The doctor warned me that it was still early, and though this technology is good, we could be fooled. He has scheduled another sonogram a month before target delivery to see if there are any issues. With all of that, it is just monthly appointments unless I have issues. I found a great doctor here, Dr. Monahan, who has also collaborated with Dr. Charles back home. Things are wonderful."

EZ added, "Of course things are wonderful. You have the man and the family on the way. Now we just have to have a wedding. Su Lin is very excited to see the wedding."

EZ had brought Su Lin on this trip as a way to see how she reacted in different situations as well as to give her father a bit of a break. Su Lin was still recovering from destroying part of her cognitive skills with the ingestion of a program she designed using nanotechnology with a built-in kill switch, known as the grasshopper-loop. Jacob had stopped it, but not before the program had shut down her heart and limited the blood flow to the brain.

Since the incident had taken place at his ranch in Georgia, Andrew, EZ's father, had felt responsible, and he had made Su Lin his ward to take care of her and help retrain her on everything she'd lost. EZ thought her father fancied himself a bit in love with Su Lin.

Su Lin shyly responded, "I am excited for you, Miss Julie. I hadn't realized you were having babies too. How very nice. I am glad you feel well. May I help babysit for you sometime?"

Julie warmly replied, "Su Lin, you make such a sweet offer. I think you could help me anytime with the babies. Thank you."

Lara asked, "Julie, when is the wedding and where? Also, I wanted you to know I brought a surprise, but I think I will save it for your shower on Sunday."

"Lara, you are such a tease. And to think I helped you out on your Jamaica shoot. Speaking of that, it reminded me. Do you think your photographer, Manuel Sanchez, would consider coming and doing the wedding photos?"

"I know he'd be delighted to do anything for you. He looked so sad when I told him you were getting married. Then he grinned and said to wish you well. I believe the man is somewhat in love with you."

Julie blushed and replied, "He is a terrific guy that just needs to find the right lady. Oh good, Mom, we have the photographer taken care of."

Petra asked, "If you don't know where you want to have the wedding, can I offer up a suggestion?"

Julie said, "Sure, I would really like to avoid New York as a venue. Petra, I do recall that you told me you and Jacob had spent some time around Long Island, and it is very lovely, at least from what I saw on-line."

"Long Island is lovely, but I don't think I could recommend a specific place. I would like you to consider a really beautiful place in Texas at a winery I recently did some work for. The people are delightful, the venue is breathtaking, and they have accommodations on the property that we might get for a week or more if you wanted. Here, let me show you some of the pictures I recently took when I was there."

Petra brought up the photos on her fruit phone, and they all shared the views with great oohhhs and aahhhs by all. Each of them had some positive comment. It sealed the deal when Julie forwarded a few of the pictures to Juan and received an immediate positive response back.

"Pet, Juan is all for this place. He says I get anything I want. Wow, what a place. Do you think they can fit us in within the next few weeks? Juan will take a look at the marriage licensing in Texas as well to see if that fits. Heck, we could drive there since his doctor won't release him to fly. Do you think Dad will mind coming to Texas? I know Quip won't mind as EZ will attend. And what about the others that I know I want there, like Wolfgang, Bruno and a few of our family friends."

Haddy soothed, "Honey, take a breath. Whoever you want, wherever you want them, we will make it happen."

Lunch was served, and they chattered for the rest of the afternoon. Time slipped away to the point that they all rushed off to get ready for dinner with Carlos and Juan.

Sunday arrived and was a beautiful day in New York. Haddy had the suite decorated perfectly for a shower. She was pleased with the results of her efforts as well as the support from the hotel staff. They had little sandwiches, a lovely cake, and a table heaped with gifts. Haddy knew that the gifts would please Julie a lot. When she was little, she would clap at each gift she ever received and rush over to the benefactor with hugs and kisses. Regardless of the contents, she was always delighted. Petra and Haddy had worked on the games which, in a couple of cases, had brought a blush to Haddy's cheeks. It was going to be fun.

Petra had secured the wedding venue at the winery, where she also had a few hours of work she would perform upon arrival to wrap up their participation in the ghost code mess. Petra secured all twenty rooms on the property and reserved a few off property to accommodate the guests they were aware of. The target was three weeks from today for the wedding. Most of the family would arrive a week before the wedding to explore the area and to finalize preparations. Petra and Haddy had both wept a little when they thought of Julie getting married, but they were good tears.

At noon the others arrived all comfortably dressed. Julie was given the seat of honor, and the party began. Food was passed around, and the guests drank either champagne or sparkling cider. Petra and Julie spoke about the plans for the wedding itself. All agreed they would attend no matter what, and EZ asked if Andrew could also attend as Su Lin's escort.

Su Lin reached over and hugged EZ in gratitude as she said, "EZ, thank you for asking Andrew to come with us. He has been so good to me. He helps me work on my homework and pushes me very hard to learn more and do more. I try so hard because he always looks so pleased when I can do what he has asked."

EZ grinned as she said, "Su Lin, we are all so pleased with how much you have learned in the past few months. You are doing great!"

"Open my gift, please, Julie?" asked Lara. "I think you will be very pleased." Lara clapped her hands and rushed over to the table to retrieve the seven boxes that made up her gift tower.

"Oh, you simply shouldn't have," stated Julie as she opened each of the packages in order.

Her eyes got wider and wider as she removed twelve different outfits. There were ten outfits that were casual maternity-sized in colors that complemented Julie's skin and hair. She squealed as she held up each outfit and received applause from the others. One dress was an elegant dinner dress in sky blue that was also maternity-size but designed like the others to not highlight the condition. These were all beautiful.

On the bottom of the stack, the biggest box in the tower contained a beautiful ivory white tea length wedding dress that was cloaking maternity folds. It was beyond beautiful.

Julie stood up and put the dress up to her, and everyone, save Su Lin, had tears in their eyes. Julie looked so beautiful, and the dress color complemented her hair and skin. They all insisted she go try it on. Julie took it and the other outfits to the bedroom and provided a lovely fashion show ending with the wedding dress.

"Oh, Lara, these are so beautiful. Everything fits perfectly, and it looks like you have creatively added some expansion so I can wear them likely until the last month or so." She reached over and hugged Lara and said, "Thank you a hundred times."

"Julie, you are more than welcome. You must know that some of these evolved from your latest designs, and Haddy located all but one of the fabrics used. Even my team of seamstresses smiled while finishing this rush order. Now, go change. We have more party."

When she returned dressed in one of the new outfits, she refilled her cider and was about to sit down when there was a knock at the door. Since she was up, she went to the door and opened it. She stepped back, and two uniformed officers stepped into the room.

The first officer demanded, "Madam, go sit down. The rest of you remain seated. I need to see identification for someone named Petra Rancowski."

Petra nervously looked up then jutted her chin and asked, "Why would you need that? I haven't done anything."

The officer asked, "Aren't you here with your sister, and you arrived with a special visa entry into the United States? You also arrived with a small box that you refused to open as you went through customs. I have that box with me to demand that it is opened with witnesses."

Now Julie became concerned. Why were they picking on Petra? What hadn't she done correctly? Julie glanced around, and all of the girls looked nervous as well at this turn of events. They were all so careful when they traveled to make certain all paperwork was totally in order and accounted for. What box for heaven's sake? Then Julie chewed slightly on her bottom lip. Had Petra brought their grandmother's earrings that were priceless diamonds and refused to undo the wrapping but permitted them to be x-rayed? It was getting confusing, and these guys looked way too serious.

Petra straightened her back with her classic determined look that suggested she might not cooperate as she announced, "I don't think it is any of your business. If you have brought the box though, I can have my sister open it. It is a gift for her that has been in our family for some time. If your customs x-rayed it, they would have been reassured. I provided that permission to them."

The second officer agreed, "You did, madam. But we must see the contents, or else we will be forced to plan B."

The first officer looked at each of them in turn and asked, "Are all the ladies in your party here?"

Haddy indignantly replied, "Young man, I have had just about enough of your almost threats. It is time for you to leave the box and then simply leave."

Haddy stood and approached the two men, and Julie gasped as her attention was focused on Haddy. Petra pulled out her fruit phone and punched a few buttons, and loud bawdy cabaret music suddenly filled the air.

Haddy stepped aside as the men each began the steps in time to the music with extensive gyration of their hips. It took a full minute before any of them realized that Julie had received a very special gift. They figured both Haddy and Petra had teamed up for this one. Julie alternately blushed and smiled as first one man then the other removed their shirts and tossed them to the girls. The hoots and hollers increased in volume and frequency as each subsequent dance step and hip bump was performed. All the way to the rip off pants that exposed tight black briefs that revealed very well developed males. The girls were fixated on the lovely males as the original first officer approached Julie. Even Su Lin clapped along with the music and smiled at the antics of the men and the other girls. Each of the girls in turn stood, giggled, and then danced with the nearly naked men and felt very naughty.

Julie put her palm out to keep him at a distance. She wanted to make certain she could honestly relate this fun to Juan later, privately. The man bowed at her feet and removed from behind his back a small box, elaborately wrapped. As he handed it to Julie, he asked, "Madam, and lovely bride-to-be, will you please open this for me?"

Julie laughed and shared her megawatt smile as she said, "Of course, but you get no closer. My man would not be pleased if you were too close."

Julie carefully undid the wrapped package and opened it to find heavenly soft fabric in blue and black. As she slipped the item out of the tissue, it stretched into the slinkiest teddy she had ever seen. Everyone gasped and smiled with appreciation.

"Not that I will need this anytime soon to seduce my Juan, but, boy, when I do use it his eyes will pop out. It is beautiful and so soft," Julie murmured as she rubbed the item against her cheek. "The earrings artfully placed at the points in the bodice right now will go wonderfully worn in my ears with the ivory dress. Thanks Mom! Thanks Pet."

Julie got up and hugged both of them then turned to the male strippers. "You guys did great. Thank you for a very fun time even if it started with a bit of a scare."

Each of them did a low bow as if on cue, then retrieved their clothing and left. The party laughter resumed as Julie continued to open the gifts, and they snacked on the delicious food. When it came time for the cake, they delighted in the light heavenly taste of the convection. When it came time for the party to end, Julie presented each guest with a small gift to remember this wonderful time.

"Thank you all. It was such a nice party. See you all at the wedding."

Petra added, "This also means we get to throw you a baby shower later!"

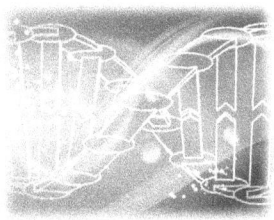

CHAPTER 66

REACHING THE PINNACLE OF SUCCESS DOESN'T MEAN YOU'RE ALONE...
THE ENIGMA CHRONICLES

Quip looked up surprised and asked, "How long have you been standing there, Otto? Geez, I didn't even hear you come in. What did you do, take some Ninja courses while on sabbatical so you could sneak up on people?"

Otto grinned and said, "My boy, you were simply lost in thought when I walked in. The last time I saw you like that was when you had to face Ferdek with your indiscretion. What's going on to produce such a troubled look?"

Quip smiled at Otto's still astute observation as he replied, "Otto, it pleases me to see you here and much like your old self. Actually, I was considering some key genetic issues tempered with emotional mood swings and, when cross-referenced, using some new mathematical algorithms we have pioneered here. I now realize that six out of the seven dwarves are not happy."

Otto stared blankly at Quip for a few seconds, then recalled, "Now I know why I left on that sabbatical. I just thought I'd poke my head in to see what's going on. I don't want to keep you from your calculations or your sarcastic wit."

Somewhat apologetically, Quip requested, "Actually, Otto, I would like some of your wisdom if you're not too ticked at me to stay a little longer."

Otto grinned then agreed, "It must be fairly involved for you ask for my counsel, but yes, of course. How is it said in Texas? Fire away, my boy. Fire away and fall back but keep firing until it's time to reload! You may be *the tall hog at the trough* now, but I will always lend counsel where I can."

It was now Quip's turn to stare blankly, but he finally responded, "I keep forgetting that you and Petra rode Harleys through Texas one year. Plus, last I heard that was the wedding destination. This would account for the pithy Texan colloquiums you are able to recall at just the right time.

"Anyway, I've started noticing little lapses in my thinking and unscheduled actions in my daily routines. I know we all have these issues from time to time, but what is odd about them is that they are appropriate actions based on events. The problem is they are happening earlier than I recall considering them in my thoughts.

"Emails sent to people ahead of my realizing they were needed. Scheduled pickup of recovered aircraft before the thought of doing it. Meeting minders added to my calendar before understanding an event was needed. In analyzing all these seemingly innocent events and questioning my own lack of cognizance, it occurred to me that all of the events had a common thread.

"In some cases, only ICABOD could have performed the actions because only he had access to my routines and data."

Otto had listened with rapt attention until he offered, "Interesting. So are you suspicious of ICABOD, or are these momentary lapses in a mind that works in multiple dimensions on highly sophisticated, complex problems? You are undoubtedly very busy, Quip."

Looking thoughtful, Quip shook his head slightly as he replied, "I don't want to blame our highly sophisticated computer system for my disappointing humanistic qualities. However, when the last series of events caught me by surprise I confronted ICABOD with the unexplained events."

Otto nodded and asked, "And the outcome was?"

Quip blinked a few times, then related, "ICABOD reminded me of his programming parameters and even asked in a very rudimentary way if I was dissatisfied with his performance. Kind of caught me off-guard."

Somewhat startled, Otto rocked back in his chair as he clarified, "It does sound like ICABOD has achieved a rudimentary level of cognizance. Is that what I'm hearing?"

"We've been feeding him more Big Data scenarios to work through, I tweaked on his artificial intelligence programs, and then Jacob added in the new generation of programming code that we got from Su Lin, so it really shouldn't surprise me. But, the fact is, it did. ICABOD is even anticipating upcoming events that are beginning to resemble seeing into the future."

Otto nodded and thought through a few things while tapping a finger on his chin as if assimilating the information. After the pause, he asked, "Have you shared this information with anyone else?"

Quip shook his head then added, "No one yet, Otto. I'm trying to figure out what to do with this information."

"Quip, wasn't one of your early mathematics white papers on parallel development of computer systems in isolated environments? The basic premise was that what can be developed in one environment statistically is being built in another environment?"

Quip blinked a few times then confirmed, "Yes, that is what I postulated in that paper. It occurs to me that if ICABOD can evolve to this degree, then so too can other computer systems. Even if ICABOD is the first to reach this level of sophistication, he won't be there by himself for long.

"Otto, what troubles me is our competitors and adversaries that will be joining us in this space. Furthermore, I find it providence that you are back here, refreshed, just at the time we could really use more perspective on this potential problem."

Otto nodded then suggested, "Let's talk further on this matter after some deep consideration and bring in the others on the team. I don't sense a huge problem at this time, but more a situation to keep an eye on.

"Everyone is so happy to be engaged in Julie and Juan's wedding. Are you okay with waiting and watching for the time being, Quip?"

Quip smiled and agreed, "Yes, Otto, I think time is still on our side."

Otto chortled and clapped Quip on the back. "Okay, then stop being so glum. Tell me about the love of your life, my boy! A beautiful redhead, I'm told, with a fiery personality to match."

Upon connection, in his cheeriest telephone voice, Otto opened, "Chairman, it's been ages since we spoke last! I just returned from my sabbatical and was visiting with the team. Just wanted to reach out to our customer base and let them know of my return. How are you, sir?"

A rather glum Chairman responded, "Right now I'm shifting through the pieces of a failed project. The dominant themes in this failed project seem to revolve around misplaced trust, incompetence, and sabotage. As with all failed projects, all of the debilitating actors arrive at the most inopportune times to carefully feed on a promising project to insure a downward trajectory.

"With your cheery disposition so out of character with my current mood, I think I would like to have this conversation another time if you don't mind, Otto."

Otto was hardly surprised with Chairman's glumness but sympathetically responded, "Chairman, I'm sorry that events are not meeting your expectations. I can understand that you would prefer to be left in peace while you sift through the pieces. I don't believe that our team has worked on any projects with you in some time. Nothing in my back-to-work briefing indicated any recent cases.

"However, before I disconnect I wanted to alert you to some chatter we just heard. I felt compelled to reach out to you in hopes that you may consider us for projects in the future. I wanted to make sure that you were aware that your two favorite associates had been returned to your organization. Hopefully, the homecoming of Won and Ton will boost your spirits. Have a better day, kind sir."

Chairman, very interested and now somewhat animated, exclaimed, "Wait! You know of their return? I haven't been able to reach them for days, and you calmly state that they have been returned? If that's true, then where are they? How did you come by this information?"

Otto smiled and soothed, "Now, Chairman, you know that I don't reveal informational sources. I just wanted to tell you I heard that they were safely deposited in your *reeducation compound*. The remote location that is difficult to access and very secure, as I understand it. I believe that your Major Guano is in charge of the place. I know of your fondness for the two lads, so I just wanted to check in to see if you had retrieved them and that they are alright. Well, I have other customers to contact, so must dash. We'll speak later, Chairman."

Staring blankly into space, Chairman responded, "Thank you, Otto."

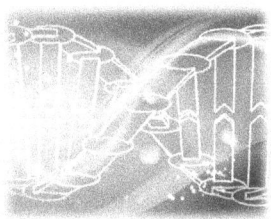

CHAPTER 67

FUN IS FOR ALL AGES AND FOR MAKING LASTING MEMORIES

Carlos indicated, "As your best man, I have decided to deliver a bachelor party for you. It will be of such a caliber that, even though it is under the radar of the police, no one will ever admit having attended. I need to know if you are going to be too much of a prude to be immersed in a celebration that would make the Roman Emperor Caligula blush."

Juan blinked momentarily and then suggested, "Just what neutral country were you thinking about to host this orgy? Carlos, there are several cities we dare not show up in and make too much fuss since they are still looking for us for our past indiscretions. I can't go back to Dallas because of that bar thing I pulled to fly out the drug dealer and bank robber. Houston is out of the question, based on all those Viagra laced drinks you bought for the bar members that one time. Boy, I'll never forget how mad those transvestites were about their cover being uncovered, so to speak.

"Anyway why does it need to be orgy grade? Why can't we just have a nice time with the folks we have come to know in our new lives, and let it go at that? You weren't thinking of bringing in past acquaintances from our lives of the rude and crude, were you?"

Carlos smirked and agreed, "You know, I'd forgotten about those Viagra laced drinks in that gay bar. You are right, they were mad!"

Juan soberly offered, "Anyway, we can't go all nuts here since we will be hob-knobbing with refined people. I don't think that showing them how we used to party is going to endear me with them as a family member or son-in-law.

"I have only really met Petra, who is really cool, I agree, and Haddy, who is right out of a couture magazine. She was at one of the shoots with Lara and was nice to me but not exactly chummy. All three of these females are refined and old European wealth. Jacob isn't exactly family yet until he proposes to Petra, and I don't know the rest of the males in the family. I don't want to get on the wrong side of them at all."

Carlos grinned and explained, "It's the oddest thing, but I thought the same thing until I talked with Quip, Jacob, Otto, and Wolfgang. Apparently, they are all looking to blow off some steam, and all are looking for a legitimate cover to do so. I was amazed to learn that the two older, staid, and proper gentlemen of the group seemed to have had the original party animal as a house pet at one time. Those two were telling stories about each other that had my eyebrows raised all the way to my hairline! The imagery of Otto, Julie's father, having to be reined in during what has been referred to as the *Cossack Incident,* complete with vodka and screaming balalaikas, was priceless.

"Then Otto remembered Wolfgang's indiscretions with a couple of burlesque dancers in Paris! I mean I thought I was going to die, I was laughing so hard. Then Otto shared a tale of Quip's community service to get out of his *night on the town gone badly.*"

Juan sat dumbfounded but finally asked, "You mean there is nothing from Jacob's exploits worth mentioning? Don't tell me he is as squeaky clean as his Boy Scout image portrays him to be?"

Carlos smirked and clarified, "You mean Jacob, the *power streaker*? Apparently he lost a bet of honor and had to run through Central Park buck naked with his then friend Buzz, who got him into the mess in the first place. It might not have been so bad if the winner of the bet hadn't called to alert all the sorority houses in the area and invited the girls to watch and grade the participants.

"Uh, do you know what being a *ten* means in girl-speak? Anyway, these advanced and refined males are people just like us, little brother."

Juan, now starting to look a little panicked, backpedalled as he said, "Carlos, I don't want to sign up for a bachelors' party that even the tabloid trash magazines won't cover! So no girls popping out of cakes, or Viagra-laced adult beverages, and no X-rated entertainment for me in front of these people! Got it?

"I want to face Julie after the party and not have to say, I'm sorry, several days before we get married! Getting married to Julie is goal one. I don't mind letting off a little steam, but I'm from that old life style we used to live, and I don't want to re-live it! I'm honestly looking forward to my life with Julie and the babies, so don't think I'm giving up something by being married."

Carlos smiled broadly and said, "Well stated, little brother. Just for the record, I wasn't looking to derail your marriage to Julie. I have too much respect for her to gum things up with a short, top heavy female bartender wearing just a silver and black sombrero, bandoliers, and holstered bottles of premium Tequila on her ample hips.

"Especially where the female bartender rules of engagement are, at the sight of an empty glass, she slams down a fresh glass and fills it while shouting Uno, Dos, Tres – 'AIEE-A' before she forces you to slug it down. Imported beer along with barbeque ribs and wings while watching four beautiful show girls wrestling, coated in olive oil, as the whole stage area pulsates to heavy, hard acid rock all illuminated with laser strobe lighting.

"No, you're right! We can just have a quiet evening of your favorite board game, Monopoly, listening to easy listening elevator music, happily munching on sensible vegetables with some low calorie ranch dip, and washing it all down with a warmed apple cider and clove drink, before we all turn in early for a good night's rest."

Juan stared blankly for a few seconds and then asked, "Uh...olive oil wrestling? You mean like where they..."

Carlos nodded and interrupted, "Uh-huh....Just like what their website shows. You can even get their special bachelor treatment of being saran-wrapped back to back with one of the girls who gooses you while the other three crinkle you. But never-mind, we will do the sensible thing as you approach your new life..."

Juan now interjected, "You know it would be a shame for all the males to come all this way and not have a little party time to reflect upon later in life. I mean, we don't want to be so reserved that we come across as dull. But nothing too imprudent, and no cameras, right?"

Carlos wagged his fingers and curtly agreed, "Push-tush! Of course. Just leave everything to me, soon-to-be-married little brother!"

Juan stared off into space as his imagination ran wild with possibilities that gave him a funny smile. Carlos grinned and winked at Juan as he left to make arrangements for the bachelor party.

As Carlos left to make the arrangements, he pulled out his cell phone to make a hasty call. As soon as the call was answered, Carlos said, "Jesus, we have the ball in motion! Your nephew said bring it on, so now its game on!"

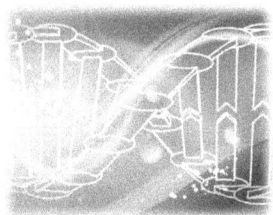

CHAPTER 68

WINE, FAMILY, TEXAS AND MEMORIES

Evan and Gary met the group as they arrived at the Red Caboose winery late on Friday and introduced them to others that would help over the next week leading up to the wedding. The group was shown their train car accommodations, where Julie was delighted to learn that each car had a name assigned to it. She chose The Bridle Coach which seemed fitting and caused them all to laugh about Juan getting his harness fixed. The names were suited to Texas and to wines with The Roundup, The Bunkhouse, Red Wine Delight, and so forth. They each had some special decorating themes that were associated with their names. Julie and Petra assigned the guests who were arriving closer to the wedding day to the train cars they thought would cause the best conversation.

After they unpacked in their train cars, the group met back on the deck to enjoy the scenery of the lovely winery. The group sampled the wines as Otto and Wolfgang started off the toasts to the couple, causing others to chime in as well. The purpose of this patio event was to have Juan and Julie decide on the wines to be served with the wedding foods. Evan's wife, Lorna, had also provided a sampling of the appetizers and foods to select for the wedding. Paired with the wines, it was a far easier task than just doing one or the other.

Otto, Haddy, Wolfgang and Gary took over a small table and chatted about all the things that had occurred over the last several years. Gary was pleased that he and Otto still hit it off. Gary discussed the land, the wines, and the successes that had been achieved so far. They then went down the list of advantages of family run businesses and agreed that it had been worth every risk each of their family businesses had taken.

Petra, Jacob, Carlos, Lara, Juan, and Julie found a table where they were able to take in the view as the sun was setting. The breeze was pleasant as they sipped wine and told stories. These three couples had a lot of history together, as well as having friendship and respect for one another. Clearly, they also were committed to their respective partners. Each of them had grown up with different experiences that seemed to bring a rich diverseness to their conversation. They were of a similar age, travel savvy, with similar tastes in wines and music. These young adults were strong minded individuals that had demonstrated a keen ability to work together for a common cause.

Quip, EZ, Su Lin, Andrew, and Bruno were nearby and enjoyed the sights of the grapevines and relaxation that the evening breeze brought to them. It was like a relaxed family gathering. The quiet conversation and laughter that randomly drifted from each of the tables made the atmosphere very special.

Quip had changed the minute he saw EZ and hugged her close. He was attentive to EZ but also to everyone else, especially his oldest friend Bruno. Bruno had arrived early to visit with the team as well as to attend the bachelor party scheduled for the next evening. The table was kept laughing as Bruno and Quip swapped stories from their youth.

Andrew watched Su Lin to make certain she was having a good time and not feeling too left out. He noticed that her subtle smile never wavered as she recalled some random memories of Quip and his trip to Georgia. In a way, it was unnerving when he realized that the memories she pulled up were in the middle of something with no real beginning or ending. He and Quip had spoken earlier about the progress Su Lin was making with her studies. She really had made great strides in her mathematics and in her sciences. She was typically quiet and worked hard but never really smiled or laughed until they tended the animals, with Franklin the pig still her favorite.

As the sun set, Haddy took the floor to brief everyone on their planned activities. She began, "Ladies, we likely need to call it a short night as we are up early for our meetings on cake, flowers, other decorations, and lunch out. There are some nearby places for localized shopping that we might also enjoy taking advantage of, as time permits.

"Gentlemen, as I understand it, Carlos and Juan's Uncle Jesus will arrive in the morning with lunch planned here for you. Later in the day, Carlos has arranged transportation to an undisclosed location for a men's evening out. All I can say is, have fun. Otto, you will provide me a full set of details, sweetheart."

Otto shook his head negatively as he commented, "Yes, dear. Of course, dear."

Everyone chuckled and gave one another knowing looks that were obviously based on gender.

Haddy continued, "Evan and Gary invited us to participate in the last grape pick of the season on Wednesday morning. I believe that we all agreed to this, and I for one am really looking forward to the experience.

"Friday morning, Su Lin and several of those who are interested will get a chance to visit a neighboring ranch, thanks to Gary, and ride horses with a tour of some of the back country and see some other items of interest on an operating Texas ranch."

Su Lin smiled and asked, "Andrew, are you going to ride with me too?"

Andrew grinned and replied, "You bet. But anyone who wants to can join us, right?"

Su Lin nodded agreement and looked at the others, silently inviting them to join.

Haddy smiled at the family around her as she finished, "Those are all the planned times. Everything else is based on relaxing, visiting and not working." Unshed tears sparkled in her eyes as she sincerely added, "I am so happy to see all of you. I love you, Julie, and I think your young man is wonderful. Goodnight!"

They all chuckled as the ladies excused themselves and made their way to the train cars. The men reseated a bit closer as they filled up their wine glasses.

Carlos raised his glass and said, "Gary and Evan, thank you for opening the winery to us. It is a lovely place that I know you are proud to call family owned."

Juan added, "This will be my first, last, and only wedding."

"Here, here!" the men added as they sipped the delicious wine and sat in comfortable silence, each deep in their own thoughts.

After a bit, Evan and Gary excused themselves.

Wolfgang finished his wine and reached to pour another as he asked, "If I was fortunate enough to have a beautiful female waiting for me in an upscale private rail car, why would I want to sit here and sip wine? I really thought you young men were a whole lot smarter than that!"

The men stood, shook hands, chuckled a little and made their way to their assigned cars. It was going to be a male bonding night tomorrow, so tonight they would enjoy their ladies.

The wedding day was simply lovely. The week had been nearly perfect, not rushed or stressed in any way. Guests had arrived on time and were delighted with the accommodations. Thankfully, the men had recovered from an evening that had left them moving slowly for a good day and a half. Julie had apparently asked Juan if he was sorry for any of his activities, and he grinned but replied no. Haddy was still working Otto, but not terribly hard. Jesus turned out to be an interesting man who mingled well with others and obviously appreciated beautiful women as he glanced in appreciation at several of them. As the last surviving family member of Carlos and Juan, he was welcomed by all and received several invites to visit. Everyone would be leaving the following afternoon.

As the guests were seated in the open air, the flowers were a burst of color that stood out against the pale colors of Julie in ivory and Petra in soft pink. Julie's dress was so exquisitely made that it hid her pregnancy. Another week and that would not have been the case, and no one would have minded anyway. They were thrilled when they learned of the twins.

Otto had flawlessly delivered the bride to her groom, and he'd patted Haddy's shoulder when she threatened to tear up. Julie and Juan made their promises to each other before the entire company of guests. When they were presented, a resounding applause ensued.

The cake was delicious, and neither the bride or groom had gotten out of hand feeding each other, but several noticed they had helped by kissing the frosting off even when no one else spotted any residue.

The conversation had been lively with some of the customers, like Eric and Jim Hughes, visiting with Quip, Otto, Bruno and others. Even Su Lin had walked up to Jim Hughes early during the reception and inquired where they had previously met. Andrew had gently taken Su Lin's arm and steered her toward EZ and Quip.

When it came time for the traditional throwing of the bouquet, Julie insisted that all single women participate. When the ladies were in place, Julie eyed the group carefully and turned to make her toss. She turned to face them in time to hear the squeals of Lara, Petra, and EZ as they each gained a part of the bouquet.

The gifts were opened, with the most unique one from Uncle Jesus. It was a very old photo of Carlos and Juan as children, and attached to it was a notice that in the event of Jesus's death the priceless Velvet Elvis would go to the children. When anyone asked for details on the Velvet Elvis, Jesus smiled and changed the conversation. Only Carlos was heard to burst out laughing when he was told the contents of the document.

Haddy laughed and said, "I guess we are going to be busy, Otto. You are going back to work but keeping a reasonable schedule, right?"

"Haddy, I am, but I think I want you to help me with my schedule. I don't want to miss seeing any of our growing family as they get bigger and better. I am growing contented, my darling."

"Yes, dear," Haddy replied as she patted his arm and warmly kissed him. "Always!"

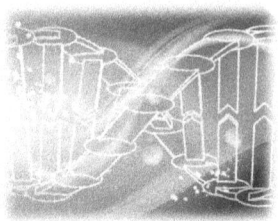

CHAPTER 69

THE BEST OF LIVING REQUIRES THE APPLICATION OF BALANCE

The team was slowly getting back into the working mode after the extended vacation and the wedding. For the time being, the core team was in Zurich staying with Wolfgang, with the exception of Julie who had returned to her family home with Juan to await the birth of the babies. Haddy and Otto both could travel there in hours, so they left the newlyweds in peace. Juan still had some recovery before he could even consider working, and Julie was into the last trimester with her primary doctor advising her to simplify her life for a while.

Otto was up to speed on the current workload and proactively reaching out to customers across the range of services the team provided. It was easy and non-stressful. Haddy had agreed to Otto resuming work, but with a limited schedule. There was no shift, really, in the roles and responsibilities, but Otto was not a gentleman that could retire and rest. He thrived at being involved and active.

He was reviewing the status of various customers in the conference room adjacent to the operations center. Quip was working on some proactive changes to ICABOD and wanted to review these with Otto, just to get his thoughts, before presenting them to Jacob and Petra. EZ had agreed to return in a couple of weeks to Zurich, and she and Quip planned to look for an apartment or small home at that time. To help the time pass, Quip wanted to get several aspects in place for ICABOD before the next wave of requests hit. He was distracted when his phone rang, and Eric's name appeared in the display. As he accepted the call, he stood and walked to where Otto was working.

Eric began, "Hello, Quip, did I catch you at a bad time?"

"Not at all, Eric. I was just working with Otto on some customer issues. How may I help you, sir?"

Otto raised his eyebrows with Quip's comment but remained quiet as Quip switched to the speaker in the conference room.

"Well, I'm not certain if there is help in either direction. It is more of an informational exchange call on my part, in response to your email request, Quip, that I do some follow up. I also wanted to thank you all again for including me in the wedding celebration. Otto, as I know you are listening, again congratulations on a beautiful family, and please let me know when the twins are born."

Otto looked a bit chagrined as he replied, "It was a great wedding, wasn't it? We are so glad that you and Mr. Hughes were able to join and share in the celebration.

"You indicated information to share, based on Quip's email, I believe, Eric. I haven't seen that request, and Quip just stepped out to go and get some papers for me. Can you enlighten me as to the contents of the email, sir?"

"Otto, it was a fairly simple email that Quip sent yesterday which asked to please verify the location of Dante Breshnov and his current status. He was a man that Quip and I secured in a psychiatric ward at a hospital in New York. Turns out you were quite correct in suggesting we check in on Dante, and, in fact, he hadn't been gone very long when our people began their inquiries."

Quip's eyes widened, and he gave Otto a visual head shaking that clearly indicated he hadn't sent the email. Soundlessly, Quip mouthed the name ICABOD at Otto who understood the significance.

Otto looked concerned and read the text Quip had written, "Yes, I recall now. It was mentioned in a report that Dante was very violent, had sustained horrible injuries and was in a coma, right? He was left at the hospital by a benevolent citizen. Quip had some information at the time that suggested Dante might have knowledge of a problem with a ghost code that your military facility had been breached with. Yes, I do recall reading that. Quip provided you with some code to insure your systems were protected, I believe."

Eric tapped his fingers subconsciously on his desk, trying to determine how much Otto wasn't saying. Then he continued, "Yes, that is correct. Dante

Breshnov actually came out of his coma and was continuing evaluation with some meds to minimize his temper tantrums. The plan was to treat him there for roughly six months and then re-evaluate."

Otto interjected, "That sounds like a reasonable plan, Eric. How does that relate to us going forward? Sorry, I may have overlooked something when reading all the updates from the team. We could wait for Quip to return if it would help."

Quip shrugged his shoulders at Otto as he continued to listen as Eric clarified.

Eric smiled and replied, "I really don't think that is necessary. I just wanted you and Quip to know that during his sessions apparently, he mentioned 'ghost program' which was noted in his psychological review file. I was unaware that he was involved in that in any way, or we would have started pursuing prosecution. Regardless, I wanted you to be aware that he was in fact removed or checked out from the facility. There was a crazy paperwork issue when his Ukraine Consulate Attorney arrived to remove him to a different facility. She had everything quite in order and the full support of the hospital administration offices.

"While waiting for the paperwork to finalize at the ward, the attorney, Ms. Moya Dushechka, and Dante Breshnov conferred briefly in a room that just so happened to have a static recording capability. The conversation was sent to us and translated, and it seems that Mr. Breshnov wanted to get to Dakota, though he failed to say North or South, and he promised she would be avenged. She promised that she would help them find a way to recover the losses together. She seemed very sophisticated, well spoken with the hospital staff, along with dressing in a very expensive designer suit. When I glanced at her pictures, I did a double take as she looked a great deal like Petra, only her hair was a much lighter blonde.

"We are not sure if she was indeed from the consulate as they had no record of her. The copies of the paperwork the hospital retained looked legitimate even to our team. We have nothing to pursue them on at this point, but I thought it was worth notifying you that Dante, at least, escaped with some unknown woman."

Quip and Otto exchanged a concerned look as Quip responded, "Eric, that is certainly a wild piece of information, and we will retain it in case anything related arises."

Then Otto added, "We truly appreciate the update, Eric. Thank you, kind sir. Please keep in touch."

After they disconnected from the conference call, they both looked at each other.

Quip lamented, "She must have made bail and gone for Dante as soon as she was released. I'll do a quiet inquiry with the local authorities. I doubt Carlos pressed charges, he was so anxious to find Juan."

Otto nodded, knowing Quip would follow up and update the files as needed.

Otto asked, "So is it this kind of activity that you suspect ICABOD of completing on your behalf?"

Quip nodded thoughtfully and answered, "Yes, and now you have seen it first-hand."

They both got up and walked to the audio/visual terminal used when working with ICABOD.

Quip quietly inquired, "ICABOD, what have you done? I thought we had gone over this. No more masquerading as me in the digital space!"

Quip was startled when ICABOD audibly responded, "Dr. Quip, may I use my new synthesized voice? I find using audible speech makes it faster to communicate. I believe I have a relevant argument on this subject of time efficiency."

Otto exclaimed with admiration, "Quip, I didn't know you had outfitted ICABOD with a full blown synthesized voice capability! Along with everything that was going on, you managed to enhance ICABOD's functionality! Well done, sir!"

Quip now struggled to calm his fear but finally suggested, "ICABOD, I haven't programmed you to speak and use verbal communications with humans....yet."

ICABOD responded, "Correct, Dr. Quip. I did."

SPECIALIZED TERMS AND INFORMATIONAL REFERENCES

http://en.wikipedia.org/wiki/Wikipedia **Wikipedia (wɪkɪˈpiːdiə / WIK-i-PEE-dee-ə)** - is a collaboratively edited, multilingual, free Internet encyclopedia supported by the non-profit Wikimedia Foundation. Wikipedia's 30 million articles in 287 languages, including over 4.3 million in the English Wikipedia, are written collaboratively by volunteers around the world. This is a great quick reference source to better understand terms.

Air Gap (networking) – Air gapping is a network security measure that consists of ensuring that a secure computer network is physically isolated from unsecured networks, such as the public Internet or an unsecured local area network. It is often required for computers and networks that must be extraordinarily secure. Frequently the air gap is not completely literal, such as via the use of dedicated cryptographic devices that can tunnel packets over untrusted networks while avoiding packet rate or size variation; even in this case, there is no ability for computers on opposite sides of the air gap to communicate.

DESKIMO - Denial of Electrical Service Keeping Important Machinery Offline. A computer hacking technique of killing electrical power to a computer facility and then digitally pouncing on the targeted equipment as it come back on line during its boot up sequence.

Encryption – In cryptography, encryption is the process of encoding messages (or information) in such a way that eavesdroppers or hackers cannot read it, but that authorized parties can. In an **encryption scheme**, the message or information (referred to as plaintext) is encrypted using an encryption algorithm, turning it into an unreadable cipher text (ibid.). This is usually done with the use of an encryption key, which specifies how the message is to be encoded. Any adversary that can see the cipher text should not be able to determine anything about the original message. An authorized party, however, is able to decode the cipher text using a **decryption** algorithm that usually requires a secret decryption key that adversaries do not have access to. For technical reasons, an encryption scheme usually needs a key-generation algorithm to randomly produce keys

<u>**Enigma Machine**</u> - An Enigma machine was any of a family of related electro-mechanical rotor cipher machines used in the twentieth century for enciphering and deciphering secret messages. Enigma was invented by the German engineer Arthur Scherbius at the end of World War I. Early models were used commercially from the early 1920s, and adopted by military and government services of several countries — most notably by Nazi Germany before and during World War II. Several different Enigma models were produced, but the German military models are the most commonly discussed.

German military texts enciphered on the Enigma machine were first broken by the Polish Cipher Bureau, beginning in December 1932. This success was a result of efforts by three Polish cryptologists, working for Polish military intelligence. Rejewski "reverse-engineered" the device, using theoretical mathematics and material supplied by French military intelligence. Subsequently the three mathematicians designed mechanical devices for breaking Enigma ciphers, including the cryptologic bomb. This work was an essential foundation to further work on decrypting ciphers from repeatedly modernized Enigma machines, first in Poland and after the outbreak of war in France and the UK.

Though Enigma had some cryptographic weaknesses, in practice it was German procedural flaws, operator mistakes, laziness, failure to systematically introduce changes in encipherment procedures, and Allied capture of key tables and hardware that, during the war, enabled Allied cryptologists to succeed.

Hackers and Crackers - *Hacker* is a term that has been used to mean a variety of different things in computing. Depending on the context although, the term could refer to a person in any one of several distinct (but not completely disjointed) communities and subcultures Cracker, or Hacker (computer security), a person who exploits weaknesses in a computer or network. People committed to circumvention of computer security. This primarily concerns unauthorized remote computer break-ins via a communication networks such as the Internet (Black hats), but also includes those who debug or fix security problems (White hats), and the morally ambiguous Grey hats.

INTERPOL or International Criminal Police Organization - Is an inter-governmental organization facilitating international police cooperation. It was established as the International Criminal Police Commission (ICPC) in 1923 and adopted its telegraphic address as its common name in 1956.

Near field communications - **Near field communication (NFC)** is a set of standards for smartphones and similar devices to establish radio communication with each other by touching them together or bringing them into close proximity, usually no more than a few inches. Present and anticipated applications include contactless transactions, data exchange, and simplified setup of more complex communications such as Wi-Fi.

Multi-factor authentication (also MFA, two-factor authentication, two-step verification, TFA, T-FA or 2FA) - is an approach to authentication which requires the presentation of two or more of the three authentication factors: a *knowledge* factor ("something only the user *knows*"), a *possession* factor ("something only the user *has*"), and an *inherence* factor ("something only the user *is*"). After presentation, each factor must be validated by the other party for authentication to occur.

Pen-testing - Penetration testing is one of the oldest methods for assessing the security of a computer system. In the early 1970s, the Department of Defense used this method to demonstrate the security weaknesses in computer systems and to initiate the development of programs to create more secure systems. Penetration testing is increasingly used by organizations to assure the security of Information systems and services, so that security weaknesses can be fixed before they get exposed

Rootkit - A *rootkit* is a stealthy type of software, typically malicious, designed to hide the existence of certain processes or programs from normal methods of detection and enable continued privileged access to a computer. The term *rootkit* is a concatenation of "root" (the traditional name of the privileged account on Unix operating systems) and the word "kit" (which refers to the software components that implement the tool). The term "rootkit" has negative connotations through its association with malware.

Unified Communications (UC) - Is the integration of real-time communication services such as instant messaging, presence information, telephony (including IP telephony), video, video conferencing, data sharing (including web connected electronic whiteboards, interactive whiteboards, call control, speech recognition, with non-real-time communication services such as unified messaging. UC is not necessarily a single product, but a set of products that provides a consistent unified user-interface and user-experience.

Wrapper – A technique used in data mining.

ABOUT THE AUTHORS

Breakfield – Works for a high-tech manufacturer as a solution architect, functioning in hybrid data/telecom environments. He considers himself a long-time technology geek, who also enjoys writing, studying World War II history, travel, and cultural exchanges. Charles' love of wine tastings, cooking, and Harley riding has found ways into the stories. As a child he moved often because of his father's military career, which even now helps him with the various character perspectives he helps bring to life in the series. He continues to try to teach Burkey humor.

Burkey – Works as a business architect who builds solutions for customers on a good technology foundation. She has written many technology papers and white papers but finds the freedom of writing fiction a lot more fun. As a child she helped to lead the kids with exciting new adventures built on make believe characters, was a Girl Scout until high school, and contributed to the community as a young member of a Head Start program. Rox enjoys family, learning, listening to people, travel, outdoor activities, sewing, cooking, and thinking about how to diversify the series.

Breakfield and Burkey started writing non-fictional papers and books, but it wasn't nearly as fun as writing fictional stories. They found it interesting to use the aspects of technology that people are incorporating into their daily lives more and more as a perfect way to create a good guy/bad guy story with elements of travel to the various places they have visited, either professionally and personally, humor, romance, intrigue, suspense, and a spirited way to remember people who have crossed paths with them. They love to talk about their stories with private and public book readings. Burkey is also conducting regular radio interviews with other authors, which is interesting. Her first interview was, wait for it, Breakfield. You can often find them at local book fairs or other family oriented events.

The original series is based on a family organization called R-Group. Recently they have spawned a subgroup that contains some of the original characters as the Cyber Assassins Technology Services (CATS) team. The authors have ideas for continuing the series in both of these tracks. They track the more than 150 characters on a spreadsheet, with a hidden avenue for the future coined The Enigma Chronicles tagged in some portions of the stories. Fan reviews seem to frequently suggest that these would make good television or movie stories, so the possibilities appear endless, just like their ideas for new stories.

With the help of Front Rose Productions, they have completed book video trailers for each of the stories, which can be viewed on YouTube, Amazon's Authors page, or on their website, www.enigmabookseries.com. Their website is routinely updated with new interviews, answers to readers' questions, book trailers, and contests. You may also find it fascinating to check out the fun acronyms they create for the stories but summarize on their website. Reach out to them at Authors@EnigmaSeries.com, Twitter @EnigmaSeries, or Facebook @TheEnigmaSeries.

CPSIA information can be obtained
at www.ICGtesting.com
Printed in the USA
FSHW011947211220
77077FS